Secrets That Kill

BY

ADAM S. DALE

**Grosvenor House
Publishing Limited**

The right of Adam S. Dale to be identified as the author of this
work has been asserted in accordance with Section 78
of the Copyright, Designs and Patents Act 1988

This book is published by
Grosvenor House Publishing Ltd
Link House
140 The Broadway, Tolworth, Surrey, KT6 7HT.
www.grosvenorhousepublishing.co.uk

This book is a work of fiction. Any resemblance to
people or events, past or present, is purely coincidental.

A CIP record for this book
is available from the British Library

ISBN 978-1-83975-221-6

ACKNOWLEDGEMENTS

Many thanks to my friend and artist, Lisa Ivory, for providing the original cover art for the book.

ACKNOWLEDGEMENTS

CHAPTER 1

Dean was certain he was being followed. As the underground train rattled from station to station, he sat bolt upright, chest puffed out, ready for the hit. He'd dared to look over several times, but on the last occasion he'd been caught, forcing him to swiftly switch his glare to the floor. Dean was sweating, not just from the heat in the carriage, but from fear.

The man was older than Dean, in his late thirties and undistinctive in appearance, but Dean had spotted him. Maybe it was only because he was on red alert after the events of the past couple of months, but he was certain this was it, the end. There just weren't enough witnesses to save him; it was the middle of a Friday afternoon and the evening commute wouldn't start for at least another two hours.

Dean had first noticed the man walking behind him as he made his way from his flat to West Hampstead station. Initially, he hadn't been overly concerned, but the man had followed Dean as he changed trains at Green Park and joined the Victoria Line southbound. Both times the man sat a few seats away, on the opposite side of the same carriage.

The train stopped in Victoria. 'Damn it,' Dean said under his breath as the young woman with a pushchair got off. No one else joined their carriage. *What are the chances?* he thought to himself as the train doors beeped and closed. Just three people left on the dimly lit carriage, including Dean and his potential attacker. The third, an elderly woman, was engrossed in a book and paying no attention to anything else around her.

Another 30 seconds passed, and the man began to stand up, causing Dean's heart to race even faster. He began walking towards him and fumbled with something in his jacket pocket as he approached. Dean's heart quickened again, and the sweat was now dripping from his face. He lifted his head up and puffed his chest out further, ready to take on the attacker. The train jerked, causing the man to stumble towards him and onto Dean's foot. He held his breath. *This is it*, he thought.

'Sorry,' the man said, as he continued past Dean and stood by the door as the train pulled into Pimlico station. Dean looked over to him in surprise; was that it? Then it dawned on him – he'd made the whole thing up in his head. As the doors opened, the man got out and several people got on. He was safe – for now.

He got off at Vauxhall as planned, without further incident, and worked his way through the gloomy station, up the escalator and reached the exit; four of them. He paused for a moment and opted for Exit 3, making his way up the stairs. His eyes struggled to adjust as he emerged into daylight, and he paused again while trying to figure out which direction to go. He worked in London every day, but in the City, not south of the river – this was completely new territory to him. He was knocked and nudged a few times by frustrated travellers as he stood trying to get his bearings. He noticed the famous British Intelligence building to the right and a rather swanky bus station in front of him.

He decided neither were in the direction he wanted and opted for left, under a railway bridge, and connected with South Lambeth Road.

The sunlight poured through the gaps in the buildings as he walked towards his destination. A collection of small businesses were built into railway arches on one side and a few tatty office buildings on the other. It wasn't the nicest part of London, far from it, but strangely, among the busy traffic and occasional pedestrian, he felt safe.

Feeling relaxed and happy should have been guaranteed, after all it was a beautiful July afternoon and he was about to embark on a two-week holiday. However, he wasn't happy or relaxed, not even close to it. Dean was worried, very worried – hence his journey today.

As he continued to walk, his pace slowed, not through tiredness but through nervousness. The butterflies had started in his stomach. He really didn't want to have this conversation, but he had to talk to someone, and he couldn't think of anyone better in this situation.

The road was now a mix of run-down shops, large building sites and small office buildings. As Dean passed a cheap looking two-star hotel, he pondered what the Grecian Abbey Hotel could possibly have done to earn its two-star status. Its pink neon sign flickered uninvitingly, like those found in a cheap horror movie.

Dean was quite absorbed by the 'real London', a side that he never saw doing his commute in and out of the financial district, with an occasional foray into the West End. The declining setting had forced him to quicken the pace, just to be on the safe side. He reached down to his pocket and checked his wallet; it's still there. No need to over-react, it's not a third-world city after all.

Having progressed for a few more minutes along the road, he stopped suddenly outside a five-storey brick building, wedged between another cheap looking hotel and a 24-hour mini-mart. He'd been keeping a good eye on the building numbers but had allowed his mind to wander as he approached his destination. Circling around, he spotted the number 12a on the brick building and slowly walked over to the door. His hand hovered over the buzzer for a few seconds, was he really about to do it? The butterflies intensified, but he plucked up the courage and finally pressed it.

After the second press, he was certain he wasn't going to get a response. Dean continued to wait, but as he did, he looked around the area, then back at the building he was trying to enter. He contemplated having to come to work here, day in and day out. He made a promise to himself there and then; he would never fall so low as to be forced to work in a place like this.

The third buzz was more successful, a woman with an Australian accent invited him up to the fourth floor. He struggled with the stiff door before making his way into the lobby. The building was run-down, with several old and dusty plastic palm trees adorning the entrance hall. The lift wasn't working, but Dean decided that he wouldn't have trusted it anyway and made a start on the stairs. The carpet was grey, well-warn and peeling away from the floor. The walls, once cream, had long since been over-ridden by an assortment of scuff marks and stains. Only every third light worked properly, and the windows were so dirty that it was impossible to see if it was day or night.

4

Dean arrived at the fourth floor and pushed open a blue-painted plywood door, with a small frosted glass pane in the upper half. He nervously crept into a windowless room, which appeared to be a waiting area. No one was immediately available to welcome him, and he decided to risk one of the wooden chairs that surrounded a low glass coffee table. He sat back, closed his eyes briefly and tried to plan what he would say, how he would say it and whether he would be taken seriously. Maybe he was being paranoid, but better to check – better to be safe.

As he sat in the drab waiting room and looked around, Dean Marchant could barely believe he'd had to come to such a place. Having worked hard at school and gone to university, he'd assumed he could have avoided visiting anywhere like this. He was very proud to be the first Marchant to graduate from university and, having joined a London bank three years ago, was progressing nicely. He was extremely ambitious, hoping to make it onto the trading floor in a couple of years – where the big money was. Growing up on a tough council estate in Birmingham, Dean counted himself as only the second Marchant to fight his way out of the Midlands city – he was about to meet the other.

At 24, Dean was physically in his peak, with a sportsman's frame; 6 foot 2 inches tall, 13 stone and muscular, but not excessively toned. His chiselled good looks allowed him to get almost any girl he wanted, however, after several recently failed relationships, he was currently single.

After five minutes the Australian receptionist appeared. She was young, early twenties and had a slim figure with straight, long blonde hair that flowed past her shoulders. Her clothes left little to the imagination, with a tight boob tube and a leather mini skirt. She wore very high-heeled shoes that compensated for her lack of height. Dean was motionless for a moment, as he stared open-mouthed at the beautiful girl now standing before him.

'Hi, I'm Tanya,' the girl said.

It took several seconds before Dean could reply, 'Er, I'm er, Dean. Dean Marchant,' he managed to stutter.

'Your uncle will be free in a coupla minutes, can I get you a coffee?'

'No thanks,' Dean replied, still fixated by the beauty in front of him.

'If you're sure. His door is second on the right, give him a coupla ticks and go on in.'

As she walked down the corridor to another office, Dean watched her every stride. When she was out of sight, he laughed to himself and thought how only his uncle could possibly have a secretary like that. He wondered how close Billy had been to her; very close, knowing Uncle Billy.

After five minutes, Dean had waited longer in the hope that Tanya would return, he wandered to Billy's door and knocked.

'Come,' a voice said from inside. He opened the thin, flimsy wooden door and cautiously made his way into the office. Billy was still on the phone as he beckoned Dean to sit down in front of him. The room was small and messy with papers scattered in almost every direction. There was a fusty smell and little light coming through the small dirty window. Dean chuckled to himself again as he moved a pile of papers and two folders from the only other chair in the room. Billy had definitely not changed.

The room was decorated with tatty, flower-patterned orange, yellow and olive wallpaper, somehow still attached to the wall. Dean couldn't quite believe he'd found something more awful than his grandparents' fifteenth-flour council flat, a true throwback to the seventies. The desk looked like a DIY flatpack job, although it was very difficult to tell with the amount of paper on it. There was a girlie calendar hanging on the wall, which Dean examined while Billy finished on the phone.

Billy wasn't an old man, in fact despite the years of hard drinking, loose women and bad drugs, he looked no older than his 46 years. Since leaving 'the force', he'd put on a few pounds, but he certainly wasn't fat. His tall frame hid the extra weight well and he still looked fairly fit. He had heavy stubble, an indication that he hadn't shaved for a few days; but he didn't need to; he worked for himself. Clients paid him for his service, not for his looks. He wore baggy jeans, a non-branded T-shirt and white trainers. His dark hair was short and combed forward, pushed up at the front; this was definitely his attempt to stay in fashion and look younger, Dean thought to himself. Billy wasn't a stereotypical private detective, but he wasn't far off. He drank, smoked, had many failed relationships, but he didn't have the appearance of a lonely, ageing, fat retired policeman.

'Not bad, is she?' Billy winked as he spoke.

'A bit out of your league, isn't she, Unc?'

Billy laughed and got out of his seat, giving Dean a firm handshake with both his hands. 'What brings you down here?'

'I had some business in this area and as I was passing, I thought I'd pop in.' He didn't sound convincing. 'I've got the day off and I'm just doing a few bits and pieces before I go on holiday.'

Billy nodded his head lightly, although Dean doubted his uncle believed him. In the three years that Dean had lived in North London, he'd never managed to find his way south of the river.

'Where you off to?' Billy asked but didn't sound interested.

'France. We've hired a house in the middle of nowhere, about two hours from Bordeaux.'

'Sounds a bit tame,' Billy responded with surprise in his voice.

'I need tame after the year I've had, hoping there won't even be phone reception. It's relaxing; lying by the pool, drinking plenty of wine and eating too much cheese. I need a holiday to be a holiday and not a twenty-four-hour all-night party.'

Billy didn't respond, instead he just made an inaudible grunt and sat back in his chair.

Dean felt pressured to keep the conversation going. 'I've only been working for three years, but if this is what the next forty are going to be like, I think I'll be dead by the time I'm your age.' Now that he was making a name for himself at the bank, the work had piled-on for Dean. From the start of January, for the last six months, it had been non-stop. Fifteen hours a day, six days a week, maybe even seven. This year it hadn't seemed to slow down for him, not even as the summer months approached. Dean was most definitely ready for a quiet, relaxing break.

'How's your dad?' Billy asked.

'Okay,' Dean said under his breath. He hated talking about his parents with Billy.

'And his wife?'

'You mean Mum? She's just fine too.' Billy never referred to Jean as anything other than 'his wife' or 'that women'. Family feuds come and go, but this one had dragged on for some 15 years. Dean couldn't even remember why, just that it had something to do with his mum and they never really talked about it. He was sure it wasn't an affair or anything sordid like that; just another stupid, pointless family feud that would never get resolved.

He'd always been close to his Uncle Billy, and despite Jean's best efforts, Dean had vowed he would never lose touch with his beloved uncle. It's easy to see why Dean was so fond of Billy all those years ago; young boys are in awe of policemen and to have one in the family gave Dean the edge over his friends in the playground. He would repeat story-upon-story to his mates, all passed on from his uncle, maybe embellished a little, but always entertaining.

Billy wasn't just any policeman either; he was Detective Superintendent William Marchant of the West Midlands Police. The local paper regularly carried news of his exploits, and every time his uncle's name appeared, Dean would beam with pride. He'd even made a scrapbook of all the newspaper clippings collected over the years of worship.

'What can I do for you?' Billy was obviously trying to move the conversation on to the real reason his nephew had come to see him.

'Oh, nothing,' Dean lied and then continued to talk, this time about their football team. Anything to keep him from the real reason he'd visited. If he was ever stuck for something to say to Billy, he could always revert to football. It was their bond years ago; with his dad uninterested in the beautiful game, it fell to Billy to instruct his nephew in the art of soccer. Aston Villa was their passion, every home game that Billy wasn't working, he'd take Dean to Villa Park to see the claret and blues play. More often than not it would end in disappointment; either a nil-nil draw, a missed penalty or a thumping defeat. But it didn't really matter to either of them – it was something that both uncle and nephew enjoyed. This was about the only time Jean let them spend together.

The Saturday afternoon ritual lasted until Dean was 15, when they fell out. They didn't speak for four years and, since they made up, things were never quite the same. There was still a bond between them, but it had diluted since Dean's idol had fallen.

It was nine years ago when Dean's world fell apart – May Day. The day the story broke about a drunken detective shooting an unarmed robber at point-blank range. The detective was Superintendent Marchant, and the robber died at the scene.

Initially, Dean hadn't believed it. He stood up for his uncle, suffered taunts at school, and had fights in the playground. Bloodied and battered, he would fight for the good name of his beloved uncle, despite what the lying papers were saying. After Billy admitted his sins to the family, Dean did two things: He vowed not to pursue his career in the police force, and he burnt his scrapbook.

There was a pause between the two before Billy made it easier for Dean. 'Why are you really here, Dean? And don't give me that crap about you just passing. Nobody with just one marble rolling around in their head would be on their way past this godforsaken hellhole.'

Dean was caught slightly off guard by his uncle's directness, initially considering a denial, before deciding to come clean. 'Okay, sorry, there is something that I might need your help with,' Dean said sheepishly.

'Why me? Why not your mum and dad?'

'Because you're a private detective and an ex-copper.'

After being kicked out of the police, Billy went off the rails. His second marriage failed when he hit the bottle, and a third came and went within a year. When he came out the other end of his decline, he was not a better man, he hadn't seen the light or found God. He was more selfish, more unfaithful and more uncaring. Even when he made up with his nephew again, things didn't improve. He became more determined to prove his bosses wrong, and he set up his own detective agency to show he could live without the police force.

He was good at his job, but on his own, without surveillance equipment, the manpower and other technological advances, it wasn't a profitable business. There are no nice little murder mysteries with four or five suspects like in the Agatha Christie novels. It's hard work dealing with society's scum and Billy had definitely developed a hardened shell.

'Are you in trouble with the police?' Billy shot back, but he didn't sound like he believed it.

'No! I just thought you would be the best person to ask,' this was a terse response from Dean, on the defensive.

'Well, spit it out then, what's the problem?'

Dean paused for a few more seconds, then began, 'Some strange things have happened to me over the past two months.'

Billy suddenly looked interested. He pulled his feet off the desk and sat upright in his tatty brown leather swivel chair. 'What kind of strange things,' he said inquisitively.

'It started with a strange feeling that I was being followed. I thought I was going mad, but then weird things started appearing in the post.'

'What kind of things?'

Dean hesitated before he responded, 'A "deepest sympathy" card, an adoption application form, a picture of me outside my flat and a subscription to a porn magazine.'

Billy let out a short chuckle when Dean had finished, causing his nephew to look embarrassed. Billy looked like he immediately regretted the laugh and tried to recover from his initial response, leaned forward in his chair and softened his tone. 'Has anything else happened? I need to know everything,' he finished the sentence firmly.

'Yeah. I think someone's been in my flat.'

'Why?'

'Things have been moved.' He paused to remember specifics. 'My post has definitely been looked at; not where I left it.'

'OK. Have you changed the locks?' Billy said with concern in his voice.

'Of course, I bloody did. I'm not some innocent bloody kid, born with a silver spoon in my mouth. I grew up in one of the toughest parts of Birmingham.'

Dean's voice got louder as he tried to prove himself and got up from his chair, looking ready to leave. Billy jumped up quickly and moved around the desk to stand in front of him, putting his hand on Dean's shoulder. As they stood there, face-to-face, Dean looked down at the floor and a tear appeared in his eye.

'Sorry,' he said warmly, but Dean shrugged his shoulder away from Billy's outstretched arm and moved to lean against the battered grey filing cabinet in the corner of the room.

'And it happened again?' Billy's tone has changed from that of a cocky older brother to a concerned parent.

'Yes.'

'Have you told the police?'

Dean hesitated before he responded, 'No.'

'Why not?' Dean stared further towards his shoes, but he couldn't reply. 'Why not?' Billy's voice was louder and more demanding.

'The letter said not to.' Dean was still staring at the floor.

Billy took half a pace backwards with surprise at this latest information. 'What letter?'

'The one I got last week, inside the "deepest sympathy" card. It said that I would die, just like Cameron did, if I told the police. Then he'd kill my parents.'

Billy was in stunned silence for a moment, clearly struggling to take in all this news. Finally, he moved over to Dean again, this time putting his arm around his head and pulling it onto his shoulder. Dean sobbed, softly at first, then more freely; the seal had been broken.

There was a knock at the door, but it opened before anyone could respond. Tanya's face poked round the door, 'I'm off to get a sarnie, do you want anything?' She didn't even flinch at the sight of a grown man crying onto another man's shoulder. Tanya had obviously seen plenty of things behind the door of that office.

'No thanks,' Billy managed, but Tanya was gone before she could hear the answer. The pair sat back in their chairs and Billy waited for Dean to compose himself.

'Sorry about that,' Dean said, as he wiped his eyes with the back of his wrist. He could have been 11 again, bruised and tearful after a fight in the playground. Now, at 24 he was still in pain, but this time the bruises were on the inside, and they would be harder to heal.

'Forget it,' Billy replied after a pause.

'What next?' Dean asked, starting to feel a lot better.

'Can you tell me who might have a grudge against you?'

'No one,' Dean replied without thinking.

'Well someone has. Think.'

Dean shook his head. 'No. No one.'

'There must be! Think. Harder!' Billy was shouting now.

'No, no, no!' Dean's voice was louder with each response.

'What about dumped girlfriends, cheated clients, gay lovers, illegitimate children? Anyone?'

Dean paused too long before replying, 'No.'

'Are you sure?'

'No!' Dean said this with more conviction, but he didn't believe it himself, let alone persuade his private-detective uncle there was nothing. There was a dark secret, something that Dean couldn't tell anyone at this point. He'd got so far, but just couldn't unburden himself that final step. Surely with what he'd told Billy already, that would be enough for him to sort it?

Billy got off his chair and walked to the window, he deliberately left an awkward silence, and Dean knew this tactic was to make him succumb and tell all. He managed to hold his nerve and remain silent, finally Billy returned to his desk and sat back in is his chair.

'You've not really given me anything to work with here,' Billy conceded.

'Sorry, but I just can't think of anything.'

'Okay. But there's not a lot I can do. Except give you the standard advice.' Billy sounded defeated.

'Go on then,' Dean said hopefully.

'Change the locks again.'

Dean was dismissive, 'I've done that already.'

'Not like this. Put three different locks on your door: a five-lever mortice deadlock, a rim automatic dead-latch with key locking handle, and a padlock. Get three different locksmiths to fit them. Only get one key cut for each lock. Never let the keys out of your sight. Get an alarm fitted. Change the code every week. What floor are you on?'

Overwhelmed, Dean managed a meek, 'Third.'

'So, they aren't getting in by the windows. But make sure you keep them locked anyway. Don't go out on your own at night, that's when they'll get you. Draw up a list of everyone you know or have known in the past. Rank them in order of who could be doing this. Tell the bottom two people on the list that you are being stalked and what's happened.'

'Why two people?'

'Because you're gonna need help moving about. If you want to go anywhere, even down the corridor at night, get someone to escort you.'

'That's ridiculous,' Dean managed, looking more worried than when he went in.

'If you don't know who is doing this thing, you have got to presume they could strike at any time.' Billy's tone was no longer warm.

'Why do I need to tell two people, though?'

'Because, if you confide in the wrong person, and they are your stalker, the other person will be able to testify against them at your inquest.'

Dean looked open-mouthed at Billy; he couldn't believe what had happened to him. He worked in the City. He wasn't a drug dealer or gangster or detective; he was a banker. He shouldn't have to watch his back or buy extra locks or put his life in other people's hands. He just managed to fight back the tears again. 'Is there anything else?' Dean said as he got off his chair and made his way to the door. He just wanted to get out of the office now.

'Yes. Take this.' Billy opened a drawer in his desk and threw something at him; Dean caught it before he knew what it was. As he looked down at his hands, he started shaking when he saw what he was holding – a gun.

'Do you know how to use it?'

'Yeah,' Dean lied. He had no idea what sort of gun it was; did it matter? It was small and looked like it would fit in his pocket, but apart from that, he knew nothing. His finger could only just get to the trigger as he held it.

'It's fully loaded; six bullets. Leave the safety on when it's in your pocket; otherwise your dad's chances of becoming a grandfather will diminish rapidly.'

Dean was still gobsmacked as he stood there, holding the gun. Different thoughts went through his head; would he have to use it to save his life? Would he have to take a life to save his own? Would he take the wrong life and spend the rest of his life living with that guilt in jail? He suddenly felt sick. 'I'd better get going. Still got some stuff to do before I leave tonight.' He went backwards through the door and was halfway down the corridor before Billy had the chance to say anything else.

Dean vomited for the first time in the toilets on the ground floor and a second time outside the building. He made his way home through the streets of South London with a lot more speed than he'd arrived, only slowing to occasionally glance behind him. Two months ago, he was a carefree young adult with no worries, no ties and no problems; now he was broken. He thought he was tough. He hadn't lost a fight since he was 12, hadn't cried since he was nine, but now he was losing a fight with someone he didn't know, and he'd just cried twice in his uncle's office.

CHAPTER 2

Dean felt safe as he walked back to his flat from West Hampstead station. The High Street was bustling with school mums and pensioners, drifting in and out of the coffee shops and convenience stores. It was broad daylight, and Dean felt confident there were too many people about for anyone to try and kill him now. They'd wait until dark when there was nobody around, and it would be over before he knew it; that gave him little comfort. He suddenly felt uneasy and turned around to see if anyone was following him, then he touched the gun in his pocket and felt safe again.

The walk was pleasant, the sun was out, and his confidence soon returned. He was going on holiday in a few hours' time and all these problems would be over, for a fortnight at least. As he approached his flat, he smiled again; maybe he had over-reacted a little and it was just a stupid joke by one of his mates?

His flat was in a neat three-block complex, surrounded by well-trimmed lawns and borders. Each block had four floors, with the top floor incorporated into the pitched roof. The buildings were no more than 20 years old, had all the mod-cons and looked impressive. They were expensive, but Dean could afford it.

As he entered the middle of the three blocks, he took a glance over his shoulder; he still couldn't see anyone.

Dean walked through the white-tiled lobby, with large false trees and modern paintings, towards the lift. There was no sign of anyone, but it wasn't surprising given that young professionals occupied most of the flats and it was still only mid-afternoon on a Friday.

He got out of the lift on the third floor and walked down the corridor. There were eight flats on each floor and Dean's was the last one on the left. As he rounded the corner, he pulled his keys out of his pocket but managed to drop them. As he bent down to pick them up, he looked up towards his flat. He froze as if he was a deer caught in the headlights of an oncoming car. His door was open – wide open! His sportsman's frame remained motionless for a minute as the reality of the situation set in; someone had gone into his flat again. Then it hit him: They could still be in there. He got that feeling in the pit of his stomach once more, but he just managed to hold off the sickness. He tried to compose himself, leaning against the corridor wall to steady his frame.

Then Dean remembered the present from his uncle and instinctively felt it in his pocket. There was the gun – at least he might get this over with once and for all. As he pulled the gun out of his pocket, he noticed his hand was shaking uncontrollably. Sweat was pouring from his forehead, and he wiped it with his upper arm. He examined the gun for a few seconds and successfully managed to take the safety off, before looking up at the ceiling and saying a quick prayer. He wasn't in the slightest bit religious, but he did it anyway. God would still have to justify his death at such a young age.

It required some effort to prise his sweaty shirt from the wall, and he slowly put one foot in front of the other. As he gradually headed towards the door, he prayed a neighbour would arrive home from work, so that they could investigate the flat together. He slowed to near snail's pace, but nobody had arrived to help him as he reached the open door.

His gun hand was shaking as he crossed the threshold into the flat, so much so that he had to steady it with his left. Although the door was open, he still needed to push it slightly to be able to get through, but as he did it, the door made a short, painful creak. He screwed his face and held his breath at the sound of the door, standing deadly still as he waited for a few seconds to see if the sound had disturbed the intruder. Finally, convinced that no one had heard the noise, Dean slowly proceeded into the entrance hall. There were no windows in this area of the flat, with the only light coming through the partially open door to the lounge. He took a quick a glance behind the front door and was relieved to see no one was there.

As he stood in the middle of the hall, he looked at the five, white beechwood doors that led off it. He contemplated which way to search the flat. To the left was the kitchen, straight on was the lounge, next to that the bedroom and then the bathroom. The door directly to the right, worried him, a walk-in store cupboard – definitely big enough for a grown man, or woman, to hide in. He decided that if he went into the kitchen first, someone hiding in the cupboard would be able to walk up behind him. But then again, he would make one hell of a noise opening the cupboard door, which was stiff.

Eventually, Dean decided to go into the lounge first, primarily because the door was already partly open and there were virtually no hiding places in there. He moved slowly forwards and, to his relief, the door didn't make a sound as he gradually opened it. Again, he looked behind the door first, convinced that was the most likely hiding place.

After satisfying himself that the lounge was intruder free, Dean made his way to the kitchen. He looked both ways as he left the lounge and walked with his back against the wall to the kitchen door. He turned the handle and unlatched it, then returned to his position against the wall. After several deep breaths, like he'd seen the good guys do in the movies, he turned quickly and pushed the door hard. As it flew open, he jumped to face the kitchen and positioned himself firmly on both feet with his gun held tightly in his hands. He moved his outstretched arms from side-to-side quickly as he surveyed the empty kitchen. He didn't need to go in, it was a galley style kitchen and he could clearly see the full length of it.

As he took another deep breath, he heard a thud from behind him. He turned around quickly, again waving his gun in an uncoordinated manner. He gulped and struggled with the sweat now dripping profusely from his forehead as he came to terms with what he'd just heard. The sound had come from the bedroom, he thought. Dean contemplated what to do next; the bedroom already concerned him more than any other room because of the built-in wardrobes and the position of the bathroom, but now he was definitely worried.

After another long pause, he built up the confidence to move towards the bedroom. He decided to adopt the same tactic as the kitchen and walked sideways along the wall to the door. The only problem this time was that the door hinged on the left, which meant Dean would have to lean across the gap between the wall and door in order to open it. He decided he would have to unlatch the door and open it in one movement, so in a split second, he jumped away from the wall to face the closed door. With his left hand he turned the handle and pushed the door open with force, pulling back for a second as he kicked the door with his foot.

He ducked, expecting a shot to come straight at him, but immediately stood up again as he realised nothing was coming. He moved into the room but didn't need to look behind the door this time as he'd heard it hit the wall.

The blow to his head came from behind as he was surveying the bedroom. A decision on what to do next was taken away from him and he crashed to the floor, managing to let out a yelp before falling unconscious on his face. His attacker had hidden in the bathroom and had quietly appeared behind Dean as he had unsubtly entered his bedroom. The intruder had used the sound of the bedroom door crashing against the wall to open the bathroom door and take their position behind Dean unnoticed. The long thin fluorescent light bulb used in the attack smashed to pieces and landed on the floor around him.

'Dean, Dean, are you alright?'

He only heard the end of the sentence as he slowly opened his eyes.

'Dean, are you alright?' the voice repeated.

He opened his mouth, but nothing came out. Before he could attempt it again, water was thrust down his throat.

'This'll make you feel better.'

Dean's head was being held up to help him take in the liquid. As he looked up towards the person knelt over him, he saw a face he recognised, even through his bleary eyes, 'Billy?' Dean's voice was croaky as he said his name.

Billy continued to ply him with water. 'How you feeling?'

'I don't know. My head hurts a bit, I think.' Dean paused as he pulled his torso up so that he was now leaning upright against the bed. 'What are you doing here?' he said as he started to become more lucid.

Billy moved from his crouched position over his nephew and twisted around so that he was now sitting next to him on the floor, also leaning against the bed. 'Looks like you've been hit across the back of the head.' Billy reached over and pulled Dean's head slowly forward so that he could examine the back of it. 'No blood, you're lucky.'

Dean chuckled, 'I don't feel lucky,' then he put his hand down to the floor and retracted it quickly when he felt the glass. 'What's this doing here?'

'Looks like it's what was used to hit you, probably strip-lighting from your bathroom.'

'So, they were in the bathroom? I can't believe they managed to get behind me without me hearing.'

'Don't put yourself down. You're new to all this stuff.' Billy forced a smile.

'This stuff.' Dean thought to himself for a moment; is that it now? Has he been forced into the underworld like his uncle? Will he forever be watching his back and walking around with a gun? The gun, where was it? Dean suddenly panicked. 'The gun!' he spluttered, 'where's the gun?' He looked at Billy like a lost school-boy.

'It's gone, I'm afraid,' Billy said sombrely. They both knew what it meant; if the stalker didn't have a gun before, they did now.

'This is serious,' Billy said sternly.

Dean nodded his head gently.

'Tell me the truth, Dean.'

'I've told you everything!' His voice wasn't as convincing as it has been in the office.

'Stop messing about!' Billy's voice was raised. He turned around, stood up and bent down to Dean. He was now pointing. 'Tell me now!' he yelled again.

'There's nothing,' Dean started to stand up as he said it.

In one movement, Billy grabbed Dean's collar with both hands, lifted him up and turned to slam him against the wall. 'Tell me the fucking truth now!'

Dean looked scared. His eyes swelled up and he tried to fight back the tears – he lost. After a few seconds, Billy put his arm around Dean's shoulder and pulled him across to the bed. They both sat down, Billy kept his arm around Dean's shoulder as he wept, then Dean dropped his head forward into his hands and planted them on his knees.

After a few minutes, Dean composed himself, wiped his eyes and prepared to reveal his secret.

The sun was still pouring into the bedroom as Billy and Dean sat on the edge of the bed. The bedroom was sparsely furnished; built-in wardrobes with large mirror doors and two bedside tables either side of the double bed. The walls were cream with just two large modern art paintings hanging on the walls. The grey carpet remained covered in broken glass from the attack.

Dean's eyes were red from the tears. He was building up to telling his uncle something that he hadn't told another living soul. Billy looked nervously at his nephew as he waited for the big confession. Finally, Dean lifted his head up, but couldn't look at his uncle. 'I've got a son.'

Billy moved his head closer to his nephew. 'You've got a kid?'

Dean nodded his head, as if disgraced.

Billy looked relieved and allowed himself a little laugh. 'What makes you think that this has something to do with the death threats? Did you shag her while she was going out with a nutcase?'

Dean shook his head. 'No. She's the bloody nutcase!'

'What happened then?'

Dean paused briefly as he composed himself to share the sordid details of his secret. 'Just after I started my second year at uni, about five years ago, I went back to Birmingham for Christmas. I met this girl I knew from school, Claire, and we started seeing each other. After several weeks of travelling from uni in Cambridge to Birmingham, it started to get tiresome, and by the February I'd ended it.'

'It goes back a few years then?' Billy interrupted.

Dean sighed, 'Yes.'

'And you've not told anyone in all that time?'

'No.' Dean had stopped crying, but his eyes remained red.

Billy shook his head and put his arm back around Dean's shoulder. 'At one time, you used to tell me every-thing. I think it's time you started to trust me again.' He squeezed his shoulder. 'Go on.'

'I got a phone call a couple of weeks after I'd finished it. She told me she was pregnant.'

'You must have been devastated,' Billy said.

'I was, absolutely devastated. Anyway, I drove straight up to Birmingham and met her. We discussed the options and we agreed it was best to have an abortion. I didn't pressure her; we came to that decision together.' Dean was trying to prove to his uncle that he'd done everything the right way, but Billy didn't look the slightest bit shocked now.

Unknown to Dean, Billy had been in this situation on more than one occasion. He often joked to friends that he probably had a few offspring wandering the planet. Dean continued, after getting the required supportive look from Billy, 'I spoke to her several times after that, but she gave me no indication that she had double-crossed me and not had the abortion.'

'When did you find out?'

'I got a phone call from her mum in the August. Out of the blue, she was just ranting at me for five minutes then put the phone down. I went straight up there and had it out with Claire. I told her I wanted nothing to do with the kid, but I'd pay what I needed to do.'

'Have you ever seen the kid?'

'No. Never,' Dean said, with no hint of regret. As far as he was concerned, he'd done all the right things. He'd been double-crossed by Claire, and she wasn't going to stop him from his ambitions. However, to a certain extent, he felt ashamed; he hadn't realised how much until he told his story aloud.

'Do you want to see the kid?'

'No,' came the firm reply, sufficiently firm that it left Billy in no doubt it was the truth. Dean didn't even think about the kid, never mind want to see him.

'And the girl, does she want you to see it?'

'She killed herself six months after the birth.'

There was a deadly silence as Billy absorbed this shock information. He had seen and heard a lot worse in his job, but he would never have expected this from his nephew. After a few seconds, he managed to utter something, 'Why?'

'Post-natal depression, or something of that sort. It's fairly common apparently, especially young single women. Her mum blamed me, her brother threatened to kill me, and her dad actually tried.'

'He tried to kill you?' Billy said, his tone indicated he didn't fully believe this.

'He drove his car at full speed towards me as I walked away from the funeral. Fortunately for me, a woman reversed out of her drive just as he mounted the kerb. Unfortunately for the woman, he hit her at 50 miles an hour, and she died.'

Billy went white with shock and couldn't speak. Dean continued, 'He was three times over the drink-drive limit and went to prison for seven years.'

'Is he out now, is that the problem?'

'No. He died two months ago in prison.'

Billy looked like he was struggling to take it all in and appeared to be finding it hard to gather his thoughts as the pair of them sat silently on the bed. Finally, he thought of a question, 'Who's looking after the kid?'

'Her mum and brother. They've never cashed a cheque I've written and never contacted me.'

'How did you know about her dad dying?'

'I got a newspaper clipping of the story in the post. Attached was a note saying, "You're next," that was the start of this stalker thing.'

'So, it's her brother then?' Billy said, not particularly at Dean, but more while in thought.

'Seems favourite,' Dean replied, but looked and felt like most of his problems had evaporated. He was relieved; he'd just poured out his soul to his uncle and suddenly felt safer. Surely now his uncle would sort this mess out? 'What do we do now?' Dean said after an extended pause. Although Dean really meant, *What are you going to do, uncle?*

Billy evidently decided to make it easy for his nephew. 'You're going to pack your bags and go on your holidays with your mates. It will all be sorted out by the time you get back.'

This was exactly what Dean wanted to hear but tried hard to suppress a smile. 'I can't go and leave you with the problem,' he said lamely, expecting his uncle's response.

'Of course, you can. Go, it will all be resolved when you get back. You're safest away from here.' That was all Dean needed to hear and he immediately relaxed; finally, he could start looking forward to his trip to France. 'I'm going to flat-sit for you. Just need to get a few bits sorted and then I'll move in for a couple of weeks.'

'Will you stay here until I leave?' Concern had re-entered Dean's voice, he didn't fancy trying to see out the next few hours alone.

'Of course. I'll stay here until you leave, then I'll pop out to get my things. Unless you hear from me, assume you're in the clear.'

'Cheers, Billy.' Dean was smiling now.

'No problem.' Dean didn't see the look on Billy's face as they hugged. If he had, he wouldn't have felt like it was all over.

CHAPTER 3

Pippa was sitting in the living room flicking through a photo album. She looked sad, but occasionally, as she saw a picture that triggered a happy memory, she smiled without knowing it. She'd been through the photo album 100 times since Cameron had died; just lately she'd managed to get to the end without crying. Her favourite picture was the one of the gang on holiday last year. Everyone was there; Dean, Beth, Graham, Marie, Stevie and Cameron – her brother. Even Ryan was there, smiling, with one arm wrapped around her and the other around Cameron.

A car pulled up outside, she put the album down and half-lifted herself off the seat to look out the window. Having checked that it wasn't them, she sat down again. Pippa had just turned 20, younger than the rest, but as mature as any of them. The group had adopted her several years ago; historically, they had been her brother's friends from uni, but after joining them on their annual holiday three years ago, they had become her friends as well. She became further integrated into the group when she started seeing Cameron's best friend, Ryan, after a holiday romance last year.

She was a pretty girl, even without make-up, which she rarely wore. At five-feet, four-inches, she always wore her trademark platform shoes to compensate for her height. She was dressed for her holiday in blue jeans and a lemon T-shirt. Her hair was blonde, shoulder-length and frizzy, tied back tightly in a ponytail. She had tiny features, every part of her face was petite, from her little nose and ears to her small mouth and thin lips. She was wearing no jewellery except her watch, and anyone that didn't know her might think she was a tomboy.

Another car drove past, and she stood up again to peek through the blinds; still not them. She slowly paced around the room, the same room she'd been in when she heard the news about her brother. She checked her watch again and cursed, she hated inefficiency and lateness. Pippa still lived at her parents' three-bedroom semi on the outskirts of Cambridge, the same town where Cameron and his friends had been to university. The living room had dated but was kept immaculately clean and tidy, with the furniture and patterned carpet looking worn and old-fashioned. There was a well-used brown three-seater sofa against the wall, opposite the window, and a matching single armchair that had a view outside. Her bags, a grey suitcase and black ruck-sack, were ready and waiting in the hallway. She'd answered the phone to her dad three times that morning, with him offering safety tips and warnings. It was harder on her parents to say goodbye to their last remaining child than it was for her to go on the holiday without Cameron.

As she put the photo album back on the shelf, she heard several honks from a car outside. Before she could get to the front door, the bell rang. By the time she opened it, Marie was standing in front of her while Graham was waving vigorously from inside the car. The women hugged and exchanged pleasantries before Pippa invited Marie in. 'Do you want a cuppa?" Pippa asked politely.

'No, best get going. Graham wants us to be in Maidstone before the others,' Marie replied.

'Are you sure Graham's parents are OK with us all staying over for the night?'

'Of course they are, plus it means we're all together for an early start tomorrow.' The car horn was sounded again, causing Marie to tut loudly.

'OK, I'm ready to go,' Pippa said as she picked up her bags and struggled through the door. Graham, now out of the car, helped load the bags into the boot and then remembered he hadn't said hello properly and leaned in to give Pippa a hello kiss, which he managed awkwardly,

'Got your passport?' Graham said as Pippa opened the rear door to get in.

'Yes. I think. Oh God, give me that bag back, I need to check now.' This scenario would be played out for the rest of the day as each person met another. Passports would have been checked 20 times before they got anywhere near France. Pippa nodded as she zipped her rucksack up again, throwing it back to Graham as she jumped in the royal-blue Ford Focus.

'I thought you were bringing your friend down with you?' Pippa enquired as she got in and adjusted her seatbelt. Marie decided to join her in the back of the car so they could gossip.

'Jack couldn't get the day off work, so he's gonna get the train down this evening.' Graham had started driving as he replied but felt the need to turn to Pippa in the back as he did this. He saw her looking slightly apprehensive and he gave a quick glance to his wife, this prompted Marie to jump in, 'I think he'll fit nicely into the group.'

Graham then interrupted before she had finished, 'Yeah, definitely. I wouldn't have invited him if I didn't think so.' Graham felt guilty for a minute as he said this, then felt the need to justify the decision to invite the stranger. 'It's not like we're trying to replace Cam, you know? Nothing can replace him. Jack's just finished with his girlfriend of three years, they were engaged, lived together and everything.' Pippa didn't need all this information, but Graham felt better for saying it.

Graham and Marie were finally married last year after going out for four years before that. They'd been friends since freshers' week, but it wasn't until Graham was in his second year at uni that they had finally realised their feelings for each other. The wedding had been formal, but still a lot of fun, with a number of stories that would be retold on the holiday. Most of the group had played key roles; Dean was best man, Stevie, Ryan and Cameron were ushers. Pippa and Beth were bridesmaids. All friends and family were together for the day, and it was more or less perfect.

Graham had put on a bit of weight since the wedding. He was average height but was now stocky, medically he might be touching overweight, but he and Marie were very content. He made little effort to disguise the geek in him, with his round-rimmed glasses and short brown hair, parted at the side. However, he was, in the right circumstances, incredibly witty and loyal – making him very popular among their group.

'My parents are looking forward to us all coming to stay, they don't get much excitement these days.' He paused as he completed a tricky manoeuvre onto the dual carriageway, then continued. 'We need to be there by 6pm to beat the others. Knowing Dean and Stevie, they'll be bang on time, and I don't want my parents having to deal with things on their own.' He paused as he completed some overtaking. 'Plus, we have to be in bed by 11pm to make sure we can get up at 4am.'

All groups of friends have a leader, and Graham was theirs. There had been no election, no campaigning and no recount, but everyone knew it. He organised, mediated and delegated almost everything. New friends that had dare contest this had come and gone; it worked well for their group. He liked organising and planning, nobody else did, and it was easier for the others not to try. Being the leader came naturally to Graham, he was a lawyer for a mid-sized practice, but at one of their more remote offices in Norwich. He was ambitious and one of the more highly paid members of the group. Despite this, he didn't spend money on fashionable clothes and cars. For the start of the holiday, he was wearing his usual smart-casual outfit, a blue polo shirt and beige slacks.

Graham's wife, Marie, had also gone to their university but had not followed her passion for photography into a career. After finishing her course, she gave it up and instead paid the bills for both of them by working as a doctor's receptionist while Graham studied law. She had soft features, nothing that particularly stood out, but had a confidence that made her attractive. They suited each other perfectly. She had straight brown hair down to her shoulders, which had subtle red highlights. She didn't have her finger on the pulse of fashion but was leagues above her spouse; wearing white jeans, Nike trainers and a navy CK T-shirt – she looked well turned out, if not stunning.

Graham tried to keep involved in the conversation for the first 15 minutes but lost the thread when the girls moved on to the latest reality show, so he turned the music up a bit and sang quietly to himself.

The girls had nodded off by the time the M25 was signposted. Graham checked the time and smiled to himself, they were making excellent progress, and the traffic wasn't anywhere near as thick as he'd expected. They were cruising comfortably within the speed limit on the inside lane of the motorway.

He didn't see the van, and certainly didn't expect the move it made – and nor should he. Marie woke just in time to see the impact; the white transit sideswiped them from the middle lane. She just managed to let out a high-pitched screech as they careered onto the hard shoulder then hit the embankment. As Graham hit the brakes, the car's back end lost grip and they swerved back onto the hard shoulder. Graham panicked and took his foot off the brake again, but he had now lost control of the vehicle as it continued to swerve between the carriageway and the grass. Then he saw the motorway bridge approaching.

Both girls, who had been screaming intermittently since the impact, let out a combined pained wail as the concrete pillars approached at pace. Graham continued to wrestle with the steering wheel as the bridge approached. He was turning right as hard as he could, frightened to touch the brakes again, but the pillars were getting closer and closer. As they all said their final prayers, they felt several jerks as the car finally pulled right and went over the edge, back onto the hard shoulder. The car continued to swerve, but Graham finally managed to bring the car under control and then to a sudden stop, just past the bridge.

He leant forward over the steering wheel, bright red, sweating and shaking, before letting out a huge exhale of air. Then he turned to his wife. 'Are you alright?'

She was sat upright, back firmly against the seat, head pressed stiffly against the headrest. She was ghostly white and had sweat pouring down her face. Eventually, she managed to respond, 'I, I think so.'

Graham turned to see Pippa who was pale but didn't look anything like Marie. 'How are you?'

'I've just seen my entire life flash before me,' she managed.

'You're not the only one!' Graham said, with a hint of hysteria.

'What happened?' Pippa asked, looking far more alive than Marie.

'Some idiot just moved into our lane without looking and knocked us off the road,' Graham said, with absolute certainty.

After a few more moments of reflection, the three of them finally started to move. Graham tried to open his door but couldn't. Up until this point, not one expletive had been uttered in the car; that changed as Graham battled hard to get out. Eventually, he gave up and clambered over the gearstick to the passenger door.

Graham, now in full control again, ordered the girls onto the embankment and then walked around to the driver's side of the car to inspect the damage. 'Bloody hell!' he shouted as he got first sight of the damage.

'Is it bad?' Marie said, her tone suggesting she knew full well it would be.

'The car's fucked!'

'He didn't even stop to see if we were alright!' Pippa said to nobody in particular.

'Of course, he bloody didn't. He would have been sued to buggery for dangerous driving,' Graham screamed.

'What do we do now?' Marie asked.

'I'll phone the police. Then we'll get a tow to my parents. Everything will be fine.' This was Graham at his best, level-headed in a crisis. Both women felt safer for him being in control, but neither would admit it.

The police arrived within 10 minutes of the call, and the girls gave their account of what had happened to a sympathetic female police officer, while Graham gave a much more detailed account to Sergeant Penny.

'Lucky escape, Mr Joseph,' he said as he circled the wrecked Ford.

'You're not bloody kidding,' Graham said with a nervous chuckle.

'From what you and your passengers described it sounds like he pulled across without looking.' Graham just grunted in agreement. 'With any luck our CCTV cameras will have caught it,' and Penny pointed towards a camera attached to the underside of the bridge.

'I'm sure we won't be that lucky,' Graham said sarcastically.

'You never know. Anyway, we've got your details; if you're okay, we'll wait for the tow-truck and check for debris. It should be here in twenty minutes.'

The sergeant returned to the squad car and completed some paperwork, while the PC walked down the hard shoulder checking for the debris.

Graham went over to his wife on the bank and put his arm around her as they waited for the recovery service. Pippa started crying, softly at first and then louder as the realisation of their near miss hit home. Graham and Marie shuffled up to be next to her.

'Are you alright?' Marie asked quietly.

'It just occurred to me, if I had died in that crash, it would have finished off my parents. If I die, they will have nothing to live for, they will be absolutely devastated. That could have finished our entire family off.'

Graham and Marie looked at each other, both waited for the other to speak before Graham finally responded, 'Don't talk like that. You're going to live a long, happy life. If we were meant to die, we would have in that crash. We were spared, what happened to Cameron was just a freak accident.'

'Was it though?' Pippa stared Graham in the eyes as she said it. Graham didn't say anything, but all three knew what she meant by that.

As he sat waiting for the rescue truck, Graham thought about Cameron's accident. It had happened six months ago in February. He'd gone on a short skiing break near the Swiss-French border with Cameron, Ryan and Dean. The friends were close, but the group dynamics usually found Cameron and Ryan together with Graham and Dean the other pair. Their 'fifth' friend, Stevie, wasn't remotely sporty or interested in skiing and had impolitely declined the offer of a skiing trip. Being truthful, Graham himself was a clumsy and uncoordinated skier, but went mainly for the social side.

Graham and Dean had discussed it at length since then – but neither knew what had happened between Ryan and Cameron ahead of the trip. Whatever it was, neither was prepared to discuss it with them; but it made for a toxic atmosphere. They had barely uttered a word to each other from the moment they got on the plane at Stansted, to the night it happened. It had completely ruined their four days away. Graham and Dean had even looked into getting an early flight back but couldn't get one for less than 500 quid.

It was on the final night that the accident happened. Graham got down to the hotel bar after a shower to find Cameron sprawled on the floor, with Ryan on top of him and Dean trying his best to keep them apart. Later, Graham had been told that Ryan connected a couple of good punches on Cameron's face, with the latter unwilling to fight back. Between Graham and Dean, they'd eventually managed to pull Ryan off him, in an attempt to save Cameron from further injury. Neither would say what it was about, but Graham later confessed to Dean that he suspected it was about Pippa; probably that Ryan had done something to upset her.

After they'd broken up the fight, Ryan walked up to Cameron and spat in his face, causing Cameron to finally retaliate; landing a perfect right-hook that clocked Ryan plum on the nose. As Ryan crashed backwards into their table of drinks, Cameron made a bolt for it and darted out the hotel before Ryan could get back up. Dean battled gamely with Ryan to stop him pursuing Cameron but couldn't, and Ryan got past him with relative ease. Ryan barged past some Spanish tourists as he charged through the door and could be heard shouting, 'I'm going to kill him!' as he gave chase. Dean tried to keep up for a while but returned to the bar after losing them both. He never saw Cameron again.

The avalanche struck about 20 minutes after the two had left the hotel. Initially, Graham had feared both of them had been killed, but after three hours Ryan returned, bruised and battered. He claimed that he had never caught up with Cameron, but Dean and Graham had never really believed him.

By the end of the following day, 16 bodies had been pulled from the avalanche, and a further five were still missing. Cameron had not been found initially, but after his parents flew out to help the search in Switzerland, Ryan flew home, apparently unconcerned about his missing friend. Graham and Dean had stayed, but as the days passed, hope of finding Cameron's body had completely gone. On the seventh day of searching, a badly mangled body had been found under a pile of rocks and mud. It didn't take long for a tearful Mr Byers to identify his son's battered torso.

By the time they brought the body home, Ryan and Pippa had split up and Graham's suspicions about the events that night seemed to have been confirmed. Ryan didn't go to the memorial service, and by the time Graham and Dean had retold the story of the ski-trip, nobody in the group wanted to see Ryan again. The general feeling among the group had been that if Ryan hadn't directly killed Cameron, he had contributed to his death by forcing him out into the mountains that night. His apparent lack of sadness and remorse at the loss of such a close friend had hardened everyone's feelings against Ryan.

'Mr Joseph,' the mechanic broke the silence that had fallen on the three of them as they recovered from the shock.

'Any chance we can get it on the road by tomorrow?' Graham asked hopefully.

He laughed. 'It's an insurance write-off I'm afraid.'

'What do we do now then? We're supposed to be going to France in that tomorrow.'

'I'm sorry, sir, but you won't be able to drive this car anywhere. We can tow you to a destination in this country.'

'Can you take us to Maidstone then?' Graham said hopefully.

'What's the point if we can't go to France in it?' Marie said with resignation in her voice.

'Well, I'm not missing out on my holiday, I'll walk if I have to,' Graham said with determination. Pippa nodded in agreement.

'If we can get down to my parents, then we can think of a plan.' Graham was not going to let this mishap stop his holiday and was in his element in this crisis.

'Okay, sir, we'll give you a ride to Maidstone. Hop in.' The three of them got into the truck as the recovery man loaded the car onto the back.

The white van had already carried on towards West Hampstead.

CHAPTER 4

'Jesus, are you all alright?' Dean was on his mobile phone as Graham recounted their near-death experience. Billy's ears pricked as he heard snippets of the conversation, while busily changing the locks on the front door.

'Well that's good of your parents, what have they got?' Dean was delighted to hear that Graham had sourced a substitute car, but in reality, he would have been surprised if he hadn't.

'A Honda, that'll be fine, what about insurance?' Billy had stopped working completely now and was staring at Dean as he finished his conversation. 'No, he's not here yet. I think he'll be about twenty minutes.' Dean turned away as he felt his uncle's eyes bearing down on him, but carried on the conversation, 'Okay, I'll see you in a couple of hours. Bye.'

Dean put the phone back in his pocket and tentatively turned to his uncle. 'What?' he said, after a few seconds.

'Nothing.' Billy got back down to the door and started working again, pretending not to be interested.

'Go on, there's something up.' Dean crossed his arms as he said this.

'Okay then, what just happened?' Billy nodded towards the phone as he said this.

'Oh, Graham had a lucky escape earlier. Some idiot van driver barged him off the road, and they nearly crashed into a bridge,' he replied dismissively.

'I see. And you don't find it strange that on the same day someone breaks into your flat and batters you over the head, your friends are nearly killed?'

'What? No one tried to kill them, it was just an accident. Anyway, the two things can't be connected, why would Claire's brother want to kill them?'

'You're assuming that Terry's your stalker. What if it's someone else?'

Dean chuckled. 'How many enemies do you think I've got? It's got to be Terry. There's nobody else it could be. Anyway, Graham has a tendency to exaggerate, it was probably just a minor prang.'

'If you say so. Just promise me that you'll take care of yourself out there.'

'Of course, but I've got seven other people with me.'

'Nevertheless, I want you to take this.' Billy reached into his bag and pulled out another gun.

'Jesus, Unc, have you got an arsenal tucked away somewhere?' Dean's attempt at humour couldn't disguise his obvious anguish at having another lethal weapon thrust into his palm. It was too much reality for him again and, as he gripped the weapon in his palm, he started to feel queasy.

Billy grabbed Dean's arm and pulled him into the lounge, before sitting him down as if ready to give a naughty schoolboy a lecture. 'Look, Dean, I'm not saying there is a connection. You're probably right that it's this Terry character. He's lost his sister and his dad and it's likely he'll want to blame someone. But, let's just keep our options open. I think that you should still go on this holiday, best to be out of the way. But I want to know exactly where you are going and the full names of everyone who is going, and if possible, their addresses and any other useful information.'

Dean looked down at the carpet as if searching for a suitable comeback, but all he could manage was a grunt of agreement.

Billy pulled out his notebook and a pen, just like a proper cop. His tone changed from that of concerned parent to a firm interrogating officer, 'Right, so who's going?'

'Graham and Marie,' Dean's voice was faint as he answered his uncle.

'Surnames as well,' Billy barked.

'Er.' Dean was momentarily stumped. 'Er, Joseph.'

'How long have you known them?'

'You can't possibly think—'

Dean was cut off mid-sentence by a stern Billy, 'Just answer the question. I'll be the judge of who's a suspect and who isn't. How long have you known them?'

Dean didn't try to resist again. 'Graham I met on my first day at uni seven years ago, our rooms were next to each other. Marie, I met once or twice in the first year, she briefly went out with someone else I knew. I got to know her properly when she started dating Graham, probably about five years ago. I was best man at their wedding.'

'Who else?' Billy demanded, almost before Dean could draw breath. He briefly thought about how tough it must have been to be interrogated by Superintendent Marchant in a small Birmingham police cell.

'Stevie Pennock, schoolteacher. Lives in Bristol at his parent's house. As with Graham, we lived in same halls at uni, known for seven years. Single.' Dean was firm now, offering only relevant information and no opinions. Billy allowed himself a small smile as he listened to Dean's response.

'Otis Cole, architect. Old school friend of Stevie's. He joined us on holiday for the first time three years ago, the rest of us hadn't met him before that. He still lives in Bristol with his parents. I don't think he has a girlfriend at the moment, but he tends to sleep around a fair bit according to Stevie.' He paused briefly and looked at his watch. 'They should be here by now actually; they're giving me a lift to Maidstone.'

* * *

They were relieved to finally see the flashing amber lights of the recovery vehicle as it pulled onto the hard shoulder. The car had spluttered to a stop 75 minutes ago, and they'd been sat on the grass verge of the M4 ever since then.

'Mr Pennock?' the recovery man said to them as he stepped out of the truck.

'Yes.' Stevie stepped forward offering a hand, but the mechanic had already turned back to get his tools.

'What seems to be the problem?' the burly, bearded man muttered as he marched over to the car. The yellow overalls and fluorescent orange jacket were well covered in grease. The badge sewn onto the overalls proclaimed his name to be Brian.

'The engine just seized as we were getting up to speed to pull onto the motorway, thankfully I was able to steer it onto the hard shoulder before it stopped completely.'

'Well done, sir,' Brian managed, with a patronising tone, as he shoved his head under the bonnet and started tugging at valves and wires.

Otis walked over to join his lifelong friend, who was standing, arms crossed and silent, next to the car, eyes fixed on Brian as he performed his assessment. 'Any idea what's wrong yet?' Otis said as he joined Stevie.

This woke him out of the trance, and he turned to his friend. 'Not yet. What happens if he can't fix it? We haven't got a back-up car. We'll have to cancel the holiday.' Otis smiled, he knew Stevie well, and he was always the merchant of doom. If there was ever a negative thought or argument to be had, it was normally emanating from his best friend.

Stevie was not a confident person, probably due to his size. He wasn't particularly tall, below average height, but weighed close to 17 stone. A few years ago, he'd grown a goatee beard, mainly to help define a chin – something he confessed to Otis, but no one else. He wasn't particularly fashionable either, but as a school-teacher, couldn't afford the best clothes anyway. His glasses were loose and often slipped to the end of his nose. In contrast to his friend, Otis was stick-thin, a result of his outdoors lifestyle, he could barely sit still for five minutes with rock climbing and paragliding among his many activities. He was of Afro-Caribbean origin, with short, neatly shaved hair and had a well-toned body, which never left him short of female interest.

Despite the obvious differences in their physical appearance, they had similar personalities and an under-lying feeling of inadequacy. For Stevie, it was a hang-up about his appearance, but for Otis, it was always his dyslexia. At school, this left them both with very few other friends and pushed them close together. It was only through the later teens that they really started to appreciate their own qualities and grew in confidence as they went to separate universities.

'Have you filled her up today, Mr Pennock?' Brian said as he walked over to them, attempting to clean his hands with a dirty rag.

The friends looked at each other. 'You ran out of petrol!' Otis couldn't suppress a laugh as he said this.

'No, no, it can't be. I filled it up yesterday evening. There must be something wrong with the fuel pipe,' Stevie was on the defensive now.

Brian interrupted before Otis could respond, 'No, you don't understand. What I mean is, the tank is full, but with unleaded – this is a diesel car.'

'What!' Stevie exclaimed with a high-pitched squeal.

'I mean, you put in the wrong type of fuel,' Brian offered unhelpfully.

'That's not possible, my dad's had this car for three years, I borrow it all the time. In fact, he's never had a petrol car, always diesel. I would never have filled it up wrongly.' Stevie was clearly outraged at this slight on his character.

Otis put an arm around his friend. 'These things happen, mate, it's not the end of the world is it?'

'Maybe not the end of the world, but it could be the end of the engine,' Brian offered, seemingly haven taken on the role of doom-monger.

'Is there anything you can do?' Otis was forced to speak as Stevie appeared to have gone into shock.

'I need to flush it out and hope that it hasn't done too much damage, I'm surprised you managed to make it this far. Can you both please move back to the verge; the hard shoulder isn't the safest place to stand.'

Otis had to guide Stevie over to the verge and almost forced him to sit down. Finally, Stevie managed to speak again, 'I know I put diesel in the car.'

'Yeah, but your car's petrol. I bet you just weren't thinking.'

'No, you have to believe me, I definitely put diesel in because the first station I went to didn't have a working diesel pump.'

'Okay, well there's nothing we can do about it now, let's just hope he can fix it.'

'But if he can't, the holiday is ruined – and my dad will kill me!'

The pair sat silent and motionless, both scared to glance in Brian's direction as he worked on the stricken vehicle. The sun was beginning to set on a fine early summer's day. The group usually borrowed Stevie's dad's car for their holiday as he always had a lovely seven-seater, with all the mod-cons. This year it was still the Ford Galaxy, in navy blue, but Stevie had been promised it would be upgraded in time for next year's holiday. Only four of its seven seats would be used for the journey down, but it provided plenty of space for everyone's luggage and would be full to bursting with duty-free beer and wine for the journey back.

Suddenly, Brian appeared in front of them at the grass verge. 'Well, Mr Pennock.' Stevie looked up like a lost child. 'It's all fixed and working fine.' Finally, he started breathing again. It took Stevie a couple of seconds to compose himself before he got up and vigorously shook their saviour's hand.

'Just remember to use diesel next time, Mr Pennock,' Brian said as he got back in his truck. Stevie half-turned to protest his innocence but clearly thought better of it.

* * *

'Where the hell can they be?' Dean was talking to no one in particular as he muttered it.

'It's no good staring out the window, they won't come any quicker,' Billy offered, then he changed his tone, deliberately sounding sceptical, 'let's hope they haven't hit any problems like Graham.'

Dean wasn't at all amused by this comment, and the glare he afforded Billy did little to hide his feelings. He'd been patient enough during the interrogation and probing of his friends. It was pretty obvious that by the time Dean had finished describing the other members of the group, it was the newcomer Jack that had interested Billy the most. A 'friend of a friend' joining the holiday for the first time, is not something that would have eased Billy's fears, and Dean knew it.

The buzzer finally broke the silence that had engulfed them after Billy's loaded comment. Initially, the sound had caused a tense Dean to jump, before he composed himself and collected his belongings. 'Finally! Right, Unc, I'll see you in a couple of weeks. Thanks for all your help.' Dean forced his hand into Billy's palm.

'Okay, take care of yourself. I'll sit it out at the flat for a few more hours and then go and get my things.' They embraced again, and Dean had to force himself out of Billy's clutches before grabbing his bags and setting off down the corridor.

He marched purposefully towards the lift with his large suitcase in one hand and a rucksack over his left shoulder. The lift seemed to take an age as he waited for it to arrive at the third floor; he was sure he could hear someone holding the door open on another floor. Finally, it came to a shuddering halt and the doors opened in front of him. As he took a pace forward, he walked straight into a large mattress, which had appeared in front of him as the lift doors opened. 'Sorry,' came the shout from someone behind the bed, 'moving-out day.' Dean managed a polite response before the lift doors closed but let out a curse under his breath as he was left behind.

He picked up his luggage and marched towards the staircase, struggling with the two fire doors that blocked his way. As he reached the bottom, he heard a beep from his mobile. 'On my way, give me a chance,' he muttered under his breath as he fought with another set of fire doors and finally got into the lobby.

'Where are they?' he said aloud this time as he opened the front door to be greeted by an empty forecourt. Then he remembered the text message. He fumbled away in his pocket, got the phone and opened the message. "Will be 30 mins – problem with car. Stevie."

'Bugger it!' he shouted across the car park as he picked up his luggage again. Dean struggled to get the rucksack in position and fumbled with the strap as he tried to get it onto his shoulder. The sun had just dipped behind the next block of flats, and it was the dark shadow cast across the car park, combined with his strap problems that meant Dean didn't notice the van speeding towards him.

Billy didn't feel comfortable letting his nephew out of his sight, but he told himself it was the right thing to do. He knew the only way to smoke out the culprit was to give him enough rope to hang himself, or herself. Could it be a woman? He'd seen plenty of women get the strength to do some extraordinary things over the years, but it didn't seem likely in this case. He had to admit that taking Dean's events alone, Terry seemed the likely culprit, but considering the other incidents involving his friends, that wouldn't fit completely.

His thought process was broken by the ringing of the landline phone. Billy went to pick it up, then hesitated with his hand hovering just above it before finally deciding to answer. The colour drained from his face as he listened to voice on the other end. Stevie wasn't able to finish his sentence before Billy hung up the phone and darted from the flat.

The sound created by the impact seemed loud enough to wake most of West Hampstead. A woman screamed from a first-floor balcony as she looked at the carnage sprawled out in front of her. Dean had missed the whole thing and only looked up in time to see the aftermath. He ran over to the red Fiat lying on its side, with a wrecked white van horizontal to it. Through the thick smoke now engulfing the scene, he didn't notice the driver's door of the van open and someone jump out. By the time he got to the wreck, the van driver was long gone. He looked into the Fiat and saw an elderly gentleman that he recognised inside.

'Mr Wadley, are you OK?'

'I think so, my legs trapped though, I can't get out,' there was definite panic in his voice.

'Don't worry, let me help,' Dean said as he tried the driver's-side door, which was now at the top of the car.

'Bloody madman, I was only reversing out and didn't see anything coming, bloody idiot must have been speeding.'

'Calm down, Mr Wadley, let's worry about getting you out.' The door was stuck. Then Dean noticed it; petrol was seeping out of the car. He froze for a moment as he realised that he was now at serious risk himself.

Before he could make a decision about whether to stay or run for it, he was rugby tackled from behind and landed face first in a flower bed. He tried to look up, but his head was being forced down into the soil. The next thing he felt was an intense burst of heat up his back as the two vehicles behind him ignited into a ball of fire.

Eventually, the grip on his neck was released, and he was able to scramble around to see the vehicles engulfed in flames.

'That's two you owe me now, kiddo.' Dean looked around to see his uncle sat next to him in the flower bed. 'And next time, leave the car wrecks to the professionals.'

'I could have got him out,' Dean protested, but he didn't really believe it. 'Poor Mr Wadley,' he said, but managed to hold back the tears.

'What about the van driver?' Billy said, although he already knew the answer to the question.

'He wasn't there when I got to the car, must have legged it.'

'He must have been driving at a hell of a speed to have caused that mess.' Dean hadn't noticed the suspicious tone in Billy's voice.

'I guess so, but I didn't see it.'

* * *

The train was late as it pulled to a stop at Liverpool Street Station. The red-haired man fought with his bags as he tried to free them from the luggage rack. After a brief wait for the doors to open, he stepped onto the platform. There were only a handful of people getting off with him, not surprising at 10pm on a Friday night.

Jack Langlan was 23 years old. A lawyer, work colleague and friend of Graham Joseph. He'd joined the office less than six months ago as an associate, working with Graham at March & Phelps; a mid-sized law firm based in East Anglia. They'd got on well from the beginning and he'd quickly been taken under Grahams' wing; even invited on this holiday with his friends. Jack wasn't exactly bursting with excitement, but then again, he was about to holiday with seven people, five of whom he'd never met. However, it was two weeks away from the office, and he hadn't had a proper break from things since the funeral. It was kind of Graham to ask him along, if only because he felt sorry for him.

Jack looked around for the sign to the underground; he wasn't a regular to London and was slightly overawed by the big city. Graham's instructions told him to get the Circle line to Victoria Station and then get on the 21:55 to Maidstone, but he'd already missed that one. In an ideal world he would have come down with Graham and Marie earlier, but he wanted to get things tidied up at the office, at least that's what he told Graham. In reality, he needed to speak to his mum; it was the six-month anniversary of the death of his dad, and he expected it would be tough for her. Two weeks would be the longest he'd have left her alone since, but what he had to do over the next fortnight was far more important than hand-holding his mother.

As he waited for the next tube to pull up, he felt a churning in his stomach. What would the fortnight hold for him? He had only one thing he wanted to achieve, well two if you count putting the past year behind him, and the first would help towards the second, wouldn't it? He jumped on the tube as the doors opened. The carriage had a smattering of people in it, a few alcohol-heavy partygoers and a couple of Japanese tourists. He checked he still had his wallet as the doors opened at Aldgate and a couple of baseball-capped teens got out.

The train pulled into Victoria Station, with Jack waiting eagerly for the doors to open. He marched out and then hesitated as he looked for the signs to the correct platform. As he started to make his way through the ticket barrier, he caught a glimpse of someone he thought he recognised. It took a few seconds, and then it registered; it was her.

* * *

As Stevie tried to pull into the car park, he could see three fire engines, four police cars and an ambulance blocking his entrance. He didn't know, but the ambulance wouldn't be rushing back to the hospital.

'What the hell's going on here?' Otis's mouth was wide open. 'There's Dean, talking to the police,' he managed as he directed Stevie to pull over onto the pavement.

Dean saw them out the corner of his eye and waved them over as he finished giving his statement to the policeman. The last thing he wanted to do was go over the whole thing with Stevie the doom-merchant, but he knew he'd have to explain the scene. Dean was covered in soil, cuts and blood, and was still shaking as Stevie and Otis joined him.

'What the hell happened to you?' Stevie was the only one talking, Otis seemed to be struck dumb by the action playing out in front of him.

'It's fair to say I've had the day from hell.'

'You're not bloody kidding!' Stevie was getting more high-pitched with every sentence.

'You're not going; end of!' Billy was arguing with Dean as he tried to clean himself up in the bathroom. He was attempting, unsuccessfully, to keep his voice unheard from Stevie and Otis, who were in the lounge.

'I am, and you can't stop me.' Dean had recovered enough to fight his corner.

'I bloody can. I'm not standing by and letting you get murdered.' Billy deliberately let the last word hang in the air.

Dean was stung temporarily by that word, "murdered", but managed to compose himself. 'I'm going on holiday to the middle of nowhere in France with seven people who'll be with me day and night – not the ideal scenario for a stalker to pounce!'

'You'd be surprised.' It was half-hearted from Billy, and Dean knew that he'd won the battle.

Dean finished in the bathroom and moved across the corridor to collect his belongings from the bedroom. As he bent down to grab his bags, he saw remnants of the fluorescent tube that had earlier been smashed over his head. His knees wobbled a little and, for a moment, he thought he might collapse. He managed to turn to his left and flop on the edge of the bed. At that second, he thought of the events of the day – his visit to his uncle's office, confessing his biggest secret, discovering a break-in, being smashed on the head, the fatal car smash. Not to mention the incidents involving his friends; one set being driven off the road and another breaking down under suspicious circumstances. Could it all be a coincidence? Billy had always taught him that coincidences didn't exist, at least as far as crime went. But how could they be linked? How could Claire's pregnancy and death possibly be linked to Graham or Stevie? His moment's reflection was finally broken by Stevie, 'Are we off then?'

'Yeah, just getting the final bits together,' he tried to sound certain, so as not to arouse suspicion. He was close to his friends, but not close enough to talk about what he'd been through. Even if he did pick someone to talk to, it wouldn't be Stevie; he'd always found it difficult to engage in a personal conversation. Dean knew that Stevie would find the conversation embarrassing and try to make a joke out of it. He'd always have a tale to tell and was, without doubt, good company, but had never been a confidant. Dean had always felt a little sorry for Stevie; among the group of five friends at uni, he'd always been the odd one out. Yes, the five of them had been close, but when push came to shove, the other four had their pairs, and Stevie would be the one left. Dean suspected that's the main reason why Stevie had invited Otis on the holiday three years ago, and it had seemed to work very well.

Dean followed Stevie to the front door, quiet now, not feeling capable of small-talk or holiday banter. He turned to his uncle, who was stood in the doorway to the lounge, and managed a weak, 'Goodbye.'

Billy didn't initially look like he was going to respond and even started to turn his back but gave in and turned to offer his hand. 'Take care.' Dean responded to the hand and thanked his uncle again.

As Dean walked down the corridor towards the lift with Stevie and Otis, who still appeared struck dumb by the incident, Billy hovered by the entrance to the flat and watched them disappear.

***

Billy checked his watch; they'd been gone for an hour. Less than five minutes after Dean had left, he'd regretted letting him go. If he'd had a car, he'd have chased after them, but he didn't. As he sat in Dean's flat, he thought about the case; would he see his nephew alive again? If he had anything to do with it, he would. But now he had work to do. If the attacker had spent time in the flat, he would certainly know about the holiday. Would he or she follow Dean to France? He had to admit to himself, it was unlikely. No, he would probably wait until Dean returned. Anyway, he'd be left shaken by the crash, maybe even quite badly injured himself. That gave him an idea, or at least a place to start; A&E. It might give a lead or two. Yes, that could well be the best place to start.

CHAPTER 5

The Ford Galaxy pulled into the driveway of the neat five-bedroom detached house, having made the journey from North London to Kent without further incident. The three occupants barely had time to get out of the car before they were greeted by a large, rotund, grey-haired old lady, with an impossibly large smile stretching from ear-to-ear. They were each hugged firmly and kissed on both cheeks by Mrs Joseph as they tried to get into the house. Having regained their breath, they were ushered into the lounge, where an inordinate amount of refreshments were waiting.

As she fussed over her guests, Mrs Joseph insisted that all of her subjects call her Grace and forced empty plates into their hands, while pointing them towards a table full of cakes and savouries. Dean was almost frog-marched towards the table, before being faced with a choice of smoked salmon sandwiches, Melton Mowbray pork pies, prawn vol-au-vents, cheese and bacon straws and freshly baked sausage rolls. He politely put a selection of food on his plate and took one of the chairs, which had been arranged in a semicircle in front of the buffet table.

Graham informed the arrivals that they were missing two people; he needed to drive to the station shortly and pick them up. Everyone was behind schedule, and sleep would be sacrificed rather than their departure time. Dean smiled to himself; Graham never changed and quite frankly, he was glad of it. He knew the holiday would feel weird this year without Ryan and Cameron, but it was nice to have some familiarity.

After finishing his plate of food, Dean politely collected a couple of the dirty dishes and made his way into the kitchen. He expected to have them wrestled off him by Grace, but instead she followed him into the kitchen. Dean carefully placed the plates into the sink and started to make efforts to wash them, desperately hoping Grace was going to insist he left them. Having waited a few seconds, he looked around to see her rooting through a large cupboard, its location meant she'd had to close the kitchen door in order to fully open the cupboard. She gave a loud tut and then closed the cupboard door as if to signal she hadn't found what she was looking for. Then she came over to the sink, picked up a tea towel and stood next to Dean as he washed the dishes.

There was an awkward silence, and Dean instantly knew she wanted to ask him something. He waited nervously in anticipation of what she had to say, eventually he decided to break the silence, 'I like the kitchen, when did you have it done?'

The silence continued for a few seconds with Dean thinking she was never going to speak, but finally Grace spoke, completely ignoring his question, 'He's not over it, you know?'

Dean stopped scrubbing a plate and looked up out of the window, although he wasn't focusing on anything in particular. He knew immediately what she was referring to but found it too difficult a conversation to have.

After his own awkward silence, he finally looked at her. 'I don't think either of us will ever get over it.'

Grace put down the tea towel and touched Dean's elbow gently. 'I know, dear.' She picked it up again and continued, 'I thought Ryan was such a nice boy. I can't believe he would have done anything like that,' her tone suggested she had some sympathy for Ryan.

'I wouldn't have believed it either if I hadn't seen it all for myself,' Dean tried to be dismissive.

'Did either of you try and talk to him?' she challenged.

'Quite hard to talk to him when he runs away from a missing friend, refuses to help in the search effort and when they finally find the body, refuses to go to the funeral,' Dean was beginning to get annoyed, and his tone didn't disguise it.

'There are two sides to every story, my dear.'

'Well, as Cameron is dead, we'll never hear his side,' Dean responded abruptly, and instantly regretted it. He looked at his inquisitor and felt sorry for barking at her. She was a caring and thoughtful woman who enjoyed making a fuss of her son's friends. Grace Joseph was a lot older than everyone else's mum, in her late sixties, she had long since retired. However, Dean suspected she had more than enough life in her to outlive all his friend's parents, and possibly some of his friends. Graham had been a little embarrassed about the age of his parents when they'd met at uni, but as he grew more comfortable with the group, he often joked about being an "unplanned planner". There was a much older sister, but Dean had never met her. She'd apparently become estranged from the family when Graham was four or five; she hadn't even attended his wedding last year.

Undeterred by Dean's tone, she continued to push, 'I know you think I'm an old busybody, but I can see how much it's affected Graham, and I'm assuming you as well, my dear.' She touched his elbow again and leaned in. 'I'm sure you'd both feel better if you met up with Ryan and discussed it.'

Dean shrugged a little to release his elbow and stepped sideways. 'I have absolutely no desire to see Ryan ever again,' he said and then calmly continued, 'but I really appreciate you thinking of us.'

He assumed his last comment would be sufficiently dismissive to end the conversation, but to his annoyance, she continued. 'I'm worried about the situation festering, and besides, something doesn't add up and—' she paused '—and I have this horrible feeling we've not heard the end of it.'

Dean had heard enough paranoia from his uncle today and wanted to get out of the conversation as quickly as possible. Then he remembered; his uncle had given him a couple of business cards. He reached into his back pocket and pulled one out. 'Grace, I think you might be right. I engaged my uncle today, who is a private detective, to look into the matter. He asked me to give his card to anyone who might be able to help. Perhaps you'd like to talk to him about your concerns?' Dean smiled to himself; let Uncle Billy listen to the ramblings of this old women while he's 500 miles away in France.

'Oh, thank you, Dean. I will you know. I will speak to him. I thought it was me going mad, but if you've got as far as engaging a detective, then there must be something in it...' she continued to ramble on, but Dean switched his attention to how he could extract himself from the kitchen, then to his relief the door burst open.

'I'm just heading off to pick up Jack and Beth,' Graham blurted out.

'I'll come with you,' Dean said a bit too eagerly. Graham was clearly surprised but grateful for the company, and they both left Grace in the kitchen, holding the business card.

Dean stood with Graham, who was patrolling the station impatiently, waiting for them to arrive. Although he was glad of Graham's organisation skills, he was now getting a bit tired of the complaining. 'They're a lot later than we planned. We need to be on the road in less than six hours' time.' Dean just nodded in agreement and let Graham carry on. 'It's alright for the others, they can sleep in the car, but I am one of the two nominated drivers and sleep would be useful.'

The platform was sparsely populated with one or two people waiting for the next train to arrive. It was a warm night, warmer than average for early July and there was still a flicker of light in the air. Dean's thoughts strayed to the holiday ahead of them, how would it turn out? Would everyone get on? It's the first holiday since the skiing incident; indeed, the first time they'd all been together since the funeral. Two people wouldn't be sitting around the dining table as usual, but for different reasons. He suddenly felt guilty, had their treatment of Ryan been justified? He and Graham were the ones that had instigated the freezing out, but then again, they were the only ones there; they only told it as they saw it.

Finally, the announcement came.

'The next train to arrive on platform two will be the 23:25 to Ashford International, this train will be calling at all stations to Ashford International.'

As the train pulled in, they began looking rapidly from side to side, eager to spot them as quickly as possible. There didn't appear to be many people getting off, a couple of drunken groups of friends stumbling down the platform as they returned from a Friday night out in town, but few others. Dean was nudged slightly as an inebriated City worker, still in his suit from post-work drinks, plodded on past. He looked around expecting an apology but soon realised it wouldn't be forthcoming, and decided it wasn't worth an argument. Graham walked towards the front of the train and looked worried as he continued to scan for them. Just as he reached into his pocket to get his mobile, he finally saw the unmistakable figure of Jack, with his thick red hair and tall frame. As he was getting ready to greet Jack, he was knocked on the arm. He half-turned, ready to give a drunken commuter a mouthful, but was greeted before he had the chance. 'Hello, Graham.'

As he completed the turn, he was met by her perfect smile. 'I made it on time.' Graham smiled, obviously relieved to see Beth standing in front of him.

'Well, if you call two hours late "on time" then I suppose you're right.' They both chuckled and then hugged, exchanging kisses in the process. Dean wandered over from his position on the platform and joined them, warmly greeting her.

Beth was undoubtedly a beautiful girl. Only five-foot-six but had a perfectly slim figure with tanned body and long flowing blonde hair. She was clever, in fact she had been to university with Graham, Stevie and Dean but was the sort of person who lived in a dreamland. Most people would describe her as dizzy; Stevie, who was the least patient, often referred to her as "bloody infuriating." She was, of course, completely inappropriately dressed to be carrying two suitcases and a handbag. The size of her bright red stilettos required her to stand supported by Graham's arm as they chatted. She wasn't the sort of girl to be shy of displaying her assets, and the only thing more revealing than her skirt was her top.

The conversation was interrupted by the arrival of Jack, who put his hand on Graham's shoulder. 'Hi.'

Graham jumped, then realising who it was, repeated the welcome. 'Good journey?'

'Long and slow. But here now,' he said with a puff of breath.

Graham finally remembered Jack didn't know the others and turned to introduce the new acquaintances, 'Jack, this is Beth and Dean. Beth and Dean, this is Jack.' Polite smiles and a couple of weak handshakes were exchanged between the strangers.

'The car's out the front of the station, I've probably got a ticket knowing my luck today.' He picked up Beth's bags without offering and marched towards the steps. 'What the hell have you got in these?'

'Just essentials, I was really good this year.' She actually believed what she was saying.

'Stevie's going to kill you. He clearly stated one suitcase and one small handbag each. There are eight of us going, you know.'

Dean smiled as he listened to the exchange. Nothing ever changed. Every year, for the past four, Stevie had stipulated a baggage allowance, and every year Beth had at least doubled it.

Graham led them down to the barrier, which was unmanned at this time on a Friday. They walked through the station entrance and out to his mum's Honda, borrowed for the fortnight after his 'mishap' earlier in the day.

'How's Robbie?' Graham said as he tried to force one of the two large cases into the boot.

'It's Dave now, but I don't think it will last.' That was no surprise to Dean or Graham. They never lasted. Since they'd met seven years ago at uni, no boyfriend had ever lasted longer than a month, although she was rarely without one. The clever ones would find her infuriatingly dippy; the thick ones didn't stimulate her, and she would reject them. Graham had fancied her from day one, the trouble was they'd hit the 'friend's zone' too early and he'd never plucked up the courage to confess the truth since.

'So, what do you do?' Beth was trying to make conversation with Jack, who had been quiet since arriving.

'I work with Graham.'

'For me, don't you mean?' Graham was teasing, clearly trying to engineer a response, fully aware Jack was subdued. The bait wasn't taken by Jack, and he sat in silence for the five-minute drive to Graham's parent's house, where they would be spending the night.

Jack and Beth suffered the same welcome as the others and were herded into a room on the left, where the group of shell-shocked and over-fed guests were waiting. Beth, a vegetarian, was ushered over to the table of meat products but knew the truth would cause Grace to implode in shame, so settled on a handful of crisps and some salad. Jack saved the day by helping himself to a plateful of meat savouries before both took their place in the circle of dining chairs. Finally, Beth was able to look up and recognise the faces staring sympathetically at her from around the room. Jack, however, was utterly bewildered; not only was he fighting with a full plate of food, courtesy of Grace, he was also being given a quick-fire introduction to all of his holiday acquaintances by Graham – with little chance of remembering them all.

As the friends scoffed on food, guzzled the drink and chatted enthusiastically, the way friends do when they haven't met for a while, Grace surveyed another success. She caught Graham's eye, gave him a nod to indicate her next move and went to join the exhausted Mr Joseph in bed. As she left, she turned to Dean, smiled at him and raised her hand to indicate she was still holding the business card.

'Did you two have a drama-free journey down?' Stevie said, but barely gave Beth and Jack any time to respond before continuing, 'it's an absolute miracle we're all here.' Stevie pushed another sausage roll in his mouth but started speaking too quickly and spat some pastry at Dean.

'What happened?' Beth enquired politely. She knew Stevie was prone to over-exaggerate and therefore wasn't particularly concerned.

'Well, first off, someone put petrol in my dad's car—'

Otis jumped in at this point, 'Yes, that someone had glasses and a dodgy goatee,' while laughing and pointing at the storyteller.

Stevie looked annoyed but pushed on, 'No, it wasn't me, anyway, they managed to flush out the engine.' He took another bite of his food. 'Then we get to Dean's flat and the police, ambulance, fire crews are all there, it looked like a war-zone.'

This time Beth did look more concerned and turned to Dean. 'Oh God, everything OK?'

Dean nodded. 'Yes, it's fine. Some idiot drove too fast and crashed into a neighbour. I was nowhere near it.' He played it down but got a knowing look from Stevie. Dean suspected he'd heard some of the post-crash conversation with Billy but wasn't prepared to indulge Stevie's desire to gossip.

Graham could see Pippa was anxious as Stevie was beginning to tell their part of the three-act tragedy and decided to intercede, with a significantly watered-down version. It took until well after midnight for the eight of them to settle into their assortment of inflatable mattresses, sofa beds and futons. Despite the problems they'd encountered on the way down to Maidstone, all of them were now firmly looking forward to the two weeks ahead of them.

However, none of them were prepared for the two weeks they were about to face.

CHAPTER 6

It took him at least 20 seconds to realise the piercing noise bolting through his head was the sound of his alarm. Dean turned over, expecting the phone to read '07:00' and was temporarily dazed to see it flashing '04:30'. It took him another 30 seconds to realise the reason for the ungodly hour alarm call; the holiday was about to start. He jolted from his makeshift bed on the floor of the lounge, waking Jack in the process and marched to the bathroom with his bag. As he made his way up the stairs, he could hear a shower running, no doubt it would be Graham, he thought to himself, he knew Graham would have to be ready first.

It took another half an hour for the rest of the group to rise from the various corners of the Joseph residence and present themselves for inspection by Graham in the living room. It was a surprise to no one that Beth was last to be ready, she occupied one of the three bathrooms exclusively for half an hour from 04:35 in order to perfect her make-up. Most of them had managed four hours' sleep, Dean managed less than two. He'd just settled into his blow-up bed at midnight when he realised he was about to try and smuggle a gun through customs. He knew that there was a one-in-five chance that the car would be searched and even less of a chance that any bag would be opened. Nevertheless, he worried, just like any normal law-abiding citizen would, and that had eaten into his sleep.

Graham checked passports as everyone filed out of the house, all were grateful that Grace was a heavy sleeper and wouldn't be around to give them 'a good send-off'. Stevie and Otis took on the role of porter, carefully loading the luggage into the two cars. Even at a quarter past five in the morning, Stevie couldn't resist a dig at the volume of luggage Beth had managed to bring along.

The passengers were divided equally among the two cars, with Graham driving the Honda as the lead car, Jack as navigator and Marie and Pippa in the back. Stevie drove his dad's Ford Galaxy, with Otis in the front, a tense Dean and a sleepy Beth in the back. Before the cars had joined the M20 Beth and Marie were asleep. Dean was wide awake.

As they pulled off the motorway and followed signs for the Channel Tunnel Folkestone Terminal, Dean could barely sit still. His fidgeting had already caused Beth to awake from her beauty sleep, which resulted in a significant chastisement. The Honda out in front moved towards one of the open booths, indicated by a green light above. Stevie followed in the Galaxy and soon both cars were waiting in line for their boarding cards. As the lead car reached the booth, Dean could see Graham in discussion with the attendant, including various gesticulations in the direction of the second car. Finally, the Honda edged forward, and Stevie lowered the window in expectation. Before he could utter a word, the attendant blurted out a garbled instruction, 'Put this card in your front window and head immediately to the departure lanes, we've got you on the next train which leaves in 15 minutes.'

Stevie managed a weak, 'Thanks,' as he complied with the instruction and drove off to follow the lead car. As they filed around the various lanes to get to the train, Dean's heart was pounding faster than ever before, he actually thought he was going to vomit as he saw the Customs sign straight ahead. He held his breath as Graham handed over the passports to the English customs booth, but there was barely a flinch from the guard as he waved the car through. This gave Dean a momentary boost of confidence as his car approached the gate. Again, the guard looked uninterested as Stevie thrust four passports in front of his nose, he managed a half-wave, which Stevie took as full clearance to catch up with the Honda. Dean started breathing again as they began moving, he even gave a silent 'Thank you, God' to the sky as they got up to the regulation 10mph.

Otis saw her appear first; Stevie was still fiddling with the card on the dashboard and would have mowed clean over her had Otis not screamed at the top of his voice. The security guard hadn't realised how close she'd been to being hit, but still had a stern look on her face as she motioned the Galaxy into a side bay. The second guard that met them was a more elderly gentleman, who looked infinitely more friendly. 'Just going to perform a random security check, sir, shouldn't take more than five minutes. Can you please all get out of the car and open the bonnet and boot.'

Stevie was clearly annoyed that this had now separated them from the lead vehicle, Beth was extremely put out that she'd been woken from her sleep and Otis was still recovering from the guard near-miss. Dean, on the other hand, was certain he was about to explode with the pain in his stomach. Sweat was dripping from his forehead, and he'd turned whiter than the cliffs at Dover. Even Beth, in her sleep-deprived trance, noticed something unusual and asked him if he was feeling OK. He managed a polite grunt before taking a position leaning against one of the stanchions that supported the sheltered area they were now standing in.

Dean watched hawk-like as the two guards performed a gentle but thorough search of the inside of the car using handheld metal detectors. He saw them go from bag to bag, waving the detector over each one as they progressed in a uniform pattern from left to right, front-to-back. Occasionally they picked up a bag as they went, Dean knew his bag was at the back on the far right, probably the last one they would come to. As they edged nearer and nearer, he felt like confessing the truth now, rather than suffer the pain another second. As the guards reached his bag, he heard it; the loud, high-pitched scream to indicate a significant metal object had been found. He missed another heartbeat as the guard summoned over his colleague to inspect the find. As they rummaged around in the boot, Dean seriously considered making a run for it and actually turned his back as they began pulling a bag out. As he prepared to dart across the forecourt, he heard Beth scream, 'Watch what you're doing with that, it took me ages to pack!'

As Dean turned around, he saw an apologetic guard holding a hairdryer in one hand and a half-opened suitcase in the other. 'Sorry, madam, just precautionary.' He then turned to Stevie while putting the hairdryer back and declared the all-clear. Finally, Dean started to breathe again.

It took him the entire length of the Euro Shuttle journey before he started to regain his normal skin colour. He was, however, pretty sure that his underwear was beyond help.

'Daylight!' Graham declared as the train left the tunnel and continued on the over-ground section of the journey towards Calais.

It was a perfectly clear and sunny morning on the other side of the Channel. The dawn clouds, evident on the English side, had been replaced by unbroken early morning sunshine in France. The announcer declared the time in France to be seven fifty-five. The group, although still sleepy from their early morning start, were buoyant as the engines started up again and the cars moved slowly out of the carriage. The start of the holiday was a welcome relief for all. It had, after all, been a difficult year for this tight group of friends.

Graham, as ever organised, had already pre-arranged a meeting point at the first petrol station if they were separated boarding the train. It took less than 15 minutes for them to meet up and start the long drive south.

The route had been mapped out by Graham and Stevie in advance, the majority of the journey would be completed on motorway, most of those being tolls, with only the last 20 minutes being a trek through the French countryside. They'd initially planned to avoid the Paris area and travel via Tours, but significant road works had forced them to change their plans. The whole journey would take between eight and ten hours, Graham had explained to his passengers on several occasions. They'd have toilet breaks built-in and a picnic site for lunch had been identified, just south of Paris. They drove initially from Calais towards the French capital, encountering very little in the way of traffic for the first couple of hours. The first leg of the journey saw them travel past great swathes of cornfields, with the plants gently blowing in the summer breeze. The fields were occasionally interrupted by a small town; identified by impressive churches and stone-built houses.

As Paris approached, the motorway extended from four lanes, to six and the urban areas became larger and more regular. They stopped at around 10 o'clock, forty kilometres from Paris, for a toilet break and to go over the route for the most challenging leg of the journey. It would be difficult to remain in convoy around the 'Périphérique', the Paris ring-road, Graham explained to the group, so both cars had better know the route and they'd meet again, if separated, at the first service area on the A10.

Although the traffic was substantially thicker than they had seen so far on the journey, they managed to negotiate Paris within an hour and stopped for an early lunch just outside Orleans, the home of Joan of Arc. Grace, to no one's surprise, had supplied a full hamper of filled sandwiches, sausage rolls, crisps, salad, cakes and fizzy drinks. As they ate in the sunlight, most of the group were in high spirits, laughing and joking and recanting stories of previous holidays. However, Dean and Jack were quieter; both sat at the end of the picnic table, opposite each other, but were not involved in any conversations. Marie had spotted this and pointed it out to Graham, but he shrugged it off. 'They'll brighten up when we get to the villa,' he declared with confidence.

'There's enough food here to last for the whole two weeks,' Stevie shouted as he loaded the hamper back into the boot of his dad's car. The girls had decided they wanted a natter for the next leg of the journey, which meant Stevie was forced to endure two hours of gossip on boyfriends, film stars and the latest fashions, while Graham was able to work on Dean and Jack in the lead car. The countryside returned as they left Orleans behind, but this time it was even more picturesque, with rolling fields of sunflowers and grapevines added to the wheat, barley and corn they'd seen earlier.

They continued to progress at good speed, with very little traffic blocking their way until they reached a small pile-up of three cars about 90 minutes from their destination, just south of Limoges, on the route nationale 21. Graham suggested a final rest-break as they slowly approached a service area, to allow the traffic to clear and to check on final directions for when they got onto the minor roads. He reminded everyone that Brantome was the closest big town to where they were staying, although that was probably about a twenty-minute drive away. Once they reached Brantome, they were to follow signs for Belaygue and that once they had driven through it, the cottage was about 12 miles south down a very minor road. 'Bloody hell! You weren't kidding when you said we were in the middle of nowhere. We can't even walk to the nearest bakery in the morning,' Beth blurted out in horror to rest of the group.

'We all agreed that we wanted to get completely away from the world for two weeks, well I think we can say we've achieved it.' Graham leapt to his own defence as a titter went around the rest of the group.

'Suits me down to the ground,' Dean said under his breath, but loud enough for most to hear.

It was half past three and the heat from the sun beating down on them made most wish they were wearing shorts. After a final debate as to the best route to go, they loaded into the two cars again, with Stevie insisting on some male company in the Ford for this final leg.

Within only a few kilometres of the re-start, the landscape changed from rolling fields to dense woodland, with the odd farm lodged in-between. Dean, who had brightened considerably during his journey with Graham, was back in Stevie's car and smiled for the first time in 36 hours as he viewed the scenery around him. This would surely be the relaxing break he had so longed for?

Jack managed to navigate the cars successfully around Brantome and through several small hamlets before they arrived in the village of Belaygue, from here he would need the specific cottage directions, and he fumbled briefly for Graham's carefully prepared itinerary folder that he had stored in the glove box.

'Okay, we need to go through the village and take the second left after the bakery. This should take us onto a small road, where we drive for about nine miles.'

Jack paused, just long enough for Graham to interject, 'What do we do after nine miles?'

Pretending to ignore him, Jack continued, 'We should see a sign pointing to the right indicating "Ferme a Cheval Blanc", take this track and we should reach a building on the right after about three kilometres.'

They progressed steadily down from Belaygue, doing no more than 30 miles per hour as the two-way road (Stevie argued with Otis that it couldn't actually be called a road, more a track) could barely take one lane of traffic. Both sides of the 'road' were covered in woodland as far as the eye could see and they weren't helped by the number of sharp bends that materialised without warning. As they got to the within a kilometre of the turning, they slowed right down to 20 mph to help look for the sign. Marie spotted it first and nearly caused Graham to drive the car into a tree as she screamed, 'There it is!'

'Bloody hell, you scared the shit out of me,' Graham responded in a suitably pained manner. By the time Graham had recovered, he had slightly overshot the turning, allowing Stevie's car to nip into the farm track before him. 'Bugger it!' Graham managed while darting a sharp look in his chief navigator's direction. Jack pretended not to notice.

The pain of not being in the lead car had clearly riled Graham, as he spent the three-kilometre journey up the farm track almost bumper-to-bumper with Stevie. They finally arrived at a clearing in the woods which revealed their home for the next two weeks. The cottage itself was surrounded by a thick forest, aside from a small paddock to the front of it, which had not been farmed or maintained for some years. To the side of the house was a patchy area of gravel, sufficient to park both cars. Further up the track, about 500 metres, was another building. It was from this direction that Pippa saw someone coming. 'Who's that?' she shouted to the rest of the group.

'That'll be Madame Bernard, the cottage owner,' Graham chipped in, almost without looking up.

As the group waited for their hostess to arrive, they surveyed the house where they would be spending the next two weeks. Although described as a cottage, the accommodation appeared large and expanded over three floors. The lowest level looked only to serve as a garage and was the smallest level as the cottage had been built into the side of a hill. What appeared to be the first floor from the front, would actually be the ground floor on two sides of the building and the second floor was partly built into the red-tiled pitched roof. As was typical for this part of France, the building was made of huge cream-coloured stone blocks, with each window on the first and second floor serenaded by brown wooden shutters. The entrance was on the first floor above the garage, which you arrived at via one of the two stone staircases that went from either side of the garage door onto a veranda. The impressive veranda was adorned with pots of red geranium and spanned the entire front of the house.

To the left was a fenced-off area which couldn't be seen from the driveway, but clearly served as the garden and outside space. There was a gate on the left of the veranda, which was evidently the external way into the garden. It was a splendid house to look at from the outside, which made the group even more anxious to get inside and start the holiday. The group were shielded from the late afternoon sun by the trees, as they waited for their host.

'Bonjour, Madame,' Graham was the first to welcome the old lady, who looked at least 70 and was sporting an old-fashioned pinny over a floral dress. She had struggled to walk the distance from her house to the cottage, and this had left the rather plump lady out of breath by the time she reached them.

'Bonjour,' Madame Bernard finally managed having caught her breath.

The rest of the group responded with a rendition of 'bonjour' before she produced a big bunch of keys and waddled towards the cottage.

'Suis moi,' *follow me*, she uttered in French, and although most of the group either didn't hear or didn't understand, they followed anyway.

She started by pulling on the garage door handle. 'Toujours garde verrouill.'

'Always kept locked,' Jack, who was passable with the language, along with Graham, translated for the group.

'Ne pas entrer,' Madame said while shaking her finger from side-to-side, the universal sign language to indicate when you're not supposed to do something. No one needed Jack to translate, but when he didn't, Graham did anyway.

Madame then moved towards the bottom of the stone steps and beckoned her guests to follow. After a lengthy amount of time taken to climb the 15 steps, she arrived at the front door, which was split into 15 panels of glass, some of which were frosted, but most were not. She fumbled briefly with the keys and then unlocked both locks on the door.

The door opened up into the middle of a large outdated kitchen. To the left was a small dining table with four chairs placed around it. A large American style fridge freezer also occupied a significant space on that side of the kitchen. To the right of the entrance was the main preparation area, with a set of olive green tiles adorning the walls above the work surface. Madame spent several minutes opening and shutting appliances, twiddling with knobs and buttons, while speaking at an inordinately fast pace. Even Graham gave up listening, never mind translating, as Madame rattled through the finer points of dish-washing maintenance.

Dean, Jack and Otis managed to break off from the main group and left the kitchen induction through one of the two other exits. They opted to take the door on the left and entered a rather grand dining room, with an antique-looking oak dining table surrounded by 10 high-backed chairs.

'Bloody hell, this is a bit better than we're used to!' Dean exclaimed.

'Hate to say it, but Graham's done us proud this time,' Otis added in a mock begrudging tone.

The dining room was long, running the rest of the length of the building, with two windows to the left, overlooking the veranda and a large stone fireplace to the right. The walls were adorned with large oil paintings, while three corners of the room were filled with six-foot imitation trees. There were also two doors on the right as they walked through the dining room, either side of the fireplace. Otis opened the first to find nothing more than a utility and storage cupboard, while the second led through to a lounge.

Ignoring the lounge, the trio headed for the French doors at the opposite end of the dining room, which led onto the patio. Thankfully, the key to these doors had been left in the lock and a swift turn by Dean allowed the three of them to enter the garden. As they strolled out, they were hit with a wall of heat as the garden seemed to be conveniently situated to allow in the afternoon sun, despite the number of trees surrounding the property. It wasn't until that moment that all three of them realised how cool the house was, despite it being nearly 5pm, they all started sweating immediately.

The garden was split-level, with the patio area being on the same level as the dining room. Another table, this time plastic, sat under a fixed canopy directly in front of the French windows and a barbeque rested directly to the left of that. Behind them, Dean noticed the gate that led back to the veranda; it appeared locked, and no key was evident. *Must be on the bunch Madame was holding*, he thought. Another set of stone steps led down to the lower garden and pool, which was just slightly higher than the floor level of the garage. As Dean looked back towards the house, he hadn't noticed Jack had already removed his shoes and shirt. Seconds later, Dean and Otis were doused unexpectedly with chlorinated water as Jack jumped in.

While the lucky trio were enjoying the freedom of the garden, Madame had taken the rest of the group through the other kitchen door, opposite the one they had entered the cottage through originally. They arrived in a small dingy windowless hallway, from which there appeared to be five options: Immediate left was the wooden staircase up to the second floor, immediately right was a locked door which the group understood was the internal way down to the garage. Madame again repeated her warning that no one was allowed to enter and edged forward to point at the remaining three doors. Also, on the left, next to the staircase, was the ground floor bedroom, straight ahead was a bathroom and on the right was a study. She unlocked it, entered the study briefly, had a quick look around and closed the door, locking it in the process. None of the group had been encouraged in, and it was again made clear this room was out of bounds as she removed the study key from the bunch.

The group were then ushered up the stairs where they arrived at a large open mezzanine area covered in shelves of old books. The area had very little natural light, with just one small skylight at one end. Several tatty old chairs were in front of the bookcases and an old piano gathered dust in one corner. Having arrived on the mezzanine, they were shown around five bedrooms and two bathrooms. The double and twin bedrooms overlooked the garden with the three single bedrooms facing the front of the house. Both bathrooms were next to each other, opposite the double bedroom.

Having completed the inspection of the second floor, the remaining four (Stevie having managed to make a break for it) were taken back down the stairs, through the kitchen and out into the dining room and lounge. As they approached the garden, Madame was obviously annoyed to see four people splashing about in the pool in their underwear. Graham, ever the diplomat, tried to apologise to Madame as she made her way back through to the kitchen, slapping the keys down on the dining table in disgust. Marie followed him briefly but got called back by Pippa and left Graham deep in conversation with Madame.

By the time Graham had returned from his attempted diplomacy with Madame, the girls were dangling their feet in the pool while the lads played water volleyball in their boxer shorts. 'Couldn't you bastards at least have waited to get your trunks out the car?' Graham was livid at being left to deal with Madame on his own.

'What did we miss?' Dean asked innocently.

'If you'd bothered to listen, you'd know,' came the terse reply from him.

'Not that much,' Marie tried to defuse the situation and gave Graham a stare, which he clocked immediately. He looked around, saw everyone, including Dean and

Jack, relaxing, walked over to the pool, took his shoes off and sat next to his wife, putting his arm around her in the process.

'Not that much to be fair,' he finally conceded, before adding; 'but she did say she was going away on Wednesday and wouldn't be back until Sunday. She gave us a number to call her son on if there's a problem. But I don't suppose there will be.'

CHAPTER 7

It took until the Sunday evening for the tiredness of the long journey, the heat of summer and months of hard labour at work, to overcome the excitement of the start of the holiday. After a slightly subdued barbeque and an obligatory game of cards, most of the group headed to bed. By 10 o'clock only Dean and Beth were left at the table playing cards, the conversation had petered-out, and Dean was struggling to think of something to say. He didn't like sitting in silence if two people were alone in a room together. After a prolonged period of enduring quiet, a thought popped into his head, and he launched into a question without going through a sufficient screening process. 'How's your dad?' but as soon as he'd said it, Dean wished he'd lived with silence – especially when he saw the look on Beth's face.

The situation with Beth's father was seldom mentioned by the group, and on the rare occasions it was, Graham was normally the one involved in the discussion. He'd been the closest to Beth at university and admitted to the lads that he'd fancied her before he met Marie. There was never any potential of a relationship, Beth was an extremely attractive blonde – although no one believed it was natural, and Graham was a geeky and unsporting scholar. However, they seemed to click in lectures, and it was courtesy of Graham that she was part of the group.

The silence that followed Dean's question felt like hours to him but was no more than a few seconds. 'He's doing OK, thanks.' Beth didn't have the slightest bit of annoyance in her voice at being asked the question, and as a result of this initial success, Dean decided to continue the conversation.

'I know it can't be easy for you or your mum, but you know we are all thinking of you.'

Dean realised how pitiful this sounded almost immediately and was about to apologise, but Beth replied before he could, 'It's not easy, but we're getting by. I know everyone finds it an awkward topic, but I don't mind talking about it.' She paused briefly, took a big swig of wine, and continued, 'At the end of the day he's guilty, he got caught, and he's paying the penalty. The only thing that bothers Mummy is losing the house, and the only annoying thing for me is having this hanging over my political career. We have no interest in what happens to him after that!'

'I'm sure that's not the case, you love him deeply, we all know that, what he did, though not excusable, was done for you and your mum.'

'How can stealing £2m from innocent people, going to prison, dragging the family name through the mud and losing all our possessions possibly be considered as doing the best by Mummy and me?' Her voice had quickly risen and had the tone that is synonymous with the start of an argument.

Dean was temporarily mesmerised, and not entirely sure how he'd ended up being the counsel for the defence in this argument. He wasn't the lawyer, Graham was. But somehow, having taken a side, he almost felt compelled to counter the prosecution's argument.

Thankfully, he bit his lip, thought for a few seconds and managed a weak apology before they returned to silence, finishing the game of cards without another word being spoken. At that point, Dean knew he would never bring up the subject of Beth's dad again, and he would warn the others against such foolishness in the future.

Just as they were off upstairs, Jack, who had gone to bed an hour earlier and was the only one with a bedroom downstairs, emerged from his room to get a glass of water. The three of them said their goodnights before they turned in. Dean hoped Jack hadn't heard him put his foot in it, mainly because he didn't want to appear an idiot, but also because it was possible Jack might not actually know about the situation with Beth's dad. However, as Graham wasn't exactly known for his discretion, he thought it unlikely Jack wouldn't have been pre-briefed.

***

The piercing bright light of the morning sun, sneaking through the cracks in the shutters, finally brought Dean back to consciousness. It took him several minutes to realise what had happened – he'd had a full night's sleep for the first time in months, he could hardly believe it.

It took him about half an hour to force himself out of bed. He heard some movement downstairs and decided to see who was up. As well as not liking silence, he hated to think he was missing out on anything. As he got up, Dean surveyed the bedroom; it was a simple set-up, with a single bed in one corner, a chest of drawers in the other and an antique wardrobe against the far wall. He'd been there for two nights and still hadn't unpacked a thing, in all likelihood he never would. He grabbed a towel and made for one of the two bathrooms on the first floor. He opened his bedroom door and was faced with the darkness of the landing-cum-library. There was only one tiny skylight for the whole area, and although the shutter was open, the sunlight barely made a dent in the dark. Not surprisingly, he failed to notice her, sat quietly in an ornate armchair, as he made for the bathroom.

'They're both free,' she said, as he had virtually entered the nearest one.

'Thanks,' he managed, before he could see who had offered him this useless piece of information. As he turned, he saw Pippa, still in her nightgown, sitting alone in the chair. The open door from his bedroom had cast a flicker of light across her face and from 10 feet away, he could see she'd been crying.

'Are you OK?' he walked over to her.

'I'm absolutely fine,' she said firmly. Had he not seen her tears, he would have believed her.

He knelt down in front of her. 'I think you've been crying, do want to talk about it?' In actual fact, he was desperate for a pee and wouldn't put up an argument if she didn't.

'I'm enjoying myself,' this was said solemnly, and Dean knew what the problem was without her needing to say anything else.

Before he could respond, she started talking at him, 'For the first time since Cam died, I'm really enjoying myself, and I feel so guilty,' another tear appeared and then disappeared down her cheek.

'You are allowed, you know,' Dean offered.

'I know, but I feel I've taken his place here. He should be with you guys; having a laugh and enjoying the sun.'

'He was your brother and he loved you. He would want you to be happy and to be here with his friends. Your friends.' Dean had forgotten about his need for the toilet and had shuffled closer to Pippa and held her hand as he said it.

She looked up, with tears still flowing. 'Do you miss him?' she whispered.

This was almost enough to make Dean well up. He paused for a moment, looking down at the floor as he thought about his response. Eventually, he thought of what he wanted to say, 'He was one of my best friends. I'd known him since I was eighteen, I'm twenty-five next month, that's seven years. Men aren't supposed to discuss feelings for each other, but the five of us were very close,' he paused briefly, 'yes, I miss him, more than I think at times. Sometimes I'll see a girl that I know he'd like, or my team would beat his, and I just want to pick up the phone and text him.' This confession had brought some moisture to his eyes, but he held back the tears as he hugged Pippa, and they both sat together for a few moments as she sobbed quietly.

He composed himself after a few seconds, wiped away the moisture and stood up, kissing her on the forehead, like a father does with a teenage daughter. 'We all owe it to him to enjoy every second of our lives. That's what he would want. I will think of him always.'

As he made a break for the bathroom, she said words that made him freeze. 'What about Ryan. Do you think of him? Do you miss him?' There was a fierceness about the last part of what she said.

Dean thought for a few moments, turned to look at her and fired out the response, 'Like I said, the five of us were very close. Me, Cam, Graham, Stevie and... Ryan.' He paused briefly before finishing, 'But some people can do things that erase the happy memories and make you want to forget them. Ryan is one of them.' Dean didn't wait for a response, turned and shut the door firmly behind him.

There was a slow and steady stream of arrivals for breakfast before Beth completed the set at around 11. Graham had already imparted his thoughts on the priorities for the day, one by one, as the group had arrived for breakfast. They needed to do a major shop having survived on scraps for the first two days, and the big supermarkets would now be open, as it was a Monday. The nearest major town, Brantome, was 20 miles away and was well worth a visit, so why not combine the two?

The plan was accepted by all without any argument, and by midday they were in the cars. Stevie drove the lead car and Graham followed at the rear. It had been a major coup for Otis to wrestle navigational duties from Graham, but the group agreed he couldn't drive and navigate at the same time. It was a rare defeat for Graham, but one the group liked to inflict on him occasionally to keep him on his toes.

As they drove away, it struck Dean how much in the wilderness they were. Usually they had a local village or hamlet close by, with a boulangerie and post office to fall back on, but this time nothing. They were in a small clearing in the middle of the forest, and it was at least 10 miles before they saw another building and a further two miles still for the nearest sign of a bakery. Dean wasn't the only member of the group pleased with this.

Brantome was basking in the heat of the summer sun, making it look all the more spectacular. The town was surrounded by rivers with traditional French buildings adorning the banks and vast colours of seasonal flowers filling the stone pots. There was an array of riverside cafés and restaurants, filled with locals and holidaymakers alike. A market was set up in one of the car parks, with stalls selling the freshest local produce: fish, freshly baked bread, gloriously ripe and delightfully misshaped vegetables. There were countless meat stalls selling everything from duck to whole skinned rabbit, causing Beth some distress but the rest much amusement. Graham and Marie stopped at a stall selling delicious looking pâtés and foie gras. He negotiated with the stallholder and was proud of his efforts in getting 5c off the price of a jar of duck liver pâté. Beth consoled herself by browsing a stall selling handbags while Otis found himself enthralled by an ancient map at an antiques stall. Dean and Jack had stumbled across a bar with a beer garden and ordered themselves jugs of Leffe.

There was little doubt, as the group joined Dean and Jack in the garden of the bar, they were all enjoying themselves and fully relaxed. By 3pm, at Graham's insistence, they finally moved a few paces, but only to find a local restaurant where they tucked into plates of trout, prawns and mussels washed down with more beer, except for the drivers. It was 5pm before they got into the supermarket by which time most were in need of an afternoon nap by the pool. This contributed to the record 30 minutes shopping trip, although they still managed to notch up a €300 bill – primarily due to the quantity of alcohol that had been shoved into the trollies.

Only Graham, Otis and Stevie stayed awake for the drive home and despite the occasional wrong turn, in large part due to Otis's six beers, they arrived at the cottage by six-thirty. Pippa, Beth and Marie made straight for the pool as the lads unpacked and started setting up the bar at the far side of the dining room.

The light had faded by the time everyone had rested and the BBQ was on the go, with Graham, Jack and Otis surrounding it in the usual show of machismo. The heat was still intense as they sat down on the patio table for their dinner of chicken, rice and salad. Beth had grilled feta cheese and mushroom kebabs but looked on enviously at the juicy chicken legs the others were devouring.

After sinking four bottles of wine between the eight of them, they moved onto games of Jenga and poker. By midnight, Dean and Graham had succumbed to the booze and gone to bed. Beth and Pippa followed shortly afterwards, and Otis had a moment with the downstairs toilet that left him out for the count. By 1am it was just Stevie, Marie and Jack left finishing another bottle of wine and discussing past misdemeanours. They had moved to the lounge and were slumped on three different leather sofas. It was an unlikely selection of the group, Jack and Stevie had never met before, and both the men were primarily friends of Graham, not Marie. In fact, Stevie and Marie had never particularly got on and at times were obviously frosty to each other.

'Have you got anyone on the go at the moment then, Stevie?' Jack managed while half-asleep. Stevie was evidently taken aback by the direct questioning from someone he barely knew.

'Er, well I, you know, it's not. Well...'

'I take that as a yes, Mr Pennock, what's her name?'

Stevie was getting redder and more flustered.

'Well, it's er, early days, I'd rather not count the chickens you know,' he took a large swig of wine.

'Good on you,' Jack responded, 'treat 'em mean, keep 'em keen,' he got up from the sofa and headed back through to the dining room. 'I'm off to bed, I'll leave you two to it.' Jack walked through the dining room, kitchen and then into his bedroom at the bottom of the stairs.

'He seems like a nice guy,' Stevie said casually as Jack disappeared out of earshot.

Marie looked across at him and smiled. 'He's not gay, you know.'

The silence seemed to last for an eternity. Stevie had gone from pink to purple and finally to crimson before he managed a stuttering response, 'I, I know. I wasn't saying I fancied him, I was just saying he was a nice guy. Jesus, this is precisely why I don't want to tell anyone – because everything I say will get twisted by narrow-minded bigots.'

'Methinks he does protest too much,' Marie said with a smirk, she was generally not a wind-up merchant, but after a lot of drinks, she was clearly in the mood for a game.

'For the love of God, I'm not in love, attracted to or in any way starry-eyed for that man!' His voice was getting higher and higher as he continued.

'I know. Just teasing. Sorry.'

Stevie calmed a little. 'Well, please don't, you're the only one who knows, and I'd like to keep it that way. Unless you've blabbed?'

'I promised you five years ago I wouldn't say any-thing and to this day I haven't even told Graham. Not that he or Dean or any of them would have a problem with it.'

'You don't know that. I've seen kids at my school hung from the goalposts just because they were rubbish at sports, so I'd rather not take the risk.'

'I think you're wrong, but it's your secret to keep and I won't say a word.'

'Thanks,' Stevie managed. He probably would have left by now, but still had half a glass of wine to drink and it would have seemed obvious to Marie that he was running away. They both sat briefly in silence, while Stevie looked at his glass and swished it slightly in his hand. He must have got a bit lax because, after a few twirls, some wine escaped from the top and landed on the rug. 'Shit!'

Marie jumped up. 'Don't worry, I'll get a cloth.' She ran to the kitchen, grabbed a towel and was mopped up the mess in seconds.

'Thanks,' Stevie said, 'I think I'd better go to bed before I cause any more damage.'

He put his glass down and was almost out of the room before Marie spoke, 'You've never really forgiven me for finding that mag, have you?'

Stevie stopped, thought about a response, but ignored it and marched out of the room without answering.

CHAPTER 8

He never believed anything he was told. Standard practice. Trust no one, believe nothing, and you don't get any nasty surprises. Not until you've been able to check it out for yourself. It was a lesson he'd learnt the hard way and he wasn't changing now, even if it was tough to investigate his own flesh and blood.

Whenever he took on a new case, he'd spend the first few days investigating his client. The initial priority was to make sure they were who they say they are, and check the facts laid out to him were actually facts. He'd seen it all, a wronged husband who was actually a stalker, a missing son who was really a sworn enemy, or stolen antiques that never existed.

His visit to the A&E departments had not managed to yield any results, and so today he was in Birmingham, Britain's second city. All of the noise and none of the charm of London, according to his secretary. Billy wasn't convinced she'd actually ever been, but that didn't stop the jibes about his hometown. He'd been a policeman here for the best part of 18 years, and he always felt a strange tingling in his stomach when he came back for a case. Despite its tower blocks, motorways and grotty pubs – he still had an affection for the place.

He'd been on the case for two days and already validated most of Dean's story. There had been a son born to Claire Mitchell three years ago, but the father wasn't listed on the birth certificate, although that wasn't unexpected. For now, he was validating Dean's story. Dean had indeed written a cheque every month, at least according to his cheque book and they hadn't been cashed, except for the last one, worth £500, which was cashed last week. This was a slight deviation from Deans' story, but he probably hadn't checked his bank account since it was cashed. Whether or not he was actually the father could wait for another day. Billy now believed Dean thought he was the father, but of more interest to him was why a cheque had been cashed now, after three years.

Billy had also confirmed that the girl killed herself six months after the baby was born, not difficult; births, deaths and marriages are easy to validate, it's those things without official records that are more challenging. Claire's dad had recently died in prison after two years inside. The odd thing was that he was likely going to be released within the next six months, the latter piece of information he'd picked up from an old friend on the parole board.

He'd spent the last day watching Claire's remaining family. The mother was Deborah, mid-forties, worked part-time at the local school as a classroom assistant. It was easy to see the last few years were taking a toll on her. She had dark bags under her eyes and greying hair. Billy was parked outside the 1930s semi where she lived, waiting for her to return from the nursery with the boy, Damian. The house clearly had previously been well looked after, brick driveway, double glazing, fancy front door, but it was also obvious that it had been a few years without maintenance. Weeds grew through the driveway, paint had faded on the walls, and the borders were overgrown.

Billy picked up his newspaper to shield his face as Deborah walked towards the house. He'd hired a blue Vauxhall Astra for the trip, which blended in perfectly to the suburban backdrop. He studied the woman trudging up her driveway with her grandson clutching her hand; she looked tired and bitter. While he could understand the sad demeanour of this woman, brought on by the events of the last few years, he didn't believe she would have the energy to stalk Dean herself. Neither did she have the money to pay someone else to do it. Billy had broken into the house earlier that morning and confirmed they lived hand to mouth. A mixture of benefits, her part-time wages and credit cards.

Of more interest now was Claire's brother, Terry. He was 23 years old and worked as a manual labourer for a small local builder. His wages covered his drinking and not much more. Billy wasn't even sure Terry kept enough back to pay for bed and board. Despite his drinking, Terry was certainly physically capable of the assault on Dean, at over six feet and muscular. However, was he really intelligent enough to torment Dean in this way? Possibly, but Billy wasn't convinced. He hadn't turned anything up at the A&E after the van crash on the Friday, and there was no evidence of any injury to Terry, so it was unlikely that he'd been driving the van that day. It didn't rule him out completely, but he had nowhere else to go, so he'd stick with Terry for now.

It was another hour before Terry returned, straight from work and in need of a bath. Based on the last two days, Billy expected him to reappear in an hour or so and disappear down the pub.

As expected, he appeared again, sporting a clean CK T-shirt and ripped jeans. From what Billy could see from his position in the car, Terry and his mum were having a heated conversation on the doorstep, she then grabbed his arm to try and stop him before he stormed down the driveway. An argument about money, Billy assumed. How wrong he was.

Billy was still watching Deborah, so hadn't spotted that Terry had picked up a flagstone from the wall and hid it behind his back. He hadn't spotted that Terry had walked up to the side of his Astra, and he didn't notice the flagstone hurtling towards the windscreen until a second before it made contact. The screen didn't shatter, saving him from a face full of glass, but cracked in a spider's web pattern, around a hole just above the steering wheel. He ducked anyway, cowering behind the wheel and momentarily in shock, this gave Terry time to open the car door and drag Billy to the ground. He took one punch to the nose and one to the stomach before he became fully lucid. He struggled gamely, but Terry's fifteen-stone frame was kneeling on his body and he had his large hands around Billy's neck.

'Another fucking reporter looking for a juicy story. I told the guy last week to leave my family alone or else. Perhaps you lot will get the message now!' Terry finished off the sentence by giving Billy another glancing blow to the side of the head and made off down the street at a jog.

Billy pulled himself up, rubbed his bloody nose with the arm of his T-shirt and put his hand through his hair. The prick had got the better of him this time, but not again. As he opened the car door, he looked at the house and saw Deborah standing at the window. Momentarily he considered going to see her but decided against it and got back in the car.

***

'Going for a fag, rack um up.'

'Sure, Terry, what your last slave die of?'

'If you ever beat me, then I'll rack um,' with that he made for the smoking shelter at the back of the pub. He clipped a couple of stools as he wormed his way through to the back, courtesy of seven pints.

Terry lit his cigarette and leaned against the wall taking a few long drags. He didn't recognise the figure that appeared to join him in the dimly lit patio.

'Light mate?' the man said.

'Sure,' but as Terry looked down to get out the lighter, he took a single blow to the head.

Billy stood over the unconscious body and smirked. 'I owed you that one, fucker.'

The cold water hit his head like a slap, but it still took Terry a moment to come around. 'Where the fuck am I?'

The hotel room was basic, a double bed, wardrobe and desk. Terry was tied to the only chair in the room. He didn't notice the gun in Billy's hand to start with, as it was masked by the towel, he was drying his hands with. 'I said, where the...' then he saw the gun, paused and changed tone, 'Look, mate, there's no need for all this, what do you want?'

Billy was going to enjoy this for a few minutes. Without saying a word, he walked over to the chair, looked Terry straight in the eyes and used the gun to point to his own battered nose. 'Look, mate, I'm sorry about that, I'm just sick of the press hounding me and Mum.'

Billy sat on the bed, staring straight into Terry's eyes. 'What made you think I'm a reporter?'

'Well, Mum said you'd been hanging around the house the last few days.'

'So?'

'Well, a couple of weeks ago this guy was hanging around. Said he was a reporter for the *Mail* and wanted to talk to us about Dad.' He'd lost any aggression and was now speaking freely.

'What happened?' Billy barked.

'I told him to fuck off and said I'd kill him if I saw him near us again.'

'And that was the last you saw of him?'

'Yes. Except...'

'Except what?' Billy was feigning impatience and waving the gun a little. In his experience, if the subject was worried, they tended to talk more.

'Except, the next day we were burgled. Broken into actually, because nothing was really taken, but Mum's files had been turned over.'

'Is that when you found them?' Billy dropped in.

'Found what?' for the moment Terry really didn't know what this guy was referring to.

'Found the cheques from Dean?'

'I don't know what you're talking about.'

Excellent, Billy thought, *the first lie*, and with that he hit Terry with the barrel, square in the stomach. Another rule of his – while the subject was telling the truth, no violence. Sometimes he longed for them to lie.

'What the fuck was that for?' Terry screamed as he struggled for breath.

'The truth. Is that when you found the cheques?'

'No!' Crack – another blow to the ribs.

'No!' And another thud, this time to the head.

Blood was coming from the top of Terry's eye and he was struggling to breathe.

'Okay, okay, give me a second.'

Billy waited impatiently. 'Go on!'

'Mum always complained about being short of money. When I saw those cheques, thousands of pounds, I confronted her. She said she didn't want anything from that man.'

'Dean?'

'Yeah, that's the twat.'

Billy ignored the insult. 'So, your mum wouldn't take the money, but you thought, well I'll have a bit of that.'

'Why not? That scumbag wrecked this family, why not make him pay?'

'Is that the only way you wanted him to pay?'

'How'd you mean?'

'Not tempted to take it further, you know, scare the shit out of him, maybe even do him in?'

'I hope that shit gets what he deserves and yeah, there was a time after Dad got sent down when I wanted to find him and rip him to bits. But Mum begged me not to, wouldn't tell me where he was living and after a while I cooled off.'

'You don't seem to be the sort of guy who listens to his mum. You didn't when she asked you not to attack me this afternoon.'

'Yeah, well in the heat of the moment I go off on one. Sorry about that.'

Billy went to the bathroom, poured a glass of water from the tap, came back in and held it to Terry's mouth.

'How'd you know I took the money?' Terry asked.

'Easy. I've been watching you for two days. You earn about 300 quid a week. Spend about 200 on beer and the rest on fags.'

'So?'

'So, you're currently wearing a brand-new 50 quid T-shirt and 100 quid jeans.'

Terry looked down at his bloody and battered clothes. 'Shit, man, you've wrecked um.'

'Tell me about the reporter.' Billy didn't want to give Terry any thinking time.

'What about him?'

'What did he look like?'

'I don't know, middle-aged guy, maybe a bit older than you?'

'Fat, thin?'

'Bit podgy I suppose, hadn't shaved for a bit, smelled of whiskey.' Billy smiled.

'What is it, man, do you know him?'

Billy bent down behind Terry and released his legs, then his arms. 'Yeah, I know him and a hundred like him.'

'Who was it, what's his name?'

'His name is whatever he wants it to be, he's me, he's my mate, he's a dozen washed-up cops.' Billy grabbed Terry's arms and lifted him up. 'You're lucky, that guy could have killed you,' and with that, he frogmarched Terry out of the hotel room.

'Don't even think about going to the cops,' Billy said as he dragged Terry through the corridors, 'one word and I'll tell them about your fraud.' He opened a fire door, not wanting to take his hostage through the hotel reception and threw him outside.

'If I see you near Dean or any of his friends, I'll kill you!' He reached into his pocket and threw him a 10 pound note. 'For a cab,' and with that, he closed the fire door and headed for some sleep.

CHAPTER 9

Dean woke late, although it took him a few seconds to realise that it wasn't the little glimpses of sunlight breaking through the shutter that had stirred him. There was a commotion coming from downstairs, raised voices and eventually Dean was able to work out that most of the shouting was coming from Stevie. *Someone probably got mud on the wing-mirror*, he thought to himself. As good friends as he and Stevie were, Dean sometimes got annoyed with his over-dramatisation of a situation.

After a few minutes hoping the noise would die down, he finally decided to give in and head downstairs. He rolled himself out of bed, stumbled across the room and ducked to avoid the ceiling light as he pulled open the shutter. He was only in his boxers, so grabbed a T-shirt and was still putting on a pair of shorts as he opened the bedroom door. He hadn't even bothered with a watch, so glanced at the clock on the landing as he meandered down the stairs. He smiled to himself; nearly 11, he must be fully relaxed by now if he can sleep in that late. The pre-holiday troubles seemed a million miles away, and with his uncle investigating things in England, Dean finally felt able to enjoy himself. Then he got to the bottom of the stairs.

As he opened the kitchen door, he could see most of the group either standing or sitting around the kitchen table. Stevie looked over as he entered the room and before Dean could even say, 'morning,' Stevie shouted, 'You'll never believe what's happened!' He was red with anger, and as Dean had a quick glance around the table, he could see Otis, Jack, Pippa and Graham were certainly not amused by whatever had riled Stevie.

'We've been attacked!' Stevie continued.

'I think that's a bit dramatic,' Graham piped up.

'Oh, is it, what else would you call it?'

Dean finally intervened, 'Okay, just tell me what's happened?'

'The tyres have been slashed!' Stevie shouted, still angry.

'Whose?'

'Both cars,' Graham continued, 'all four wheels.'

It hit Dean like a heavy punch to the stomach. He went pale and if he hadn't sat down, his wobbly legs would have certainly given way. He didn't hear any of the subsequent chatter that was being repeated for his benefit. Instead he sat, frozen, as he tried to compute what he'd just been told. He didn't need to hear the endless theories being spouted by the group or the remembered stories of other holiday disasters. Unlike everyone else at that table, he knew what this meant. He didn't know why and maybe not who, but he did know that whoever had attacked him before they'd left, had followed them down to this quiet part of France. He couldn't even comfort himself with the 'it's a coincidence' fall-back position that everyone would no doubt try and soothe him with if they knew the whole story. As a rule, he didn't believe in coincidences, and certainly not this many in quick succession. He'd spent enough time with Billy as a kid to know a coincidence seldom was that.

The others were so embroiled in conversation that Dean managed to get himself out of his internal mire sufficiently to re-surface back to life before anyone noticed he'd gone.

'Who do you think did it?' Graham asked Dean directly.

Dean had to force a shrug. 'Kids I suppose,' he managed, feebly.

'Well unless any of us did it, that's the only sensible possibility,' Graham said.

'Kids! Where the fuck did they come from? We're in the middle of a forest, in the middle of fucking nowhere!' Stevie barked, unwilling to end the debate yet.

Having been given every possible doomsday scenario by Stevie over the last half hour, Graham was no longer in the mood to continue with idol gossip. 'Ultimately it doesn't matter who did it, we just need to figure out what we do next.'

Before Stevie could argue back, Dean, who was grateful for the opportunity to end the 'whodunit' debate, jumped in, 'I agree with Graham, let's plan a way forward.'

Stevie thought about continuing but decided it wasn't worth going up against Graham and Dean. Everyone knew that agreement between the unofficial leader and his deputy meant arguing was futile.

Stevie, Otis and Jack took Dean to see the damaged cars as Graham went upstairs to tell Marie and Beth the bad news. Graham and Dean had agreed that everyone should meet back in the kitchen at 11.30 to plan the next steps.

Seeing the slashed tyres on both cars caused Dean's legs to wobble again. He knew Stevie was right, there was no one within a twenty-minute drive, so it couldn't be kids. Dean also knew that he couldn't frighten the life out of everyone else, just to ease the burden in his own mind.

As he headed up the stone steps back to the kitchen, he had a thought and suddenly changed pace. He ran through the kitchen door, pushing past Beth, who had emerged bleary-eyed, and charged up the stairs to his room. He rummaged around his suitcase and breathed again as his hand hit a cold bit of metal. 'Thank God,' he muttered, but was a little annoyed it had taken him that long to remember the gun.

He stood in the middle of his room for a few moments holding the gun awkwardly. There was no way he could keep this on him without it being noticed – the weather was glorious, and everyone was wearing appropriate clothing; a pistol would stick out. He cursed the sparsely furnished room as he wandered about aimlessly, then decided to stuff it into one of his pillowcases. Not ideal, but it would have to do for now. Now late for the meeting, he grabbed his watch and phone for the first time on the holiday and trotted downstairs at pace.

'Sorry,' Dean said as Graham, seated at the head of the table, gave him a look. There were enough chairs for all eight of them, with some having been moved in from the dining room, but Jack and Dean decided to perch on opposite worktops as the others sat around the table.

Graham began, 'Firstly, does anyone have any signal at all?' a mixture of shaken heads and 'no's' were given by the group. Beth was the only one who needed to get up and find her phone, causing both Graham and Stevie to tut loudly. For someone so dizzy, it was difficult for the group to imagine how she was so intelligent. She returned in moments to confirm in the negative, and Graham was able to continue.

'Okay, the landline doesn't work either, so I guess we'll have to try Madame Bernard.'

'I have done, she's not in,' Jack said, impressing the group with his initiative.

'Oh, well, we'll have to try again,' Graham said, and the others could tell he was slightly put out that Jack had been ahead of him.

'Her car isn't there, I went as soon as Stevie showed me the tyres.' He looked at Stevie, who nodded his corroboration of the story.

'Perhaps she went away?' Marie said.

'No, not likely, she said she was going away tomorrow, until Sunday,' Graham dismissed his wife's comment out of hand.

'Yes, but that relies on your rather patchy French,' she hit back.

'You should trust that I know the difference between "Mardi" and "Mercredi",' Graham hit back.

As much as Dean enjoyed the light relief of seeing a real-live husband-and-wife tiff, he decided to intervene in the interests of getting them out of the predicament. 'I think we should assume she'll be back today, but nonetheless, have a back-up plan in case she decided to go early.'

Graham looked like he appreciated Dean's interjection and was quick to move on from the argument with Marie, 'Agreed. I think we need to pretty much stake out her cottage so that we don't risk missing her but have another plan.'

'But what is the other plan?' Beth said.

Graham continued, barely acknowledging her, 'We've got plenty of food, so that's not a problem, but we can't just sit around waiting for someone to show up,' and then he nodded towards Otis as if giving him permission to speak.

Not being at university with the core group, Otis still felt a little like an outsider and started nervously, fidgeting in his pocket before producing a map. 'I've had a look at this, and I reckon we're ten to twelve miles away from the nearest village.'

'Is that all! Let's put a few sandwiches together and set off before noon,' Marie said sarcastically. Graham gave her a look of disapproval, before asking Otis to continue.

'Yes, it's a long way, but not impossible in three to four hours.'

'And who's going on this mild stroll through the country?' Marie questioned.

'Well, I'm very experienced at this kind of thing, so me. I can read a map and am fit enough, but...' Otis paused.

'But what?'

'I can't speak a word of French,' he admitted.

'Oh fabulous, so you get to the nearest phone and then the AA will end up in Monaco!' Marie threw back at Otis.

There was a slight pause, before Graham responded, 'No, because Jack and I will go with him.'

Marie chuckled, and then realising he was serious, decided to argue, 'No way, you're two stone overweight and don't even walk to the pub.'

'I have to. Jack and I are the only ones who can speak enough French to send out the rescue truck.'

'Why not, Dean?' she continued to argue against her husband's participation, 'he's far fitter than you.'

Dean stepped away from the worktop he was leaning on, in order to join the debate, 'I don't speak French very well. Jack and Otis can support Graham on the walk, and I'll stay here with the girls and Stevie. I have some self-defence training, so if the youths come back again, I can make sure we keep this place safe.'

Dean didn't believe it was 'youths' for one-minute but decided to keep up the theory that had been established.

The debate raged on for a few more minutes, but eventually they all agreed on Graham and Otis's plan. Stevie and Beth were despatched immediately to the steps of Madame Bernard's cottage for the first shift of the stakeout. Otis suggested the boys didn't set off until 3pm after the worst of the heat was over. They all agreed and determined that the best-case was they'd reach the nearest village by the time the restaurants opened.

The girls fussed around the boys, preparing a couple of bags full of baguettes, pâtés, crisps and plenty of water. As the time got nearer for the three men to head off on their journey, the tension in the house grew. Marie had made it very clear to Graham that she believed he shouldn't be going but had long given up the fight and moved on to support and instructions. Beth and Stevie returned from their stint at Madame Bernard's to wave them off and the group gathered outside the house to say their best wishes. 'They're hardly heading up Everest,' Stevie joked but got no more than a few polite titters. Marie gave Graham a final hug, and then he turned and joined Otis and Jack, who had already taken a few steps forward to try and encourage Graham's departure.

It was just after three, and each man was carrying a rucksack loaded with provisions for the journey. Otis, who was a scout leader in his spare time, had made them all pack a change of socks, T-shirts and a bed sheet. Jack and Graham had wondered why the sheet was needed but opted to go with Otis's advice, with little argument. All three had been given four litres of water, meaning the packs were heavier than they would have liked, but it was a baking hot day.

The first part of the journey was about three miles of dirt track through the forests, which mercifully kept them in the shade. They passed the occasional clearing, where trees had been removed, although in their four days in the house they had not seen any sign of another human being, never mind actual felling in the area.

Jack and Otis adjusted their pace to allow Graham to stay in touch. Although they could have gone considerably quicker, Otis declared he was relatively happy with the progress they were making. To hit any sort of life by the time the breakdown trucks were still operating, he told them they needed to get through this section, to the rough tarmac road, within an hour.

It actually took just under that hour for them to reach the end of dirt track and through to a single-track concrete road that crossed at 90 degrees in front of the road they were coming from. 'Let's rest here for a bit,' Otis said. Graham, who was slightly overweight and out of shape, looked red-faced and breathed heavily as he sat on the verge. The worst-case scenario was the twelve-mile hike to the nearest village, but there was always the hope they'd manage to flag down a passing car.

They were still surrounded by forest as they set off again, turning right on the concrete road and managing another 30 minutes before Graham's pace slowed considerably, causing Otis to offer another five-minute break. This time Graham just collapsed by the road, not bothering to even catch up the 30 metres he'd fallen behind. 'He's really struggling,' Jack said as he and Otis perched on a fallen tree.

'Yeah, we'll need regular breaks, it may take us longer than four hours.' They chatted for a few minutes, questioning the wisdom of bringing Graham along, before they agreed to keep moving.

Otis had started heading over to Graham when he heard something. He stopped and stepped further out into the road. No, he must have been wrong. He carried on, then stepped out again; he was sure he could hear something, but it was impossible to see as the road wound around the forest. He looked back at Jack, who had obviously heard it as well. 'Is it a car?' Jack shouted.

'Dunno. Let's hope so,' Otis shouted back. He carried on walking towards Graham, who had now managed to stand up and step forwards into the road.

He looked up at Otis as he came toward him. 'I think it is, you know.'

'Fantastic!' Otis shouted. He made his way into the centre of the road, he could hear it getting closer, but wouldn't get sight of it until it was 150 metres away, due to the bend in the road. He looked back at Jack again, who was waving him forward.

To Graham, it seemed like the three of them had been waiting an age, but finally the white Peugeot 206 became visible to Otis first, as it came around the corner. It was doing a fair pace but appeared to slow down as it saw Otis waving his arms violently; he'd now moved to a position of safety on the edge of the road in case the car hadn't spotted him. He gradually edged back into the road a little more as he became confident the car was slowing down and he turned back again to Jack to give him the thumbs up.

Graham noticed it first, then Jack, but unfortunately Otis was still facing Jack when the car started accelerating again. It was the look on Jack's face that made him turn back towards the car. There was just enough time for Otis to take two steps back towards the edge of the road, but as he did this the car swerved. Not away from Otis, towards him.

***

Dean was glad his shift on the doorstep of Madame Bernard's was with Pippa. She hadn't really registered with him before, being Cam's younger sister, he'd not thought of her as a woman, but she certainly was now. She had long, flowing golden hair that touched the top of her bare shoulders. She was wearing a tight-fitting top that had only the slightest of straps – *Jesus, how she's grown up*, Dean thought to himself.

They talked about nothing in particular to start with, but Dean got a sense that Pippa wanted to take the conversation in a different direction, so brought his assessment of the British political process to a close. After a prolonged silence, Pippa finally started to speak on her chosen subject, 'Thank you for yesterday.'

'What do you mean?' Dean knew but liked a bit of false modesty.

'For talking to me like a grown-up. For not being frightened to discuss Cam. For treating me like a real member of the group.' She laid it on a thick, but Dean appreciated it and put his arm around her, giving her a friendly squeeze.

'Firstly, you are a member of this group. Stop thinking of yourself as an outsider. Secondly, I like remembering Cam, talking about the things we used to get up to together and finally, you can always talk to anyone of us about your brother. Perhaps not Stevie, he's not the "talk about your feelings" sort of person.' They both laughed, and Dean removed his arm from her shoulder.

After that unexpected openness, there was more silence, so Dean made an excuse about hearing a noise and went for a patrol around Madame Bernard's house. He felt weird about the feelings he was starting to get for Pippa and fancied a little bit of space. Could he really be feeling something for her? Did she feel the same way? How would the group react? And then his thoughts became more sombre; how would Cam have reacted? Then he remembered Ryan.

How could he have forgotten that? In all the emotion of Cam's death and blame that was put on Ryan, the group had put very little focus on the fact that Ryan was Pippa's boyfriend. To the outside world, it would have made a great tabloid magazine article, 'My Boyfriend Killed My Brother,' but to the group, and in particular to Dean, it was one friend responsible for the death of another.

Dean remembered Cam's reaction when Pippa and Ryan announced they were seeing each other. There was a huge fight between the two friends, but Pippa had eventually talked her brother around – she could always talk her brother around.

As Dean completed his walk around the house, he saw the vision that was Pippa on the doorstep. He looked at her beauty and realised he was falling for her. 'Sorry, Cam,' he said out loud – but to himself – and jogged over to sit next to his dead friend's sister.

* * *

Both legs snapped immediately as the car drove through him. His body flew up, with his head cracking the windscreen first before his torso landed onto the bonnet and his entire frame rolled over the car, landing with a deadly thud on the road. The car, having slowed down once, didn't do so again – it swerved back into the centre of the road and sped away. For a moment there was silence.

Jack, who had thrown himself into the verge, picked himself up and started running back down the road towards Otis's body. Graham, who had stood rigid by the roadside throughout the whole incident, just started saying 'fuck' repeatedly under his breath.

Jack reached the body first but stood for a minute as he thought what to do. 'Otis. Otis, mate, are you OK? Otis, Otis mate, come on.' He bent down and went for the pulse. Otis was lying on his back with huge cuts over his head. Jack bit his lip to stop himself being sick and managed to fumble around the neck to locate the pulse. 'He's still alive,' Jack shouted over to Graham.

This seemed to spark a frozen Graham into life, and he charged over to Otis. 'Otis, wake up,' they kept repeating.

Neither was proficient in first aid, but Jack said he knew a bit from his rugby days, so Graham reverted to assistant for now. 'Get the bags,' Jack barked at his friend, and obediently Graham went off to collect all three, which were scattered about the road.

Jack pulled out some water and tried pouring a little into Otis's mouth. Graham appeared, having picked up the last bag, and surveyed Otis properly for the first time. 'Shit, look at his legs!' Jack hadn't noticed this so far, but when he looked down, he could see the bone sticking out of his right leg and a significant amount of blood covered his whole lower body.

Jack stared at the mangled legs for a few seconds, then, in a controlled and quiet manner, vomited.

After allowing himself the brief pause, Jack grabbed some of the water to wash his mouth out and regained his composure.

'What should we do?' Graham said, panic-stricken.

'Any phone reception?' Jack asked hopefully.

Graham pulled out his mobile again, looked at it and shook his head. 'I've been checking every few hundred metres.'

'Damn it!' Jack paused before continuing, 'I can head off as planned to get help and leave you with Otis,' he offered.

'No way,' Graham was firm, 'there is no way we should split up at this point.'

'But how the hell are we going to get him to a hospital?'

'The last thing we want is for you to get taken down as well. We must stay together. Plus, it's another eight miles at least to the nearest village.'

Jack looked at Graham for a few moments and then dared ask, 'Was that deliberate?'

Graham thought for a second, but was too frightened to admit his fears, so just shot back, 'Fuck knows. Let's get him sorted.'

Jack nodded in agreement and then started to form a plan of action. 'First off, we'll have to stop the bleeding and get him as comfortable as possible before he regains consciousness.'

Graham agreed, and the two friends began work tending to Otis's wounds. They used one of the sheets Otis had insisted on bringing, tore it into strips and used several strips to bandage his cut head. As they attempted to move the broken bones in his legs, Graham vomited but carried on without acknowledging it to Jack. They both used several strips to build padding around the protruding bone in Otis's right leg, with several more strips used to keep them in place. Jack, using Otis's penknife, cut a couple of large sticks to use as a support for his legs. They tentatively placed two sticks, one either slide of his right leg, and used more strips to tie them to the leg. 'We'll have to do the same to the left leg,' Jack said as they looked on at their handiwork.

Jack moved over to the left leg and gently moved his hand down it. 'Two breaks,' he declared after a minute, but neither break had forced the bone through the skin. They repeated the exercise with the branches and strips of cloth and eventually stood up to review their work. They looked across at the other, each of them covered in blood – hands, t-shirts, arms, even their faces.

Graham felt sick again but held it in and then checked his watch. 'It's taken an hour to stabilise him – what do we do next?'

Jack checked his watch to verify the information. 'It's nearly five thirty, it took us an hour and a half to walk this far.'

'I reckon we carry him back,' Graham suggested confidently.

'Are you kidding? You struggled to make it this far yourself!' Jack shot back.

'What's the alternative?' Jack shrugged his shoulders, giving Graham the opportunity to put forward his plan. 'If we eat now and abandon all the bags, save for a couple of litres of water, we can carry him back using the other two bed sheets.'

Jack nodded before Graham continued, 'At best, it will take us double the time to get back, which means we might just do it before nightfall.'

Having eaten, they laid the sheets out on the road-side, doubling up both before attempting the difficult part. They stood each end of Otis and paused, neither wanting to move him for fear of waking him. Jack grappled with his shoulders and Graham the legs. 'Ready,' Jack said, Graham nodded, and they gently lifted him onto the makeshift stretcher. Both were grateful that Otis had a slight frame, weighing less than 10 stone. Jack checked he was still breathing as he gently lowered the head down and was relieved to feel Otis's breath on his cheek.

Graham then grabbed two bottles of the water and lay them down on the stretcher in-between Otis's crushed legs. 'All set,' Jack said.

Graham nodded and Jack counted down, 'Three, two, one, lift,' and both groaned as they bent down to pick up the stretcher. Graham stumbled a few paces, but Jack was able to follow his movement before they began to find a rhythm and cautiously moved back along the road they had walked down earlier.

***

The conversation had become more awkward, more pointless as each waited for the other to make a move. Dean struggled to think of anything interesting to say, his heart was pounding faster with the anticipation of what might be, then she helped him out, 'It's getting a bit colder,' she said, giving Dean the opportunity to put his arm around her.

'Is that better?' he offered and with that Pippa moved closer into Dean, encouraging the hug.

After a few minutes, in which neither said anything, she turned her head towards him. 'Do you think we should have another walk around?'

Dean gently shook his head. 'No,' and slowly moved in to kiss her. She gradually turned her whole body towards him and put her hands around his neck as he released his arm from her shoulder and put his hands around her waist.

After a minute, they withdrew and giggled a little. Dean then put his arm around her shoulder again, and they said nothing for the remainder of their shift.

***

As they reached the turning onto the dirt track, they collapsed. It had taken over two hours and seven stops for them to walk a third of the journey back, and now it was nearly eight. 'We'll never do it,' Graham managed after a few minutes, his red face was nearly crimson and his breathing still fast and wheezing.

'We will. Think positive,' Jack said, as he handed him some more water, 'it might take us until the morning but—' at that point Jack was interrupted by a groan from Otis. They dropped down to their knees and leaned over Otis's body. 'Otis, mate, you alright?'

Otis cried.

'Don't worry, Otis, we're getting you back to the house, you gave us quite a fright.'

'It hurts,' Otis managed.

'Yeah, we know. We need to get you back home asap,' Graham said before Otis slipped out of consciousness.

Otis waking had given Jack and Graham fresh impetus to get going, and they both agreed to start off straight away. As they gently lifted their patient, Jack checked to make sure he hadn't woken again. They tentatively began making their way down the uneven mud-track road.

Thankfully, Otis didn't wake for the next couple of hours. Every time they stopped, they gently laid his stricken body down, checking the blood was clotting and that he was still breathing.

At about 11pm they had to take an extended break. 'How much longer?' Graham panted as he took a long swig of water.

'I reckon another hour should do it.' Jack was lying almost flat, with his head resting on a fallen tree.

'I think it was,' Graham said after a few more minutes.

'Was what?' Jack barely managed, with an uninterested tone.

'Deliberate.' Graham let the word wallow in the humid night air.

Jack sat up, suddenly interested. Although tired, he was desperate to have this conversation. 'Seriously?'

Graham just nodded.

'But who? Why?' Jack was anxious to get the theories.

'I don't know. But I'm pretty sure there's something going on with some of the others as well,' Graham offered.

'What do you mean?'

'I don't know exactly. Initially, I thought it was because it was the first holiday since Cam died. But more and more it's felt like something is wrong, and I just can't put my finger on it.'

'Maybe the car didn't swerve on purpose?' Jack said hopefully.

'No. You saw the same thing as me. It slowed down, realised who was in the road, then sped up and swerved to hit him.'

Jack couldn't argue – it was exactly what he'd seen. 'Do we tell the others?'

'Yes, the moment we get back.'

Graham was in charge again.

After a few minutes of silence, they both agreed to carry on for the final mile and gradually lifted Otis's body up.

It was the intensity of the scream that hit them both, making them drop the body straight back down.

'Don't do it,' he begged. His agony was conveyed through the pained scream, louder and more intense than ever before.

Graham bent down beside him and stroked his head. Both he and Jack had been stunned by the ferocity of the scream, but quickly regained their composure.

'Please don't move me again,' Otis howled.

'We have to,' and with that Graham nodded to Jack and they lifted his body.

The scream returned, louder and more frightening than the first time, but they both ignored it. As they marched down the dirt track, both men sobbed as they listened to Otis beg them to kill him.

They just kept going.

CHAPTER 10

'Where are they?' Marie said again.

The remaining five had given up stalking Madame Bernard and were sitting around the kitchen table nibbling on crisps and nuts, although none of them were particularly hungry.

Dean and Pippa deliberately sat apart and tried not to make eye contact. Dean, a handsome, toned and fit man, who had plenty of conquests to his name, was surprised how awkward he felt after a simple kiss. None of the other three had spotted the awkwardness amid the tension created as they waited for news of the adventurers.

'They should have been back by now,' Marie said again, checking her watch and then the kitchen clock, to make the point.

'It's only been nine hours, give them time,' Dean comforted.

'They said three to four,' she threw back tersely.

'Yes, but if it took four hours to walk to the village; they won't just find a mechanic, sat ready to go in his pick-up – and then immediately get teleported back here. Give them time.' Dean tried in vain to ease the worry.

'Knowing Graham and Otis, they're probably holed up in a bistro with a three-course meal inside them,' Stevie said, unusually trying to ease the tension. Marie just huffed and got up to pour another glass of wine. If doomsday-merchant Stevie was trying to play down the situation, they knew it must be bad.

Dean was worried. More worried than he let on to the others. The events that occurred pre-holiday were swirling around in his head. He stood up from the table and walked out of the house through the kitchen door but wedged it open so that he wasn't completely cut off from the others. He stood on the veranda above the stone steps, looking down at the trashed cars. He contemplated what to do, what could he possibly do? He felt an enormous amount of guilt for the predicament he'd put everyone in.

* * *

Jack saw the light first, but by the time he'd managed to get the words out of his dry mouth, Graham had already seen it. Never before had either of them been so happy to see a little flicker of yellow, half a mile away at most. The pace picked up, especially as their patient was comatose.

It had been a torturous eight hours. Nearly one o'clock in the morning and they'd spent a third of a day carrying a badly injured friend across uneven ground in a foreign country.

They'd debated what to say every time they'd stopped. Finally, they'd agreed the truth – as far as they knew it. Otis had been deliberately run down and left for dead. It all had to be linked to the slashed tyres and maybe even the pre-holiday car crash. Someone was determined to get them – they were all in danger.

Graham had thought the worst, what he dare not say to Jack; what if the house had been attacked while they were out, and his wife and friends slain? It was a distant possibility, and one he didn't want to say out loud for fear of having Jack concur and increase his fears. So, he pretended, outwardly, that the house represented a safe haven. He also knew that returning to the house empty-handed would feel like they'd been sent down to the starting square of a snakes and ladders board.

Dean saw them first. As they turned the corner and came past the last of the trees, the white of the bed sheet reflected off of the near-full moon.

'They're back!' he shouted as he ran down the steps to the driveway. 'They're back,' he shouted repeatedly with excitement and charged towards them. The others jumped up from their seats, Marie knocking over a glass of wine in the process but ignored it as she charged for the door.

As Dean reached them, Jack lowered his end of the sheet, collapsed onto his knees and put his face in his hands. Graham carefully placed Otis's head on the floor and found the energy to run and meet his wife as she descended the steps. Marie had barged passed the others on the steps and ran out with arms open, ready to squeeze the life out of her husband. The others followed; joy, relief for a brief second, then they heard the cry from Dean as he stood over Otis. 'Pippa!' he screamed, 'Pippa, get over here quick,' but she was already on her way.

The trainee nurse was only just 20 years old but was now immediately responsible for the life of a friend. On-the-job training was best, her teacher had always said, now she was about to get some real practice.

There was mayhem. Questions flying about, Stevie panicking about his best mate, Marie relieved at her husband's return, mass disappointment at the mission's failure. For Dean, in particular, it was a blur. He and Stevie assumed the role of support carer for Otis as Pippa barked orders authoritatively. Dean vaguely heard talk of a car swerving deliberately in the background but didn't take it in. Pippa demanded Otis be taken to a bed, and Dean was despatched to clear Jack's belongings from the only lower-floor bedroom. He didn't protest, too exhausted to do anything other than swig the water that Beth and Marie were bringing.

Pippa surveyed the damage to Otis's legs and checked the cut on the side of his head. She asked Jack and Graham for details on his consciousness over the last nine hours and concluded, unsurprisingly, that he needed to get to a hospital ASAP.

She carefully removed the patchwork splint and tourniquet that Graham and Jack had applied to the legs so that she could see the extent of the damage. She felt faint but held it together – this was the worst set of injuries she had encountered in her short career. She summoned over Dean and Stevie again. 'We need to get him into the bed, and I'll have another go at setting the legs,' she paused briefly and wiped her forehead, leaving a light dusting of blood, before continuing. 'Obviously both legs are broken, one of them is a compound fracture. He really needs a hospital now!'

Dean looked at her, still shocked. 'Are you sure we should move him in this condition?'

Pippa's response was terse, 'Well, we can't leave him out here, can we? Let's get on with it before he comes around again.' She directed Dean and Stevie, who both flinched when they got a better look at the state of Otis.

As they began to lift him, he started to wake, causing them to start lowering him again.

'Don't stop. Keep going!' Pippa shouted at them, and they obeyed without question, carrying him up the outside steps to the kitchen and then through into the bedroom. Pained screams silenced the group, but having momentarily paused once, Dean and Stevie continued without stopping as Pippa barked orders at them. When they reached Jack's bedroom, they laid him down gently.

'What now?' Stevie asked.

Pippa surveyed the scene, and for the first time, Dean thought she looked rattled, so he decided to put a comforting hand on her shoulder. 'Can I do anything?' This brought her out of the temporary daze and led to more orders. Someone was despatched to her bedroom for a medical kit, another for hot water and another for towels. Stevie just knelt by his friend's bed and held his hand as Otis screamed uncontrollably.

One by one, the requests were delivered to Pippa. She took the scissors from her bag and started cutting away at Otis's trousers. 'We need to set the legs and continue to stem the bleeding.' Everyone who had now gathered around the bed agreed, but they all knew that only one person was going to do it.

Pippa looked in her bag and let out a groan of disappointment. 'Pathetic,' she said under her breath. Even Dean could see a few bandages and some antiseptic was not going to cut it here. Nevertheless, he was impressed with how Pippa continued with authority, despite this obvious setback. 'Has anyone got a sewing kit?' she barked, Marie nodded and was despatched. Graham left with his wife to be sick again.

It took all of them to hold Otis down as Pippa reached into his open wound and moved the bone roughly back into place. She tied the bone to a section of the grill she'd had Dean break off and douse in antiseptic. Then she began to tie the skin together with a standard needle and thread. A chair was broken to supply external support to both of Otis's broken legs as bandages were liberally wrapped around both of his lower limbs.

'That's the best I can do for now,' she said as one by one the group released their grip on Otis's body. She gave him off-the-shelf painkillers, knowing they would make virtually no difference. He continued to cry out in pain as the group made their excuses and left the room in silence. Several of them were splattered in blood, Beth and Jack had tears rolling down their faces.

Over the next hour, the group showered and changed as they tried to get the stench of blood off them. Eventually, they reconvened in the kitchen and spent another hour arguing and debating over Graham and Jack's accounts of the day. The conversation, often heated, only halted when squeals of pain could be heard from Jack's former bedroom. The only person missing was Stevie, who was watching over his best friend.

The conclusion was damning; they were being targeted, that was without question. There was no doubt the attack on Otis was deliberate. The tyres had been slashed, obviously deliberately. What had originally seemed like an accidental crash on the motorway, now seemed suspicious, especially when paired with the incident at Dean's flat. Had Stevie been at the table, he would have thrown the fuel incident into the mix as well. Dean still couldn't bring himself to tell them about his stalker.

By 4am they agreed to try for sleep, knowing full well that it was unlikely for anyone.

Stevie didn't move from Otis's side.

CHAPTER 11

As expected, it had been difficult for most of them to sleep. Otis had been crying for what remained of the night – moving from periods of loud sobbing to outright howling screams. Stevie had continued to sit with him all night and looked horrendous as the group started assembling in the kitchen for breakfast, this time at eight o'clock – not eleven as in previous mornings. As Stevie collapsed in a chair, he declared that Otis was now sleeping, as he started to pick at a stale croissant.

Dean doubted if he'd slept more than an hour and outwardly put it down to Otis, but he'd spent the night with the numerous conspiracy theories whirling around his head.

Graham looked equally terrible, having dragged Otis home yesterday, but as Beth and Pippa arrived at the kitchen table to join the others, he held a conference. 'We have to get Otis to a hospital today, that's our number one priority,' Graham said with authority. Everyone agreed, although only Pippa and Stevie could be bothered to nod.

'The way I see it, we have no transport, no immediate access to a telephone and no way to contact a single other person apart from Madame Bernard. She has to be our priority today, it's quite clear that we're not easily going to be able to find another way out of this place.'

'How far did you walk yesterday before the accident?' Stevie enquired.

'About three miles, why?'

'And in all that time you didn't get any mobile reception?'

'Of course not,' Graham shot back.

'You're telling me that in this day and age there is at least a three-mile area of France without mobile signal?' Stevie's tone hovered between questioning and accusatory.

Jack and Graham looked at each other before rounding on Stevie, 'I'm not sure what you're trying to say, but there was no signal at any point of our walk. You probably wouldn't have noticed while you were sipping wine from the comfort of the poolside, but there are no fucking houses around here!'

'So?' Stevie shot back, undeterred.

'Well, fuck-wit, if there are no houses, there is very little point in putting in a mobile infrastructure, is there?'

Stevie looked like he was going to continue the debate but managed to read the mood of the group and shut up.

Beth, who had been staring ashen faced at the table, looked up. 'Do we still think someone is deliberately trying to trap us here?'

'We don't know, Beth. But it seems the most logical explanation for the situation we are in,' Jack said in a considered tone.

'But why?'

'At first I thought youths—' Jack offered.

'But that seems unlikely now this has happened to Otis,' Graham interrupted.

'I suppose it is possible the two events are not linked?' Pippa said hopefully.

Dean couldn't bear to involve himself in the conversation, as far as he was concerned it was down to him. He wanted to tell the group, but didn't, he couldn't. He felt like a coward.

'If it was just the tyres and Otis, I could possibly buy it as a coincidence, but what happened before the holiday – it all must be linked!' Graham offered little comfort in his assessment, and there was no counter argument from the group.

The seven of them said little for a minute, before Beth spoke again, mainly to try and change the subject, 'What time is it? Can't find my watch.'

'I think I saw it in the lounge last night,' Marie offered. The chair scratched on the tiled floor as Beth moved it back and headed out of the kitchen.

Graham looked at his watch. 'It's nearly nine now. I suggest we get ready and split into two—'

The scream stopped Graham in his tracks.

Dean reacted quickest, kicking his chair over as he made for the dining room door. Jack and Stevie followed close behind as the rest of the group charged through. Dean had knocked over two more chairs on his way through the dining room to the lounge, which slowed down the rest of the group and almost tripped up Graham. A vase smashed. 'Bugger, that's the deposit gone,' he said, as he became the last member of the group to arrive in the lounge.

Beth was in tears, staring at the wall opposite the window. Dean had run up to her and got his arm around her shoulders before turning to see what she was staring at. One by one, the group had come to a stunned stop, looking at the wall. 'Think that vase is the least of our problems,' Jack managed.

The wallpaper had been vandalised with red paint – a message had been left for the group:

SECRETS KILL – DEAN MURDERED HIS
SON'S FAMILY

Beth was inconsolable. 'He was here, he was in the house. Oh God, he's going to kill us!' she wrestled herself clear of Dean and ran to Graham. 'He's going to kill us!'

'Don't be stupid,' Graham rebuffed.

'What do you mean, don't be stupid? He's been in here – in this house, while we were asleep.' She started screaming uncontrollably.

'Calm down, calm down,' Graham tried, but to no avail. In the end, Marie moved to her husband's side and quickly slapped her across the side of the face. Beth squealed and pulled her hand to her face, which had already started to turn red.

The rest of the group were silent as they waited for her reaction, but Marie spoke first, 'Sorry, but we all need to get a grip.'

The group waited another few seconds for a reaction from Beth, but she was stunned into silence. Marie carefully pulled Beth's hand down from her face, kissed it and apologised again before hugging her. To the group's relief, Beth responding by putting her arms around Marie and the two hugged for a few more seconds.

'Stevie,' Graham hollered, as he now felt able to move on.

'Yeah,' Stevie offered quietly, still stunned.

'You were down here with Otis all night. Did you see or hear anything suspicious?'

'Funnily enough – No! I was too busy trying to comfort my best friend who has just had both his legs crushed!' It wasn't said with anger, more disbelief.

No one had yet paid attention to what the message actually said – it was enough that there was a message at all. Dean knew that would change soon. His heart was pounding, he felt dizzy and nervous, almost like he felt before an exam – only ten times worse. His legs started to wobble, and he held the mantelpiece to stop himself from collapsing.

'OK,' Graham said, realising that his line of questioning with Stevie was going to prove fruitless, 'it's obviously not someone that knows us particularly well. I mean, Dean doesn't even have a son.' As he said it, he gestured towards Dean. The group, who had been looking away from him and towards Beth, finally turned to focus on the subject of the message. All assumed Dean would jovially 'false confess' to having probably knocked-up half of West Hampstead and laugh it off as a crazed manic; then they saw Dean's face.

Finally, his legs gave way and he collapsed into the nearest chair. His head was in his hands and he didn't even try and fight back the tears this time. The group looked around, stunned at Dean's reaction.

Finally, Graham broke the silence, 'Dean, it is bollocks, isn't it?' this was now said, more in hope than expectation. Marie pushed passed her husband and knelt by Dean. She put her hand on the top of his head and stroked it gently as she asked him softly and calmly to tell them what was wrong.

He looked up and nodded, wiping the tears from his eyes with the back of his hands. 'I'm sorry,' he said, but this time nobody interjected. They stood silent with all eyes fixed on the man sobbing in front of them. 'This is all my fault. The attempt on your lives before the holiday, the damage to the cars, Otis being run over; it's all because of me.'

'I find that very hard to believe,' Marie said, still softly, 'why don't you start from the beginning.' And he did. He told them his secret. He told them about Claire's unexpected pregnancy, a girl he hadn't been seeing long enough to introduce to the group. He told them about the agreed abortion and about the double-cross and his decision to have nothing to do with the baby.

The room was filled with shocked faces. 'Why didn't you tell us?' Graham said.

'Because I was ashamed of what I was doing – abandoning my child. I thought you'd think I was wrong.'

'Don't be silly, you tried to do the right thing and she double-crossed you,' Marie said, hugging him tighter.

'I don't understand how this ties-in with the madman here?' Graham questioned.

'Well, there's more,' Dean continued, 'she died by suicide six months after the baby was born.' There were gasps around the room, but he continued, it was about to get more shocking. 'Her dad tried to kill me but ended up killing someone else and was sent to prison.'

'How did he try to kill you?' Beth enquired. Dean looked up at the group and paused for a few seconds. 'How?' she asked again.

'He got very drunk and tried to run me over.'

'That's it then. It's her dad,' Beth barked.

Dean shook his head. 'No, it's not her dad – he died in prison a few months ago.'

The room was stunned into silence again. Eventually, Graham, who couldn't think of anything useful to say, declared that he needed a drink and charged into the dining room to pour himself a large whiskey. He downed it and paused for thought as he leant on the bar.

'I can't believe all this happened to you and you didn't say a word,' Stevie said.

'We all have secrets,' Marie said sharply in Stevie's direction, and he quickly retreated.

'Yeah, but this is a secret and a half,' Graham said as he came back into the room, 'I still don't understand how this links to us here and now? If the dad is dead, who in the hell is doing this to us?'

'A few weeks ago, I received a sympathy card with the newspaper article about her dad dying in prison and the words "You're Next" in it.'

'But who from?' Graham challenged.

'I assumed her brother, but I'm not sure he's clever enough to do all the other stuff.'

'What other stuff?' Marie said as the husband and wife provided an interviewer tag-team.

Dean continued to tell the story about the stalker and the events that led up to him seeing his uncle – but not beyond. He decided to omit the subsequent attack on his life in the flat; the group had enough to worry about already.

As he finished the story, there was a question. 'Is that everything?' a voice asked, although Dean didn't know or care who it was.

'Yes,' he responded meekly.

'Are you sure?' Then he recognised Graham's authoritative voice – but he didn't respond with enough conviction the second time to convince Graham or anyone else.

'Tell us everything,' Beth took over the questioning.

'Okay, there is something else, but I didn't think it was going to help us,' Dean conceded. Pausing to get the strength to tell the rest of the story.

'Just tell us,' Beth shouted impatiently.

'I'm going to. Give me a chance.' For the first time, Dean was starting to get defensive. During the last silence, Marie had retreated from a position of support to stand with her husband. Dean surveyed the group and realised they needed to know. They deserved to know the truth, and so he told them about his break-in, about being hit on the head, about the attempt to run him over in the car park. He told them everything there was to know. He had no secrets left.

'You selfish bastard!' Stevie shouted, 'If you'd told us all this at the start, maybe Otis wouldn't be lying in bed with two broken legs!'

'It's not Dean's fault,' Pippa intervened for the first time in the whole conversation.

'Like hell it's not,' Beth chipped in, 'we could have called the police in England. We could have stopped Dean coming on holiday, we could all be safe.'

'He wasn't to know what was going to happen,' Pippa argued back.

'Bollocks – we're all up shit-creek because of him!' Stevie shouted as he pointed towards Dean.

'Easy now, fella,' Jack stepped in to defend Pippa.

'You can fuck off. You're not even part of this group anyway,' Beth fired back.

'Fuck off yourself, you stuck-up bitch!' Jack shouted back at her.

'Hey, leave off her.' Graham pushed himself past Beth and in front of Jack.

'What you gonna do, tubs? Hit me?' Jack smirked as he said it.

'Don't you speak to my husband like that.' Now Marie was involved.

Jack turned his back on Graham, Marie, Stevie and Beth and shouted a colourful insult, before walking out the room.

Dean had watched the argument peter out and stood up from his chair. He'd confessed all and felt much better. He was also now not in the mood to take shit from anyone. He tenderly touched Pippa's elbow as he whispered a thank you in her ear.

'Do we all feel happy now?' Dean said and spoke over Stevie as he tried to carry on the argument, 'it's not going to help our cause if we start fighting among ourselves is it? We need to work together to get out of this mess.'

There was a pause as Marie, Beth and Stevie waited for a response from Graham. Eventually it came, 'You're right, let's figure out what to do next.'

Stevie wasn't quite ready to let the argument die, but rather than go against Graham, he marched out, giving Dean a long stare. 'Going to check on Otis,' he said sternly.

The remaining five sat down in the leather chairs and tried to ignore the daubing on the wall. Graham started, as usual, 'If it is this brother of Claire's, what's going to be his next play?'

'Well, I assume he's ultimately aiming to get me – and you lot are just in his way,' Dean said.

'So what do we do then?' Marie asked.

'Well, I've been thinking about it. I think I should offer myself up as bait.'

'No way!' Pippa blurted out before anyone else could respond, but Graham dismissed her out of hand.

'Let him speak. How would you do it?'

'I was thinking that I should set off from the house on my own, let him try and pick me off.'

'That's just ridiculous. We won't let you do it,' Graham said, even before Pippa could, 'you'd be picked off in minutes, you wouldn't stand a chance.'

'I might if I took my gun with me,' Dean said.

'Yeah, but you haven't got a clue how to fire it. No way we're letting you go out there on your own.' Graham wasn't about to lose another friend, although Beth was a little less bothered.

'What choice do we have, I say let him go.'

'No way,' Pippa barked back, and Beth didn't dare start another argument.

The group decided on a comfort break and Marie went off to make tea and coffee for the group, while Dean thought he needed to feel the comfort of his gun.

'There is something we're overlooking,' Marie said as she returned to the lounge with a tray of warm drinks and some left-over pastries.

'What's that, darling?' Graham's tone suggested he was not optimistic his wife was going to add something useful to the debate.

'Well, if Dean is the target, why was our car hit in England?' Graham looked annoyed that his wife had thought of this – there was no satisfactory answer.

'Maybe they're not linked,' Beth said, clearly still keen to pin their situation on Dean.

'No, they have to be linked. It's too much of a coincidence otherwise.'

Graham dismissed Beth but couldn't immediately think of an answer to Marie's question. 'There is no reason for Claire's brother to come down to Cambridge and target us a few hours after trying to kill Dean,' he continued.

'But if he's a psycho?' Beth was losing the argument, and everybody knew it.

'In which case, sending Dean out on his own is not the answer either. If he's trying to pick off Dean's friends and family as some sort of sick revenge, he's not going to stop just because we've sent Dean out on his own as bait.'

'What's the next step then?' Dean asked, quietly relieved they wouldn't let him fall on his sword.

'Pippa, is Otis in any immediate danger?' Graham was crafting a plan.

'I've stopped the bleeding but there is a significant risk of infection and of course he's in considerable pain; however, I'd say he's got a couple of days before an infection would become life-threatening.'

'And we've got enough food to last for a good few days,' Graham said.

'Hold on, you're not thinking we sit it out here, are you?' Beth panicked.

'That's exactly what I'm saying. We've got to think about the safety of all of us. We went out yesterday and he picked us off.'

'But we're here for another ten days, Otis won't make it that long.'

'I'm banking on Madame Bernard being around this morning, she's not supposed to go away for the weekend until later today. If we don't get anywhere with her today, then we'll think again.'

'What do we do, stake out Madame Bernard's house again?' Dean enquired.

'No. I don't want to split up the group today. We stay together. We'll roll one of the cars back to block her driveway. If she wants to get in or out, she'll have to come and see us.'

Marie and Dean nodded in agreement. 'I'll go and explain it to the others,' Graham said. They knew Stevie wasn't going to take it well. Dean was grateful Graham was doing the talking.

CHAPTER 12

The trip to Birmingham wasn't a complete waste of time, but it hadn't given Billy any real leads. He'd confirmed Dean's story, which wasn't unexpected, and ruled out the Mitchell family of being involved in the stalking. Whoever was behind this had gone to enough trouble to hire a private detective. He also knew that if the detective was half-decent, he'd never find him, and even if he did, he'd never reveal anything about his client. He suspected that the detective was not behind the break-in; that was probably down to our mystery man or woman.

He'd swapped cars before leaving Birmingham, annoyed at the loss of his deposit which ordinarily he'd charge to a client. Christ, how he hated personal jobs. He hated anything personal. His marriages had crumbled; in truth, the first well before he left the force, with many women and two more wives having crossed his path since. Billy was mid-forties, single and had no desire to change that situation. Despite his age and lifestyle, he was still good-looking in a rugged sort of way. Often appearing unkempt, in fact his facial hair wasn't completely unplanned, it covered a few scars from his time in the force and some he'd picked up afterwards.

As he drove back down the M6, he thought about his nephew; they'd been so close once – he'd done the fun stuff with Dean at weekends when his dad hadn't been bothered. The brothers had never really gotten on. Billy was six years younger than Jeremy, and he always felt Jeremy resented him being born, as it took the attention away from the boffin.

While the older brother had been somewhat academic, the younger sibling was not – his focus had been on sports and girls. Not that Billy was stupid, he was very clued-up about the ways of the world, but the two of them were just so different, they never got on. Billy was always hurt that Dean rejected him after he was thrown out of the Force but put it down to Jeremy's influence. The argument that the brothers had the day Billy left Birmingham was so ferocious, there was no way back for their relationship.

Billy thought for a minute. He'd really love to pay a visit to Jeremy and tell him to his face that Dean had turned to his waste-of-space uncle for help when he really needed it – but he couldn't do that to his nephew. A call came through from Tanya, interrupting his thoughts. 'Yeah, girl, what you got for me?'

'I've got the list of people he's gone on holiday with, their parents' names and addresses. I've sent it to your phone.'

'Jesus, girl, you know I don't know how to work that thing.'

'Well, learn – you dinosaur,' and with that she put the phone down.

Billy cursed, she was loyal and dependable, but sometimes stubborn. Not unlike himself – if he was honest; perhaps that was why they got on so well.

Having ruled out the Mitchells, Billy now had to look down other avenues. After hearing about the crash

Dean's friends suffered before they left for the holiday, he felt a connection had to be probable. If this person was coming after Dean and his friends, was his nephew the primary target or just one of many within the group? Billy had put out a lot of calls to old friends in various police forces for CCTV footage of Graham's accident. It seemed too much of a coincidence that a white van had been involved in the crash outside Dean's and was also involved in Graham's incident. It was taking longer than anticipated for the answer, but he was rapidly coming to the conclusion that this threat was beyond just Dean's life.

Billy pulled over at the services and went in to get himself a coffee. He really wanted something stronger but promised himself he'd stay dry while he was trying to save Dean. This was not a promise he would likely keep, but the best of intentions had been laid out. He paid for a coffee and a stale muffin, cursing the high prices under his breath, generating an unamused look from the rather plump lady serving him. He glanced around the large canteen, half-filled with a mixture of travelling salesmen and old aged pensioners. He smiled to himself and thanked the lord he didn't have a nine-to-five job or had reached the age where a cuppa and a teacake in a service station was the highlight of his week.

He wrestled with his phone as he struggled to get it out of his pocket and then stared at it for a minute as he tried to remember what Tanya had taught him. He pressed a few buttons and even surprised himself by managing to find the email she'd sent through.

Tanya had done far better than expected. She'd not only checked the basic details that he'd been given by

Dean but also managed to pull out some preliminary background. Billy spent a few minutes cross-checking the information that he'd just received from Tanya with the information Dean had given him a few days ago. Although Tanya was a shared resource in the office complex, he definitely managed to monopolise more of her time than was fair, partly because she enjoyed the work and partly because they were close. They weren't officially dating, and she certainly knew him well enough not to expect cosy nights in by the fire, but when both were in the mood, they'd meet up of an evening and keep Billy's neighbours awake until the early hours.

The background was stuff he'd probably have known if he'd been closer to Dean over the last few years, but Billy was starting with virtually no information about his nephew's adult life. Dean's closest mates were Stevie Pennock and Graham Joseph, from when they'd all met at uni seven years ago. Graham's wife Marie and Beth Stringer had also been at uni with them. Otis Cole was a school friend of Stevie and seems to have been integrated into the group some time ago. From his initial scan through the email, the two names of immediate interest to Billy were Pippa Byers and Jack Langlan. The latter because he was new to the group, a work colleague of Graham's, who Dean hadn't even met before the holiday. He'd start with Pippa though, as her backstory was far more interesting to him than anything else he'd seen so far.

He swigged down his coffee and, ignoring what was left of the muffin, headed for a comfort break. He spent a few minutes searching for his Astra, before remembering he'd switched it for a grey Mondeo. He rummaged through his notes and, having found the right page, punched the Byers family address into the satnav. The drive to Cambridge would take him just over an hour – giving him enough time to construct his strategy. On the way he phoned Johnny Oaten, a friend who had his own agency and one of the few people in their industry that he trusted. He'd concluded that he needed some help to cover all the bases in this case, if he wanted it resolved before Dean came home. Johnny answered the phone with a booming, 'Hi, matey,' as Billy gave him the headlines from the case, before despatching him to investigate the other person of interest – Jack Langlan.

Billy got to the Byer's house just after midday, having driven down the road a couple of times, he pulled up opposite the adjoining semi. Sweat had been building on his forehead during the journey, with the aircon struggling to take the edge off what had become a gloriously sunny day. He scanned the road; no cars on the driveway, then checked his watch, if they both worked full time, he'd not expect them home anytime soon. Ideally, he'd like to catch Caroline Byers first, Pippa's mum. Generally, he found women more willing to answer questions from strangers, whereas men tend to hold back more. He studied the house, it was probably worth a bit, being on the outskirts of Cambridge, but they hadn't really taken much care of it. The lawn looked like it was due a cut, with more weeds than grass and the drive hadn't been re-laid for several decades.

On the way over he'd decided on his tactics – honesty. Well, pretty much honesty. He figured they'd clam up if they felt they had no skin in the game. If he could lay out a possibility of their daughter being in trouble, it might encourage them to be forthcoming. A couple of neighbours walked past him as he waited, giving him some funny looks. In the end he concluded that he was drawing more attention to himself by sitting in the car, so decided to get out and walk up to the house. He slowly made his way up the drive, taking in as much as he could, without making himself look even more suspicious. He'd just reached the badly worn front door, with white paint peeling off it, when he heard a car pull up behind him. He turned and raised his hand in a semi-wave and smiled. It was Caroline.

'Can I help you?' Caroline said sternly as she got out of the old beige Volvo. She had the look of a school-teacher. Probably she'd once been attractive, Billy thought, but she'd plumped up a bit and had her greying hair in a ponytail. Wearing a brown skirt, white blouse and carrying a cardigan over her arm, she marched with purpose up to Billy.

'Yes, I was looking for Mr and Mrs Byers,' Billy said with confidence as he studied the woman in front of him.

'Well, you've found Mrs Byers, but I'm sorry, we don't entertain cold callers.' She barged past him and unlocked her front door.

'No, I'm not, that's not why I'm here.' He'd been taken aback by her assertiveness. Billy had expected someone more timid, not sure why, he just built up a picture of a middle-aged woman still grieving over the loss of her son. But this woman was tall, stocky and confident – maybe he'd need to wait for Mr Byers after all; rarely did both halves of a couple have the same temperament.

'Well, what is it then?' She was picking up the post and sifting through it, barely looking up at him.

'Well, it's about your daughter.'

Caroline stopped looking at the post and finally focused on Billy.

'What about Pippa?'

'Can I come in please?' Billy asked, 'I think we should do this inside.'

'No. You can tell me who you are first,' Caroline barked back at him.

'Sorry, I should have called in advance. I'm Dean's uncle. Billy Marchant,' with that, he pulled out his driving licence to confirm his name.

She looked surprised. 'Oh, well, I guess you'd better come in then.'

Billy wiped his feet as he came in. The hallway, like the outside of the house, was dated. A tatty patterned carpet adorned the floor and snaked up the stairs. However, unlike the outside, it was clean. No dust, no dirt, just tired and old.

'Please go into the lounge.' She ushered him through the first door. 'Tea or coffee?' she offered, but in a tone that suggested to Billy she'd rather not be bothered.

'Coffee, with milk and two sugars please,' he replied and could hear her mumble under her breath. No doubt she was uttering her disapproval about him having sugar in his coffee. 'If she knew my other vices,' he said to himself.

He hadn't wanted a drink, but he liked to get the subject out of the way so he could have a casual look around. The room was big, but like everything else, dated. He noticed a relatively new photo album stuffed onto the bottom of the bookcase – he'd love to get his hands on that. As he wandered around the room, he could see some photos of the family. One or two of the kids together, some of other relatives.

'Please have a seat,' Caroline was a little less forceful as she brought in the coffee. She'd obviously found a pack of biscuits at the back of a cupboard and thrown a few on a plate. 'I'm afraid I only have an hour for lunch.'

'I'm sorry to drop in like this, but I'm worried about the kids, and I'm hoping you can help.'

'Well, now you've got me worried, so you'd better spit it out.'

'Have you spoken with your daughter since she left on holiday?' Billy sipped his coffee.

'Derek did, that's my husband, she phoned to let us know she'd reached Maidstone and then a couple of texts once they were in France.'

Billy nodded and produced a smile to put her at ease. 'Did she tell him about the incident with the van on the way down?'

'She mentioned they'd had a bit of prang, but she said it was nothing to worry about. Why?'

'I went to see Dean on Friday, to say goodbye ahead of his holiday, and he mentioned that some strange things had been happening to him.'

'What things?' She was quieter and inquisitive now.

'Some threatening letters had been sent to him, and he'd had a feeling someone had been in his flat but hadn't taken anything.'

'Sounds nasty, I hope he's OK because he's a nice boy. But what has this got to do with Pippa?'

'I just wondered if you'd had anything similar happening to you, your husband or Pippa?'

She looked down for a split second – a tell. Billy knew that whatever she was about to say next was a lie.

'No. Nothing like that. We'd never have anything like that… we're good people.' Billy nodded as if to confirm he believed her; he didn't. He stood up and walked up to the window without saying anything else. Silence – a powerful tactic, he wanted her to speak next. 'I don't understand why you'd think we'd have these things happening to us. We're good people.' Billy nodded again.

'Can I use your loo?'

'Er, yes, it's upstairs, straight in front of you at the top of the stairs.'

Billy thanked his host and bounded up the stairs, but rather than head into the toilet, he turned right at the top of the stairs. Faced with three doors, he opened the first, empty, no carpet, no bed, no curtains – nothing. The second door was the master bedroom and the third led to what was obviously Pippa's bedroom. He put his head inside first, then gradually eased his way in, hoping the floorboard wouldn't creak as he was now above the lounge. Having glanced around briefly, he cautiously opened her bedside drawer and grabbed a small diary that had been poorly hidden underneath some make-up. He decided against investigating further as he didn't want to risk being discovered and losing Caroline's trust. He moved quickly to the bathroom, flushed the toilet and headed back downstairs.

As he entered the lounge, he put on a stern voice and added an impatient tone, 'Mrs Byers, a white van forced your daughter's car off the road on Friday. Forced off, not an accident. There are about a dozen witnesses to it.' He moved around the room as he said it. 'Two hours later, a white van crashed outside Dean's flat as it attempted to run him over.'

The colour drained from her face, he sat back in the chair and leaned forward to her. 'As well as being Dean's uncle, I am a former detective superintendent and a current private detective. I don't believe in coincidences, especially when I'm talking about the lives of my loved ones. I am asking for your help to save Dean, Pippa and their friends.'

At that moment Derek arrived home. 'Home, love, what's for lunch?' he shouted as he unlocked the door.

'In here, darling,' she managed, but tears were forming in her eyes.

He walked in, a slender man wearing a cheap suit and scuffed shoes. His receding hair was combed over slightly. 'What's going on?' he demanded. 'Who's this?'

'I'm, Billy Marchant.' He stood up and offered his hand, but it was ignored by Derek as he went over to comfort his wife.

He spoke softly to her, 'What's the matter, love?'

'Mr Marchant is Dean's uncle. He thinks our Pippa might be in some trouble. Tell him,' she urged Billy.

Billy repeated part of the story he'd just told Caroline, but he didn't get very far before Derek shut him off, 'I don't believe it. For one, if the accident had been that bad, Pippa would have told me. And for another, they wouldn't have been able to carry on to France.'

Billy attempted to protest, with some support from Caroline, but to no avail and he found himself on the doorstep within a few seconds. Physically, he could have put up a far greater fight, but he'd learnt enough from this first visit to make the trip worthwhile. As he headed slowly down the driveway, he could hear raised voices through the rotting windows. By the time he reached his car, Billy was heavily in thought. There was something not right about the house. He couldn't quite put his finger on it, but it played on his mind; he'd be back.

Time was not on his side. It had taken him nearly four days to get this far, Dean had been gone since Saturday, and now it was late on Wednesday. He had to start making progress and quick. He knew what he wanted, he just had to wait for them to go to bed. He'd driven as far as the nearest pub and waited for darkness.

He'd just ordered a 'speciality' burger and chips when he got the call. The call that closed down a lot of avenues but opened up so many more. It was from Jill, a former colleague at West Midlands police who now worked for the Cambridge police. He'd worked his charms on the phone a couple of days ago and got her to pull the CCTV ten miles either way of Graham's crash – to see if a white van with the same number plate as Dean's crash could be spotted. She confirmed what he had suspected for the last couple of days; it was the same van. She promised to give Billy a day's grace, but then she'd have to tell the enquiry team about the connection. He promised her a weekend away, and she upped it to three days' grace.

As he sat in the pub, working his way through the burger, he checked Pippa's diary again. There was nothing of interest or note, it was more of a calendar than an intimate confidant. He opened his notepad and flicked through the pages again as he contemplated his next move. He knew he'd have to consider all eight of the friends on the holiday. Who would want to harm them? Were all three of the people in Graham's car targets or just one person? What about the incident with Stevie's car? He didn't believe in coincidences, but it didn't make sense that the stalker would switch from tampering with the fuel in Stevie's car to full-on attempted murder in Graham's car.

Suddenly, he got the urge to speak with Dean, and he flicked through buttons on his phone until the ring tone appeared: straight to answerphone. 'Damn it!' he said loudly, causing a few people to look over at him. He'd spoken with Dean on the Saturday and received a text on Monday, but he just wanted to hear his voice to confirm he was OK. He finished his burger and headed back to the bar. He'd been on cola all evening but needed a whiskey to steady himself ahead of his next move. He paid, downed it in one swallow and left, the promise he made himself earlier in the day, now broken.

He parked two roads away – far enough for the car not to get noticed, but not too far for him to run if he needed to. He walked past the house, noticed there were no lights on and carried on for about 200 yards. It was nearly midnight, and he didn't imagine the Byers would be up past 11 on a weekday night. As he walked back to the house, he marched up the drive to the lounge window, which was to the right of the front door. Using an old shoehorn he found in the back of his rental car, he released the flimsy lock and quietly opened the window.

He was out within 20 seconds, holding the photo album in one hand and shutting the window with the other. With any luck they wouldn't even notice it was gone.

It took him an hour to get back to Dean's flat, but rather than go through his loot, he went straight to bed;

he'd had a couple of close calls on the way back, hitting the rumble strip on more than one occasion. He decided a few hours' sleep were needed, then he'd go through his prize with a clear head in the morning.

CHAPTER 13

Most of the group had decided to try and enjoy the sunshine on the terrace rather than wallow inside. It was a glorious day and the royal blue pool looked too good to resist. Stevie was still sulking following an argument with Graham and sat on his own in the shade, pretending to read a book. He'd disagreed over the decision to stay in the house rather than seek help for Otis, but he'd shown immense loyalty to his friend, something that was highly respected by Graham and Dean. Pippa had agreed to stay inside with Otis to help give Stevie a break. Part of the agreement in staying at the house for the day was that no one would be left alone – and that included Otis. As a further safety measure, all windows and doors that didn't face the terrace had been firmly locked and bolted. Despite the heat of the day, none of the group had argued.

Marie and Beth had initially not bothered to put on their swimwear, but eventually changed when the temperature hit 30 degrees. Dean made a simple lunch of grilled chicken, tomatoes and boiled potatoes. He took in trays for Otis and Pippa as the others sat around the patio table – which was mercifully in the shade. The boys guzzled lagers while the girls polished off a bottle of white wine. For a wonderful few hours that lunchtime, they felt like they were back on holiday, and not stuck in hell.

As the day drew on, the group knew there was little chance that Madame Bernard would appear. At about four o'clock, Graham finally relented and allowed a group of three to leave the house to investigate her cottage.

Dean was selected to investigate as he possessed the only gun. Graham selected himself, and Marie insisted that she wasn't going to let her husband out of her sight after yesterday. Jack was left in charge of the house, all doors to remain firmly locked until the secret code was knocked on the kitchen door. If they didn't return within an hour, assume the worst, although there wasn't actually a viable plan for that scenario.

The three of them walked along the mud driveway up to the ramshackle cottage where their would-be-saviour lived. Paint was peeling off the walls, doors and windows. The roof had an assortment of missing tiles and the gutter had grass growing from it. The land around Madame Bernard's cottage had been cleared of trees completely, which meant there was no shade for them as they tentatively approached the front door.

Graham lifted his hand but paused momentarily before finally knocking on the door. As he did, a patch of blue paint peeled off. There was a stain on the doorframe where a doorbell had long since disappeared. His gentle knock grew to mild hammering within a minute. They waited but didn't expect a response.

'Let's do a walk around the house,' Dean suggested after a minute, and the others duly followed him as he set off. They paused at each dirty, cracked window as they passed, squinting in as best they could, but seeing very little. The first one they reached was the kitchen, which looked tired and old, but not messy or unclean.

On the right side of the house, they tried the kitchen door, which was made up of 12 small mismatched panes of glass, although none were broken, several were cracked. Next, they went past what was the bedroom. Again, it was tired and old-fashioned, but not messy. The bed had been made and clothes were not on show, although the antique-looking oak wardrobe was slightly ajar with a dressing gown hanging over the door. They ignored the frosted window of the bathroom before they reached what was a large living/dining room that stretched the length of the house. At the back of this room was a rotting set of French windows. Dean firmly tried them; locked. He looked in again – nothing out of place or out of the ordinary. Graham and Marie turned to head back around to the front of the house, certainly not expecting what happened next.

The sound of glass smashing sent them cowering down to the ground as if hiding from heavy shelling in an air-raid. As they looked around, they could see the cause of their shock; Dean had kicked in the French windows and started to head inside.

'What the hell are you doing?' Graham shouted as he got back up and dusted down his shorts.

'Looking for a working phone line,' Dean responded, in a tone that suggested breaking and entering was an everyday occurrence.

Graham didn't argue and turned to help Marie up before following Dean into the house.

The room had two sofa chairs near the now-damaged French window and a four-seat dark wood dining set at the opposite end. There were bookshelves on the two sides, stuffed full and bursting, although none of them were decipherable to Dean or Graham. Marie finally joined them, having figured out it was probably safer than being outside on her own. There were several coffee tables, stained with old cup marks and water damaged, but again not obviously newly dirty or out of place. The three of them agreed that the room, while not in great shape, was 'as it should be'.

There was a small TV on a fold-out table and next to it a good old-fashioned phone. Marie spotted it first and managed to pick it up before her husband. She pressed it firmly and hopefully to her ear before declaring it was dead with some disappointment but little surprise. Graham took it from his wife and pressed the receiver several times, just to make sure; still nothing.

Dean followed the phone cable from the receiver to the wall connection. 'It's not been cut,' he declared.

'We'd better go and report back to the others,' Graham said. Dean wanted to continue to explore but doubted they'd find a working phone, so agreed to retreat.

'We're gonna have some explaining to do when she gets back,' Graham said, without a degree of worry. Dean couldn't be bothered to say anything. For some horrible reason, he doubted they would see Madame Bernard again, but he decided not to share his fear with the others.

As they got to the end of the mud-track that led down from the cottage, they paused momentarily. The holiday cottage was completely obscured by trees when at Madame Bernard's, so it was with some relief to Dean that nothing untoward had occurred while they were out.

'Still there,' Dean said, half-joking, as they walked past the damaged cars. He shook his head as he was reminded of the destruction and made his way with the others up the outside steps to the kitchen door.

Three knocks. Two knocks. One knock. Dutifully, Jack opened the door – albeit tentatively. 'All OK?' he said eagerly. Beth, Pippa and Stevie appeared from different doors, nervously hoping help had been found.

'Nothing,' Dean said sadly.

'Bugger. You mean she's not in or not answering the door?' Stevie questioned.

'She's definitely not in.' Graham followed on, before explaining the details of their excursion. A moment of silence fell upon the group.

'Definitely blown the deposit I'm afraid,' Dean said, repeating their earlier joke and a few of the group politely laughed.

'How's Otis?' Dean asked Pippa.

'He's in a bad way,' Stevie piped up before she could answer.

'Well, he's no worse than earlier,' Pippa said slightly more positively, 'but he could really do with some proper help sooner rather than later.'

Dean walked over to the kitchen window, looked out and then checked his watch. 'It's nearly six, we can't do any more today.' There were general mutterings of agreement from the group. 'I think we have to assume Madame Bernard's not coming back until Sunday.' More agreement and nodding from around the kitchen table. 'And we can rule out anyone else coming to our rescue. Ergo, we have to get ourselves out of this.'

'That's all well and good, Miss Marple, but how are we supposed to do that?' Stevie was not the sort to come up with solutions, he much more enjoyed picking holes in other's suggestions.

'I have a plan, but you're not going to like it,' Dean said, still standing. Other than Stevie, the rest of the group were sat around the kitchen table. Graham and Marie were holding hands, and it looked like she'd managed to persuade Graham to relinquish temporary control, allowing Dean to carry on.

'Go on then,' Stevie barked.

'First light tomorrow, say six am, I head off with Jack to get help.'

'No!' Pippa shouted, 'it's far too dangerous.'

'She's right,' Graham followed, sombrely.

Dean looked at Jack. 'I'm up for it. We're like sitting ducks here,' Jack agreed.

'Why you two?' Graham queried.

'Well, we're the fittest—' he paused briefly '—and I have the gun.'

'I think I should go as well,' Graham offered.

'No way. You're not going again after last time!' Marie shouted back at him.

'They need me,' he argued.

'Actually, Graham, we don't need you,' Jack said, and the air was sucked out of the room as the group waited for an explosion from their leader.

Thankfully, Dean intervened more tactfully, 'You're not as fit as Jack and me. We can probably cover more ground in the day.'

A coup was taking place, and everybody knew it. 'But you can't speak French,' Graham argued.

'Oh, for God's sake, Graham, you can't speak French either,' Stevie barked at him. The coup was completed.

Graham appeared hurt, but Stevie looked like he couldn't have cared less. They all wanted a plan that would help Otis – and Dean was delivering it.

After more silence, Dean attempted to appease his best friend, 'Jack is as good a French speaker as you, maybe even slightly more experienced. Between the two of us, we should be able to muddle by.'

'You can't afford to just muddle by, we're talking about Otis's life,' he argued, meekly.

'For God's sake, Graham, they don't want you to go, just live with it,' Marie barked at her husband, causing him to retreat to the lounge.

As Graham sulked, the rest of the group made plans for the following day. He was offered a way back into the discussion on several occasions but declined to input. His stock answer became, 'You guys decide and tell me what you want me to do.' He obviously hated it, but even his wife recognised he wasn't a wartime leader. Dean was the Churchill – he'd secede power back to Graham after this was all over.

Jack and Dean finished packing their bags ready for the next day – plenty of water, fruit, chocolate and the gun. Beth and Marie prepared a simple supper of Brie, Roquefort, tomatoes and ham. The bread was long gone, but as the group gathered around the dining table, there was no complaining.

After supper, Jack sat with Otis to discuss the route that they should take. The map was still covered in Otis's blood, but Jack had managed to clean it sufficiently to define a route. Otis gave him his compass, which had survived the accident, albeit with a crack.

As he was about to leave Otis's bedside, Jack felt his arm being pulled back. Otis had something he wanted to tell Jack but didn't want the others to hear, so he quietly whispered to Jack to close the door.

Having obeyed the command, Jack returned to the bedside. Otis was in pain but clearly wanted to tell him something. 'It's not Dean's fault,' Otis said.

Jack nodded. 'We know that, it's clearly some lunatic who has a grudge against us.'

'I think I know why I was run down,' Otis managed, but grimaced in pain as he said it.

Jack looked around to make sure nobody had come into the room, then leaned closer to Otis. 'Why?'

'I think it was my girlfriend's dad.'

Jack didn't say anything and allowed Otis to continue, albeit slowly, as he paused every few words to cope with the pain. 'He said he'd kill me. He didn't want me to go out with her.'

Jack tried to brush it off. 'Why? Because you're black? You know what, that is so old-fashioned. In this day and age—'

He was cut off by Otis tapping his arm. 'It's not because I'm black—' he paused again before finishing '—it's because she's fifteen.'

Graham and Marie went to bed early and promised to be up to see off the adventurers. The others joked for a while about Graham's diminished responsibility as they tucked into a nice bottle of Chateau Bel Air. It had been purchased at the market in Brantome by Beth as a gift for her mum, but she'd decided to crack it open; their need was greater right now.

They headed off to bed around midnight, Dean clutching his bag tightly as they went around and made sure every window and door was locked and bolted. They were determined that the bad guy wasn't getting in tonight.

It was stifling, but nobody slept with their window open.

CHAPTER 14

Dean had set his alarm but didn't need to. He managed four hours' sleep, waking just before five. It was still dark outside as he lay in bed, contemplating the day ahead. He reached down and checked his rucksack was still there; yes. His hand was shaking a little.

He jumped out of bed, wearing only his boxers and grabbed a towel from the back of the chair. He walked over to the door and gradually opened it, peering through the gap as he did it, nervous as to what he might see when he left his room. The process was useless, as the inner room, which led to five of the bedrooms, was pitch-black. After five nights, he thought he knew the way to the bathroom without putting the light on, but cursed as he stumbled, first into a stool and then a pile of encyclopaedias. He finally made the bathroom and closed the door before pulling the light switch. He didn't want to wake anyone else, least of all Jack who was now sharing with Stevie. He could hear Stevie's snores from the next room and felt sorry for his fellow explorer.

Dean felt better after the shower and decided to shave for the first time since coming on holiday. He looked at his reflection in the mirror. *Is anyone my age supposed to look so rough?* he thought to himself. The loud bang bought him out of his thoughts. 'Bugger,' he heard from the library. He wrapped the towel around his waist and opened the door.

'Bloody stool,' Jack whispered to no one, then saw Dean at the door, 'you finished?' Dean nodded. They stood for a moment, both knowing what the other was feeling, because they were both feeling the same anxiety. These two would save the group today – or not.

As Jack closed the bathroom door, Dean decided he wasn't risking the walk across the library-cum-landing in the dark again and switched the light on. He almost made it back to his room before he noticed it. He only just caught it out of the corner of his eye; red paint splashed across the beige patterned wallpaper. A shiver went up his spine, and he took a few steps back.

MARIE KILLED THE BABY

The words didn't mean anything to Dean, it was the fact that it has been written at all that nearly caused him to collapse. He ran into his bedroom and opened the bag, the gun was still there. He grabbed his shorts and T-shirt and quickly flung them on before going back onto the landing. He read it again, and this time tried to make sense of the words. Rubbish, it has to be, Marie wouldn't kill a baby. He'd known her long enough to know she wouldn't do that. But there was a big 'but,' the statement about him had some element of truth: could this one be right too?

He knocked on Graham and Marie's bedroom door. 'Oh, is it time to go?' a voice said.

'No, but I think you need to come and have a look at this.' By the time Graham and Marie had risen, Jack had finished in the bathroom and was standing with Dean looking at the graffiti.

As she appeared from her room and spotted the message, Marie screamed. Never before had Dean heard a scream like it. It was a scream that told of real pain, not physical – like Otis's – but emotional. Dean knew immediately the statement was true. Beth, Pippa and Stevie quickly appeared in the airless room and stood with a mixture of shock and anger, looking at the new statement of torment that had been left for them to take in.

As she regained a morsel of composure, Marie surveyed the room – with six faces looking back at her, she quickly bolted back into her bedroom. Graham looked at Dean with horror on his face and shrugged to indicate he knew nothing of this, before rushing in to see his wife.

'Otis!' Stevie shouted, and the group raced downstairs to check on the invalid. He was awake and grimacing as they entered the room one by one.

'What's going on?' he questioned.

'We've had another break-in,' Stevie said grimly.

'Oh no, is everyone alright?'

'Physically, yes,' Beth said.

'There's another message,' Stevie continued, 'about Marie.' The discussion moved into speculation about what it could mean.

Dean slipped out of the room, with Jack following him. 'Let's see how the hell he got in,' Dean said.

They walked from the tiny stairwell into the kitchen. Dean checked the door. 'Locked, and the bolt's still on the top of the door.'

Jack was tugging at the window over the sink. 'Locked and it's not been forced.' Dean looked and nodded in agreement. They walked out of the kitchen into the large dining room. This had two windows down one side of the room and French windows at the end by the bar. Having satisfied themselves they'd not been opened, they moved through the door into the lounge. Dean flinched as he saw the previous night's writing on the wall again.

There was only the large window facing out to the pool area, and they quickly confirmed this had not been forced.

They circled back through the dining room and kitchen until they were at the bottom of the tight staircase again. Both turned 360 degrees to see if they could glean a new aspect. There was the door behind them that led back to the kitchen. The two doors on the right were padlocked. From surveying the outside, the group had earlier agreed the first of those doors led down to the garage. The second of those doors was the study, but it was firmly locked, so ruled out. The remaining two doors, straight on, led to the downstairs bathroom and to Jack's room (now Otis's).

They could hear the speculative conversation continuing in Otis's room as they headed into the bathroom. The window was in need of a lick of paint and the latch on the window was loose, but the section of window that opened wasn't big enough for anyone to crawl through. They headed back into Otis's room.

'Is your window closed?' Dean asked.

'Stevie did it last night,' Otis replied.

'We've just been trying to figure out how he got in and quite frankly we can't see how he managed it.'

'I didn't hear anything, and I've been unable to sleep most of the night,' Otis managed in-between grimaces.

'Could he have come in upstairs?' Beth asked.

Dean nodded, it's possible, but that means through one of our bedrooms, as the bathroom windows upstairs are only tiny.' The group looked around among themselves, and nobody dare speak as that thought ran through each and every one of them.

Eventually Jack broke the silence, 'Breakfast?' he said loudly, 'I don't know about anyone else, but these break-ins are making me very hungry.'

Dean laughed, grateful for the subject to change. 'Me too, lead on.'

Despite the shock of the latest break-in, the group followed Jack's lead and filed into the kitchen. They all seemed to take this latest intrusion more calmly than the previous night, with the obvious exception of the absent Marie and Graham. After bowls of cereals had been prepared and orange juice poured, the five of them sat down to breakfast. No one spoke until Graham appeared at the door, looking ashen faced.

Dean saw him first, bolted up and over to him, putting his arm around his shoulder. 'You alright, mate?'

'Not really.' He was handed a cup of coffee by Pippa and sat at the kitchen table with the others ready to listen.

'Marie and I have been speaking and she has asked me to tell you what I'm about to.' He paused and took a swig of the coffee, then continued, 'You may remember that before we started going out, Marie and I had been friends from the start of uni.' He looked over to Dean and Stevie for reassurance that they remembered the history. Both nodded. 'Well, it wasn't until the summer after the first year at uni we started going out. Before then, Marie and I had been in lectures together but not really mixed our friendship groups.'

Stevie nodded again. 'Yes, I seem to remember the Law Society Ball. That was the first time I think I met her.'

'She came to one of our parties before then I think,' Dean remembered, 'wasn't it around the end of the exams?'

Graham nodded. 'Yes. My exams finished a couple of days before the rest of you, so Marie and I ended up going on a pub crawl together.'

'Wait a minute,' Beth interrupted, 'I remember now, we'd finished and had two or three days of non-stop drinking and partying.'

'That's right,' Graham said.

Beth continued, 'Well, there were four of us – us two, Marie and...'

'Cam,' Graham finished the sentence for her.

Pippa looked over to Graham. 'What are you saying?'

Graham struggled to get the words out, and Dean put a reassuring arm around his shoulder, allowing him to say what he had to. 'For about three weeks, Cam and Marie went out together. I was incredibly jealous as I fancied her like mad, and Cam knew it. Knowing the connection Marie and I had, he ended it. She was gutted about it, but Cam told me it was because he knew I fancied her. I never really believed that he'd done it for me, but I was grateful, and we agreed we'd never mention it to you guys.'

'And then what happened?' Pippa enquired. She was definitely the most interested, now her brother had been brought into it.

'Nothing, as far as I was concerned anyway. Later in the summer, I finally plucked up the courage to ask her out and that was that.'

'But there was something else?' Pippa asked suspiciously.

'What I didn't know until today, and that I've just been told by my wife, was that...' He paused a second and Dean, who'd not sat down for any of this, put another reassuring hand on his shoulder. 'Was that, she became pregnant via Cam.'

Dean, Stevie, Beth, Jack and Pippa all looked around at each other, shocked at what they were hearing.

'She had an abortion,' Graham said as he focused his gaze on Pippa. He was telling her about the death of a potential nephew or niece and looked apologetic.

'I didn't know any of this,' Pippa said, as she extended her arm to stroke Graham's.

'Cam reacted very badly when he found out, apparently. He accused Marie of murdering his child and threatened to tell her parents. In the end, she believes that when he saw how happy we'd become together, he decided not to rock the boat.'

Graham stood up and moved to leave the room. Before he left, he turned back. 'Marie asked me to tell you, because of the situation we all face at the moment. But she would prefer that it is never mentioned again after we get out of here.' The group nodded in agreement as he left the kitchen to comfort his wife.

* * *

'We were supposed to leave three hours ago,' Jack said, as he found Dean sitting thoughtfully in a comfy chair in the lounge.

'Dean. Earth to Dean. You alright?' Jack said sarcastically, after failing to get an initial response.

'Sorry, mate, I've just been thinking about something.'

'Haven't we all. Shocking news about Marie isn't it,' Jack said.

'I think it's best we don't talk about it,' Dean shot back, catching Jack a little off guard. The two of them had bonded quite well on the holiday, having not previously known each other, but this was a scolding that had been unexpected.

'Where is everyone?' Dean asked.

'Scattered about, I think.'

'Can you gather everyone in Otis's room please,' Dean ordered.

'Yes, sir,' Jack managed and went off to complete the order he'd received.

Dean walked up to Graham and Marie's room with purpose but paused before knocking on the door. He was sure he could hear crying. He thought for a minute – should he knock? Then he remembered the mess they were in and firmly banged the door. He barely waited for a response before entering.

Marie had been crying, as he'd suspected; she had the tell-tale sign of red and puffy eyes. Graham looked like he might have shed a couple of tears as well. Both looked up at him and were about to tell him to get lost, when he spoke quickly and with authority, 'Sorry to interrupt, but I've been thinking. There's potentially a much more serious threat than we have already imagined. I need you both downstairs now in Otis's room.' He left no doubt what he wanted.

Downstairs the others were gathered around Otis. Jack perched on the windowsill, Stevie sat on the chair,

Beth and Pippa on the edge of his bed. 'What is it?' Pippa asked as Dean walked in.

'We need to wait for Graham and Marie,' Dean said sternly. They duly arrived and stood in front of the wardrobe – Marie kept looking down, holding Graham's hand firmly.

'Thank you,' Dean started, 'I've been thinking about what's happened this morning, and something's been bothering me.'

'What?' Stevie asked.

'Well, the person that's tormenting us seems to know a great deal about us. More than most of the rest of us knew.'

'Agreed,' Stevie said, 'so what?'

'And this morning, Jack and I couldn't find any evidence of a break-in.'

'Certainly not an obvious one,' Jack added.

'Well, before I head off into those woods and leave six of you undefended behind. I want to make sure I know what we're dealing with.'

'I don't follow?' Stevie really hadn't a clue where Dean was going with this.

'Well, a horrible thought occurred to me. I hope I'm wrong. I pray I'm wrong. But there is another possible explanation we may have overlooked.'

'What do you mean?' Beth sounded just as confused as Stevie.

'He's saying it could be one of the eight of us,' Graham chipped in, having realised where Dean was going with this.

'Don't be ridiculous,' Stevie exclaimed.

Dean took over again, 'It's merely a hypothesis. If we look at the facts – no evidence of a break-in, Otis heard nothing in the night, we're in the middle of sodding nowhere, and the mystery person happens to know a great deal about us!'

'Do you really think one of the eight of us is the tormentor?' Graham said solemnly.

'In all honesty, no. But we have to address it as a possibility,' Dean said.

'I agree. We have to consider it,' Graham concurred.

'Aren't you forgetting something?' Jack's tone suggested he was a disbeliever of this theory, 'the person driving the car wasn't one of us.'

This didn't stump Dean. 'I've thought about that. It is possible it was an accident, or the person in the car was in league with one of us. Whatever the explanation for Otis being run over, I'm not prepared to rule out the possibility that one of us is involved.'

Dean paused for effect and waited to bat back any other naysayers. In the end Beth spoke, 'So if we buy into this as a possibility, what do you want to do about it?'

'Well, I have a solution, but I don't think you're going to like it.'

'Go on,' Graham gave Dean the confidence to carry on.

'I propose to do a room-to-room search, not limited to, but including all of our personal possessions.'

'Fuck off. You're not going through my things,' Jack exploded, 'who made you dictator-in-chief anyway?'

'It's a bit extreme,' Stevie said.

'I don't feel comfortable with that. What do you expect to find?' Beth added.

'I'm not sure. But I believe if one of us is involved, that person would have left some kind of evidence.'

'I tell you what, you are not going through my things,' Jack repeated.

'Why, something to hide?' Dean was harsh.

'Because you are not the boss. Who's to say it's not you. Who's going through your shit?'

'He has the gun,' Graham said casually.

'What's that got to do with anything?' Jack shot back.

'Don't you see; he has the gun. If he wanted to do anything to us, he could do. We wouldn't stand a chance.'

'So what? It doesn't mean he can go through our things.'

'We need to put our lives in someone's hands. Quite honestly, I can't think of anyone better.' Graham smiled at Dean as he said it. 'This is my best friend, and I'd trust him with mine and my wife's lives. Which is exactly what I'm doing now.'

'Thanks.' Dean was humbled by the vote of confidence from his friend. 'I propose everyone stay here while I search. Afterwards, everyone is welcome to go through all of my things.'

As Dean tried to go out of the room, Jack moved in front of him. 'You are not going through my things!' He was angry, shoving his finger right into Dean's face.

Nobody expected the punch – not from their good friend Dean. But he connected a gut-thumper, flooring Jack, who caught Otis's leg with one of his flailing arms, causing the invalid to yelp.

'Sorry. But I'm doing this,' Dean shouted, then looked to Graham. 'Keep him in here,' and tossed him the gun. 'Careful, it's loaded, and the catch is off.' Graham nearly fumbled it as he tried to regain his composure. As Dean left the room, Jack was struggling to get back to his feet and muttering obscenities. Graham locked the door behind Dean.

He was going to start in Jack's room anyway, the little incident downstairs had only made him more determined. It was difficult for Dean to imagine his long-term closest friends, such as Graham and Stevie, being responsible for this. It was much easier to think it could be a complete stranger.

Jack was now sharing a very simple room with Stevie following Otis's accident. Two wooden-frame single beds at opposite ends of a dark room with a small window, one old wardrobe and a bedside table each. There was a scruffy rug that barely covered any of the rough floorboards.

Dean guessed which was Stevie's bed by the pile of pills and potions that adorned the bedside table. He moved to the other one, starting with the bed itself, which hadn't been made following the early start. He checked under the two pillows, inside the pillowcase, inside the duvet cover and under the mattress. He wasn't sure if he was relieved or disappointed.

He found Jack's holdall and carefully lifted all the items out one by one. He'd unfold a T-shirt, shake it down and then gently fold it back. He reached the bottom of the bag; nothing. Good on you, Dean thought. He opened the wardrobe – empty, neither man had hung up a single item of clothing. He was about to move on to Stevie's stuff when he remembered he hadn't checked under the bed –schoolboy! Billy would be very disappointed.

He bent down, there wasn't much space underneath, but he pulled out an old sock and dirty pair of pants. He winced as he dropped them into a pile. He shoved his hand as far under the bed as he could and then gradually shuffled himself along the floor to take himself the full length of the bed. He'd almost reach the top of the bed when his finger brushed it, a piece of paper. He shoved the bed, knocking over Jack's bedside table and shattering a glass of water. The displaced bed had revealed a batch of papers. Dean picked them up, but before he could read them, the commotion began downstairs, followed by a bang.

The gun had just gone off.

CHAPTER 15

He was groggy when he came around. The banging had seemed far away in his dreams, but now it seemed closer. BANG, BANG, BANG. It took him a few more seconds to realise it was the front door. He forced himself up and stumbled into the corridor. BANG, BANG, BANG. 'Yes, yes, I'm coming, give me a fucking minute!'

As he opened the door he was confronted by a jolly, chubby, ginger-haired man. 'Fuck me, Johnny. What the hell are you doing here at this time?'

'It's not early, matey, it's gone six and I've got some really big news for you – about this Jack character.'

Johnny barged past Billy and flopped onto a chair in the lounge. 'Jack who?' Billy was still coming around and was struggling with the cheeriness and volume of his friend.

'Jack Langlan, your nephew's mate – or not – as the case seems to be.' And then Billy remembered where he was and what he was doing. For a few blissful hours he'd forgotten all about the last five days.

'I'll put the coffee on while you get ready,' Johnny said loudly. Billy looked down at himself and realised he was nude, but for a pair of CK boxers.

Coffee and toast were waiting for him when he returned to the lounge. 'It had better be good, Johnny,' Billy said with his hair damp from the shower.

'Oh it is, matey,' Johnny took a big bite out of his buttered toast. 'I did some research on his family. Basic stuff on google etc., before I went up to Norwich.'

'Get to the point.' Billy was tired and impatient.

'Well, his dad took his own life earlier this year,' another bite of toast.

'Another death,' Billy said under his breath.

'Another?' Johnny questioned.

'Oh, don't worry, carry on.' Billy was getting another pain in the pit of his stomach.

'Well, by all accounts, Jack's dad had been pushed to the brink of suicide after he was conned out of his savings by a dodgy business venture.' He paused for effect, before continuing, 'It gets better. The person who ripped him off has recently gone to prison for fraud.'

'Tell me there's a link,' Billy asked hopefully.

Johnny nodded with a smirk. 'You gave me a list of names to cross-check and I got a hit. The bad boy was David Stringer.'

'Beth's dad!' Billy shouted.

'None other!' Johnny smirked and then took another bite of toast.

'It can't be a coincidence,' Billy muttered as he paced around the room, while Johnny continued to munch his way through the toast.

'Nope. I reckon this Jack character is a clever boy. He did work for the same law firm as Graham a year or so before his dad's financial problems, but at the Peterborough office.'

'He asked for a transfer to Norwich?'

'Yep – two weeks after his dad's suicide.'

'But how was he able to link Beth and Graham?' Billy was still walking around the room.

'I think it was one of our people.'

'You think this kid organised for a private detective to do a background check on Beth and then linked her to Graham?' Billy's tone suggested he didn't believe this.

'It's one of the possibilities.' Johnny brushed the crumbs off his jumper. 'Or it is a genuine coincidence.'

'Okay, but as far as we know, this Jack character doesn't have any link or beef with the others?' Billy was thinking aloud.

'No. He has no link to the others – that I've been able to establish to this point. And as far as I can tell, of the people he's on holiday with, he's only met Graham and Marie before. What you thinking, matey?'

'I'm thinking something else doesn't add up. Jack has nothing against Dean or Stevie or Otis. He may have been happy to see Graham's car run off the road with Beth inside, but she wasn't in the car. Why go to all the trouble of moving jobs and getting invited on the holiday – only to bump off half the attendees before they get there?' Billy had stopped pacing but was now staring out of the window.

'So, you're not worried about Jack?' Johnny managed as he struggled to get himself up from the sofa.

'You don't think I should worry that a vengeful man has managed to lock himself up in the middle of nowhere for two weeks with the daughter of the man responsible for his dad's death?'

Johnny's smile left his face.

CHAPTER 16

Initially, the screams had covered the sound of Jack bounding up the stairs, but Dean had heard them in just enough time to position himself behind the bedroom door, with a lamp in his right hand.

Jack's anger had overwhelmed his judgement. He burst into the bedroom with the gun in his right hand and waved it around in front of him, searching for Dean. He paused for breath as he surveyed the room, unaware his prey had taken up a position behind him.

The lamp shattered into more than 100 pieces as it connected with the back of Jack's head, sending him crashing to floor and the gun flying out of his hand. Dean was relieved that Jack had gone down straight away and didn't fancy taking the burly man on in hand-to-hand combat.

His heart was racing, but he remained in control – he was getting used to this now. Dean grabbed the gun and put the safety on. Now he needed to stop Jack moving when he woke up. He spotted a belt on the floor and tied it around his wrists so that Jack's arms were firmly behind his back. He started looking for another for his legs.

'Fucking hell, have you killed him?' Graham appeared at the door.

'I really hope not,' Dean said. As he looked at Graham, he spotted what he wanted. 'Take that off!' Dean barked as he pointed at his belt and Graham dutifully obliged. They tied it around Jack's ankles together.

'Is everyone OK down there?' Dean asked as the adrenalin started to wear off.

'Bastard jumped me. I don't know how he managed it,' Graham tried to cover his shortcomings.

Dean just smiled. 'But everyone's OK?'

'Yes, scared shitless, but OK.'

Stevie and Marie appeared at the door next. 'Well, that's all sorted then. Bastard!' Stevie said loudly.

'Did you find something?' Marie asked, and Dean grabbed the papers from the back of his shorts, where he'd stuffed them in a rush.

'Think so, haven't read it yet.' Just as he said it, Jack started to wake up. The group took an involuntary step back as they saw him starting to writhe around. Dean was the first to move over to him, kneeling next to his head, which was face down on the floor.

'Fucker!' Jack managed, 'let me go.'

Dean grabbed the ginger hair on the back of Jack's head, allowing him to lift it up enough so that he could look him straight in the eyes. 'I have the gun. I will use it if I have to. In fact, right now, I feel like blowing your fucking head off, so don't move.'

Pippa, who had just appeared at the door with Beth, gasped as she heard this different side to her new flame. Dean looked at her and wished she hadn't heard it but turned back to Jack. 'Do you understand?' he said through gritted teeth.

Jack didn't say anything but nodded as best he could, given that Dean still had his head held up by his hair.

Dean, Graham and Stevie helped pull Jack onto the bed, still with his arms and legs tied together. They weren't gentle, causing Jack to wince with pain as he shuffled into position, eventually they supported him with a pillow.

It was nearly midday, and the searing hot sun poured in through the tiny window of the first-floor bedroom where they were assembled. Jack had some bruising beginning to appear on his face and there was some blood on the back of his head, although this had been stemmed by Pippa who'd used a pillowcase to stop the dripping. The rest of the group (apart from Otis) were stood in a crescent around Jack's bed. The room had been thoroughly trashed, which had given Stevie an excellent opportunity for more moaning.

Dean stood with the papers in his hand, still unread. 'Do you want to tell us what these say, or do you want me to read it out to the group?'

'This is nothing to do with you lot, just her,' Jack barked.

Although he couldn't move his hands, there was no doubt that the movement of his eyes had picked out Beth. The group look at her and she felt compelled to shrug. 'I've not seen him before this holiday,' she managed, feeling under scrutiny herself at this point.

'That's right, screw over the little people then forget them,' Jack said with venom.

'I'm sorry, I really don't know what you mean.'

There was a momentary pause. 'Stop it, Jack. Leave her alone and tell us what these papers say.' Graham was obviously stunned by this latest turn of events, given he'd brought Jack into this group for the holiday.

Jack forced himself more upright before replying, 'What those papers say, in plain simple English, is that her family killed my dad.'

There was a long enough pause following the latest shocking revelation that meant Beth felt compelled to answer. Ordinarily, something as outrageous as this would have been dismissed out of hand by the rest of them; but not now. Not this week. 'That is ridiculous, my family has never killed an animal, never mind a human being. I'm a vegetarian for goodness sake!'

'Read it,' Jack shot back, 'the one dated January this year.' Dean flicked through the pages until he found a piece of plain A4 paper with a newspaper article glued on it. At the top of the page was the date scrawled in blue.

Dean started to narrate, as instructed, and read every word without a sound from a member of the group:

MAN'S SUICIDE LINKED TO WINE FRAUD

A Cambridgeshire businessman and father of two, Roger Langlan 55, took his own life earlier this year after being swindled out of his home and savings by two men that have recently been found guilty of fraud.

The coroner recorded a verdict of suicide, but said it was likely a result of losing his highly successful farming business. Mr Langlan lost out after investing heavily in the fake wine import business set-up by Tom Watkiss and David Stringer. In his verdict the coroner said, 'The shame of being conned out of his money by these two men was more than he could bear. I believe the guilt of losing the family home and his business was the single biggest contributor to Mr Langlan's death.'

Watkiss and Stringer were sentenced to five and a half years each in September for organising a wine fraud in which they used fake wine labels and cases to falsely inflate the selling price of cheap wines they'd imported from Moldova.

As Dean finished, he looked around the room. The group were silent, most looking down at their feet. Jack staring at Beth, who was sheet-white and, without warning, fainted. Graham wasn't quite quick enough to catch her, and with a thud, her head hit the open door.

'Shit!' he exclaimed as he fumbled after her. Pippa pushed past Stevie and Marie to get to her, but Beth came around within a few seconds.

'Whiskey,' Pippa ordered in the general direction of Stevie, and he shot off down the stairs to get it. They helped Beth onto the other bed in the room, sitting with her head between her legs. She was obscured from Jack due to the number of people crammed into the small room. The whiskey arrived and was handed to Pippa who then helped Beth pour it gradually into her mouth.

Satisfied that Beth was in safe hands, Dean, Graham, Marie and Stevie re-focused their attention on Jack. 'OK, I get that you're angry with her dad, but why the hell are you taking it out on all of us?' Dean asked.

Jack seemed shocked. 'I'm not,' he managed as it became clear he hadn't connected his revenge to the predicament they were all in.

'Come on, what do you take us for? You were caught red-handed with more of this scandalous tittle-tattle.' Stevie was in an unforgiving mood.

'I'm telling you the truth. What reason would I have to cause any of the rest of you harm? I'd not met you before Friday!'

Graham's mind had started firing, he had a lot of questions he needed answers to. 'Okay, if we believe that, you must have gone to a lot of trouble to get yourself invited on this holiday.'

Jack had some sorrow in his voice now. 'Okay, I admit it. I did contrive to get myself invited. I found out that someone I worked with was friends with Stringer's daughter and I wanted to get some sort of revenge.'

'You expect us to believe that?'

'Yes. Because it's true. I asked for a transfer to the Norwich office, which was unsurprisingly accepted as no one ever wants to go that way and made sure I sought you out. I admit our friendship was formed from a lie, but the truth is, I did grow fond of you and Marie.' The anger had drained from him now and he was almost begging to be believed. 'I had no plan for how I was going to get the revenge, I didn't go looking to get on this holiday, I just thought our paths would cross if the two of us were friends. But when you invited me on the holiday, it felt like a gift, it felt like I was meant to take some sort of vengeance.'

This landed heavily on Dean. 'Vengeance?' That seemed a hard word. Surely, he wasn't planning on killing her.

'And what form was this vengeance going to take?' Graham asked, who now assumed the role of 'bad cop'.

'Not physical. I wasn't going to hurt her. I was going to torment her, mentally. Ironically, I was going to do something along the lines of the graffiti that happened to Dean and Marie. Originally, I planned it for Saturday, that's why I took the downstairs room. But I bottled it. To be honest, I'm not sure I would have gone through with it in the end.'

'But why should we believe you?' Marie asked.

'I have to admit it looks bad, but I have no reason to do this to any of the rest of you. And, I was definitely

181

not the person driving the car that hit Otis.' He looked at Graham, who reluctantly nodded.

'It's true, he couldn't possibly have been driving the car. 100%.'

'So, where does that leave us then?' Marie asked.

'At the moment, nowhere further on,' Graham replied. Dean went over to Jack and grabbed his arms, looking at Graham to get agreement, which he did, Dean then released Jack's arms, followed by his legs.

'How's your head?' Dean asked of his victim.

'A bit sore, I guess.'

Dean put his hand on Jack's shoulder and then thrust the gun into his hand. 'This is your chance, mate – if you really are the bad guy, shoot me.'

The room froze as Jack looked at the gun in his hand, he felt the weight of the gun, lifted it up and pointed it right at the centre of Dean's forehead.

Within a second, he flipped it over and handed it back to Dean. 'Only kidding.' And the room breathed again.

For the sake of equality, Dean searched all the other bedrooms, while the other members of the group had reconvened in Otis's room. It was of little surprise to him that he didn't find another source of information that could lead them to their tormentor. He declared openly to the group that he was satisfied that it was an external party involved. Secretly he still wasn't convinced, but why add more stress to the rest of them?

They settled down a simple lunch of tuna pasta bake at 2pm, the cupboard was beginning to get a little threadbare now, but they all ate swiftly and without complaint. It was agreed that it was now too late for Dean and Jack to head off as they had originally planned. Jack, in particular, needed a rest following his bang on the head.

The group tried to enjoy the remainder of the day as best they could. Beth had said very little since the incident with Jack earlier. She was clearly devastated by the impact her father's crime had on another family, and although both Pippa and Marie had tried to speak with her, they were unable to get much conversation. Ultimately, she decided to keep a distance from Jack and opted to say very little for the rest of the day.

After a light supper of ham and cheese, washed down with the final bottle of red, the discussion started on plans for the following day. A row had erupted earlier between Graham and Marie, and it wasn't until after supper that the rest of the group found out why; Graham was going to come on the expedition again. He promised he'd keep up and wouldn't slow them down. Marie had been made to support and agree to this proposition. He'd also worked on Beth and Stevie. No official vote was taken, but Dean accepted defeat graciously. He did however promise Graham an unrelenting day tomorrow.

They packed their bags and agreed that whatever happened overnight, they would go on their 'search for help' tomorrow.

They double-checked all windows were locked, and dining chairs were placed up against all door handles as a precaution. However, Dean still slept with his gun in his hand.

CHAPTER 17

Johnny's revelations had distracted Billy, causing him to temporarily forget about the photo album he'd retrieved from Pippa's house. He invited Johnny to have another coffee and threw him the remote control as he went to find it.

Billy sat in one of the armchairs and encouraged Johnny not to distract him as he flicked through the photos. It was clearly Pippa's album, starting with her sweet-sixteen party four years ago. Lots of pictures of her with friends and some with her brother, Cameron. Billy had picked up the key details from Dean on what happened with Cameron – Tanya had managed to fill in a few more blanks.

As he got past the middle of the album, he started to notice a few photos with her on nights out with Cameron's friends; Dean, Graham and Stevie. But some photos had been taken out. One or two random ones to start with, then more, until several pages had no photos in, just the glue where a photo had once been placed. As he got to the back of the album, some photos returned, this time with Pippa on holiday – presumably, last year. Then he reached the last page, just one large photo, a holiday photo with the whole gang from last year. Billy studied it for a second then ripped it out and walked over to the window to get a better look. Nine people; Dean, Graham, Marie and Stevie he recognised from a photo Dean had on his wall. Otis, he spotted having met him when they picked Dean up on Friday. Beth must be the third girl. Pippa was in the middle of two men, one of which was Cameron, but who was the other? He flicked through the photo album again and was able to tick off everyone from the group photo in at least one other photo, except this mystery fella with his arm around Pippa.

'Johnny,' Billy eventually broke the silence.

'Yes, matey.' He flicked off the TV.

'I need you to follow up on something else for me.'

'Sure thing, what is it?'

'See this man in the photo, Cameron Byers, he died in a skiing accident earlier this year. I want you to go over it again. I want to know every detail.'

'Will do.' And with that, he was gone.

Billy trusted Johnny like no one else in the business. Which isn't saying a lot, given the business is rife with cads, drunks and nomads, but he was glad for his help. He decided to flick through Dean's things to see if he could find any photos of the mystery man. If any photos existed, they were probably online, but he hadn't got time to faff around with technology. He spoke with Tanya and asked her to run through Dean's Facebook page and print off any likely candidates that he'd review later.

Having waited for the rush hour traffic to subside, and another failed attempt to reach Dean, Billy began to make his way over to Graham's parents' house. A ninety-minute drive around the M25 to north Kent. He'd been so distracted on the drive with thoughts of the case that he'd had a couple of near misses. He pulled up outside a handsome detached house in the suburbs of Maidstone and waited for a few minutes. He was hopeful Ted and Grace Joseph would be more receptive to his visit than the Byers had been yesterday. His original plan was for Johnny to cover off the Josephs, but Billy was sufficiently impressed with Johnny's work on Jack, he trusted him to cover off the history on Cam. In any event, Billy had an urge to see the last place the kids had been physically verified alive and well.

He could have comfortably parked on the driveway but preferred the road in case he was in need of a quick getaway. There was no car on the drive, but it could conceivably be in the garage, which was at least double width. The house, unlike the Byers semi, was very well maintained and tended. There were at least half a dozen gloriously colourful hanging baskets adorning the front of the house, with traditional summer favourites, geraniums, petunias and begonias. There was barely a weed in the garden, and all paintwork had been carefully maintained.

Billy rang the bell, causing a rather elaborate musical rendition of 'Rule Britannia' to play. He waited, but nothing. He didn't fancy ringing the bell again, so banged loudly on the door this time; still nothing. He peeked through the letterbox, there were a couple of letters on the floor. He wandered around the side of the house and tried the gate; it was locked. He shoved it, and it gave a little at the bottom, so he reached over the top of the gate and found the bolt. It took a few more seconds to wiggle it loose before he managed to unlock it. He'd already noted the alarm and wasn't planning to break in; it probably wouldn't help in getting the Josephs to cooperate. He just wanted to check the place out, and he'd come back after lunch. The pathway opened out onto a large and immaculate back garden, with borders full to bursting with shrubs and plants, all meticulously trimmed. Then he noticed something, a half-full washing line with some clothes drying and a basket on the ground with some of the damp clothes still in it.

He looked at the back of the house, noting there were three ways in if he wanted to risk it. A back door that seemed to lead to the kitchen. A lounge patio window and French doors to a fancy conservatory. He tried the kitchen door, which flung open and bashed into a cupboard. 'Shit!' he shouted. He tentatively poked his head through the doorway, almost apologetically. 'Hello, Mr and Mrs Joseph, anyone home?'

He shouted again as he moved his whole body into the kitchen, 'Mr and Mrs Joseph, are you in?' Nothing. He quickly scanned the kitchen, spotting used breakfast dishes and open jam pots on the table. He reached into his jacket and pulled out his gun. Instincts told him when something didn't feel right, and this really felt odd. From the front of the house, no evidence of anyone about, from the back, it's as if the house is full.

He had two doors to choose from and picked the closest. He opened it gradually while holding his gun up against his chest. He slowly entered the dining room, which offered no obstacles or hiding places for an assailant. He swiftly moved to the other end of the dining room and opened the next door, which led out into the hallway. Of the five doors he was now faced with, he assumed one led back into the kitchen, another to the toilet and the third was a cloak cupboard. Two doors of interest remained, he took the first on the right and gradually opened it.

He saw her body before he'd fully opened the door. She was slumped on the sofa, head covered in blood and eyes still wide open. He rushed in, not noticing the second body in front of him, which tripped him up and made him collapse in a heap in front of the fireplace. His legs wobbled as he stood up and took in the scene from his position in the middle of the room. He picked up his gun, although it was evident the time for this had long since passed. Billy's breathing suddenly became heavy and he started sweating. He realised just in time that he was about to faint and crouched down, putting his head between his legs. He breathed big breaths before he attempted any more movements. After a few seconds he looked up, seeing the carnage in front of him again and suddenly he started to feel a flow of warmth coming up his throat.

He managed to get most of the vomit in the nearest bin, but he was ashamed of himself. He'd never reacted like this in any of his cases, ever. But this one was different, he had skin in the game. This thing was real now, real dead bodies, real murder, real danger for his nephew.

He pulled himself together and started making mental notes of what he could see. The woman, Grace he assumed, had been clubbed around the head with a poker from the fireplace. Not difficult to see, the weapon was on the floor. It did for both of them. He suspected that Grace had been sitting with her murderer having a cup of tea. Ted was probably finishing break-fast and ran in when he heard the noise. Our murderer (Billy had just upgraded him from stalker in his head) was stood behind the door and took him out as he rushed in.

What was disturbing was that after having killed them, the murderer had decided to continue to pummel their heads and faces, making them almost unrecognisable. Billy continued to survey the room, the blood on the walls and carpet had long since dried. He estimated they'd been dead for about three days, meaning it was probably Sunday morning when the killer struck. Just a day after Dean and his friends had been there. He prayed that he wasn't going to find the body of his nephew and his seven friends stacked in different rooms of the house.

Billy decided to survey the rest of the house, but the caution he'd shown in reaching the lounge was gone; the murderer was not in the house after three days. He actually prayed that he or she *was* in the house still – at least he wouldn't be in France with the kids.

After five minutes of banging open doors and marching around the house, he concluded the carnage had been confined to the lounge. He picked up his phone and was about to call the police but rocked it in his hands as he thought about what to do. If he called them, that would be the end of his investigation, he'd be wrapped up in police interviews and Christ knows what else. No, he needed to get what he could out of this house and get out, hopefully without being seen.

He started in the study and sat at Mr Joseph's desk. Bank statements, share certificates and household bills. The Josephs had plenty of money, but beyond the house, didn't seem to spend a great deal of it. Then he stumbled across a separate bank book and flicked through; regular payments out of £1,500 a month to someone called V.J. Joseph – odd, as his research suggested Graham was an only child. Maybe it was a poorly sister of Ted's, or even his elderly mother. He found details of the mortgage, which had been paid off; they'd moved into this house when Graham was a baby.

He mooched about for an hour in the study, looking for anything useful, before he felt he'd exhausted it. There were a few things missing that he might have expected to see in the study and decided there must be a safe with some really private papers. Psychology suggests anything really personal will be kept in the bedroom – it's safe and close throughout the night. He headed back up to the master bedroom and worked his way through the wardrobes until he found it – a small safe hidden at the bottom of Ted's shoe cupboard. He thought about trying to blow it open with his gun but had an idea. He reached into this pocket and pulled out his notes from Tanya. Graham's birthday 6th July, he punched in 0607. 'Bingo.' He was proud of himself – first time. He reached in and pulled out all the documents then gradually laid them out on the super king-sized bed.

Billy quickly discovered who VJ was; Verity Janet Joseph, born 40 years earlier to parents Edward and Grace Joseph. An estranged daughter that they still support financially? She'll soon be the prime suspect for a double murder, he thought to himself. Billy found their wedding certificate, 44 years of marriage and both their birth certificates. The final one he picked up was the winner – Graham's birth certificate; born in Brighton, Sussex. Mother – Verity Janet Joseph. Father – unknown.

'The grandparents bringing up a grandchild as their own, not exactly original, but highly interesting nonetheless,' he said aloud to himself.

He kept hold of Verity and Graham's birth certificates but returned everything else to the safe. He straightened the bed and then went back through each room of the house to make sure there was no evidence of his visit. He grabbed a dustbin bag from the kitchen and put the soiled wastepaper bin inside it. He went back out the kitchen, shutting the door and through the side gate – locking the gate by reaching over the top again. No doubt exactly the same way the killer had left the scene.

Billy waited 30 minutes and called the police. He didn't need to worry about Verity, there was little chance she was responsible for the murders, let alone Dean's misery. In the event she was involved, the police would have her whereabouts quick enough, and Dean would be safe anyway.

He phoned Johnny from the car, it was rush hour in the evening, and his journey around the M25 was painfully slow. He told Johnny about the fate of the Josephs and what he'd managed to learn about their history. Johnny said he was making some good progress on Cameron and they agreed to meet back at Dean's flat in the morning. Billy decided to make one more stop before he went back to Dean's flat.

CHAPTER 18

'I told you to stay the hell away, now get lost.' Not the most welcoming response Billy had heard, but not the worse by a very long way. Mr Byers was blocking the door to stop an attempted entrance. Mrs Byers was hovering by the lounge door in the background looking on anxiously.

'I need to ask you one question, and then I'm gone.' Billy was terse but still reasonable.

'I said, we're not interested, now leave us alone.'

'I can't do that, Mr Byers. Your daughter and my nephew's lives are in immediate danger.'

'We don't believe you.' Mr Byers wasn't giving an inch.

'Have you heard from Pippa since they got to France?'

'That's none of your concern.' Mr Byers was being annoyingly stubborn. Billy knew they had plenty to hide and he wanted to know it all at some point, but for now, there was one question he wanted answering.

'Your daughter called you from Mr and Mrs Joseph's house on Friday to let you know she made it.'

'If you know that, why are you asking?'

'Mr Byers, on the news this evening you're going to hear about a double murder in Kent. The dead couple is Mr and Mrs Joseph.'

Mr Byers was clearly dumbfounded. Billy let that statement sit in the air for a few seconds. Eventually, Mrs Byers spoke first, 'Derek, please let him in.' He looked around at her, still speechless, but eventually moved his frame out of the way to allow Billy into the hall.

'Thank you, Mrs Byers, I don't expect you to trust me until you see the news tonight, but for now I want to know the answer to one question; who is this?'

As he said it, he whipped the photo of last year's holiday from inside his coat and thrust it in Caroline's face, with his finger pointing at the mystery face beside Pippa.

'Ryan. Ryan Curtis. He was a uni friend of Cameron's.'

'Mrs Byers. One more question if I may?' She nodded. 'Was he at this time or at any other time dating your daughter?' She nodded.

He thanked them both and turned to the door to leave. Before he did, Caroline spoke again, 'Will you save our daughter?'

Billy looked around and, with a solemn tone, left them with another thought that would haunt them that night. 'Mr and Mrs Byers, I know there is a lot you are not telling me. The more I know, the best chance I have of saving all those kids down there. It may be too late already, but I'm going to do my damnedest to get them back alive.' He handed his card to Caroline. 'Call me when you want to talk, but don't leave it too long.'

Billy didn't wait for a response or look back at the tatty, tired house. If he had, he might have seen Derek slide down the back of the front door sobbing uncontrollably, and Caroline kneel beside him, hugging her husband, with her own tears hitting the floor.

***

Billy knew the Byers would phone, but for now he just wanted to locate Ryan. It had taken Tanya a matter of minutes to piece together who Ryan was; uni mate of the boys, same halls as Cameron and Dean and friend since day one. He had lived in London but seemed to have given up his job in February, and no one had seen much of him since. She'd managed to locate his parents address in Nottingham, which meant another long drive in the morning.

Billy picked up a Chinese takeaway on the way back to the flat and a four-pack of beer. He felt exhausted, but the thought of this nephew's fate kept him going. He sank the first beer before he'd even unpacked his chilli-beef and egg-fried rice. The second beer went as he munched down a couple of prawn crackers and the third washed down as he ate his meal, with his feet up in front of the news. He was asleep by the time the news of Mr and Mrs Joseph broke.

CHAPTER 19

Dean was woken by a bang and shot up, dropping the gun onto the floor in the process. 'What was that?' he said aloud, as he became more lucid, then realised that the sound was coming from outside; thunder, heavy rain and lightning. He opened the window and shutter and was nearly blown back into the room by the wind. Heavy rain washed through the window, and he heard the thunder again followed by a dart of lightning that illuminated the room. Forcing the window closed, he turned on the light and checked his watch, it was 4.15am.

'Bugger,' he muttered under his breath. He wasn't sure what annoyed him the most, being woken up that early or the fact that it was pouring down. Why didn't they do the walk yesterday?

Dean lay in bed until 5am and then decided to get ready. Whatever happened, they were going on the rescue mission today. After yesterday, he decided the lights were going on everywhere he went. He walked onto the landing, expecting the worst, but thankfully he wasn't greeted by any more graffiti. He washed quickly and sprinted back to his room, the temperature had dropped, and he was suddenly feeling cold. He re-packed his bag – change of clothes, waterproofs and a flask would be required now. If only he had those things. He put on a pair of jeans and shoved a change of socks and shorts in his bag. He had a coat, but it was a light jacket, ideal for chilly summer nights, not for thunderous storms!

As he made his way downstairs, he started to get a knot in his stomach; he would be surprised if they hadn't had a visitor. He quickly moved into the kitchen, through the dining room and finally into the lounge. Nothing. Well, nothing new. He circled back into the kitchen and put the kettle on.

'Have you checked on Otis yet?' A voice said from the bottom of the stairs, just out of sight. It was Graham, up early and eager to prove he was worthy of the expedition.

'No, can you pop your head around the door?' Dean asked.

Graham knocked gently and slowly nudged the door open. 'Still alive,' Otis said sarcastically. He'd barely slept, with the pain again causing his insomnia.

'I'll bring you a cuppa in,' Dean shouted from the kitchen.

He delivered on his promise and took in a cup of tea to Otis. 'What, no milk?'

'Sorry, mate, that's all gone now. I'll bring us some back after our walk today,' Dean joked.

'Thinking about it, I'm not sure you should go out in this weather,' Otis said seriously.

'Whatever happens – we said yesterday, and I stick by it. You need a doctor and imagine how grumpy Stevie is going to get if we run out of food.'

'Please be careful. That man is a psycho.'

Dean waved the gun at Otis. 'I'm ready,' he said.

It was six o'clock and everybody was up, ready to wave off the heroes. 'Perhaps you should give it another hour to see if the rain stops?' Marie begged her husband.

'This is in for the day by the look of it,' Jack said as he peered out of the window.

'I really don't think you should go out in this, it's still dark.'

'We'll be fine, darling,' Graham said and gave Marie a reassuring kiss on the cheek.

'Remember what we said, lock the door and put the chair up against it,' Dean bellowed at those staying behind as he opened the kitchen door. The rain flew in horizontally and drenched him before he'd even set foot out of the door. All three of the explorers muttered obscenities as they left the kitchen and headed down the stone steps to the driveway below.

Stevie assumed charge of the house, shutting and locking the door. Then he wedged a kitchen chair up against the door handle. 'God help us if they don't come back.'

The driveway was exposed to the elements, making it a real struggle until they made it to the mud track road. The trees kept them sheltered from the worst of the weather, and they moved at a brisk pace. Dean was wearing his summer coat and was drenched from head to toe by the time they'd walked the first of the 12 miles. Mud had splattered up the back of his legs as far as his jacket and his shoes were barely recognisable. Graham fared little better, although he had brought a raincoat with him, which meant his torso and head remained partially dry. Jack had opted for shorts, initially viewed as a strange decision by the others, but now seem-ed most sensible as the others dragged damp jeans around with them.

They walked another half a mile before stopping under a cluster of conifers for a break. They managed to find a felled tree to perch on and Dean checked his watch. They'd walked for 40 minutes and done just two miles. Not a bad pace. All being well they'd be at civilisation by lunch. Jack pulled the map out from under his coat. They'd not needed to look at it yet, but the water had seeped through, causing some damage. 'Try not to open it yet,' Graham said, 'it will tear if it's wet.'

Jack forced it back in his inner pocket. 'I'm pretty sure I know the way.' They sipped water and had a biscuit each as they caught their breath.

'What was that?' Graham shot up and looked around. Jack and Dean hadn't seen anything.

'It came from over there.' Graham pointed into a thick part of the forest, darkened by the rows of conifers.

'I'm sure it's nothing,' Jack offered.

'Come on, let's get going,' Dean ordered, and they picked up their rucksacks and moved away.

Graham looked nervously behind him. 'I thought I saw...' he muttered to himself, but the others had already moved away, and he jogged a few metres to catch up.

Dean and Jack chatted while walking a few paces ahead of Graham, who had started to struggle and certainly didn't have the energy to keep up and partake of light conversation.

'I think it's another mile or so until we hit the concrete road,' Jack said.

'OK, let's try and make it that far before we stop again.' They both looked behind them.

'Is he going to be OK?' Jack asked.

'I don't know, but let's keep going at our pace.'

They couldn't have moved on more than another quarter mile before the rain picked up pace again. This time they were more exposed as the trees had cleared where felling had already taken place. Graham had now fallen a good 30 metres behind. There was a loud bang, causing the three men to duck. 'Fuck!' Jack exclaimed. 'It's just the thunder,' Dean comforted, but as they looked up, they saw the bolts of lightning filling the sky. Crash. Another rumble of thunder.

'We need to get into some cover,' Dean suggested.

'But you're not supposed to shelter under trees in a storm,' Graham argued. However, the other two were already moving swiftly across the clearing towards a batch of oaks. Graham opted to join them but really struggled across the uneven ground. As a lightning bolt flashed past him, he tripped over a tree stump and landed on his face in a wet patch of mud and twigs.

Dean, having already reached safety, darted back out to rescue his friend. Jack, who was still making his way to the cover, looked back but decided to carry on towards the trees.

'You alright, mate?' Dean asked as he reached Graham.

'Fuck it!' Graham shouted as he lifted his muddy face out of the ground. Dean tried not to laugh as he helped him up and supported him as they made it to the trees.

Jack and Graham were breathing heavily as they sat on the ground, propped up against different sides of the same tree. Dean patrolled the ground on the edge of this section of the wood, looking up at the sky. 'Come on, give us a break,' he kept repeating to himself. He turned and looked at his comrades, even Jack was struggling in this weather. How were they going to make it another 10 miles? He looked at his watch. It was nearly seven thirty, and their pace had slowed considerably since the last stop. He'd let them rest for another 10 minutes and hope the weather turned. It surely couldn't keep this up all morning.

Dean continued to walk around and found himself about 40 metres away from the others when he heard the rustling. He jumped around. 'Who's there?' he said. Nothing. He turned back and checked on Jack and Graham – still OK. He heard the rustling again. 'Who's there?' he repeated, and he reached into his pocket for the gun as he took a few paces towards where he thought he'd heard the sound.

'Everything alright?' Jack shouted as he could see Dean waving his gun around.

Dean felt a little foolish. 'Think I just saw a fox,' he lied. He headed back to the others, occasionally slowing to look over his shoulder.

'It's not slowing down much,' Jack shouted as the noise from the rain seemed to increase again.

'I think we give it another ten minutes and then start walking again,' Dean said as he finally sat down and perched himself up against the same tree.

'I need a piss,' Graham announced after another couple of minutes.

'Afraid it's a fair walk to the nearest toilet,' Jack joked as Graham trudged off.

As he sat under the trees, soaked to the skin, Dean allowed his mind to wander. He remembered the optimism they all had at the start of the holiday, how they enjoyed winding Graham up by not always doing exactly what he wanted. He now appreciated how hard it was to be the leader. Then he allowed himself a nice reflection as he remembered the kiss with Pippa. Could it be that something good would come out of this terrible mess? He was smiling.

'What the hell is he doing, taking a dump?' Jack said, which woke Dean out of his daydream. It took a second for him to fully come around.

'Graham, come on, mate, we need to get going,' Dean said as he stood up.

'Graham, don't fuck about, we need to get going!' Jack shouted.

Dean's heart started beating a little faster. 'Graham, come on now!' He turned to Jack. 'Where did he go?' and whipped his gun out again. Jack pointed out the general direction and they set off calling Graham's name every few seconds. They trudged through the woodland, which seemed to get thicker as they moved deeper and deeper.

'Graham, for God's sake. Where are you?' Dean was beyond panic and into hysteria now. His best friend was missing, not a day after he'd promised his wife he'd look after him.

'I don't think we should go any deeper,' Jack said after 10 minutes. Dean agreed, and they decided to sweep around the section, without venturing further in. The shouts of Graham's name dropped from every second to every minute. By the time they'd swept the area three or four times, Graham had been missing for an hour. They reached the clearing from where they'd started.

'What do we do now?' Jack asked.

Dean wasn't with it; he was mortified that he'd lost Graham.

'Dean. Dean. What are we going to do?' Jack repeated.

Dean shook his head. 'I, I don't know.'

They both stood in the rain. Jack waited but Dean was still in a daze. 'We should keep going,' Jack said, bored of waiting for his shell-shocked leader.

'What?' Dean said in horror.

'I said, we should keep going to the village.'

'And forget about Graham?'

'I didn't say that. But there are seven other people to think about,' Jack argued.

'Yes, and only one that is out here on their own,' the passion in Dean's voice temporarily put a halt to Jack's protests.

They continued to walk aimlessly with no real pattern, and Dean checked his watch again. 'We need to find him, it's the number one priority. Nothing else matters.'

Jack looked at Dean and made his decision. 'I'm going on, alone if needs be,' he said calmly, but forcefully.

'Don't be ridiculous. You'd be picked off within an hour,'

'You mean like Graham was?' This seemed to shock Dean back into reality and he thought for a moment. Jack took this opportunity to continue, 'What good will it do if we keep searching for him? If he's been taken by Mister X, then he's gone. If not, he's lost, and he'll be safer than the rest of us. In that event, he'll probably find his way home.'

Dean looked at Jack and then over to the area they'd last seen their friend. Dean wiped his eyes, grateful that the rain had disguised his tears. Finally, he'd seemed to come to his senses, and without speaking, nodded at Jack's assessment.

They both started to move forward without speaking, Dean checked his watch again, it was nearly 10 o'clock and they'd only managed just over two miles. As he left the clearing and re-joined the mud track, he started walking quicker and quicker until eventually he was in a near-jog. Jack tried to keep pace but was struggling, even though the rain had slowed to a drizzle.

They'd cleared another mile before the weather deteriorated again; first the dark clouds rolled in, then the rain got faster and finally the thunder started. Then it struck.

The lightning bolt smashed into a batch of conifers just in front of them. Two of the large trees came crashing down, one across the road in front and the other headed right for them. 'Run!' Dean shouted as the flaming tree aimed for them. Dean jumped right and Jack left into a ditch. Bang! The tree connected with the mud road and sparks shot in every direction.

Dean shook himself down as he struggled back to his feet. 'Jack, Jack mate, are you OK?'

He stumbled around the top of the burning tree to the other side of the road. 'Jack, are you OK?' He began to panic again. 'Please, God, I can't have lost another one.' He ran around the trees. 'Jack. Jack!'

'I'm here,' came the shout, finally.

'Thank fuck. Are you OK?'

'I think so.' But as he tried to get to his feet, he screamed in pain and collapsed to the ground again. 'Argh, my bloody ankle hurts.'

Dean sat him down and examined it. 'I don't think it's broken, just twisted.' He thought for a minute.

'Damn it!' he shouted eventually, 'we're done for the day. We'll have to go back to the house.'

'Go on without me,' Jack offered, hopeful that Dean would decline. He wasn't disappointed.

'No way. We've already lost one person today – I'm not losing another. Besides, out there on my own, he's going to pick me off before I get much further.'

'It's gonna take ages to get back with my ankle like this. We must have walked three miles.'

'We'd better get going then,' Dean said and with that started yanking Jack up from under his shoulder.

The thunder clapped again, and the rain continued to flow down as Dean helped Jack up the embankment and onto the road. The slow journey back had begun.

* * *

'How long have they been gone?' Beth asked in the general direction of Stevie.

'They should have made it to the village by now,' Marie offered, after it became obvious Stevie wasn't going to respond. The three of them were sat at the kitchen table, supping their fourth black coffee of the day.

Stevie kept his focus on the kitchen door. He'd taken his responsibilities of gatekeeper very seriously and had barely left his position near the kitchen door since the boys had left seven hours ago.

'Twelve miles is a long way, isn't it?' Beth said.

'I wish Graham hadn't gone now,' Marie responded.

'I bet they'll be downing wine in a café,' Beth tried to comfort.

'Knowing Graham, they'll be munching through a pile of steak as well,' Marie joined in.'

'Oh, did you have to mention meat.'

'Ha, you know they'll be thinking of you while they're eating.'

The girls paused their inane conversation, before Beth broke the brief silence again, 'What time is it?'

Stevie jumped up from his chair. 'Oh, for fuck's sake, will you stop babbling on, you're doing my nut in. They'll be back when they're back, and your bloody prattling on isn't going to change that.'

Beth was stunned into silence by the tirade of abuse from Stevie. Marie, more used to his outbursts, just smiled. Slightly embarrassed, Stevie retreated to Otis's bedroom, leaving his post unguarded for the first time that day.

'What did I do wrong?' Beth asked after Stevie left.

'Nothing. You know what he's like. Just ignore it.'

'I don't babble on do I?'

'Maybe just a bit,' and Marie laughed. She grabbed the coffee mugs from the table and took them to the sink. As she walked over to swill them out, she froze. Looking out of the kitchen window, she could see shadows coming towards the house. Eventually she reacted.

'There's someone coming,' she shouted at the top of her voice. 'There's someone coming!' she repeated as she scrambled across the room to shout towards Otis's bedroom. Stevie and Pippa came bounding out.

'Who is it?' Stevie questioned.

'I can't see for certain.' The four of them sprinted over to the kitchen window to peer out.

'It's Dean!' Pippa shouted with relief in her voice, and she ran over to the door and began opening it.

'No, wait!' Stevie bellowed and forced the door closed. 'We need to wait. Just wait for them to get here. We don't know who else is out there.'

'It's Jack as well!' Marie said as she continued to monitor progress, 'they must have left Graham in the village.'

Stevie and Pippa shot looks at each other, suggesting both knew immediately something was wrong.

There were three knocks, as had been pre-agreed with Dean, and with that Pippa grappled with the door to open it again. As the door flung open the four warm and dry members of the group stood in a semicircle staring at two extremely wet and weary men standing in the rain, one being held up by the other.

Dean supported Jack as they took a couple of paces forward into the kitchen and then stood solemnly, silent, staring at Marie as the water trickled down his body onto the floor.

'Where's Graham?' Marie asked. Her heart was pumping fast.

Dean looked down at the floor.

Marie took a couple of steps towards Dean. 'Where's Graham?'

Dean looked up, and it was then that Marie could see the water dripping down his face wasn't rain, but tears. Her voice got louder and pierced the air as she repeated, 'Where is Graham? Where is he? Where's my husband?'

The rest of the group were silent.

'What has happened to him?' Marie was screaming now.

Dean still couldn't speak. Then he felt a hand gently grasp his shoulder, he turned to see Stevie who quietly repeated the question, 'Dean, what happened? Where's Graham?' the unusual softness in Stevie's voice sprung Dean temporarily out of his daze.

'He's gone,' he eventually managed.

'What do you mean he's gone?' Stevie asked.

'We lost him.' Dean was pale and barely able to speak.

'What do you mean you lost him?' Marie screeched. She moved back in front of Dean. 'He's your best friend, you can't have lost him!' Tears poured down both their faces and she started thumping Dean in the chest as she shouted at him, 'You're supposed to look after him, you can't lose him. How can you lose him?' After a few seconds, Beth and Pippa pulled her away from Dean. He collapsed on a chair, planted his head on the table in front of him and sobbed uncontrollably.

As Beth and Pippa tried to ease Marie out of the room, she spotted Jack, who had himself collapsed on the kitchen chair previously used to prop the door shut. 'Was it you?' She broke free from Pippa and moved halfway across the room, pointing at Jack and still crying. 'It was you, wasn't it!' she shouted. Jack looked stunned.

Pippa tried to put her arm around Marie, but she wriggled free and continued, 'Did you kill him?'

'No, of course not!'

'It seems convenient, we find you plotting against Beth, you go out with Graham and all of a sudden he's missing.'

'Marie, come on.' Pippa tried to pull her away.

'No, I want to know what he did to my husband.'

'I did nothing. He went for a piss in the woods and didn't come back.'

'And you just thought, sod it, let's leave him to die in the middle of nowhere!' With that she broke down, uncontrollably crying, hunched on the floor and repeating, 'You killed him! You killed him!' With each sentence, her voice became quieter until there was barely any sound at all.

Pippa and Beth moved over to her, managed to coax her up off the floor and gradually encouraged her out of the kitchen and upstairs.

The three men remaining in the kitchen stayed quiet for several minutes, stunned by the emotional breakdown they'd just witnessed. Eventually Stevie broke the silence, 'You two must be desperate for a hot drink, coffee for two coming up,' and he started to busy himself with the kettle. Dean managed a weak, 'Thanks,' as his friend pottered about.

Dean knew they were in real trouble if Stevie was being kind and thoughtful; it just wasn't in his nature.

She was face down, sobbing. Her brown hair, matted and misplaced, covered the parts of her face that weren't buried in the pillow. Beth and Pippa had managed to get her onto the bed and now watched over her as she grieved.

They had tried to comfort her. 'He'll turn up, he's not dead yet,' just didn't seem to cut it. Marie feared the worst. They all did.

The coffee arrived and Stevie sat down across the table from Dean. Neither Jack nor Dean mentioned the lack of milk.

'What happened?' Stevie asked.

Dean took a swig of the coffee, grimaced and nodded his head at Stevie. He then told him the story of their day.

CHAPTER 20

He was in his car by five, having slept for eight hours, and arrived in Nottingham before seven. Billy had missed the call he expected from the Byers and resolved to make them sweat – he'd phone them back later. Last night he'd engaged 'Bean Associates', a local firm in Nottingham that he'd worked with before, to watch the Curtis house. Time was against him, and he simply didn't have the ability to do everything himself. Normally he hated sub-contracting out, mainly for the reliability, but also for the cost – although usually he'd bill it on to the client. He'd instructed Arlo Bean to ensure Mr and Mrs Curtis were at the house when he arrived, which meant Mr Curtis's front tyres had suffered a rather violent act of vandalism overnight.

Billy jumped in Bean's car, which had prime position on the road outside the Curtis house. Being a built-up street of terraced houses, with cars jammed in on both sides, Bean wasn't noticed as he kept watch. The debrief was short but insightful; Mr Curtis was a civil servant working for the council, Mrs Curtis was a homemaker. They had two sons, with Ryan being younger by three years. Neither lived at home, so far as Bean had been able to establish.

Billy was in no mood to be messed about by Ryan's parents – it was Friday, and Dean has been gone for six days. He already knew this journey would end in France at the address his nephew had given him before his holiday, but he also knew he needed as much ammo as possible to understand what he was facing. Whatever happened, he would go to France on Sunday – Tanya had already booked his Eurotunnel tickets.

The terraced house had a small front garden, he walked through an iron gate and within two paces he was at the front door. His knock was firm and impatient. After only a few seconds, he knocked again and then again. 'Coming,' came the cry from a woman inside.

She half-opened the door to try and disguise the fact she wasn't ready yet, but Billy could see she was still in her dressing gown. 'Can I help you?'

'Yes, I'm looking for Mr and Mrs Curtis as a matter of urgency.'

'Well, I'm Ava Curtis and Tom, my husband, is upstairs.'

'Can I come in please?' He remained firm.

'I'm, well, not really…'

Billy interrupted, 'It's about your son Ryan, and it is very urgent.'

Ava quickly relented and let Billy in. She was a good-looking woman, with dyed-red hair, held back by a band. She invited him into the lounge and shouted for Tom to join her.

'Are you from the police?' she asked, almost in defiance, rather than concern. In fact, she didn't seem worried about Ryan at all, which Billy knew meant she'd seen him very recently.

'No, Mrs Curtis, but be assured, they are going to be here very soon.' Suddenly, her demeanour changed, and she started to look worried. Tom Curtis, a round, pot-bellied man appeared with a rolled-up newspaper under his arm. Billy, who hadn't bothered to sit down, walked over to Mr Curtis, introduced himself and offered a hand.

Ava moved over to her husband and put her arm around his waist, as if for protection. 'How can we help you?' Tom said as he ushered his wife into a sofa next to him, without shaking hands. Billy removed his offer of a hand and sat opposite the Curtis's, with a tired-looking coffee table separating them.

'Mr and Mrs Curtis, I am a private detective and I also happen to Dean Marchant's uncle.' The look on their faces changed from slight concern to one of annoyance. 'I believe your son and my nephew were at university together and until very recently were close friends.'

Tom spoke with a tone that matched his expression, 'That's right. They were friends, until your nephew and his other friends cut him off. Blamed him, unfairly, for the death of the other lad, er, Cameroon?'

'Cameron Byers,' Ava corrected Tom's deliberate mistake.

Tom continued, 'And do you know why they blamed him for the accident?' Billy remained motionless but liked that they were more willing to talk, which usually meant they were telling the truth. 'Apparently the boys had an argument and Cameron ran off, then came an avalanche. Like Ryan could have caused an avalanche, for crying out loud!' Billy nodded sympathetically in agreement. 'Look, Bill, what's this about?'

'Mr Curtis, yesterday I discovered Graham Joseph's parents murdered in their home in Maidstone.'

'Who is Graham Joseph?' It quickly became clear to Billy that Tom liked to play stupid.

'It's one of those boys that our Ryan was friendly with,' Ava offered, 'now you mention it, I did see that on the news this morning, an elderly couple were murdered in Kent. Lovely looking house as well.'

'Okay, but what's that got to do with Ryan? You're not saying he killed them, are you?' Tom challenged.

'No. Absolutely not. It's just that I need to speak with him to see if he can help out or has any information. You see, I'm very worried about Dean and his other friends, as I've been made aware of a potential threat to them all.'

'Well, I'm very sorry, but we haven't seen Ryan for ages, have we, love?' Ava shook her head, confirming they'd definitely not seen him. The first lie.

'Okay, but I wondered if you could answer a few more questions?' Billy asked.

Tom nodded and surprisingly didn't seem keen to get rid of Billy. Indeed, apart from the one lie, he felt the Curtis's had been the most truthful of any of his interviewees so far.

Billy listened on for 20 minutes as they described how Ryan had been best mates with Cameron and how he'd been going out with Pippa for a while. He believed them when they said they thought she was a lovely girl, but that Cameron was a bit odd. Billy understood and sympathised when they described their bitterness towards Ryan's friends for dumping him when he needed them most. They described with some emotion how Ryan had suffered a breakdown after Cameron's death and quit his job and flat in London.

'Where is he now?' Billy asked, knowing the answer would be their second lie.

'We said before, we don't know.' Tom was still firm on this.

'Does he still have a room here? I just wondered if there might be a couple of clues about what's been going on?'

'No, we turned it into a guest room when he moved down to London.'

Billy believed them again.

The breakdown truck arrived, and Tom went out to talk to the mechanic as Ava made some tea. As Billy waited for her return, he walked around the well-appointed room. It was a typical front room lounge for a Victorian house, small but with lots of character and charm. A traditional fireplace dominated one wall and a large mirror hung on another, opposite the sash window. The fourth wall had family photos – lots of them, mainly of the boys at school or sports clubs. Ava came back in with tea, still in her dressing gown.

'Are they close?' Billy asked, pointing at a picture of her two sons.

'Yes, always got on very well,' Ava said proudly, 'I'm sorry Ryan fell out with his friends, they seemed to get on very well together. Lovely holidays they all had.'

'Mrs Curtis, you may end up being very grateful that they did fall out. If they hadn't, Ryan would be on holiday in France with the others and we don't know what will become of them.' With that, Billy gulped down his tea, grabbed a biscuit from the tray and made his way out of the room. 'I need to go, Mrs Curtis, here's my card. You've been very helpful.' He meant it.

Billy thanked Tom on his way down the drive, who looked a little bemused to see him leave so abruptly. He jumped in Bean's car, 'I know where Ryan's been staying.'

They had travelled about 15 minutes to the other side of Nottingham, less attractive than the last place, now 1950s maisonettes lined the street. They parked outside a run-down mini-mart and looked up at the flat belonging to Glen Curtis, Ryan's brother.

'We believe he lives here with a friend, it's a three-bedroom flat, so perfectly reasonable to assume Ryan's been staying here since he left London,' Bean summarised.

'What does he do for a living?' Billy asked.

'Plays in a band, gigs most nights. Has a police record – possession of cannabis.'

Billy looked at his watch – nine thirty, probably still in bed. He thought for a minute. 'Bean, we might need to play this one a little differently.'

The door came down with one kick. 'POLICE! Don't move!' the two men marched to the second floor of the maisonette and hit the first bedroom. As suspected, a rough-looking man in his Y-fronts was struggling to comprehend what was happening as he stumbled out of bed. Stoned and hung-over, Billy guessed – this is exactly what they expected and wanted.

'Police, this is a drugs raid, put your hands behind your back.' Bean cuffed Glen and dragged him down the stairs into the lounge.

Billy did an initial check of the other two bedrooms to confirm that no one else was in. Glen's flatmate was a nine-to-five worker and had long since left for the day. Billy checked on Bean and his prisoner, the latter was denying everything under the sun, from 'they're not mine,' to 'it's recreational use only.' He left Bean, who was doing his best impression of an undercover policeman, with Glen, and returned upstairs for a more detailed snoop around.

Billy immediately dismissed the flatmate's room and went to bedroom three. There was an unmade single bed in the corner of the small room. At the end of the bed was a desk strewn with papers and dirty mugs of tea or coffee. The small wooden wardrobe had a few garments hanging in it, but most of the rest were scattered, unwashed, across the brown and green patterned carpet. Billy pulled back the thin, dusty red curtains and opened the window. He cleared some used crockery from the chair and sat down.

He fingered through a few of the papers and pulled out an A4 sized black journal that hadn't been immediately visible. He opened it up, and his heart skipped as he saw the title that had been written and underlined at the top of the page. This was followed by a list of seven names:

<u>SECRETS FOR REVENGE</u>
GRAHAM JOSEPH
MARIE JOSEPH
BETH STRINGER
DEAN MARCHANT
PIPPA BYERS
STEVIE PENNOCK
OTIS COLE

The list of names had been written in the same black ink. Next to each name was a tick, written in a different pen, indicating to Billy that these had been added over time – presumably as and when a secret had been discovered.

As he glanced through the book, he could see each person had been allocated four pages, with notes below their name, scribbled over time. Some words highlighted or sentences starred. Billy heard some commotion from downstairs and knew he didn't have long. He grabbed all the bits of paper, along with the journal, and shoved it in a bin bag. He had a rummage around the rest of the room but couldn't find anything else of interest. The used cups and plates had gathered mould, suggesting it had been a few days since anyone had stayed in the room.

Billy bounded into the lounge. 'DC Hunter, can you release the suspect for now, I've found some suspicious items for testing at the lab.' Bean struggled to contain his smile.

Billy turned to Glen. 'Mr Curtis, where are the other two people who live here?'

'Jim's at work and Ryan's been gone since Saturday.'

Since he believed him, there was little point in holding him any longer. 'OK, but we may need to speak with you again, please don't leave town.' Billy suspected that's exactly what Glen would do.

They phoned for the sixth time around midday, and this time Billy decided to take the call. He agreed to meet the Byers at Dean's flat early the next morning. He was hoping to catch Johnny before then, having already had to delay him in favour of his trip to see Glen. As he drove back down from Nottingham, he kept looking at the bin bag on his passenger seat. The clues that were inside the journal may finally lead him to the culprit, the tormentor of his nephew.

The journey on the motorway was slow; every few miles there was a shunt or tailback, meaning it took over three hours to reach Dean's flat, by which time he just wanted to close his eyes and dream of a beach in Hawaii. He'd never been, it was his dream, maybe when this case was over, he'd go. If only he could persuade Tanya to come along with him.

He forced a cold meat sandwich and black coffee down his neck and spread out his loot on the dining table, which was in a poorly lit corner of the large living space. He wandered into Dean's bedroom and grabbed the bedside lamp and returned to his makeshift desk. He picked up the journal and immediately went for the pages marked 'Dean Marchant'.

It was obvious to Billy that Ryan was bitter at what had happened, he was obsessed at every little detail of the lives of his former friends. He slowly read through the notes about Dean, but there was nothing he didn't already know about his nephew. As he got to the last note, he got the confirmation he needed:

'4th July – found the holiday address in Dean's flat. Knocked him out when disturbed. Checked he was still breathing. Got away cleanly.'

Billy read it again. The stalker was confirmed – but was this angry young man really a killer? In one way it was looking ominous, but Billy took comfort from the fact that Ryan had checked Dean was still breathing. He picked up an A4 pad and ripped off a sheet. He titled it 'Ryan's confirmed movements' and wrote down the estimated time of the attack on Dean – c.3pm on Friday 4th July.

He closed the journal as he thought for a few minutes. He suddenly had hope. He was sure this guy didn't want to hurt Dean. Not physically anyway. Emotionally he was ripping him apart, but there was no evidence he wanted to harm his nephew.

Billy opened the journal again and this time read through the section about Beth. It confirmed what he'd suspected since Johnny's digging – Jack Langlan had been given Beth's details by Ryan himself. Ryan had engineered a meeting in a pub in Peterborough and started talking about his friend's dad being a criminal who'd just been sent down. Billy noted that Ryan was gleeful when he discovered Jack worked in the Peterborough branch of the same law firm as Graham.

Billy had spent very little time focusing on Stevie and Otis, and although interested in their secrets as he read through their pages of the journal, he concluded quickly that they had little significance on the overall case. He had made a note on the 'Ryan whereabouts' sheet which confirmed Ryan had put the wrong fuel in Stevie's dad's car on the morning of the 4th July.

Billy was, however, much more interested in the details of Marie's pages. The report on Marie started fairly mundanely, some details about Graham and Marie's work patterns and habits. Ryan had quickly worked out when the best time was to break into their house, and he'd done so three times, according to the journal. The second time he'd found a locked briefcase at the bottom of Marie's wardrobe, but hadn't the time to open it. The third visit was set aside purely to review its contents. Ryan described how he forced open the lock with a penknife, although he wasn't careful enough to do it without damaging the case. If she used it regularly, she'd see it had been tampered with – he concluded in his notes.

Ryan described the assortment of papers he found, but one was highlighted and underlined with red ink. 'Receipt from "Women's Choice Clinic" – invoice dated six years previous', next to this he wrote in big letters 'At this time Marie was dating Cameron!!!!'

Billy ripped off another two pages and put Cameron's name in the middle of one and Ryan's name in the middle of the other. It was clear to him now that the key to the mystery lay with these two young men. Both had more connections with the other group members than any of the friends now at risk.

On Cameron's page he drew a series of arrows off and wrote comments on each:

- *Pippa – sister*
- *Marie – Ex-girlfriend who aborted baby?*
- *Graham – friend now married to ex.*
- *Ryan – best friend. Dating sister.*
- *Dean – Close friend from uni.*
- *Stevie – Close friend from uni*

The linkage to Beth and Otis was tenuous, so he excluded those names for now.

He replicated this for Ryan's page:

- *Pippa – Girlfriend & Cameron's sister*
- *Cameron – Best friend and Girlfriend's brother.*
- *Beth – Briefly dated?*
- *Dean – Close friend from uni*
- *Graham – Close friend from uni*
- *Stevie – Close friend from uni*

He studied both pages for a few more minutes and then picked up the journal again. He read quickly through Graham's pages and was impressed that Ryan had managed to chase down the location of Graham's real mum, although there was no evidence that he'd done anything with this information.

He hadn't yet seen an entry for Pippa. He flicked through again but still couldn't see anything. Yet a tick had been written next to her name, indicating he had indeed found something on her. Or did he know it before he set out on the revenge mission?

Billy's head began to pound, so he walked to the kitchen and hunted out a couple of paracetamol and poured himself some water. He went back to the table and glugged down his drink as he stood looking over the pages in front of him. He sat back down and ripped off a fourth page from the A4 pad, he titled it 'Incidents', but before he could add anything else, there was a bang on the door. Billy checked his watch; it was just gone five.

Johnny had a takeaway bag under one arm and a pack of beers in the other as he wobbled in and plonked himself on a sofa, at the opposite end of the room to where Billy had been working. 'Want One?' he offered, as Johnny grabbed a handful of fries from inside the bag. Billy shook his head – he knew better than to take food off his friend.

'How's it going?' Johnny spat bits of burger out of his mouth as he said it.

'Okay. All the evidence seems to point to this other mate of Dean's – Ryan Curtis.'

'Ah yes. His name came up in the Cameron incident,' Johnny managed as he took another bite of burger.

'That's right. Dean and his mates blamed Ryan for Cameron's death and cut him off.'

Johnny nodded. 'You don't sound convinced on this Ryan character just now.' Johnny was surprisingly perceptive.

'Well, to be honest with the evidence I've got on him he'd be tried, convicted and hanged in court, but...'

'What?'

'It just doesn't seem likely to me. I don't know the kid, but what I've read and heard...'

'Not feeling it in the gut, matey?'

'Nope.'

'In that case, we keep going,' Johnny said as he finished his fries off with one big handful, tilting his head back to devour them in one go.

'Beer?' Billy said, in awe of the food demolition going on in front of him.

'I'll use the ones I brought, don't like that swill you drink.'

'You can stay the night. Dean's got a decent sofa, and I'd appreciate someone to bounce ideas off.'

'No Tanya?' Johnny laughed as he said it.

'Not this time. I need a clear head.'

Billy returned with his beer and sat on the next sofa across from Johnny. 'Did you turn anything else up on the Cameron death?'

Johnny nodded and reached into his pocket for his notepad. 'Few things of interest. Confirmed the time and date of death was this past February on the mountains. Coroner concluded death was by massive head and chest trauma as a result of the avalanche.'

'The compacted snow did it? I thought most people suffocated?'

Johnny nodded and took a swig of beer. 'Usually yes, but our Mr Byers was particularly unlucky, he made it away from the worst of the snow but was hit by several falling trees.'

Billy grimaced. 'Nasty.'

'He died at the scene and was taken to the St Moritz mortuary where he was later identified by his father, Derek Byers.'

'How many people died?' Billy questioned.

'Well, you may remember it was a particularly bad one, 19 people were confirmed dead, and two bodies have not yet been recovered.'

'Twenty-one dead people as a result of a bit of snow. Remind me never to go skiing.'

Johnny took another sip of his drink. 'If you don't mind me saying, I think your nephew and his friends were being a bit harsh in pinning Cameron's death on Ryan.'

Billy didn't respond but thought for a minute, then asked a question almost to himself, although loud enough for Johnny to hear, 'Can a person flip like this and start killing just because their mates have cut them off?'

Johnny stood up and shook off the crumbs. 'You said this character had a breakdown. It's possible. And if the evidence points to it...'

Billy took a deep sigh and returned to the table. He sat down and started scribbling on the fourth bit of paper, listing the key timings of the events.

Johnny walked over to him and stood over his shoulder as he jotted away. Then the large fat man hit the jackpot. 'I think you've missed something.'

'What?' Billy said, frustrated.

Johnny picked up the first piece of paper and waved it in front of Billy. 'If Ryan was hitting Dean over the head at 3pm in West Hampstead, how on earth could he be driving a white van and forcing Graham's car off the road in Cambridgeshire twenty minutes later?'

It took him a few seconds to compute what Johnny had just said. 'I'm a fucking idiot!' Billy shouted and smashed his fist on the table. 'A fucking idiot!' he repeated.

'No, you're just tired,' Johnny tried to console him.

'It's been staring me in the face for the last week. If we link all the incidents together, no one person can be doing it.' He was shuffling bits of paper about on the table, as he continued to talk to himself.

Johnny nodded. 'Question is, matey, is it two people acting independently or two working together?'

CHAPTER 21

The rain slowed by seven, but the clouds didn't lift and the darkness that had engulfed them all day, remained. Over the course of the afternoon Otis, Beth and Pippa had been given the details of Graham's disappearance. No one had dare speculate about what their next move would be. It was agreed that over dinner, a new plan would be formed.

Pippa cooked some pasta on the stove and, having found some tinned vegetables, threw this in to add some flavour. Dinner was served with tap water in the dining room. Nobody complained.

Stevie was the first to break the silence, 'How's Marie?' The question was directed at Pippa, who had spent a large part of the afternoon with her.

'She's obviously still upset, but she did say she'd come down later,' Pippa informed them.

'I can't believe she had the nerve to blame me for Graham going missing,' Jack said.

'She didn't know what she was saying,' Pippa defended her.

'Yes, but we all know she's just feeling guilty,' Jack responded.

'How do you mean?' Beth said.

'Well, come on, he shouldn't have come with us. He was slowing us down. She was the one that supported his decision to come with us, when Dean and I both knew it would be a nightmare.' Jack kept talking, with his back to the dining room door, and hadn't noticed the others around the table had stopped looking at him, instead they focused behind him.

Marie had appeared at the door. The tears had stopped, but the puffy eyes were a giveaway. The group held its collective breath as they waited for an explosive confrontation.

'You're right,' Marie said as she entered the room.

Jack, shocked, jumped up from the table and started to mumble an apology before she interrupted, 'He shouldn't have gone with you. You both knew that, and I should have stopped him. I'm sorry I blamed the both of you.'

Dean stood up from the table, walked round to Marie and hugged her warmly. Neither said anything for a moment as they held the embrace.

'What's the plan to get out of here now then?' Marie said as she finally released herself from the hug and took her seat at the table, helping herself to a small bowl of the pasta as she sat.

Dean looked at Jack, both surprised at how composed she looked, just a few hours after the disappearance of her husband.

'Come on, the only way we have a hope of saving Graham is to get some help ASAP. So, what's the plan?' She completed the sentence as she shoved a fork-full of pasta into her mouth.

Dean wasted little time in sharing his latest idea. 'For various reasons, the walks to the nearest village has been a spectacular disaster. If we keep attempting it, then it seems likely we'll be picked off one by one.' Jack and Marie both nodded in agreement.

'But what else can we do?' Stevie challenged.

'Well, thinking about it, we all agree that the mystery person is not one of us eight. So, there must be a ninth person involved.'

'So what?' Stevie barked as he interrupted Dean's flow.

'Well, we're twelve miles from the nearest village and we've not seen or heard a car or motorbike nearby.'

'So?'

'So, it must mean that the culprit is based somewhere near the house.'

'Where?' Stevie was beginning to annoy the others.

'If I knew that, all of our problems would be solved. But my best guess is that he or she is holed up in an old barn or shed or something like that.'

'Makes sense,' Marie said.

'Which means, if we can find where they're holed up, we'll be able to stop this thing.'

'Hold on a minute, you want us to go hunting around this place looking for the den of a crazed maniac? We'll all be killed!' Beth said what most of them were thinking.

'What's the alternative?' Marie said, as keen as any of them to make a breakthrough.

'We have another week until the holiday is due to finish. At that point, we may be lucky enough to have another group arrive, but maybe not,' Dean said.

'Plus, there is no way that Otis will make it another week. I'm already worried about infection in his leg,' Pippa supported.

'And we're rapidly running out of food,' Stevie agreed, reluctantly.

'Well, there is no way you're getting me wandering around out there with a lunatic on the loose,' Beth was defiant.

'That's fair enough. I was thinking four of us go out in one big group, leaving two people with Otis,' Dean said.

The group looked around and nodded. 'If we all agree, I propose Jack stays with Beth and Otis, as he can't walk on his ankle at the moment.'

Beth looked at Jack and back at Dean. It was obvious she wasn't happy about being left with the man that wanted to torment her but having made a big thing about not going exploring, she wasn't able to backtrack now. The cruel side of Dean quite enjoyed seeing Beth uncomfortable. Stevie smiled as he also lapped up Beth's discomfort.

'Agreed then,' Jack said.

'I'm proposing we only go out if it's light and we only go out in one-hour bursts.' He grabbed a spare bit of paper from the sideboard and drew a circle with a dot in it. 'If the dot is us, we should cover this off in segments. We'll walk out and back, covering off each area at a time, let's say six segments, this way we should be able to spot any place the bad guy is using as a base.'

'How far out?' Stevie asked.

'Probably about half a mile, no more. That way we should be able to do each segment in an hour.'

'I have a bad feeling about this,' Beth said.

'So do I,' Dean responded, 'but I see no other choice.'

Nobody disagreed with him.

What remained of the light outside had faded by 10 o'clock, as the group put the final refinements to their plans for the morning. No one was really ready for bed, but with the alcohol all gone and limited food supplies available, there was little to do. 'Monopoly?' Beth asked as she picked it up from the sideboard.

'I'm going to bed,' Marie said, still raw from the day's events.

'I'm going to check on Otis,' Pippa managed to excuse herself, but the others agreed – it was something to pass the time and take their mind off things.

As she walked into his bedroom, Pippa heard Otis cry out. 'You alright?' she said as she moved over to his bed.

'No. It's really hurting.'

'I should probably try and change the dressing, trouble is, I don't have a great deal to play with.'

She hunted around his bedroom and found a clean sheet on top of the wardrobe, she cut it into smaller bits and dunked it in the last of the TCP. As she tried unwrapping the old bandages from the leg, the blood started to flow again. 'Shit!' she shouted, then looked at his worried face. 'Sorry. I'm going to leave the old ones on, just cover them with the new.'

Otis yelped a few times as she applied the new dressings over the old. 'The good news is you're not going to bleed to death,' she said she applied the sheets.

'What's the bad news?'

'We're out of drugs.'

'It doesn't matter. A couple of paracetamol doesn't really cut it when you've got a bone sticking out of your leg.' Somehow, they both managed to laugh.

'It's going to be alright. Dean will figure a way to get us out of this,' Pippa said.

'You like him, don't you?' Otis replied.

Pippa was embarrassed. 'Is it that obvious?' She unconsciously flicked her blonde hair back as she said it.

'Pretty obvious. Even to me.'

Pippa smiled, and Otis felt at ease. He loved having the attention of this pretty young nurse. Okay, there was no chance anything was going to happen between them, but nevertheless, he could still enjoy his time with her.

As Pippa finished the dressing and tidied up Otis's bed, he started crying. 'Oh God, sorry did I knock your leg?'

Otis shook his head and tried to speak through his tears, 'I'm sorry.'

'Don't be silly. What have you got to be sorry about?'

'I think this might all be my fault,' as Otis said this, Pippa sat back down on the edge of his bed, this time nearer his head.

'How can it be your fault, Otis?' She said it softly and with warmth in her voice.

'I think I know who might be doing this to us?'

'Who?'

'Candice's dad.'

'Who's Candice?'

'She's my girlfriend. Or was my girlfriend.'

'Why did you split up?'

'Well, we'd been going out for a while, and one day she said her parents were out, so would I like to go round her house.'

'So, she was still living at her parents?'

'Yes, only we were in bed together, and her parents came back early.'

'They caught you?' Otis nodded.

'I take it her dad wasn't very happy?'

'You could say that. He threatened to kill me if he ever saw me again. I thought he was going to kill me there and then. If her mum hadn't been there, I honestly think he would have done.'

'It seems a bit of an extreme overreaction,' Pippa sympathised.

'Well...' Otis paused; he found the next bit hard to say. 'It turns out she was only fifteen.'

She didn't mean to, but this bit of news caused her to be physically taken aback. She half slid off the bed and managed to save herself by grabbing the bedside table and standing up.

Otis quickly tried to justify himself, 'I didn't know she was fifteen. Of course, I wouldn't have done anything if I had known. She told me she was eighteen when we met in the nightclub. I mean, she was in a nightclub, why wouldn't I believe her?'

Pippa recomposed herself and sat back on the bed. 'It's okay.' Otis looked relieved again to hear the reassuring voice of his nurse.

'But I still don't understand what our situation has got to do with Candice?'

'Her dad threatened to kill me, and someone did actually try to kill me.'

Pippa gave him another smile and held his hand. 'Otis, this has nothing to do with you. Why would Candice's dad take the trouble to come down to France, research all the secrets from our past and torment seven perfect strangers, just to get revenge on you?'

He thought for a moment. 'I suppose you're right.'

She got up and gave him a gentle kiss on his forehead. 'Try to get some sleep.' She turned the light off as she left.

For a few glorious minutes, Otis forgot about the pain in his legs as he enjoyed the tingling on his head that the kiss had left behind.

'Ah-ha, three houses on Trafalgar Square, that's 800 pounds, please,' Jack said gleefully towards Stevie.

'Bollocks! I bloody hate this game,' he shouted as he handed over the remainder of his cash and property.

'I'm going to bed now,' and with that he marched out of the dining room and could be heard banging about in the kitchen trying to find a clean glass for some water.

'Goodnight,' Dean shouted to him as he heard Stevie fill his glass and head upstairs. There was unintelligible mumbling from him as he disappeared.

'He took that well,' Jack said, happily.

'In actual fact, he has taken it much worse in the past,' Dean laughed. For a moment, the four of them had forgotten about their troubles. The game had worked; it had gotten them through to nearly midnight without them thinking about their predicament.

'My turn,' Jack shouted. 'Six; oh no,'

'Mayfair, two houses, 600 pounds,' Beth said smugly, but as she put her hand out to collect it, they were immersed in darkness.

Beth screamed first and darted up off her seat, knocking her chair back onto the wooden floor with a crash. This made Jack and Dean jump up, the latter grabbed his gun, which had been resting next to his drink on the table.

'You alright?' Dean said in the general direction of Beth, although he couldn't see her.

'Yes, I'm alright,' she replied.

'The lights are off in the kitchen and stairs as well,' Dean said as he tentatively tried to make his way around the large dining table.

'Must be a power cut,' Beth said.

'Let's hope so,' Jack replied.

Dean hit a chair and then bumped into the sideboard. 'Shit, I can't see a bloody thing.'

He thought for a second, but before he had a solution Beth screeched, 'What's that noise?'

Jack and Dean went quiet and listened, there was a gentle thud, thud, thud, coming down the stairs.

Dean took the safety off his gun and held it with both hands in the general direction of the door. Thud, thud, thud. Gradually the noise was getting louder. The floorboard outside the kitchen squeaked and then the slow plod of feet on the kitchen tiles. It wasn't immediately obvious, but Dean felt sure he could see a speck of light ahead of him.

'Who's there?' Dean shouted, 'I've got a gun!'

There was a slight pause.

'For God's sakes, I lose at Monopoly and get shot in the same day,' Stevie said as the other three in the room groaned.

'You bloody fool, I could have shot you. How did you get down without breaking your bloody neck?'

'My phone, obviously. God knows why we're listening to you if my survival instincts are better than yours!'

Dean was annoyed and embarrassed at the same time. 'I remember seeing some candles under the sink,' he said as he and Stevie headed into the kitchen. The others slowly followed him, all failing to avoid walking into a piece of furniture along the way.

'Here they are,' Stevie shouted as the others started to gather behind him.

'Matches?' Dean decided to test the resourcefulness of Stevie.

'Gas hob,' he replied without a pause. He lit the hob and one after another they lit half a dozen candles.

'Thanks, Stevie. Legend.' Dean had enjoyed seeing Stevie assume responsibility, but now it was time to take it back. 'We need to prioritise securing the house. We'll go around together and check every door and window.'

They all agreed, and one after another, each window was checked and double-checked. Each door was bolted and had a chair shoved up against the handle. After securing the downstairs, they popped in to check on Otis, who was groaning in pain, but he promised them he was okay and despatched them to bed.

As the four of them headed up the stairs, Beth stumbled and dropped the candle she was holding. 'Bother, sorry,' she said quietly in an effort to avoid waking Marie and Pippa. Stevie let out an annoyed tut but managed to avoid saying anything nasty.

As they got to the top of the stairs, Beth tapped on Marie's bedroom door. No response. They agreed to let her sleep – no sense in waking her to tell her the power was off. They exchanged their 'goodnights' as they headed into their own bedrooms, with Dean offering to check on Pippa. He tapped gently on her door, paused briefly and then turned to leave her alone when she responded, 'Come in.'

He slowly opened her door. 'Sorry to wake you. I was just checking you were OK. The power's gone off.'

'Yes, I heard the commotion, I'm fine.'

'Goodnight.' Dean slowly turned to leave.

'Don't go,' she said before he could make his exit.

'What is it?' He moved in closer.

'Sit down, please.'

As he sat on the corner of her bed, he could see her pretty face, long blonde hair and big green eyes through the flickering candlelight, and he knew he had to kiss her. And that's exactly what he did.

He didn't leave her room that night.

CHAPTER 22

The rain had relented completely by the morning, with sunlight trying to squeeze through the gaps in the shutters. Dean woke first, taking a few moments to realise he wasn't in his own bed. He looked to his right, and he could see the beautiful girl lying next to him, still sleeping and with a smile on her face. Dean gave her a kiss on the head and gently tried to free his right arm from underneath her body. He struggled to get yesterday's boxers on and having finally managed to protect his modesty, he grabbed the rest of his clothes and headed for his own room.

Having showered and changed, Dean made his first port of call, Otis. He knew the bloke was virtually unable to sleep with the pain, and he desperately wanted to find help for him.

'You awake?' Dean said as he entered the room, the door was only ajar.

'Yep,' Otis replied.

'Fancy a cup of coffee?'

'Not really, but I'll have one anyway.' He was trying to stay upbeat. 'Did you sleep well?' Otis asked.

Dean smiled. 'Not bad actually, mate. Not bad.' He headed into the kitchen and put the kettle on. As he waited for it to boil, he thought he'd check the rest of the downstairs and walked through into the dining room. He couldn't see it from his initial survey of the room.

He walked into the lounge and was confronted with the scrawling from two days before. But thankfully no new messages on the wall. He passed back through the dining room to the kitchen, missing it again.

He picked up the kettle and paused; the water was still cold. And then he remembered about the power going off. 'Shit,' he said out loud.

'It's going to be a few more minutes,' he shouted towards Otis's room, as he pulled a pan from the cupboard and popped it on the stove.

Eventually he completed his task and took the coffee into Otis. Dean filled him in on the plan for the day and told him about the power going off. As he left the room, he promised Otis he'd get some help soon.

Dean poured himself some cereal and softened it with some tap water. 'Food is food,' he said to himself and forced it down.

'Morning,' Stevie was surprisingly chirpy as he entered the room.

'Morning, mate, power's still off,' and Dean pointed towards the pan of hot water.

'Yes, never mind. Any nasty messages this morning?'

'Not that I've seen. All seems pretty calm.'

'I've got a good feeling about today. I think we'll get out of here before nightfall.' By the time Stevie had boiled the pan again Beth, Marie and Jack had emerged.

'Where's Pippa?' Stevie asked.

'I heard her in the shower just now, so she'll be down in a bit,' Beth responded. Dean became embarrassed, but thankfully nobody noticed.

'Black coffee and dry cereal for all,' Stevie boomed as he plonked the cups on the table.

'Umm, you are spoiling us, Mr Pennock,' came the sarcastic response from Marie.

Dean thought about asking how she was feeling but decided not to. He wasn't prepared to spoil the more jovial mood that seemed to have emerged this morning, but he could tell by her puffy eyes that she'd been crying throughout the night.

As the group munched through their breakfast, Pippa appeared. 'Oh, hi, Pippa,' Dean said, now totally embarrassed.

'Morning,' she said with a smile and winked at Dean.

As he fussed over Pippa, the others started clearing away. 'As loser, I'd better pack away the Monopoly board,' Stevie said and headed into the dining room. Moments later, he returned.

The rest of the group were involved in different conversations and hadn't seen the look on his face as he stood in the doorway. 'You bitch!' The chatter stopped and everyone looked at Stevie. 'You fucking bitch!' It took a few seconds to realise he was looking at Marie. 'You couldn't keep your fat mouth shut, could you?'

'What the hell's going on?' Dean moved over to Stevie.

'She's never liked me. Slander, that's what it is. Slander!'

Marie looked shocked. 'What are you on about?' she questioned, appearing genuinely confused.

'What you've scrawled onto the table – you spiteful bitch.'

Dean stepped in. 'That's enough, Stevie. Show me what you're on about.' He virtually manhandled Stevie back into the dining room and immediately spotted the words scratched into the dining table:

STEVIE IS GAY

The others filed in to see the message. Stevie was still bright red with anger.

'What's this got to do with Marie?' Pippa said eventually.

'She, she's the one...'

'The one what?' Pippa asked.

'I'm the one that's known all along that Stevie is gay.' Marie stepped forward.

Stevie went from red to purple and attempted to deny it. 'I'm not a poof, it's all lies!'

Dean put his arm around Stevie. 'I hate to break it to you, mate, but we've all known for a very long time. It's about the least shocking revelation we've had on this holiday so far.'

He looked stunned. 'She told you?'

'No. No one told me, or Graham or Ryan or Cameron for that matter. We've known you for seven years and we've always suspected. But, mate, it has never bothered us.'

'But there hasn't been a break-in. It has to have been one of the people in the house that did this,' Stevie argued.

'Maybe. Maybe not. Someone is doing this and if it's not one of us, then someone is getting into this house at night.'

'Why don't you seem bothered by that?' Beth asked.

'Well, those of us that went to bed last night are still here this morning. Right now, I take comfort in the fact that the worst thing this person is doing is vandalising the house,' Dean said in a matter-of-fact way.

'How can you say that's the worst thing? Look at Otis, look at Graham,' Marie shouted.

'Yes, but these things happen when we leave the house, not when we're in it.'

'And what's the next plan of action?' Jack asked.

'We're going to leave the house.'

Dean really was bothered about someone coming into the house unknown, but he wanted to be as blasé about it as possible, so as to help reassure the rest. He'd checked and double-checked everywhere last night, and he couldn't figure how they'd managed to get in. Maybe it was one of his friends that was doing it, but he doubted it. Somehow, somewhere, this person was getting in. Tonight, if he made it to tonight, he'd find out how.

By eight o'clock the four explorers were ready to leave. No provisions, no bags to carry. They were planning on being back every hour and they didn't want anything to slow them down. Jack and Beth were given their instructions. Open the door to no one. Only open on three knocks. Four knocks meant they were under duress and don't open. No windows to be opened. Feed and water Otis.

It was a cool and fresh morning, but bright, as the sun overpowered the light clouds. Everywhere was still damp from the previous day's rain.

Functionality was the key; the girls were wearing shorts and trainers, T-shirts and a cardigan apiece. Dean also wore shorts, but Stevie wasn't going to be persuaded away from his jeans.

As they set off down the driveway, they all took a look left towards Madame Bernard's, hopeful of seeing her return. Nothing. They were going to cover the ground from south to south-east on their first excursion, with the boys having seen little to help them on their two previous trips north.

They turned right onto the dirt track, where previously they had been turning left to head north. Every way they looked they were surrounded by trees. The group followed the track for about 10 minutes before Dean stopped the group and pulled out his map. He'd marked off each segment, and he estimated they needed to break through the woods at this point and walk another 15 minutes before sweeping around and re-joining the same track further up. Eventually, Dean took a deep breath. 'Come on, no time to waste,' and marched off on his own, desperately praying the others would follow him.

'Ouch!' Dean turned to see Marie struggling to free herself from a bramble.

He returned to help free her. 'You alright?' he asked as he released her leg.

'Fine. Let's keep going,' she barked. Dean and Pippa looked at each other – his heart melted when she eventually gave him a smile. He winked back at her and did a double-check to make sure no one had seen him. However, Marie and Stevie were seemingly oblivious to the birth of a new romance among the group.

The group continued until they reached a section of the woods that had been cleared. 'This is as far as we need to go,' Dean declared. 'We'll follow the outside of this cleared section back to the road.' He neither waited for a response from the others nor expected an argument. Since Graham's disappearance, there was no one who came close to assuming leadership of the group. As unsuccessful as the other excursions had been, they still seemed to have faith in Dean.

* * *

The silence was excruciating. Circumstances had dictated that the two of them had been left alone; well almost alone. Otis still occupied the downstairs bedroom, but Beth and Jack had been unable to utter a word between them since the others left. They sat at opposite ends of the lounge, reading, sufficiently far away not to have to speak to each other, but close enough for reassurance.

It had taken some persuading, but Beth was now reasonably confident that Jack wasn't behind these events. Nevertheless, she didn't completely trust him.

'Coffee?' Jack offered eventually.

'No, thanks,' Beth managed, relieved that the silence had been broken. 'I'll check on Otis,' she offered.

As Jack filled a pan from the sink, he thought he heard something outside, he moved the net curtain to get a better look. He couldn't see anything and assumed it must have been wishful thinking.

Then he heard it again, only louder. It took him a few seconds to pinpoint what the sound was. An engine! It was a car!

'Beth! Beth, come here!' he shouted back towards Otis's room. 'It's a car,' he added, as she entered the kitchen.

'Oh, thank God,' Beth said as she moved over to the window.

'There it is.' Jack pointed as a small blue Ford Fiesta pulled up on the gravel driveway.

Beth peeled away from the window and ran in to tell Otis the news. Jack stayed focused on the car as whoever was inside waited a minute or so to emerge. Eventually the driver's side door started to open, and a man got out, at least it looked like a man; whoever it was had a hoody top on and jeans, skinny and slight. Could be a woman, Jack thought to himself.

He charged over to the kitchen door, which led onto the veranda, and went through the long process of unlocking and unblocking it.

Finally, he opened the door and looked squarely at the face waiting in front of him.

***

The four of them had been out for nearly an hour, now about 10 minutes' walk from their house, having broadly covered the south to south-east segment.

'Can't wait to get back and eat that nice bowl of dried cereal again,' Stevie muttered to himself as they trudged across a clearing, still muddy from the previous day's rain. Dean chuckled to himself and cruelly found himself thinking that Stevie could do with a few days of food shortage.

They headed into another wooded section, just as the clouds appeared again and a few spots of the rain hit the ground. 'Nearly home,' Dean shouted as he looked back, but hadn't realised he'd left them 30 metres behind.

'Come on, you lot! We've got more of the expeditions to do today.'

Stevie looked over at him and mouthed something quite unpleasant.

Dean slowed to let them catch up, but as he looked around to check on their progress, something in the distance caught his eye. He did a double-take. Bright red, in the middle of the woods? 'Back in a sec!' he shouted as he bolted off to see what it was. He ignored the cries of 'WAIT!' from the other three.

Dean ran about 100 metres in the direction of the red object. But he managed to lose his bearings as he swerved to avoid one large tree and paused with his hands on his hips as he turned in circles to see if he could find sight of it again.

After a few seconds he decided to run on again, no plan, just run and hope; he froze when he saw it.

'Where the hell did he go?' Stevie questioned.

'Dean, where are you?' Pippa screamed in a panic.

'The bloody idiot, what on earth did he think he was doing?' Marie added.

'Let's wait here a few minutes, he may come back,' Stevie offered, but both women threw him a worried look.

He circled it a couple of times, splitting his time between focusing on the bright red tent and looking behind his back. The tent was zipped shut; he kept looking at it. He knew what he needed to do, but his heart was pounding fast, and his legs started to give in. Dean pulled out his gun. 'Okay, let's do this,' he said to himself.

He bent down gradually and started to unzip it, pausing every few seconds to look behind him. As he edged the zip to the top, he took another look around before poking his gun and then his head into the tent.

Firstly, he noticed a dark green sleeping bag laid out on the floor, second, he spotted a grubby looking rucksack in the corner of the tent. Finally, he saw stars as the large tree branch connected with the back of his head.

CHAPTER 23

He didn't know if it was the distant screams of his name or the now fast-flowing rain that woke him up, but he came around with a sore head and wet clothes. As he tried to get up, he managed to shout, 'Here!' as loud as he could but stumbled back down to the ground again. He held his head in his hands and tried to get the thumping sound out of his mind.

'There you are. Thank God!' Pippa shouted, as the women fussed around him.

'You're soaked, what happened?' Marie questioned. Stevie kept standing and paced around the area.

'I found a tent,' Dean managed.

'Where?' Stevie was impatient.

Dean stood up successfully this time and looked around, still a little dazed. 'It was here. Right here.'

'Well it's not now, are you sure?' Stevie was being deliberately argumentative.

'Yes, look here, the peg marks.' Dean pointed to the ground. 'And look, a chocolate wrapper.' Marie grabbed it from a nearby shrub.

'Bloody hell, you found him,' Stevie puffed out his cheeks as he said it as if all their problems had been solved.

'You're lucky to be alive,' Pippa hugged him and didn't care if Stevie or Marie saw it.

'It's not luck. If he wanted me dead, I'd be dead. He had the opportunity, and for the second time, he didn't take it.'

'Second time?' Stevie was intrigued.

'When I was hit over the head the day before the holiday – when I walked in on him breaking into the flat. He could have killed me then but didn't.'

'You're saying "him" as if you know who it is.' Pippa looked Dean directly in the eye as she asked the question, almost afraid of the answer.

Dean nodded and paused before grasping her hands in his.

'Who the hell is it then?' Stevie barked.

Dean looked around at Marie and Stevie before focusing back on Pippa.

'I recognise the tent and backpack from when we went fishing together.' Stevie and Marie looked at each other and tried to say the name, but both stuttered before Dean managed to beat them to it, 'Ryan.'

Dean knew this would hit Pippa hard, she'd been desperately in love with Ryan and it had broken her heart to lose both Cameron and Ryan at the same time, earlier in the year. Dean kept hold of her hand tightly and willed the colour to return to her face.

She spoke softly, 'Why?' then repeated, 'Why would he do that to us?'

Dean, equally softly, replied, 'Isn't it obvious? We cut him off. All of us, to a man, and woman. We turned on him, blamed him for Cam and dumped him.'

The four of them fell silent as they thought about it.

They didn't see the hooded figure, a few metres away, behind a large pine tree. He smiled to himself as he heard this conversation and gently jogged off without making a sound.

'We'd better get back and tell the others,' Stevie said after a few minutes. Dean was hugging Pippa tightly as tears continued to flow down her cheeks. Stevie's words seemed to resonate with her, and she pulled herself up out of Dean's arms, grabbed a hairband from a coat pocket and tied her long, flowing golden hair back into a ponytail.

'Stevie's right, it won't do any good moping around here, let's get back to the others.' She said it firmly, surprising the others with her resolve. Dean smiled to himself; God, he was falling more in love with this woman every hour.

They were surprised, and not a little unnerved, at how quickly they got back to the house from their unscheduled stop. 'There it is,' Stevie said unhelpfully as they emerged from the last patch of woodland to see the back of the house.

'Never thought I'd say this, but I'm glad to see it again,' Marie said. Everyone agreed.

The house and garden were surrounded by a large fence, so they made their way around to the front of the property and looked up at the farmhouse from the drive.

'It's still standing at least,' Dean quipped.

'Let's hope everyone inside is as well,' Pippa added.

They walked up the drive, and then the steps to the veranda. Dean went to tap on the door but turned to Pippa. 'How many was knocks was it?'

'Four,' Marie said impatiently.

'No, no, four was for "under duress",' Stevie barked. But before the argument could continue, the door unlocked and opened in front of them.

'What the hell happened to you?' Stevie exclaimed. Jack was standing at the door with a now-red tea towel covering a cut above his left eye.

The others stood looking at Jack before Pippa pushed past them. 'For goodness sake, sit down,' she said and manoeuvred Jack to the kitchen table.

As the others filed in, Dean started shouting, 'Beth, Otis we're back are you okay? Beth, Otis. Beth!'

'They're not here,' Jack managed, his head facing down towards the table as Pippa tried to tidy his wound.

Dean moved next to the table but didn't sit down, instead he and Stevie towered over Jack as he sat. 'What do you mean they're not here?' Dean said.

'What have you done with them?' Stevie shouted.

'Nothing,' Jack managed, through tears.

'Well, where are they, Jack?' Marie moved over and sat opposite Jack at the table.

'I don't know.' His tone was getting defensive.

'What do you mean you don't know?' Dean was pointing his finger close to Jack's face.

'Ease off, Dean,' Pippa said, as she finished tying the makeshift bandage around his head, 'let him speak.'

Dean and Stevie sat down, Pippa finished off washing her hands and joined the others at the table.

Four faces now glared at Jack as he composed himself.

'We're all waiting,' Marie said with anger in her voice.

He breathed in heavily and began. He told them about hearing the car and shouting for Beth. He told them about opening the door to a face he didn't recognise, and he told them about a blow to the head and waking up on the kitchen floor in a pool of his own blood. Then he told them about discovering Beth and Otis missing. As he finished telling his story, he looked up at the remaining four faces in front of him.

Marie spoke first, 'You expect us to believe that?'

'What do you mean?' Jack shot back.

'Well, come on, he's been caught red-handed with evidence that he wants to get revenge on Beth. He's left alone with her, and she goes missing. He was the one out with Graham when he went missing. It all makes sense, he's behind it all.' Dean tried to put his arm on Marie's shoulder, but she shrugged it off. 'Come on, what you waiting for? Tie him up or something. We all know it's him!' Marie was nearly hysterical at this point.

'Except, we know it's not him, don't we?' Dean said. Jack looked up hopefully.

'What do you mean?' Marie shot back.

'We know that Ryan is behind this, we've just seen the evidence.'

'He's right,' Pippa supported Dean.

Marie looked angrily at them both. 'Just because you're fucking him now, doesn't mean you have to agree with everything he says!' Marie barked, without thinking.

A temporary moment of silence engulfed the tired, eighties kitchen, as an embarrassed Dean and Pippa went different shades of rouge.

Jack broke the ice, 'Who's Ryan and what's he got to do with it?'

They paused and waited for each other to speak. No one really wanted to retell the story, but one of them would have to now.

Stevie plucked up the courage. 'He was a friend of ours from uni. We were basically a gang of five; Dean, me, Graham, Pippa's brother Cam and Ryan.'

'Oh, he was the guy responsible for Cam's death?'

'Don't try and change the subject, you're still the prime suspect,' Marie said, pointing at Jack from across the table.

Jack ignored her this time. 'But what's this Ryan got to do with our situation?'

'We've just found his tent, about ten minutes south of here,' Dean explained.

'So you think, how do you know?' Marie was still not relenting. 'What if he did away with Ryan before the holiday and is now coming after the rest of us?' She was standing behind her chair by the time she finished the latest rant.

Dean pushed his chair back calmly, went over to his best friend's wife and held her tight. She resisted initially, but eventually she relented and allowed Dean to hug her as she broke into tears. He kept hugging her as she sobbed so hard, she could barely breathe. 'I miss him,' she kept repeating. Dean tried to offer some comfort by promising to find Graham, but he was unconvincing. He didn't have confidence the remaining five would get out alive, never mind find the three that were now missing.

He instructed the other three to leave through subtle motioning of his eyes and eventually encouraged Marie to sit back down at the kitchen table.

'Is it Ryan? Do you really think he could do this?' she said as the tears stopped flowing and she wiped her eyes clear.

'He's involved somehow, there is no doubt. But is he capable of kidnap and maybe worse? I'm not so sure.'

'I have a plan though, which might provide some answers tonight,' he said with little confidence. He felt sure Marie didn't have any confidence in another of his plans either.

The others hadn't asked about it, and he certainly didn't want to worry them by revealing something he didn't have to – but he wouldn't lie. He kept planning on what he'd say if they asked, as he lay across his bed, trying in vain to have an afternoon nap. 'I lost the gun.' No, that sounded like he was incompetent. 'Ryan has the gun.' Definitely not, that would put the shits up everyone. 'The gun was taken.' Yes, that sounded more like it.

So, playing it back in his head, what's the follow-up question anyone would ask?

'Who took it?' Answer: 'Ryan.' Next follow-up: 'You mean the same Ryan that hit you over the head at your flat and took a gun off you then as well?' 'Yes, that Ryan.'

'So, the Ryan that is stalking us, threatening us and potentially kidnapped three of our friends, has two fully loaded guns on him?' 'Yes, that's the one.' He even chuckled to himself as he played out the conversation in his head. God, he hoped no one would ask about the gun.

He was running the conversation scenarios through his head when the announcement came from Pippa that dinner was ready. He walked down the stairs with little enthusiasm about what he was going to eat.

'Hmm, smells nice, what's on the menu?' he said as he entered the kitchen.

'Don't be sarcastic, it doesn't become you,' Pippa said as she greeted his entrance to the kitchen with a peck on the cheek and a quick hug – no need to be discreet now. No need to hide their feelings. Life's short. Theirs could well be shorter than most.

Stevie and Jack were fighting, and losing, with a hot pan of something as they tried to drain its contents over the sink. The obligatory swearing could be heard from Stevie.

'I've made a sauce for the pasta,' Pippa declared boastfully. She swished the saucepan in front of Dean, who evidently was supposed to be impressed.

'Looks good,' he said politely, 'what's in it?'

'Tinned tomatoes and garlic. Lots of garlic,' Stevie shouted as he struggled over to the table with a large bowl of undercooked pasta.

Jack placed a jug of water in front of them. Dean made an exaggerated look around the table. 'What a feast,' he said aloud, and everyone laughed.

'Where's Marie?' he asked, as he grabbed a large spoonful of the pasta and dropped it on his plate.

'She's not hungry, I checked on her earlier,' Pippa said as she attempted to pour the lumpy tomato sauce onto Dean's pasta.

As they struggled their way through dinner, Dean decided to tell them of his plan. 'He's getting in the house – of that I'm convinced,' Dean said.

'Why didn't he attack us then?' Stevie asked a very reasonable question.

'I don't know. Maybe he is working alone, maybe not. But I do know this, if he wanted me dead, I would be.'

Stevie agreed and enquired about the plan. Dean turned around to get a notepad and pen from the sideboard. He wrote on the piece of paper. 'We're going to take turns to stay up tonight.'

'No way,' Pippa declared.

'Shhh,' Dean muttered and beckoned them in closer as the huddled around the table, 'it's possible there is a listening device, I don't know.'

Stevie laughed. 'This isn't James Bond, you idiot.'

Jack offered some support to Dean. 'It is possible,' he whispered, 'after all, he seems to know when the last of us has gone to bed.'

'In that case, let's talk in the garden,' Pippa suggested.

They left the kitchen together and walked through the dining room towards the French windows that lead onto the patio. They decided not to venture too far from the open door once outside.

'I don't like this idea at all,' Pippa declared.

'It is a bit risky,' Stevie agreed.

Dean turned to Jack. 'What do you think?'

He paused for a second, before responding, 'We've always been one step behind him, this might just swing the advantage back to us.'

Dean looked around, the group of three stood in front of him in the evening sunshine. 'It is a bit risky. Jack and I will take turns. Three-hour shifts from midnight to six. Me first, then Jack.'

'I know you've got the gun, but it's still risky,' Pippa said. Dean ignored the comment about the gun, he'd tell Jack about it later.

'Stevie and Pippa, the two of you make a big scene about going to bed at midnight, then come and wake me up and I'll come down and hide in the dining room.'

Pippa and Stevie, still unconvinced by the plan, eventually nodded their agreement.

This gave Jack little choice, but Dean counted on him still wanting to prove his innocence to the rest of the group.

As they prepared to return to the house for the washing up, Marie appeared in the dining room. She'd run down the stairs and was so anxious to say what she wanted she couldn't make herself understood to the others.

'What is it?' Pippa said, the whole group was now concerned.

'I, I think I've just seen someone at Madame Bernard's house.'

'What?' came the response from all of them.

'I was just washing my face in the bathroom when I noticed the curtains move in her front window.'

'Are you sure?' Stevie doubted.

'Yes, I didn't believe it at first, but then I watched it for a few minutes and there was definitely a figure inside.'

'Bloody hell,' Dean said, 'better take a look.'

'Hold on, you can't see her cottage from this house,' Stevie challenged. The others looked at each other, realising Stevie was right.

'The trees completely obscure the view of her cottage,' Dean agreed.

'Well, I saw it!' Marie looked embarrassed but defended her position. 'I'll show you.' The five of them marched through the kitchen and up the stairs to the main bathroom. They gathered around the tiny window and peered out. Marie was right, you could see the cottage through a small gap in the trees.

'That's weird,' Stevie offered, 'many apologies.'

'Some trees have come down,' Jack said, as he continued to stare through the window.

The others all gathered around the window again, and sure enough, they could see three or four felled trees lying across Madame Bernard's front garden.

'Was it the storms?' Pippa asked.

'Who knows, but it's definitely worth a look,' Dean said. He glanced around the bathroom. 'I'll take Jack with me.'

Pippa shot back first, a split second before Marie could, 'No you won't,' she was definite in her tone.

'Why not?' Dean queried.

'Quite simply, if anyone is alone with Jack, they go missing or get injured,' Marie jumped in.

'Don't be ridiculous!' Dean shot back. A brief argument broke out between four of them while Jack remained silent.

Eventually, he offered a solution. 'Let's all go. Safety in numbers and all that.' He shrugged his shoulders as he said it to indicate he didn't believe it would offer any safety at all.

There was some muttering among the other four, but in the end, there was very little to argue with, and one by one, they all agreed.

'Dean's got the gun, so the rest of us should grab something sharp from the kitchen,' Jack suggested.

Dean took a big breath and realised it was time to come clean about the gun.

As he explained about waking up in the wet field without the gun, he was surprised, there was limited angst among the group as Dean made this latest confession. Stevie, as expected, had offered the most damning assessment. However, they were all becoming accustomed to bad news and took it in their stride.

They returned to the kitchen, and each one of them found a suitable defensive implement. The armed group then stepped out onto the veranda together and waited as Stevie locked the door behind him.

'You realise this is the first time we've left the house empty since this saga began,' Stevie offered but drew little response from the group.

They walked slowly, looking like a gang of vigilantes as they marched up the driveway towards the run-down bungalow. The earlier rain had been replaced by searing hot sunshine, despite it being nearly seven in the evening. Dean held a carving knife in his hand, Stevie a rolling pin, Jack had picked up some scissors, and the two women had grabbed the sharpest vegetable knives they could find.

'Looks even shittier than before,' Dean commented as they arrived at the porch. Dean approached the blue door again and, having paused for a few seconds to seek approval from the others, knocked firmly three times. The door wobbled with each knock. Every one of them held their breath and waited for a response. Nothing. Dean tried again, another three firm knocks. The hinges creaked, but the door just about held firm. Still nothing.

'OK, no one's home,' Dean said, 'let's head round the back to the broken window.'

'At least no one that admits to being home,' Stevie said, half under his breath.

They marched around to the back of the cottage, dodging the broken bit of drainpipe and arrived at the damaged French windows. They stared into the house from the garden, all of them clearly nervous, although no one admitted it.

'OK, watch out for broken glass as you step in,' Dean commanded as he moved in. He extended his right arm, which held the carving knife, and sheepishly, slowly, cautiously, entered the sitting room.

Dean moved gradually into the middle of the room as the others nervously joined him. He stood in the same spot, but circled around, trying to see if there were any noticeable changes. The two sofa chairs were exactly where they were before, near the broken window. The cluttered room was untidy and unkempt. Something attracted Dean's attention and he walked over to the round dining table, at the opposite end of the room from where they'd just entered.

'Someone has been here,' he said.

'How'd you know?' Marie said with more than a hint of concern in her voice.

Dean pointed at the nearest dining chair. 'This chair wasn't here,' he paused briefly before continuing, 'I remember because there were only three chairs around the table.' He walked around the table, focusing on its contents. 'Someone pulled this chair over from near the fireplace and cleared a space at the table to do something. Before, this table was completely covered in stuff, but see, the space in front of this chair is now clear.'

Everyone looked and nodded in agreement. Dean walked over to the phone and picked it up as Marie had done days before, more in hope than expectation. 'Nothing,' he said.

'It's been cut,' Jack offered.

'That doesn't make sense,' Marie said, 'it didn't work before, but it hadn't been cut. Now someone has gone to the trouble of cutting this line.'

'This place is bloody creepy,' Stevie said, 'let's go back.'

'No, we need to look at the other rooms,' Dean commanded.

Dean studied the surroundings; there were two doors to choose from. For simplicity, he chose the nearest one. He led the way into what was a small lobby that housed the front door. There was another internal door, opposite to where they'd come from, and a smaller door to the left that they all concluded was probably a cupboard.

Dean motioned with his knife arm, indicating that they should follow him into the opposite room. The door squeaked as he gradually edged it open. It was a bedroom, outdated, like the rest of the house: a pink carpet, dirty wallpaper and a bedspread in various floral patterns. The room more than hinted that it hadn't been updated in decades. The five of them entered and stood at the end of the old wooden bed, surveying the room. One window to the front of the property and a door that presumably led to a bathroom. On the opposite wall to where they'd come in was a dark wooden Victorian wardrobe. It was monstrously large and dominated the room.

Feeling brave, Jack made a beeline for the bathroom, followed by Dean and Marie. Stevie stood by the bedroom door to 'keep an eye out', and Pippa wandered around the bedroom.

'Just a bathroom,' Jack shouted back.

Pippa reached the wardrobe and tugged on one of the doors, fully expecting it to be locked. It wasn't. As she pulled it, the door flew open and a large object knocked her onto the bed, landing on top of her. Her screams prompted Jack, Dean and Marie to charge from the bathroom and Stevie to give up his post by the bedroom door.

'Get it off me!' Pippa screamed as she tried to free herself from the object on her, unaware of what it was.

Marie screamed and then froze as she returned to the bedroom, but Dean and Jack kept going and fought with the thing to release Pippa. As they pulled it off her, they noticed she was splattered with blood. Dean and Jack had one hand each on the object and, having noticed the blood on Pippa, turned to focus on the thing they were holding.

The 'thing' was Madame Bernard – minus a throat. The boys dropped the body instantly and made for the door, Dean grabbing Pippa from the bed as he made his way past. As they entered the lobby, Stevie tried and failed to open the blue front door and after a few seconds, gave up and followed Jack and Marie back through the sitting room and out via the broken French windows.

Dean and Pippa landed last, with the five of them slumped in a heap on the grass outside the cottage. They were all huddled together.

Pippa was still screaming.

Dean paused for a minute, panting for breath, before Pippa's screams focused his attention. They'd landed either side of Jack's large frame, and Dean had to scramble over that obstacle to reach his new girlfriend. Pippa was rolling around on the ground with her arms and legs flinging about randomly. Dean was able to avoid a couple of whacks from her arms as he positioned himself astride her, managing to pin her arms to the ground. She struggled violently and managed to free her left arm, which connected with Dean's nose. The blood dripping from his nose added to that of Madame Bernard's, and Pippa was more hysterical than ever.

Dean ignored his injury and managed to pin her arms down again, but her head was still moving ferociously. The others eventually regained enough composure to come to Dean's aid, with Marie putting her hands over Pippa's head and leaning in, repeating reassuring words, 'It'll be all right, it'll be alright.'

Stevie, having finally managed to get up, watched stony-silent as the others tried to calm her down.

Eventually the adrenalin subsided from Pippa, and the physical convulsions were replaced with a continuous sob. Jack, who held her legs, and Marie, slowly released their grip, encouraged by Dean's head moves and they stepped away. Dean moved to lie beside her body and cradled her as she continued to cry.

Having moved a sensitive, but safe distance away, Jack, Stevie and Marie stood silent and watched Dean comfort this pretty, but distraught, young women.

The light had started to fade by the time Dean had managed calm Pippa down. He tried to wipe away the tears, but every time he did it, he managed to spread the blood around even more. He sat up and took off his T-shirt, revealing his toned body and used it as a cloth to make a better job of cleaning her beautiful face. Eventually he coaxed her off the floor and wrapped his arm firmly around her as he manoeuvred her back around the garden of Madame Bernard's cottage and onto the driveway. The others had managed to get 10 metres or so ahead, giving Stevie time to open the door before Dean and Pippa rose up the steps to the veranda and finally into the kitchen.

Dean sat her down at the kitchen table as Jack put a glass of water in front of her. Pippa sat motionless, staring straight ahead at nothing. 'Marie's gone to run her a bath,' Jack said.

Stevie was by the door, double locking it and checking it twice.

After a few minutes of complete silence, Marie appeared. 'Come on, let's get you in the bath.' She helped her up off the chair. Dean attempted to help, but Marie was quick to assume control. 'I'll sort her out, you lot double-check the house is secure.'

Dean was more than a little relieved to be let off the hook on this one. He turned to the kitchen sink and splashed his face with water, attempting to remove the blood – at least it was his own.

'Are we completely fucked?' Stevie said as Dean dried his face with a handy t-towel.

'Probably,' Dean said calmly as he finished drying himself.

'What do we do next?' Jack asked.

Dean responded matter-of-factly, 'We wait,' and with that, he bounded upstairs to put on a new top.

Chapter 24

Billy barely slept. He kept going over the possibilities in his head; Ryan couldn't have been the driver of the van. But if not him, who was he in league with? His brother seemed unlikely. In fact, he hadn't met anyone over the last week that was capable of murder.

At 5am, he finally gave up trying to sleep and headed to the little galley kitchen to make some coffee. He could hear Johnny snoring heavily on the sofa. They'd stayed up until after midnight mulling over theories and ideas, managing to down a dozen beers in the process.

He put on the radio. The news had moved on from the double-murder in Kent, but something in the headlines triggered his memory of the Josephs. He thought of the horrible discovery in their house two days ago and he got a knot in his stomach. If the stalkers were capable of that, they were capable of doing anything to Dean.

He'd already made his mind up that he was going to France tomorrow, regardless of what the Byers were going to tell him later. He'd had a call and several texts from Dean at the beginning of the holiday, but nothing for four days and he wanted to see him in person; he certainly wasn't going to wait another week. He'd also have to deliver some very sad news to Graham about his parents' death.

He took his coffee and headed to the lounge, ignoring Johnny and sat down at the table to sift through the documents in case he'd missed something else. He picked up Ryan's diary and flicked through it again. He couldn't see anything that he'd missed. 'Damn it,' he said to himself and slammed the book shut.

He showered and changed into his usual jeans and T-shirt before Johnny stirred. He threw some bread in the toaster and shook Johnny from his slumber. 'Rise and shine, the Byers will be here within the hour.'

It took Johnny a few minutes to reappear from the bathroom, looking even more dishevelled than usual, his red eyes giving away his previous night's drinking. Billy chuckled when he saw the state of him. 'You need to lay off the beers.' Johnny just grunted and sat down at the table, grabbing some toast and shoving it in his mouth without bothering to butter it.

It was just before eight when the buzzer went. Billy nervously answered the intercom, thankfully it was the Byers, and he buzzed them in. It seemed like an age for them to arrive, eventually he heard footsteps down the corridor and poked his head out to see the slender Derek Byers and plump Caroline Byers coming cautiously down the corridor.

Billy invited them into the lounge, and they sat down as Johnny was despatched to make tea for everyone. The Byers sat together on the sofa, nervously holding hands as they waited for Billy to speak. He looked at them, they both appeared worse than him, which gave him some comfort.

'Mr and Mrs Byers, I hope now you realise I'm genuine and acting in the best interests of your daughter?' Billy started.

'Is Pippa OK?' Derek asked without answering the question.

'As far as I know.'

'As far as you know? And you want us to trust you?' Derek was sharp.

'Mr Byers. I spoke with Dean on Sunday and had a text on Monday, and he makes no mention of any issues, so I have no reason to suspect a problem.' Derek just nodded. 'However, I can't get hold of him and haven't heard anything from him in five days.' Billy paused before he turned to Caroline. 'Have you heard from Pippa?'

She answered without interval, 'She phoned when she arrived in Maidstone and then on Sunday after they got to France, but nothing since.'

There was a pause, gratefully broken when Johnny came in with the tea.

Billy took a sip of tea. 'OK, I assume we can all agree that something funny is going on with the kids and we need to work together to figure it out.'

'Who says there is something funny going on?' Derek barked again.

Billy's patience finally snapped. 'Look, if you want to carry on playing games, then you can both just take a running fucking jump out that window. If you weren't worried, you wouldn't have driven from Cambridge to West Hampstead to be here at eight in the morning.'

The Byers were both stunned by Billy's rant and a little embarrassed. He softened the tone slightly. 'I just want to make sure my nephew is safe, and in doing so, I should keep all the kids safe. To give me the best chance, I need to know everything. And I mean everything. If you can't give me that, then you're no good to me.' He paused and walked over to them before continuing, 'But know this, I will blame you both if you don't tell me what I need to know to save the kids... and then I'll kill you both.'

Derek shot up. 'Are you threatening us?'

Billy turned to look at him and moved his face to within an inch of Derek's. 'Yes!'

'Come on, Caroline, we're leaving,' he said bravely. He hadn't spotted that Johnny had blocked the lounge door with his large frame. Derek grabbed her hand and yanked her up off the sofa. 'Excuse me,' he requested hopefully to Johnny.

Johnny just shook his head.

Derek turned to Billy. 'Are you going to keep us hostage?'

'If I have to. What is so bad that you don't want to tell me, even though your only remaining child is in danger?'

Caroline looked at her husband. 'Derek, please!'

He looked at his wife, at the lines on her face and bags under her eyes. Then looked back at Billy. 'Is she really in danger?'

Billy just nodded.

The four of them sat down again, the tension disappeared, and Derek started talking. 'We love our children, Mr Marchant. Sometimes parents are blind to the shortcomings of their kids, but that's natural, isn't it?' Billy wasn't going to interrupt; he got the sense that Derek had a lot to say. He just nodded and let him continue.

'He was a brilliant boy; sporty, athletic, a great academic. He loved computers and always dreamed of a career in the IT field. We were so proud of him when he got the job in London.' Caroline was holding firmly onto her husband's hand.

'They always got on very well. She was five years younger than him, but he doted on her from the day she was born. We'd had a couple of miscarriages after Cameron and we thought it might not happen, but he was more thrilled than either of us when she was born.' Tears started slowly trickling down Caroline's face.

'They got on well and even when Cameron got older, he still spent a great deal of time with Pippa, however…' Derek took a deep breath, 'when he was about thirteen, I caught him being inappropriate with her.'

'Inappropriate?' Billy queried.

'Mr Marchant, I'm not going to go into details, but let's just say, it's not the sort of thing a brother and sister should be doing with each other.'

Billy was shocked but managed a small nod.

'Must have been horrifying,' Johnny interjected.

'We sorted it out. He went for counselling and we monitored things carefully for a good while afterwards. Eventually we got on with our lives and we never mentioned it again. We assumed that Pippa wouldn't remember much about it.' He paused and caught his breath.

'He went to uni down the road, but stayed in halls, and we were thrilled when he started seeing that girl.'

'Marie,' Caroline reminded him.

'Yes, Marie – but it didn't last long, and she ended up with one of his mates, which hurt him.'

Billy nodded. 'Did you know that she aborted his baby?'

The Byers looked at each other and shook heads. 'No, we didn't know that,' Derek responded, 'did Cameron know?'

'Yes, we think he did know,' Johnny added.

'That might explain it,' Caroline said to Derek.

'Explain what, Mrs Byers?' Billy interjected.

Derek picked up the conversation, 'you have to realise that, had we known what was going on, we'd have called the police this time.'

'What was going on, Mr Byers?'

'Well, it appears that the abuse started again after Cam went to uni – in the holidays and at weekends. She was fourteen, he was nineteen.'

'How did you find out?' Billy and Derek were almost in a private conversation between themselves with Caroline and Johnny looking on.

'It was Ryan.'

'Ryan?'

'I went to Switzerland after the avalanche. Everyone was blaming him for the argument that sent Cam on to the mountain. I went to see him, just me and him. He wasn't going to tell me, but I begged him to, forced him to.'

'And he told you about the abuse?'

'Ryan told me that before the skiing holiday, Pippa had broken up with him. She couldn't bear to be intimate with him because of the abuse.'

'Did he say how long the abuse had lasted?'

'It stopped when Cam moved to London, so lasted until she was sixteen, probably about two and a half years.'

'How did you feel?'

'Angry, devastated. I couldn't even look at him when I went to identify the body, I was so disgusted with what he'd done.'

'Did you tell Pippa you knew?'

'No. Ryan and I agreed that Pippa wouldn't know he'd told me.'

'And you didn't tell Caroline?'

He looked at his wife and shook his head. They were both crying by now. 'He told me all of it after your visit this week,' Caroline managed.

'I think you're both very brave to have told me this. Thank you,' Billy's voice was soft and caring. He seldom used this tone.

'I have a few more questions if you don't mind?' Billy continued. Derek nodded.

'Have you seen Ryan since Switzerland?'

'As it happens, he came to see me a few weeks ago,' Derek said.

'Why was that?'

'He said he wanted to know if Pippa was OK and how I was feeling.'

'Do you find that odd?'

'Not really. He's a really nice lad. We've known him for seven years, first as Cam's best mate from uni and then when he started seeing Pippa.'

'How did he seem to you?'

'He seemed OK actually. He'd moved on and mentioned he started seeing a new girl.'

'Really. Did he mention a name?'

'Yes, he did, now let me think, oh what was it? Ah, that's it, Lilith. I remember because it was the same as an old aunt.'

'Lilith. OK.' Billy nodded.

'Mr Marchant, for what it's worth, I think Ryan is a remarkable lad. He was harshly disowned by his friends and Pippa. He kept his dignity, he kept Pippa's secret, and he moved on with his life.'

Billy looked over at the table in the corner of the room, strewn with Ryan's paperwork and looked back at Derek. 'Yep, sounds like a nice lad. I'd like to meet him.'

Billy looked at Johnny and he knew what to do. 'Right, Mr and Mrs Byers, you've been a great help, but we need to make more enquiries. We'll be in touch when we know more.'

Derek was taken aback by the sudden ending of the interrogation. He stood up and shook hands with Billy. 'Please look after our daughter.'

'I'll do my very best, Mr Byers.'

Derek took Caroline's hand and held it firmly as they left the flat.

Before the door had even closed behind them, Johnny looked at Billy. 'Did you...?'

Billy was packing up his bag. 'Yes, I heard it. We need to go now. Got your passport?'

Johnny patted his jacket pocket.

'I'll phone Tanya from the car and get her to move the tunnel booking.'

'Well, we know who was in the van,' Johnny said as he grabbed his bag, 'we just don't know where they are now.'

'I've got a bloody good idea where they are – and it scares the shit out of me,' Billy said as he slammed the door behind him.

Chapter 25

By nine it was completely dark outside, still and calm. The rain of the previous nights was mercifully absent. A light wind created only the slightest rustling of the nearby trees.

Candles had recently been lit by the group as they sat together in the lounge. Pippa had re-joined them, not because she wanted the company, but only because she couldn't bear to be alone tonight. It had already been agreed that she would spend the night with Marie in her room, as Jack and Dean alternated the watch downstairs.

They'd also agreed on their final survival plan for tomorrow – should they make it through the night. They'd set off together in the morning for the nearest village. They all agreed it was the only way now that virtually all supplies had diminished, and they didn't have to worry about injured friends. Marie had put up a half-hearted appeal to remain behind in case Graham somehow found his way back to the house, but given the events at Madame Bernard's, no one expected that to happen anytime soon. In the end, Marie hadn't taken too much persuading to join them. They knew the risks; both previous attempts to reach the nearest settlement had resulted in casualties. However, they comforted themselves that if they all went together, perhaps some of them might make it to safety. It was the only plan they had – but they still had to get through the night.

Jack and Dean left for bed at 10 o'clock, leaving the girls and Stevie with candles burning. In the event, Dean couldn't get close to sleep and re-joined the group downstairs an hour earlier than planned, at 11. Shortly afterwards, Marie, Stevie and Pippa were des-patched to bed, on the instruction to make as much of a show of it as possible. Dean blew out the last of the candles and assumed a position in the dining room, in front of the bar. They'd all discussed and agreed the perfect position earlier, and this gave Dean a view of both the lounge (through the open door) and into the kitchen. Crucially though, it kept him out of view from a window.

He sat on a couple of threadbare orange cushions, with his back firmly leant against the bar. He had a carving knife in his hand, the rolling pin next to him on his left, and two more kitchen knives to his right. At the very least he hoped to create enough noise to spring a response from those upstairs.

Initially he'd worried about dozing off, but there was no fear of that. The nervous tension kept him alert, with every rustling of the trees in the wind causing his heart to beat ten times faster.

Never had time moved so slowly for him. By 1am he was numb from sitting on the floor for 90 minutes, despite the cushions, then the cramp in his left calf kicked in. He bit down hard on a cushion to stop himself from screaming out. After the pain subsided, he shuffled around, attempting to make as little noise as possible, but knocked the rolling pin, which made a thud as it hit a leg of the dining table. 'Damn it,' he said under his breath as he scurried across the floor to retrieve his weapon.

He returned to his place in front of the bar and did some stretches to try and ease the stiffening of his muscles. He hadn't allowed his mind to wander up until now, keeping hugely focused on the task in hand, but as he got comfy again, for the next phase of the stakeout, he started to contemplate their predicament.

He still couldn't fit all the pieces together. He was convinced Ryan had caused their recent misery, but the attempted murders were a bit of a stretch to believe possible from a former best friend. The van that came at him the day before the holiday was almost certainly the same one that tried to force Graham off the road. Then there was the car that had mowed Otis down. All three acts would definitely be seen as attempted murder. But equally, Ryan had two opportunities to finish him off: firstly, in the flat the day before the holiday and secondly, in the tent earlier. Both times he ended up being knocked out, but it would be stretch to call it attempted murder. But if it wasn't Ryan, who had done the more unforgivable acts? And if he hadn't been involved in the disappearance of the three missing members of the group, who was it? Dean had to admit to himself that he didn't 100% trust Jack. He'd never met him before, and he had beef with at least one member of the group. Could he be working with Ryan? Possible. But to what end?

He continued to throw up more theories in his head; what if Graham had somehow gotten involved in it? Upset about the discovery that his wife had previously aborted Cam's baby. Could his disappearance be staged? And what about Beth? He didn't know her as well as the others and her dad had a criminal record.

He cursed himself for getting carried away. Right now, he was focused on Ryan. This made him angry with his former friend. Why resort to this? To what purpose? Dean suspected there was something Pippa wasn't telling him, but he wasn't prepared to push her on it.

He thought about Cam again and his tragic death; he missed him. The group seemed to function well with the five of them in place, Graham as the organiser, Stevie as the sceptic, Dean as the pragmatist, Ryan as the intelligent one, Cam as the communicator. Dean thought about uni and how he'd probably only have got half the number of women he did if he hadn't got Cam as his wingman. Cam just had the confidence to go and chat to women, which always seemed to open the door for him and Ryan. More often than not, it would be Cam who didn't take a girl home, but he always seemed comfortable chatting with them, even if it didn't lead anywhere.

Dean had moved on to reminiscing about a particularly funny night after the Law Society Ball when the sound of a click interrupted him. He sat bolt upright, grabbed the rolling pin and re-confirmed his grip on the carving knife. Did he really hear it? Perhaps not. His heart started racing faster as he waited for another sound. Then came a creaking. He couldn't see a thing, but he daren't move and risk frightening him away. Where was it coming from? It sounded very close. The creak echoed through the silent room, like a door being opened, but the two doors in the dining room were already fully open. Then he saw it – a flicker of light. But where from? He scanned the room and finally spotted it was coming from under the dining table. How could that happen? Then he realised; it was a trapdoor – a bloody trap door under the table! How could they not have spotted it?

Dean's heart was pumping so fast, he feared his legs were going to give way as he quietly stood up. He had to wait for the right moment, to make absolute sure Ryan wasn't able to escape back through the floor, but equally, he needed to give himself the advantage. Ryan wasn't expecting anyone to be in the room. Even if he had the gun, surely the element of surprise was an advantage, wasn't it? He held his breath as the moment of truth started to approach. He heard a thud and took that to mean the trap door had now landed open on the wooden floor. Then he heard some shuffling, indicating Ryan was climbing up into the room. The torchlight thankfully focused on the wall to Dean's left but jolted around as the intruder made the ascent. Dean waited until he thought the intruder's torso was fully in the room and then in one swift move, he grabbed the nearest chair and swung it as hard as he could under the table, in the general direction of where the light was. He connected with something and then heard a pained 'argh' from the intruder. The torch rolled and hit the wall, rebounding back and offering enough light for Dean to see a figure on the floor. He didn't waste any time and turned the table on its side, creating a loud crash as the fruit bowl and several used glasses connected with the wooden floor.

Dean was angry as he charged over to the person on the floor. He jumped on him and then began repeatedly hitting him with the rolling pin. More cries of pain from the invader. Then, somehow the intruder managed to wriggle free and, with a spare arm, connected a punch on Dean's chin which sent him flying back into the upturned table. It took Dean a few seconds to realise what had happened, but before he was in a position to react, the shape was on top of him. He closed his eyes and waited for the hit to come. It didn't. Instead, he heard another bang and the intruder came crashing down next to him. Then Dean saw a figure above him.

'Alright?' Dean was relieved as he recognised Jack's voice.

'Quick, pass the belt,' Dean said as they both charged over to the face-down body before it could get back up. They jumped on him and managed to tie his hands together.

By the time they'd secured him, the rest of the group had appeared at the door and begun lighting candles.

'Who is it?' one of them asked.

'Maggie Thatcher,' Jack replied sarcastically. Dean chuckled but couldn't speak as he tried to regain his breath.

'Bring some light over here,' Jack said. Marie and Stevie came towards them tentatively. They placed candles on the seats of a couple dining chairs and the four of them stood over the figure. Pippa remained by the kitchen door.

'What did you hit him with?' Dean said as he regained his breath.

'The toaster,' came the reply from Jack.

'Ouch,' Stevie murmured.

Dean wiped some blood from his nose as Marie enquired after his health. Dean nodded confirmation he was OK. *It'll hurt like hell in the morning though*, he thought.

Dean looked at Jack. 'Shall we do this?' Jack nodded and the pair of them bent down and rolled him over. The final turn of the body seemed to take an age as they grappled with his tight T-shirt, each of them eagerly wanting to see who had been tormenting them.

Ryan landed with a small thud as they finished turning him onto his back. Dean and Jack shuffled backwards as they tried to focus on the body. Jack looked at Dean. 'Is it him?' Dean looked hard, not surprised, but still in shock as the face of his former friend looked back at him. His long jet-black hair was matted with the blood that covered his face, but he was recognisable to Dean, Stevie and Marie.

'Is it him?' Jack said again. Dean nodded, with Jack looking at the rest for confirmation.

'Yes,' the other three agreed. Pippa, who had maintained her distance from the group, struggled with confirmation that her ex-boyfriend was behind their misery. She started to feel faint and quickly backed out of the room and collapsed on a chair in the kitchen.

'Is he dead?' Marie asked.

'No. He's breathing,' Dean replied, almost disappointed.

The four of them decided to secure Ryan further, lifting him into a dining chair. They used the cord from a toaster and kettle to tie his ankles to the chair legs and then tied his torso to the chair with a bed sheet. Then they manoeuvred him away from the window, up against the opposite wall.

'He looks a lot different,' Marie said, as they stood back and examined their work.

'He's lost a lot of weight, he's really thin,' Dean said.

'And he hasn't had hair that long since our first year at uni,' Stevie added.

'The missing teeth and blood-splattered face don't help I'm sure,' Jack said to try and lighten the mood. Nobody laughed. Ryan's face had taken the full force of Dean's initial strike, leaving him with a broken nose and two badly chipped front teeth.

'Shall we get some water?' Marie said.

'Why?' Stevie questioned.

'Isn't that what they do in the movies when they want someone to wake up. Throw water in their face?' she replied.

'Do we want him to wake up?' Jack asked.

'Well, if it's all the same to you, I'd quite like to find out where my husband is,' Marie said, putting her own spin on sarcasm.

Without further discussion, Stevie shot out the room and filled a saucepan with cold water. He didn't pay any attention to Pippa slumped at the kitchen table as he returned and offered the pan to Jack, who passed it along to Dean. He looked up at everyone and paused. 'Ready?'

They all nodded agreement. 'Go,' he said, and threw the entire contents over Ryan's head.

He spluttered to life, struggling to adjust to the scene in front of him. The group gave him a few seconds to come around. In the meantime, Dean had picked up the carving knife and rested the point of the blade under Ryan's chin.

'You bastard!' Dean said as Ryan's eyes started to focus on him. Dean had moved close up to his face; he spotted the nose was broken and still dripping blood. There was at least one tooth missing and another damaged. He also had a large cut across his forehead.

'Where's Graham, you bastard?' Marie shouted.

Ryan was still struggling to come to terms with both the pain and his situation. He was unable to speak, not least because his mouth was full of blood.

'Anything to say?' Dean asked as he pressed the knife further into Ryan's flesh. Ryan flinched with pain and Dean released it slightly.

'Sorry,' he managed, but inaudible to any of them.

'What was that?' Dean barked and then pressed the knife into him again.

Ryan managed a slightly louder, 'Sorry,' this time and Dean released some pressure from the knife again.

'Sorry!' Marie shouted and moved forward, past Jack. 'Sorry! You utter scumbag. Sorry! Never mind about sorry, where's my husband, you bastard?' and with that Marie lost control and started hitting Ryan about the head. Dean moved the knife away as he let her vent her anger. He had absolutely no intention of trying to stop her. Eventually she relented on her own.

'I don't know what you mean,' he said and as he recovered from another battering, he spat some more blood out.

'Don't lie to us, Ryan,' Dean said, 'we know you're behind all this.'

'I am. I mean, it's true. I've been stalking you guys, but I haven't done anything to Graham.' He struggled as he spoke, Marie moved forward to hit him again, but Dean managed to stop her this time.

'Tell the truth!' she barked at him.

'I am. I admit that I've been a proper bastard, stalking you guys – mainly you, Dean, well, all of you really.' He spat blood out again. He asked for water but was universally refused and was ordered to carry on. He struggled to breathe but managed to continue, 'I admit it. Being cut off by you guys and dumped by Pippa. I felt like I had nothing left, so I made it my mission to make your lives a misery. I followed you, learnt your secrets and joined you down here to reveal it all.'

'So, I ask you again,' Marie interrupted, 'where's Graham?'

'I don't know. I mean, I haven't done anything to him. I swear. I just wanted to make your lives a misery and ruin your holiday.'

Marie was getting angry again. 'Oh, for God's sake, let me at him and I'll make him tell us.'

Stevie and Jack held her back as Dean pulled a chair over, placed it in front of Ryan and sat down. He retained hold of the carving knife, but toyed with it in his hand, rather than thrust it under his chin again.

'I could let her at you. It's very tempting,' Dean said, calmly, 'I need you to give me a reason to believe you.'

Ryan tipped his head back as if to think but struggled with the blood in his mouth and had to bring his head forward to cough it up.

'For crying out loud, at least treat him like a human being,' Pippa said as she appeared from the kitchen and thrust a glass of water at Dean. The forcefulness in her voice stunned the group temporarily, and Dean obligingly took the water without thinking.

Ryan looked at his ex-girlfriend. 'Pippa,' he was almost shocked to see her.

'Was it going to be my turn tonight, Ryan?' Pippa barked at him, but he just shook his head. 'I don't believe you. You were going to come here tonight and ruin me, weren't you?'

He was as shocked as everyone by her outburst. 'No, no, I would never do that to you. I swear.'

'Who were you coming for tonight, Ryan? Who was to be the latest victim?'

'It was Otis's night,' he replied sheepishly.

'You really are a piece of work, Ryan!' Pippa yelled and she stormed back into the kitchen as she said it.

Dean looked at Marie and realised she needed answers on Graham; otherwise, she may well kill Ryan.

'OK, Ryan, enough with the bullshit, we need some answers now,' Dean said this as he dripped some water into Ryan's mouth. Good cop time, he thought. Marie, who was now holding the rolling pin, was definitely bad cop.

Ryan enjoyed the water and tried to compose himself. He wrestled with his arms and realised for the first time that he was going nowhere. He shook his frame and adjusted his arms as much as he could, getting as comfortable as possible. 'Alright, look, I'll tell you everything, but then will you at least loosen my arms?'

'That depends on whether we believe you,' Dean said sternly. He had to hold back a potential protest from Marie with this offer but managed it like a true diplomat.

Ryan nodded, paused briefly and then began, 'So, I hit a low point about a month after Cam died and you guys cut me off.' Dean and Stevie looked a little sheepish, but Marie's stare didn't break. 'I thought about suicide, almost did it, but someone intervened. An angel, almost at the critical moment, stopped me from jumping.'

Dean and Stevie looked at each other as the story unfolded. 'Anyway, she talked me down and she helped me recover, she was a trained counsellor. She told me that I had to move on with my life, but sometimes, in

order to move on, you have to put the past to rest first.'
He paused briefly. 'And that's when it hit me; the way
I could move on was to make you guys feel as low as
I did.'

Stevie interjected, 'Great advice from the counsellor;
where did she train, North Korea?'

'It wasn't Lilith's fault. I think I took her advice a bit
too literally.'

'Did you shag her?' Jack asked without thinking.

'No!' Ryan protested, 'but we did become close
friends over the next few months.'

'So, she helped you?' Dean shot back.

'No. I didn't tell her exactly what I was doing. She
helped me out here or there, but only because she
thought I was trying to make peace with you guys.'

'Where is she now?' Stevie asked.

'She found out I was planning on coming down here
to see you guys. She told me that if I did come down,
she wouldn't be able to see me again.'

'So, she dumped you,' Stevie said.

'Guess so,' Ryan replied regretfully.

There was a pause before Dean broke the silence, 'I
think we're getting a little off-topic,' he could sense
Marie's impatience. 'You didn't jump, this counsellor
saved your life and you decided to get even,' he said,
forcefully.

'Yes. So, I started with you, Dean. Sorry. I broke into
your flat a couple of times, found out some info on you
– enough for me to ask questions of Claire's family in
Birmingham. I made sure her brother found out about
the cheques.'

Dean didn't say anything but nodded, indicating
Ryan should continue.

'I broke into Graham and Marie's to see if they had any secrets I could use. Cam had hinted heavily about the situation you were in when we were at uni, although he never actually came out and said it. But it gave me enough to know what I was looking for.'

Marie didn't speak, just kept her eyes fixed on his face.

'We all knew about Stevie, so I didn't even have to bother searching through his flat.' He paused again to catch his breath; he was in full flow now but still struggled with the blood in his mouth. 'I watched Otis for a bit and was able to get the low-down on his girlfriend.'

Stevie was intrigued. 'We don't know about that yet,' he said, almost wanting the gossip.

'And we don't need to know about it,' Jack added quickly, wanting to keep Otis's secret.

Ryan decided not to expand on the Otis story but moved his attention to Jack. 'I sought him out,' Ryan said, clearly nodding in the direction of Jack, who looked confused and ready to deny everything. 'You don't recognise me, do you?'

Jack shook his head.

'I guess you guys must have bashed me about good and proper. How many teeth have I lost?'

'One and one's chipped,' Dean said, almost gleefully.

'You're the guy in the pub!' Jack shouted as he finally recognised the face. Dean and Stevie looked suitably confused.

Jack turned to explain. 'This is the guy that told me about Beth and how her family were living off my dad's profits. He gave me her name and everything.'

Ryan chuckled a little. 'I never dreamt you'd end up moving offices, befriending Graham and coming all the way down here. I have to admit it, I was impressed.'

It was all Marie could take, and she snapped, racing forward she caught Ryan plum on the left eye with the rolling pin with the first hit, which knocked his chair over and then clobbered him a couple of other times on the arm. Eventually, Jack and Dean managed to restrain her before despatching her to the kitchen with Pippa.

The boys stood Ryan back up. 'This situation is not funny, Ryan. I swear to God, if you don't start making sense, I'm going to let her at you with this knife.' Dean was trying to get control back.

'I realise that,' Ryan said sombrely, before continuing, 'I knew you guys were going on holiday, so I did a couple of stupid things that day,' he paused, almost unable to admit it.

'Go on,' Dean encouraged.

'Well, firstly, I knew you'd be taking Stevie's dad's car, so I put the wrong fuel in the tank. And then, I needed the address of the place you were staying down here, so I broke into Dean's house, but—'

'I came back early, and you smacked me on the back of the head,' Dean interjected.

'Yes,' Ryan said, looking ashamed as Pippa came back into the room.

'Did you try to force us off the road?' she asked calmly while standing three paces back from the boys, who were all now sitting down on chairs in front of Ryan.

'No. Of course not. I wouldn't hurt you.'

'And we're supposed to believe that?' Stevie said.

'I think we're going to have to,' Dean said, sounding disappointed.

'Why?' Stevie asked, surprised.

'Because, when I was getting smacked over the head with a light fitting, Graham's car was being driven off the road in Cambridgeshire.'

Stevie and Marie, who had returned from the kitchen, looked disappointed. Pippa perked up and move forward towards the boys, almost excited now. 'That's right! It couldn't have been Ryan.' Dean looked at her, he had a sinking feeling in his stomach. Pippa appeared very keen for Ryan to be proved innocent – innocent of the bigger crimes at least.

Dean paused for a few seconds as he tried to recover his thought process. 'I'm also assuming, Jack, that this is not the person who knocked you out earlier?'

Another light-bulb moment for Jack. 'That's right. I'd recognise the face, and it definitely wasn't him.'

Marie interjected, 'And we should take your word for it, Jack? A minute ago, you didn't even recognise that he was the one who led you to Beth.'

Dean nodded and turned back to Ryan. 'Let's get one thing clear, you are not innocent. You may not have done some of the terrible things we've been subjected to this holiday, but you are certainly not innocent.' He focused his gaze on Pippa as he said it, desperate to get her to realise how bad Ryan was.

He nodded. 'I realise that – but give me a chance and I'll make it right.' Dean looked at him, his former friend, and wished he didn't believe him.

Stevie pushed past Dean to stand in front of Ryan. 'Did you slash the tyres of the cars?' he pointed as he shouted at him. Ryan nodded.

'Did you run over Otis, even if it was an accident, in your car?' Dean asked.

'No!' Ryan shot back impulsively. 'I haven't even got a car. I came down on a moped.'

'Well, that's something,' Dean said, 'at least we can get word to a village tomorrow.'

Ryan shook his head. 'Afraid not. It got nicked a couple of days ago.'

'Very convenient,' Marie said, and stormed back to the kitchen; even she seemed to be reluctantly accepting Ryan wasn't responsible for Graham's fate.

'What about the gun?' Dean asked.

'Oh, I didn't bring that to France, I wouldn't have dared trying to get it through customs.'

'What about the one you took yesterday?'

'How many guns you got, Deano?'

Dean shot him a look, which suggested he'd better not be flippant.

'I didn't know you had another gun.'

'You took it yesterday. We were searching the area and we stumbled upon your tent, about ten minutes south of here. I know it was your tent because we used to go fishing in it.' Dean was getting agitated.

'Yes, it sounds like you found my tent.'

'I went in and then you hit me on the head again and took the gun.'

'That wasn't me. But it was weird, though, because I couldn't find my tent when I got back to it yesterday, I thought I'd gone mad because it wasn't quite where I thought I'd pitched it.'

'This is simply not believable,' Stevie said.

'I moved the tent every day, so as not to get caught. I just assumed I'd not remembered the right place,' Ryan replied.

285

This didn't make sense to Dean. He could fathom that Ryan wouldn't want to kill him, but why would the van driver, who clearly wanted him and the others dead, not kill him if he had the chance?

'Look, guys,' Ryan spoke, 'I know it doesn't look good for me and I have done some terrible things, but it looks like we're all in a lot of trouble here. If anyone is going to get out of this, we're going to have to work together.'

'What do you think, guys?' Dean said to the others in the room.

'Well, we know he didn't kidnap Beth and Otis. He wasn't the one that ran Graham off the road—'

Stevie was in full swing when Marie jumped in 'But he was the one that tormented us, stole from us, vandalised our house and car and left us without any means to get away from this hell.'

'All true, but what's important is that we do what's best to get the six of us out of here alive.' Then he looked at Marie as he continued, 'And then come back with support to find the others – including Graham.'

Marie was clearly unhappy. 'You guys are all crazy, we'll wake up dead tomorrow, mark my words.' She marched out as she finished and went to bed.

Dean and Jack turned the chair around slightly, allowing them to undo the belt and sheet that was keeping Ryan in place. As his arms were released, he stretched them out and rubbed his wrists, which were marked from the restraints.

He stood up and started checking his mouth with his fingers. 'Bloody hell, you made a right mess of my teeth.' No one responded or offered any apology.

Ryan walked over to Pippa, but as he reached her, he couldn't think of anything to say. In the end, Pippa spoke first, 'Does it hurt?' as she moved a tissue towards his mouth. He flinched backwards to avoid the nerves being touched.

'Leave it. I'll be alright.' There was another awkward pause. 'It's nice to see you again,' Ryan said as they stood opposite each other, close enough for him to touch her arm. Dean could see there was chemistry between them but didn't want to believe she could fall back in love with him after everything.

'Right, Ryan, we need to let you in on the plan for tomorrow,' Dean interrupted. Pippa seemed reluctant to leave but slipped off to bed at Dean's insistence, while the boys moved through to the kitchen to go over the strategy for the morning. Ryan wasn't fully on board with Dean's plan but had no sway over the group and certainly wasn't going to start throwing his weight around yet.

Dean checked his watch. 'Jesus, it's nearly three-thirty. I think we'd all better try and get some sleep.' He looked at Ryan. 'On the basis we don't fully trust you yet, I think you'd better pull a mattress into my room. We've got a long walk ahead of us tomorrow.'

And with that, he virtually manhandled Ryan out of the door and up the stairs.

CHAPTER 26

It was a glorious morning. The sunlight seeped through the shutters and eventually caused Dean to stir. He'd finally made it to bed at four o'clock and taken until five to drop off. As he woke, it took him a few seconds to remember the events of yesterday. He bolted upright and looked down towards the mattress on the floor: Empty. He shot up, wearing only boxer shorts and charged to the door.

He immediately feared the worst; did he make a mistake in trusting Ryan? He cautiously crept along the dark, dusty landing. And then he heard voices coming from downstairs.

There was no screaming or shouting, which was a relief, and he started to relax. He went back into his room and threw on a T-shirt and shorts before making his way downstairs.

'Hello, sleepyhead,' Jack said as Dean emerged into the kitchen.

Jack and Stevie were at the kitchen table drinking black coffee. Dean could hear voices in the dining room, and he walked over to investigate. Ryan and Pippa were sat at the large table, deep in conversation. He thought about disturbing them – he wanted to disturb them but decided against it and turned back into the kitchen.

'What time is it?' he said, still distracted by the scene in the dining room.

'Oh, nearly nine,' Stevie said.

'What? Bloody hell, we should be on the move by now.'

'Take it easy, fella,' Jack said, 'we figured you needed the sleep. Anyway, we expect the walk will take about four hours; that gives us plenty of time.' Dean was annoyed, but more at the sight of Ryan and Pippa talking than the lateness of the start.

'We'd better get going soon. Where's Marie?'

'Getting ready,' came a reply from the dining room.

Dean raised his voice and moved to a position between the kitchen and dining room, to ensure he was heard by Pippa. 'OK, guys, we need to be ready to go in fifteen minutes.'

'I'm going to get ready. Jack, can you sort the water bottles out. Remember, we're taking the bare minimum with us.'

He stopped, expecting some response, but the other four just sat staring at him for what seemed like an eternity.

'OK, boss,' Ryan said, breaking the silence.

'I'll get on with the water,' replied Jack, and with that Dean's authority was restored. He left the others to it and headed up to finish getting ready.

He desperately wanted to know what Pippa and Ryan were discussing and could hardly think of anything else as he splashed some water on his face and brushed his teeth. Dean hadn't expected to fall for Pippa; to him she'd always been Cam's younger sister, but having become smitten with her, he was terrified of losing her.

They were all assembled in the kitchen by the time Dean returned. Ryan, Jack and Dean were wearing shorts, t-shirts and trainers. As ever, Stevie was sticking with jeans. Pippa had opted for three-quarter length trousers, and Marie was sporting a crop top and shorts.

There were six rucksacks lined up by the door. 'Water and the rest of the cooked pasta in each bag,' Jack said.

Along the worktop, six weapons were laid out: the trusty carving knife, the rolling pin and an assortment of vegetable knives.

'I've got the map,' Ryan said, sporting a severely bruised face and a large gap in his teeth. 'If we're heading north, this is where I pitched the tent last night, so we can drop in and pick up some snacks. Not a lot, but better than the cold pasta.'

'That's great,' Pippa said. Her enthusiasm cut into Dean's stomach. He wanted her to hate Ryan for what he'd done to them.

'I found these,' Jack announced, 'they were among Otis's things.' Jack placed two walkie-talkies on the table. 'They may come in,' he said, obviously proud of his resourcefulness.

'Let's go,' Dean declared and one by one they each filed out onto the veranda, picking up a rucksack and a weapon as they left. Stevie was last out, he had the key in hand and instinctively went to lock it, but having thought about it, decided to drop the key into a nearby plant pot.

As they descended the stone steps and walked onto the drive, all of the group looked back at the house that had held them captive for the last week. They all hoped it would be the last time they'd see it.

It was nearly nine thirty by the time they set off. The temperature had already reached 24 degrees Celsius, with the July sun beating down on them. Ryan led the way with map in hand and Pippa to the side of him. Dean opted to follow-up the rear, doing his best to encourage the out-of-shape Stevie to make firm progress. The most important thing was to stick together, which meant it was vital no one twisted an ankle, or worse, on the uneven ground.

They followed the dirt track at a solid pace, the same route that Dean, Jack and Graham had taken a few days earlier. They were surrounded by trees on both sides, which had the advantage of keeping the worst of the sun off them, although they were all twitchy – concerned at who or what might jump out at them.

The trees, a combination of firs and oaks, stood deadly still as they passed them, no inkling of a breeze on this scorching day. They discussed the route and knew they'd have to tackle the road, which had claimed Otis earlier in the week. All of them knew the risks but had accepted them. Working out the estimated timings; they figured about 40 minutes to Ryan's tent and 90 minutes to the intersection with the concrete road and then up to a further three hours for the nearest village.

They walked for nearly 30 minutes when Stevie started to fall a couple of paces behind the others. 'You alright, Stevie?' Dean asked.

He nodded with a grimace. 'A little out of shape, but I'll be fine.'

Dean shouted to the front of the group, still led by Ryan, to slow down, and after a few mumblings, they allowed Stevie to catch up.

Dean scolded Ryan and reminded the group they needed to stay together. 'We'll have a rest when we get to the tent,' Dean said.

'Why'd you pitch the tent so far away from the house?' Jack asked.

'I figured you guys were on to me,' Ryan said, 'I thought someone had been in my tent yesterday, but I had no idea they'd actually moved it.'

Marie looked at Dean but didn't say anything. She still didn't trust Ryan and, to be honest, Dean didn't completely trust him either. He knew Marie was letting him know of her distrust, although neither spoke.

As the trees cleared on both sides to reveal lush green pasture, Ryan stopped. 'It's definitely around here somewhere,' he declared.

He pulled off the track, to the left, and walked a couple of hundred feet. Still visible to the rest of the group from where they remained on the road.

'He could be leading us into a trap,' Stevie said quietly, as the five watched Ryan wandering in the distance.

'Don't be ridiculous,' Pippa shot back, 'if he'd wanted to kill us, he had plenty of chances last night,' she continued.

The others looked at each other and then focused on Dean. His heart sank. He knew for certain from that passionate defence that he was losing her back to Ryan. He moved himself a few metres away from the others to avoid their glares, pretending he was keeping an eye on Ryan. At that moment he decided he wouldn't fight it. If Pippa wanted Ryan, he wouldn't stop her.

The silence among the remaining five standing on the road was awkward. Pippa edged herself away from the others, still with an eye on Ryan in the distance, and stood by Dean. He pretended not to notice her arrival, keeping his face fixed on Ryan, without really focusing on him.

They stood for a minute before she spoke, 'I think we need to talk.'

Dean looked at her and smiled politely. 'It's not the right time. Don't worry about anything. Let's get through this and then we'll talk. It's really alright,' and he put his arm around her shoulders, briefly, and kissed her on the cheek. Enough to give her comfort, but sufficiently dismissive to make her realise he knew the score.

Ryan started walking back to them. 'Sorry, guys, I've got it wrong, it must be the next clearing.' There were some moans among the group, but they all gathered the bags and weapons again and followed Ryan.

As if to make a point, Pippa deliberately held back from Ryan this time and folded in with Stevie, who quickly returned to the back of the group.

The landscape returned to woodland on both sides of the track, all of them thankful of the shade the trees offered again. It was 10:15, and the spell out in the open had made them all heat up considerably.

They reached another clearing within 10 minutes, and Ryan confidently declared that this must be the place. The clearing was much smaller than the last one, probably only 50 metres before the trees returned. 'I'll take a look, wait here,' he said and signalled them to stand still.

Stevie waited for Ryan to get out of earshot before commenting, 'Looks like you've lost your job as captain, Dean.'

Dean forced a chuckle. 'Hey, I'm not interested in it. If he wants to lead us, then good luck to him. So long as we get out of here alive.'

He had to admit to himself that he was annoyed someone else was taking over, both in his command of

293

the group and with his girl. He felt like a defeated lion, losing his pride, but kept alive to endure the embarrassment of failure.

Ryan turned around suddenly and started running back to the group. 'Have you found it?' Pippa shouted.

He was too out of breath to answer immediately as he returned. He bent forwards to recover but shook his head to indicate he hadn't found the tent.

'I've seen a...' he gasped for breath '... a building. There's a building over there. Well, more of an out-house.' He sat down.

The rest looked at each other, with Dean speaking first, 'We should take a look,' he said firmly.

'No way,' Pippa said, 'we're not investigating strange buildings. We said we were heading straight to the nearest village.'

'We've not seen any buildings around here at all, so far. It could be where they're holding Graham and Beth.'

Marie, who had said virtually nothing all day, in protest at the inclusion of Ryan in their group, found herself agreeing with Dean. This caused some anxious murmurings from Stevie and Jack.

'Let's at least all walk over there and decide what to do when we see it,' Dean compromised.

They all agreed and followed Dean, trudging across the field. The rain of the last few days had made it muddy in places and they struggled to get across as they hit some soggy patches.

Dean saw it first, as they passed a row of trees.

The building looked like a barn; made of stone, one storey high plus a tatty pitched roof. There were gaps where windows may once have been, but not in a very long time. The building was no more than ten metres long and five wide. From where Dean stood, he couldn't see a door.

All six of them stood for a few seconds looking at the building.

'Pass me the walkie-talkies,' Dean said to Jack, who obliged without comment. Dean messed with them briefly and got them both working.

He handed one to Pippa. 'Wait here with this and I'll go and take a look.'

'No way,' she shouted back at him, and for a minute he got a buzz – she was worried about him. In part, that's why he'd suggested it.

'We said we'd all stick together,' Stevie argued.

'I'll go with him,' Ryan said.

Marie reacted first, 'No, don't do it, Dean. He can't be trusted.'

Dean looked at Marie, Ryan and then Pippa. 'I'm going in with Ryan. If Ryan comes out and I don't, you know he's the killer.' He looked back at Ryan and smiled before he continued, 'Then you'll have to kill him to save yourselves.' Stevie and Jack laughed at the humour. At least they hoped it was humour.

Dean gulped some water down and passed it to Ryan. He took a sip but grimaced as the water seeped through the gap in his teeth. Dean hid a smile and had little sympathy for his former friend.

After taking in refreshment, Dean summoned Ryan and they slowly headed towards the building. The others were about 20 metres back from it.

'Testing, testing, over,' Dean said into the walkie-talkie. Pippa was surprised and fumbled it as she tried to respond, dropping it on to the floor.

'Testing, testing, over,' Dean said again as Pippa battled to pick it up.

Finally, she responded, 'Er, what do I say?'

'Received, over,' Dean said. By now they'd reached the nearside wall – no immediate sign of a door.

The building was surrounded by forest on three sides, with only the side visible to the others facing onto pasture.

Dean, holding the carving knife, motioned to Ryan and they slowly moved around the building clockwise. Dean patted the wall, it was solid enough, although the stone exterior was covered in moss.

Dean turned the corner first, followed closely by Ryan, who was holding the rolling pin as his weapon of choice. Still no door, although above them was a small opening in the wall, nothing more than 20 centimetres wide and slightly above head height.

'Fancy a go at getting in there?' Dean whispered.

'I've got more chance than you,' Ryan responded. Neither of the men were fat. Ryan was now extremely thin, probably about ten stone and six-foot tall. Dean was slightly taller and with a strong frame, not particularly muscly, but in reasonable shape.

They cautiously turned the next corner, but still nothing. 'Perhaps there's a secret button to press,' Ryan joked.

'Fourth time's the charm,' Dean said as they turned the final corner to reveal the entrance to the building.

There was a hole in the wall, the shape of a door, but no sign of a door or even the doorframe. There was another of the small holes above the door. They both peered through the gap in the wall; it was a mess of chopped wood, damp hay and a few old rags. The floor space was about five metres squared. It looked like a mezzanine had once hung from the walls, but it had collapsed and now sat at 45 degrees, creating a triangle between the floor and the one remaining wall it clung to.

'Shall we risk it?' Ryan said.

'In for a penny,' Dean responded, and they both took their first tentative steps inside.

The other four stood nervously, looking at the building.

'I said all along this was a mistake,' Marie muttered, in-between taking chunks out of her fingernails.

'I'll check in with them,' Pippa said, 'Everything OK? Over.'

There was an anxious wait as the seconds passed. Pippa was about to ask again when the walkie-talkie crackled into life, 'All OK, just going in. Over,' came the response from Dean.

'OK, take care,' Pippa said, before remembering she was supposed to say over and adding it late.

Stevie tutted and moved away. 'We're wasting precious time; we need to be getting to the village.' He wandered about 15 metres away from the others as he moaned about the pause. The others took little notice, they were very used to Stevie's outbursts.

He continued to walk slowly, meandering, through the open pasture until he was about 50 metres from the others. He looked back and realised he'd left himself further from the others than he'd wanted.

At that moment he saw something in the distance. It was north of where he was and slightly further away from the track.

'There it bloody is, the dope,' he said out loud, but not loud enough for the others to hear from the distance.

He could see some blue coloured material about 200 metres away. He shouted to the other three, but they couldn't quite hear what he was saying, so Pippa moved to close the gap and Stevie did likewise. They were about 20 metres apart by the time she could decipher what he was saying, 'I can see his bloody tent from here.'

'Are you sure?'

'Well, in the middle of the green forest and green field, I'm guessing the blue bit of plastic over there is his tent.'

'OK, wait for Ryan to come back and we'll all head over together.'

'We're wasting time, I'll go and get it and come back,' Stevie said impatiently and marched off before he could hear the response from Pippa.

Jack came over to join Pippa and she explained the conversation she'd just had with Stevie.

'You'd better radio to Dean and tell him,' Jack suggested.

She complied, putting the walkie-talkie to her mouth and pressing the button.

Dean and Ryan had reached the far end of the building and found no evidence of anyone having been inside for a very long time. 'Dean, come in. Over.' He stepped over a rotten piece of wood before answering.

'Yes,' he replied sharply.

'Stevie has found Ryan's tent. He's just gone to get it,' Pippa said.

'OK, we're coming out now. There's nothing in here to worry about,' Dean replied.

Dean moved to step over part of the mezzanine but tripped and put his foot through the rotten wooden frame. 'Damn it,' he shouted and dropped the radio.

Ryan picked it up and spoke into it with an American accent as if mimicking a spaceman. 'Just waiting for Dean to relieve himself,' he joked.

'What?' came the reply from Pippa.

He laughed as Dean struggled to get his foot out. 'I could help you,' he said, 'but that wouldn't be as amusing.'

Ryan sat down on a log and toyed with the radio again. 'Still waiting for Dean,' he said.

'Hurry up,' came the response from Pippa.

'Anyway, I'm a bit gutted that Stevie managed to find my tent before me. He's not renowned as the most observant.'

'Even he can see a blue tent in the middle of a green field,' Pippa joked back.

Ryan paused. Dean looked up. They both realised at the same time.

'Pippa, did you say blue?' Ryan said, as Dean finally freed himself.

'Yes, he saw something blue in the distance.'

Dean's stomach churned; Ryan was already heading out the door.

'Pippa, my tent is red. Do you read me? MY TENT IS RED!' he was shouting.

Pippa took a few seconds to compute the information, but by the time she turned to Jack, he was already charging across the field in the direction of Stevie.

Marie, who still stood almost equidistant between the outbuilding and Pippa, was stunned as she saw Dean come bounding around the corner and towards Pippa. 'What is it?' she cried, but Dean ignored her as he charged past.

Ryan followed, also ignoring her as he sprinted towards Stevie. Dean reached Pippa, who was crying by now. 'Which direction did they go?' he shouted, slightly out of breath.

Pippa pointed in the general direction that Stevie and Jack had gone. Ryan caught up with Dean, and they both ran together in the direction of the tent.

'I can see it!' Dean said and continued at pace towards it. As they approached the tent, they both slowed. Dean moved his knife in front of him and started walking. They could see neither Stevie nor Jack from the direction they'd approached the tent.

Dean stayed a few metres away from the tent but started gradually to move around it.

Then he saw it, a pair of shoes.

He continued to move slowly around; his heart moved faster as he saw the shoes were connected to a pair of ankles.

He moved further and could see the legs, and then the torso; it was Stevie. He ran the few metres remaining to see him in full.

He let out an involuntary scream, 'No!' as he finally saw the full scene. Stevie was lying flat on his back, blood pouring from his neck. His throat had been slit.

He didn't even notice Jack at first, but he was kneeling over Stevie and looked up at Dean as he approached. 'He's dead!' Jack said coldly.

Dean dropped beside Stevie and grabbed his hand to check for a pulse. Tears started rolling down his face.

As Ryan arrived at the scene, he froze, watching as Dean's tears flowed faster and his cries got louder.

Then came the most spine-tingling, horrific scream of all. Marie had arrived beside Ryan and let out a sound that Dean would never forget. The scream was full of horror, driven by both the sight of a friend slain before them, but the realisation of the fate that had more than likely afflicted her husband.

Without thinking, Ryan put his arm around Marie as she stood next to him, and for a few seconds, she allowed Ryan to comfort her. Jack stood up and looked at himself, he was covered in Stevie's blood. This caused Marie to remember herself, she shrugged away Ryan's arm in disgust and moved a couple of paces towards Jack.

'You!' she shouted, as she pointed at him, 'you did this!'

Jack looked too shell-shocked to put up an argument.

Marie turned to Dean. 'He was with Graham when he went missing. He was with Beth and Otis when they went missing, and now he's first at the scene when Stevie is killed!'

Dean was stunned by the accusation and said nothing, instead he put his arms out towards Marie in an attempt to provide comfort. She wasn't in the mood for it; she moved closer to Jack and screamed in his face again, 'Where's Graham? What did you do with him?'

'I, I, I don't know. I'm sorry, I don't know,' and with that he collapsed on his knees again and sobbed some more.

'He did it, Dean, I know he did.' Marie's anger turned to fear and finally to tears and this time she allowed Dean to comfort her. They hugged. As Dean embraced Marie, he looked over her shoulder, towards Ryan and then down at a crying Jack. Panic hit him.

'Where's Pippa?' he shouted and broke the embrace with Marie.

Ryan turned 360 degrees as he instinctively looked to find her.

'Oh my God,' Marie exclaimed. Jack jumped up, and between the four of them, they started scouring the nearby area. 'Pippa! Pippa!' was shouted by each of them as they moved in small circles looking for her.

Jack came to his senses earlier than the others. 'Stop!' he shouted and motioned to the others, 'we must stay together.' But Ryan and Dean were both distraught at the thought of losing Pippa. They continued roaming the area, calling her name.

Jack moved in closer to Marie. 'Speak to them, Marie. Stop them or we'll all be picked off.' She looked at Jack and grabbed his hand, pulling him with her as she followed the rough path back to the outbuilding Dean and Ryan were heading for.

'Dean, for God's sake, STOP!' she screamed. A different tone to the horrified scream a few minutes earlier, but sufficient to get his attention.

Dean stopped and looked at her and Jack coming towards him.

'Dean, we must stay together,' she said more calmly.

Something clicked inside Dean's head and reality set in. He turned back to Ryan, who was now approaching the outbuilding again.

'Ryan. Stop!' he yelled. But he was ignored.

'Bastard,' Dean said under his breath and summoned all his strength to run the 20 or so metres to catch Ryan.

Ryan was looking away from Dean towards the building when the hit took his legs away from him. He planted his face in the mud as he came crashing to the ground and was winded in the process.

It took him a few moments to realise he's been rugby tackled by his love-rival. Ryan wriggled, but Dean pinned him to the ground as Marie and Jack caught up with them.

'Get off me, you lunatic,' Ryan shouted as he continued to fight against Dean, but he was far bigger and stronger and eventually Ryan relented.

Marie bent down to him. 'We have to stay together, whatever happens now. We're getting picked off every time we split.'

'But she's gone,' Ryan said, and his voice cracked.

Dean rolled off Ryan and sat on the grass with his head between his legs as he caught his breath. Ryan sat up, and Marie put her arm around him as she sat down. 'I know we'll find her.'

Jack joined them on the floor, and for a few minutes the remaining four of them sat quietly.

CHAPTER 27

The clear blue skies were gradually being replaced with patches of grey clouds, and the cover of the trees added to the fading light, despite it only being 11.

While they were having a breather, Dean had formed a plan of action in his head, but he knew it wouldn't be popular with at least half the group.

He raised his head and spoke calmly and clearly, 'We have to keep moving, keep going to the village.'

Marie and Ryan looked at him in horror, but he spoke again before they could argue, 'We've got to make some more progress before the weather turns completely, it's another three to four hours on foot. We have to keep going as planned.'

Marie was mortified. 'What about Graham? Or Pippa,' she looked at Ryan as she said this, hoping for support, 'do we just abandon them?'

'No, but we can't help them if we can't help ourselves,' Dean agreed.

'Not good enough, we don't leave them behind,' Marie barked.

Dean grabbed the map that had fallen out of Ryan's pocket and threw it at Marie. 'Okay, tell me where they are and we'll go and get them,' he said sharply.

Marie was temporarily muted. She picked up the map but didn't know what to do with it. She looked at Ryan for comfort, but he could only shrug his shoulders.

'It's the only way,' Jack said.

'But,' Marie tried to argue but failed to put any words together.

Ryan finally offered verbal support to Dean's plan. 'As soon as we get to the village, we can get the police swarming around here,' he said, with little conviction in his voice.

Marie looked at all three men in turn and realised she'd lost.

Having got everyone on board, Dean offered more details to his plan. They would go back to the blue tent and search it for clues and then head back onto the road. This time, nothing would distract them. Nothing. They'd stick to the road and get to the village as quickly as possible. They'd managed only two of the twelve miles so far and spent over two hours in the process. The next ten had to be quicker.

Dean got up first, followed by Jack. They picked up their rucksacks, looking sadly at the two they left behind. Sentiment had to take a hike, they needed to travel light for the rest of the journey.

As they reached the tent, Dean picked up his carving knife from where he dropped it beside Stevie's body. Each of them struggled to see him again, but no one was leaving Dean's side as he collected their weapons. He dished them back out to the group and moved to the front of the tent. The tent was open, and he was easily able to confirm that no one was in it. He crawled in, but it was completely empty. 'Nothing,' he declared, and he returned to join the other three standing guard outside.

The four of them walked with purpose back along the field and re-joined the track just as the rain started. None of them flinched as the rain kept coming, slowly at first, then faster and faster still. They were all covered in mud and beyond caring what they looked like. The only thing they had to worry about now was survival.

The track continued into a heavily wooded section. They walked in pairs, with Dean and Marie at the front and Ryan and Jack behind. All four of them held their weapons firmly as they marched.

The next mile passed with relative ease and with no further incident, although the rain had persisted. Each of them was soaking wet, but still no one complained.

They reached a tree, which had fallen across the track. 'This is where we got caught last time,' Jack said. 'I twisted my ankle, jumping to avoid this,' he continued.

Dean suggested they all had a five-minute break and used the tree as a makeshift bench.

Despite being wet, they all reached into their bags and gulped back some water. Dean looked at his watch. 'It's nearly one, we've probably got three hours to go; if we keep at this pace, we'll be OK.'

He was trying to keep spirits up. No one believed it would be quite that simple.

'Need a pee,' Jack said to the others.

'You're not going anywhere,' Dean barked.

'Just do it here. I won't look,' Marie said. Jack obliged but moved a few paces away and turned his back on the group as he relieved himself into the verge. As he finished, he paused and focused into the woods.

Dean, who had been keeping a watch on Jack's back, wandered over. 'What is it?'

'I think I can see something over there,' Jack said.

'Oh no. We're not moving off this road,' Marie scolded, 'we all agreed.'

Dean moved next to Jack and looked into the woods. 'He's right, there is something in there.'

'It's a trap,' Marie argued.

'I agree. Let's keep moving,' Ryan said.

'Last time we left the road, we lost two of the group.' Marie wasn't giving up this time.

'It won't take a minute, we'll all go together,' Dean said. 'Leave your bags here, take your weapons. Make sure we stick tight together.'

There were a few mutterings from Ryan and Marie, but they had little choice but to follow as Jack and Dean gradually edged into the woods. This part of the woodland had thick brambles, causing problems for all of them, who were wearing shorts. As they cautiously moved through, the occasional "ouch" could be heard as a branch pinged back and scratched someone.

They moved only a couple of dozen metres before they saw it. Dean spotted it first and stopped dead in his tracks. Marie, who was right behind him, carried straight into the back of him, but Dean didn't notice. As she released her foot from a bramble, she saw it too.

'Marie, wait!' Dean shouted, but he couldn't stop her as she charged towards it.

Jack and Ryan soon realised that 'it' was actually 'him'.

Marie reached him first and threw herself on top of his lifeless corpse. Graham was lying face down under a tree, with a knife still firmly planted in his back.

Dean was momentarily stunned but quickly flipped into survival mode. He shouted at Jack and Ryan to keep a lookout as he knelt beside his best friend, putting an arm around his widow.

They knelt together over his body as the rain washed over them. Marie gently stroked the side of his face that

307

was visible, the rest was planted in the ground. Her tears mixed with the raindrops although she wasn't hysterical. They'd all feared this moment since he went missing. Dean kept his arm firmly around her.

After a few minutes, she turned her body into Dean, and they hugged tightly. 'Who's doing this?' she kept repeating. Dean and the others had no answer.

Jack and Ryan did their best to keep watch, but it was tough not to be drawn to the emotional scene playing out in front of them.

Ryan separated from Jack and moved ahead of where Graham's body lay. He was just as devastated at the death of another former friend; no one could see the water running down his face was a mixture of both rain and tears.

'Help me turn him over,' Marie said as she finally broke out of her hug with Dean, 'I want to clean him up a bit and look at him properly for the last time.'

Dean didn't say no, but his failure to respond immediately prompted gentle pleading from Marie. He agreed without much of a fight and summoned Jack over to help him turn Graham's frame over.

Dean was no pathologist, but it was clear to him that Graham had been dead a few days. His skin was ice cold and there was no colour in him whatsoever. Worryingly for Dean, he was becoming less affected by the sight of dead bodies, even dead friends. In the space of 24 hours, he'd now encountered three bodies in various states of decay.

'He must have died the same day he went missing,' Dean said gently, 'I don't think he would have suffered. It looks like he was stabbed from behind; there's no sign of a struggle.' He had no idea about whether Graham had suffered in his last moments, but right now he was focused on Marie and making her feel marginally better.

She barely heard Dean, instead she focused on trying to clean Graham's mud-soaked face with a jumper that she had in her bag. It was a fruitless task, but no one had the desire to tell her.

'Dean, look at this,' Ryan said from his position just ahead of them. Dean obligingly picked himself up from ground and walked over to him. Ryan was pointing out another building, barely visible through the trees.

'What do you think?' he asked while waiting for a response from Dean.

Dean paused, afraid of what they might do next. 'I don't know,' he said finally.

'I've been driving around this area on my moped for the last week and didn't notice this,' Ryan offered.

'We said we'd head straight to the village,' Dean said, as he looked back at Marie.

Ryan moved in and whispered to Dean, 'Yes, but what if they've got Pippa in there? She could still be alive.'

Dean had started to accept Pippa wasn't going to be found alive. Ever since they found Madame Bernard and especially since Stevie's death an hour ago, Dean had reconciled himself to the fact that missing meant dead. He was still trying to come to terms with the fact that Pippa was missing.

'Do you really think that whoever is doing this is going to let us get out of here? We've three more hours of walking.' Ryan paused. 'We have to find this person and kill them before they kill us.' He wasn't giving up easily with his pleading.

Dean let a tree take his weight as he thought about this. It was a tough one; Ryan had a point, but another detour would not end well, of that he was certain.

He looked back at Marie and Jack again and then back at Ryan. 'If we do it, we go together – all four,' he said finally.

'Go where?' Jack had joined them.

Ryan pointed over to the building.

'Oh shit,' was Jack's only response.

Dean moved back over to Marie and put his arm around her again as he bent down besides Graham.

Jack and Ryan stood watching again as Dean quietly told her about their next move. 'I'm not going. I can't leave him,' she said loud enough for the others to hear.

Dean looked up at Ryan and Jack.

Ryan moved closer. 'We have to. We have to end this now, before we're all picked off.'

Marie looked back at Graham's body and then back at Ryan, tears still rolling down her face. 'I really don't care anymore. Let them kill me as well.' She hugged Graham again. 'But if this is going to be the end, I'd rather spend this time with my husband.'

They tried to persuade her, but to no avail.

'We're not leaving her alone,' Dean said as he re-joined the men.

'I'll stay with her,' Jack said reluctantly, producing his knife again to show willing. Dean wanted to argue but had no energy left. The reality of what Ryan had said hit home. Running was not an option now, they had to confront this killer head-on.

In the end, Dean managed a half-hearted, 'Are you sure?' to Jack, but barely waited for a response.

There were no big goodbyes or promises of a return with the police. Jack and Marie wouldn't have believed them anyway.

They had nothing but their weapons on them and no reason to take anything else. Only Marie had brought her bag with her, the men had all abandoned theirs by the side of the road when they rested.

Jack crouched down, with his back leaning up against a tree as he guarded Marie. He signalled to Dean and Ryan that he was ready for them to leave.

They approached the building slowly. It was only partly visible from where they'd found Graham, and they had to make their way through more woodland before the building revealed itself in full.

As they rounded the last tree, they stood in a small clearing looking directly at it. It was a wooden barn; much larger than the brick outhouse they'd searched earlier. Probably about 30 metres long and 20 wide. It was two storeys high with a steeply pitched roof. No windows visible on the sides, but the front of the barn had huge double-doors. Directly above the doors was a hatch in the second storey.

Surprisingly, the barn looked in good condition, no rotten panels or peeling paint. There were tyre marks that led through the clearing and into the doors. The barn was in use – recent use.

Dean spotted the tracks first and pointed at them. 'Looks like a tractor,' Ryan said. Neither had a clue about the countryside, but a tractor looked plausible. They edged closer to the barn and could see the tracks led away through a thin gap in the woodland that fed to an open field.

'Well, we've found a working farm,' Dean said, with Ryan nodding his agreement.

They kept edging closer to the barn, looking behind, to the side and around them at regular intervals. Their weapons firmly held in their outstretched arms.

As they approached the front, they could see the barn doors were huge, about twice the height of a human, with large iron hinges. There was a latch, but no lock. As they reached the doors, they paused for a second, then turned around again. Was anyone watching them? Was anyone about to jump out on them? Dean doubted they'd find a couple of helpful, English-speaking farmers alive inside.

'Ready,' Dean whispered as he put his hand on the over-sized latch. Ryan nodded and Dean held his breath as he gradually pulled the latch down. The squeak from the hinge was loud, loud enough for Dean to pause. 'Don't stop,' Ryan declared, and Dean held his breath some more as he finished opening the latch.

They both stood back a couple of paces as they contemplated opening the doors. They looked at each other again for reassurance, and both moved together to grab the doors, one each.

Both ducked as they finished opening the doors, as if someone was going to shoot directly at them. They stood up but didn't venture in immediately. Ryan took another quick look behind them as Dean absorbed the scene. The barn was obviously used as a store. Half of the barn was open, right up to the pitched roof, two clear floors. The other half, to their left, had a mezzanine platform that ran the whole length of the barn, supported by a dozen or so vertical wooden stilts. In the middle, a wooden ladder provided the only way up to the mezzanine.

Under the mezzanine, the area was mainly littered with bales of hay and the odd pile of wood. The open side of the barn had a two small tractors and some farm tools. A couple of tin barrels were leaking a black substance, most likely diesel, Ryan speculated. The barn had been used recently, judging by the footmarks on the floor, although no immediate evidence of anyone there at the minute.

Neither of them contemplated calling out to see if anyone was in. They'd trespass and face the consequences, as necessary.

Finally, they stepped inside.

* * *

As she held her dead husband's body, Marie felt the cold metal of the pistol touch the back of her neck. She froze. Despite never having seen a gun before this holiday, she knew instinctively what was pressed against her skin.

* * *

They were both covered in mud and drenched from the rain. Having moved a couple of paces into the barn, they stood still again. Dean wiped his forehead but smeared more mud across it. Ryan swept his long black wet hair out of his face. They both looked up at the ceiling and then scanned around the barn. It was dark, with most of the light coming through the open door. Each end of the barn had a manhole-sized hatch on the first floor. The nearside hatch was closed, but on the far side had come loose and was banging in the harsh weather.

Neither spoke, instead they motioned to each other as they gently strolled around the right-hand side of the barn, which didn't have the protection of the mezzanine. The equipment, from ploughs to rakes and tractors all looked well used, but not out of commission. The second of the small tractors had no sign of rust, probably only four or five years old, Dean thought. They walked about halfway down the right side of the barn before moving over to the left side, which had the mezzanine above it. They both looked at the wooden ladder. Neither said anything, but they both knew there was an inevitability they'd end up climbing it; eventually.

They walked under the mezzanine and started to examine the left-hand side of the barn. Mostly, it was neatly stacked piles of hay bales, each pile consisted of about 12 carefully bound bales.

They were back at the front of the barn, having examined both sides of it, up to halfway back. Dean poked his head out of the open barn doors but could see nothing. The rain could be heard beating a loud tune on the wooden roof.

They moved back towards the centre of the barn when something caught Dean's eye. He pointed over to the far left of the barn, at the opposite end to where they'd come in. Ryan couldn't see what Dean was pointing at, causing him to break the silence. 'That pile of hay's been knocked over,' he whispered to Ryan.

He nodded and feigned intrigue but followed Dean over anyway. As they approached the disturbed pile, they slowed and reaffirmed the grip on their weapons.

The light was poor at this end of the barn as they strained to see where they were heading.

Ryan saw it first, a blue piece of material. He touched Dean's arm and pointed him to what he'd seen. They moved over even more slowly. Whatever it was, was under a bundle of hay. They both pulled level with it and counted under their breath, 'One, two, three' and quickly pushed the hay away.

It took them a few seconds to figure out what they were looking at. 'Oh God,' Ryan gasped when it sunk in.

They both just looked at it and stared.

The blue that Ryan had spotted was overalls. The person wearing them was lying face down with blood covering most of the back of their head.

'Who is it?' Ryan asked.

Dean couldn't speak. This victim had suffered the most violent death of the four so far. As he scanned the area, Dean could see an axe covered in blood near the body. He noticed several big holes in the back of the person's head, enough to make the brain visible.

Dean knelt down and threw up. Ryan somehow managed to keep his composure.

'Is it Otis?' Ryan said as Dean wiped his mouth and stood back up.

He shook his head. 'I don't know, but I don't think so.'

He scanned the body again but tried to avoid the head. 'Otis's not built like this, he's really skinny. Plus, the leg's not broken, oh and Otis is black!'

'Let's turn him over to see,' Ryan said.

'No way,' Dean argued back, 'I'm not touching it.'

Ryan couldn't be bothered to argue and grabbed the nearside arm, pulling it up to flip the body over.

The face belonged to a white man in his late forties or early fifties, greying hair and a moustache.

'Do you recognise him?' Ryan asked. Dean shrugged. 'Must be a local farmer,' Ryan suggested.

Then, the body rolled further backwards, knocking into another stack of hay bales, which toppled over in turn, before knocking over a scythe.

Both winced at the noise it created and shot around to see if they'd disturbed anyone.

As he looked over the newly created mess, something else caught Dean's eye. He moved another of the bales and edged forwards to see it.

'Jesus!' he shouted this time, as Ryan came to join him.

They saw the next two bodies lying face up this time. Less mess, but definitely dead. A teenage boy and a woman, the same age as the dead farmer they'd found minutes earlier.

'This is seriously fucked up,' Ryan said.

'Who'd do this to a boy?' Dean responded.

They both struggled to view the scene and moved a couple of steps away, frightened of what else they might come across next.

'We're not going to get out of this alive,' Ryan said. 'Whoever's doing this is a complete nutcase,' he continued.

Dean just looked at him and sat down on a bale. Ryan sat opposite him, directly on the floor.

Neither said anything for a couple of minutes.

'What next?' Ryan said eventually.

Before Dean could answer, they could hear some banging above them. Or could they, was it just the weather? They stood up and listened without speaking. Dean held up his hand to indicate neither should talk.

Then they heard it again, banging, almost directly above them on the mezzanine. The dust from the wooden floorboards landed on their heads.

They both started running towards the ladder in the middle of the barn. Dean reached it first and placed both hands on it to block Ryan. As he moved up a couple of rungs, he turned back to Ryan. 'Wait here,' he said firmly, 'if anything happens to me up there, run for the door and go and get Jack and Marie.'

Ryan looked at the door and back at Dean. He was obviously as petrified as Dean. 'Don't come back – save yourself,' Dean finished.

Ryan didn't fully compute what Dean was saying but nodded obediently and watched as Dean swiftly climbed the ladder. As he reached the top, Dean looked down to check on Ryan – he'd done as he was told.

The upper mezzanine was covered in hay, mostly loose but with half a dozen full bales at the far end, obscuring the area from where the banging had been coming. Dean moved swiftly along the floor, the boards creaking every time he pressed his foot down.

He got past the last bale expecting to see the most horrific sight.

* * *

The rain continued to lash down over the barn, joined by riotous claps of thunder. Outside, rainwater gushed over Graham's body as his corpse lay alone, next to the tree where he'd been found earlier.

* * *

'Thank God!' Dean shouted as he ran over to Beth. Her hands and feet were tied together with rope, and her mouth was gagged by a dirty rag – but she was alive.

Next to her was Otis, lying down, also gagged and his hands tied together in front of him. His crushed legs had been left without constraint.

Dean removed Beth's gag first and undid her hands, which were tied behind her back. 'Are you OK?' he asked as he finished untying her hands, before moving onto her feet.

'Oh, Dean, thank you,' she said. She started crying. 'It's been terrible.'

He was half-listening as he moved over to Otis and removed his gag. 'Argh,' Otis complained as Dean knocked into his leg.

'Sorry, mate.' But he quickly moved on to release his hands.

'We need to get you out of here,' Dean said as he looked at Otis's legs.

The scream came from Beth. Dean hadn't kept watch behind him as the figure emerged from the other side of the stack of hay bales. He shot round and grabbed his carving knife, expecting to see a mystery figure.

It was Ryan.

Beth screamed again. 'Get him away from me,' she cried.

Dean looked at her and then back to Ryan.

'Don't worry, it's only Ryan,' he said and let slip a half-laugh.

Otis shouted impatiently, 'It's him, Dean, it's Ryan, he's one of them,' and finally Dean realised what the two captives were telling him.

CHAPTER 28

Ryan looked shocked, he'd frozen solid and couldn't muster a denial. He was fixated on Beth and Otis, now discovered alive, and seemed unable to compute what they were saying.

Dean stood up, paused briefly as he turned to face him, and then charged straight at Ryan, knocking him backwards against the wooden slats which acted as railings to the mezzanine. Ryan crashed through and was half over the edge as Dean jumped on top of him and connected a punch with his nose. The nose cracked again, and more blood shot out, covering the hay below. Dean remained firmly on top of Ryan, holding his T-shirt tightly as they both balanced over the edge of the mezzanine.

'Where is she? you bastard!' Dean shouted in Ryan's face. Ryan could barely breathe, never mind speak. He was in pain, confused and choking on his own blood.

'Where is she?' Dean repeated, but Ryan still couldn't speak. Dean stood up, with his legs astride Ryan's body and lifted him up by filling both fists with Ryan's T-shirt.

'Next time, you go over the edge. Now, where is she?'

Ryan managed a tame, 'I don't know,' before the anger overcame Dean. He pushed Ryan's body further over the edge of the mezzanine and released his right hand from Ryan's T-shirt. In one move, he formed a fist with his hand and connected a heavy punch to Ryan's chin. As he landed the punch, he let go of Ryan with his left hand and jumped backwards, allowing time to escape and watch him fall backwards and connect, back first, onto the ground below.

Dean leant over to see the damage. Ryan didn't move.

'Is he dead?' Beth said as she ran over to join Dean.

'I hope so,' Dean responded and headed back to check on Otis.

As he examined Otis's leg again, Beth spoke, 'Where are the others?' Dean tried to ignore the question.

'We'll get you out of here, Otis, I promise,' Dean said.

Beth touched Dean's elbow to make sure she got his attention. 'Where are the others?' she repeated.

Dean looked at her. He thought about lying but decided there was little point at this stage. 'Graham and Stevie are dead.'

The words landed on Otis and Beth like a hammer to the head. Despite what they'd both been through, clearly neither had expected their friends to be dying.

Dean knew this was particularly hard on Otis, who'd been Stevie's lifetime best friend. Otis let his head flop back, put his hands over his face and let out a loud scream.

'What about Marie, Jack, Pippa?' Beth looked at Dean, clearly hoping for better news of those three.

'Jack and Marie are outside, they're OK. Well, at least they were when we came in here.'

'And Pippa?'

Dean looked back to the hole where he'd just thrown Ryan. 'She's missing.'

Dean paused temporarily, before re-focusing on Otis. 'Beth, I need you to help me lift Otis up, we need to get him out of here.'

'Leave me,' Otis said, 'you don't have time. Take Beth and get Jack and Marie and go.'

Dean looked at him with surprise. 'I'm not leaving you; besides, I've taken care of him now,' and he pointed to the hole in the mezzanine.

'But he's got a gun,' Otis said, 'you need to go now.'

Dean looked at Beth and then at Otis. 'No, he hasn't. Anyway, I've just knocked him out.'

Then somebody spoke behind Dean. 'I think he's referring to me.'

Dean froze. He recognised the voice but couldn't immediately place it. Nevertheless, a chill went up his spine.

He didn't turn around straight away; he was still trying to recognise the voice. He looked over at Beth, who was sheet-white with fear. Dean thought she looked like she'd seen a ghost. Then it hit him; a ghost – the voice was from a ghost.

He turned around slowly, but still couldn't immediately see who he was looking at in the poor light.

Dean wobbled, before taking a couple of paces forward. He hadn't even bothered to pick up his knife, he was completely mesmerised by the figure in front of him. He got to within three metres of the figure before he was finally able to make him out.

He stopped and looked him up and down. And then he spoke quietly and calmly, 'You're dead.' There was no emotion in his voice, the last few days had drained it from him. Instead, Dean just stood in front of him, unable to think of anything else to say.

Cameron smiled back at Dean with an enormous grin. He was a similar build and height to Dean. His hair was starting to recede, and he'd cut it short, not bothering to hide its retreat. He held Dean's gun in his right hand and spoke with no emotion, 'Not quite dead; disappointed as I know you are with that.'

The shock of seeing Cameron alive and well had made Dean forget their predicament. And about Pippa. Just for a minute, but then he remembered her.

'Where's Pippa?' he barked sternly.

'Oh, lovely Pippa. Everybody loves my sister.' He smirked again, causing Dean's emotions to start bubbling again. 'Don't worry,' Cameron continued. 'she's right here.' He motioned to his left and out from behind the bales of hay shuffled in Pippa. Her shoulders were hunched over, her hair dirty and partially covering her face. Her top was torn. Her hands and feet were bound together.

Dean made a move towards her but was stopped by the gun being thrust at him. He took a pace back and turned to her as she approached. 'Are you OK?' She looked at Dean, he could see some bruises on her cheek and cuts around her mouth. She nodded slightly before hunching her shoulders up again and lowering her face to look at the floor.

'Take a seat over by Otis,' Cameron said to Pippa. She moved slowly past Dean and he put out his hand to support her. 'Don't touch,' Cameron barked. 'You can sit down too,' he said to Dean, who stared him in the eye, before reluctantly sitting down beside Otis.

Pippa finally managed to lower herself next to Beth. The four of them sat among the hay and watched Cameron as he moved a few steps closer.

'Not much of an audience,' he said to them sarcastically, 'let's see if we can do something about this.' He disappeared behind the hay bales for a few seconds and muttered something that the group couldn't hear.

Slowly another figure emerged. It was Jack, his hands and feet also bound together, with his mouth gagged. Dean barely had time to register Jack's arrival, before Marie emerged a few steps behind Jack, equally restrained.

Jack was pushed next to Pippa and sat down, as instructed by Cameron, with Marie moving next to Dean. Cameron walked over to Marie and removed the rag that had gagged her before repeating with Jack.

He stood back from the group of six, which was now roughly sitting in a semicircle. 'That's more like it,' he said, with another smirk. He then pulled over a bale of hay and sat on it, so that he towered over his audience.

He paused for effect. 'Now, where to begin.'

'Firstly, I should thank my accomplices for bringing us this far together.' He waited for a response from the audience, but no one gave him the satisfaction. Having failed to get the invited question back, he continued himself.

'Yes, two key people have supported my efforts to reunite us.' He paused again, before casually saying the names, 'Ryan and Jack.'

Jack was stunned and looked guilty as Dean shot him a glare that could kill. Beth couldn't resist the bait. 'I knew it was him all along,' she blurted out.

'You bastard!' Marie shouted at him before Dean finally snapped and jumped over to Jack, moving his arm back, ready to throw a punch.

Cameron caught his arm. 'Easy, tiger. Take a seat.' And he virtually threw Dean to the ground.

As Dean recovered from the fall, he looked at Jack again, leaving little doubt he would make him pay later.

'Not very trusting of our friends, are we, Dean?' Cameron said, almost like a scolding parent.

'But given who your friends are, that's probably for the best.' Cameron sat back down on the bale.

He waited for a few seconds, toying with the gun, before continuing, 'When I said I had accomplices, I didn't say they knew what they were involved in.' He chuckled to himself. 'That's what made this whole thing so beautiful.' He laughed again before continuing, 'Ryan started this whole thing off without knowing it.'

'You mean with the secrets and stalking,' Marie interjected, but Cameron looked at her with disdain.

'No, dear. Jesus, you're thick,' he snapped at her.

'I bet Dean can work it out. He's pretty smart,' and with that Cam got back up off the bale and walked over to him, still wielding the gun.

Dean looked to the floor as he thought for a few seconds. 'You mean when he started to see Pippa?'

'Bingo!' Cameron shouted excitedly, 'you always were the smart one, Dean.'

'I don't understand,' Beth said directly to Dean, barely acknowledging Cameron. Dean didn't respond. Instead, he looked over at Pippa. Tears were quietly rolling down her face.

Dean hadn't worked it out until now, hadn't allowed himself to think it of one his best friends, but the pieces had finally come together in his head. He knew the frostiness that had descended on the group when Ryan started seeing Pippa. Originally, he'd assumed it was just an over-protective brother, but over the course of the holiday, it had all started to make sense. The emotion of Pippa and how quickly she'd bonded with Ryan again – she clearly didn't really blame him for Cam's death. Dean knew she'd been hiding something from him, but now it all fell into place, but he wasn't about to rake it up in front of her.

'Come on, Dean, you're so smart, tell Beth what she's too dumb to work out.'

Dean looked at him in disgust. 'No.'

'Oh, Dean, you do disappoint me.' And he moved over to Dean, placing the end of the pistol directly in the middle of Dean's forehead. 'Tell them!'

Dean gritted his teeth and closed his eyes, waiting for it to end. 'No!' Cam clicked the pistol back, ready to shoot. Dean closed his eyes tighter.

'Dean, tell him,' Pippa begged.

Dean opened his eyes but couldn't turn his head to see Pippa as the pistol was too firmly planted in his face.

'Are you sure?' he managed.

'Yes, please tell them,' Pippa shot back without pausing.

'OK, but get that fucking gun out my face,' Dean said.

As Cameron slowly turned his outstretched arm away from Dean's face, Jack shot up from his position on the floor and charged his body at Cameron. In doing so, Jack managed to knock Dean backwards into an upright post, causing him to bang his head and lose consciousness for a few seconds. Jack had landed square on Cameron, who'd managed to retain hold of the gun. Unable to release his hands and feet from the rope, Jack was only able the writhe around on top of Cameron, the significant weight difference preventing Cameron from immediately defending himself.

Beth, having initially frozen, and as the only other person not bound, finally moved, but as she approached Jack, a shot rang out.

* * *

The car stopped in the road, it had to; there was nowhere to go – the tree was blocking their way. Billy got out first and instinctively put his hand through his hair as the rain continued to fall.

He walked up to the fallen tree. 'Fuck it,' he said out loud and motioned to Johnny, who was showing no sign of getting out of the vehicle. He groaned and gradually prised his large frame out of the car, sandwich in hand. Billy stepped around the tree. 'Someone's been here recently,' he declared as he inspected some footprints in the mud.

'We're in the middle of nowhere,' Johnny shouted as he waddled his way over to the tree.

Billy roamed the area before spotting three of the rucksacks by the side of the track. 'Here.' He motioned over to Johnny, who attempted a jog to join him.

Billy opened one of the bags and inspected it. 'Just a few basic provisions, nothing of particular interest,' Johnny declared as he leaned over Billy's shoulder.

'But why abandon it here?' Billy muttered. From his crouching position over the bags, he spotted more footprints out into the woodland.

'Come on,' he said to Johnny quietly, 'you'd better get your gun out.'

* * *

Dean heard it as he started to come around. Beth jumped for cover. Pippa screamed loudly.

Jack fell backwards, landing on Dean's feet. He had a gaping hole in his right shoulder as blood gushed through his T-shirt. Cameron got up, sweating and angry.

'You fucking fat bastard,' Cameron said as he regained his composure, pointing the gun at Jack, ready to finish him off. 'I'm gonna fucking kill you for that,' he said.

Expecting the worst, Jack, who was already in significant pain, tried to move away from Cameron.

'Please don't, Cam,' Pippa pleaded with her brother.

Cameron looked at her, 'why shouldn't I?' he said angrily.

There was a momentary pause as Pippa plucked up the courage to say it, 'Because I love you and you love me. And if someone you love asks you to do something for them, you do it.'

Cameron looked at Pippa, then looked back at Jack, before returning his glare to Pippa. He smiled and withdrew the gun. 'What a load of claptrap,' he laughed, 'did you get that from a romance novel?'

He moved back into the centre of the group, still laughing to himself. 'OK, I'll leave him alive, for now.' He paused and looked around at the faces scattered about the floor.

Jack was wrestling with the pain in his shoulder, but doing his best to keep quiet, as he clearly didn't want to draw attention to himself again.

'So, I guess you all know what this is about now?' He looked at the group and they all nodded some acknowledgement.

'No one, but no one, comes between me and Pippa. When this is all done and dusted, the two of us will disappear from here and never be seen again.'

'You actually think you'll get away with it?' Marie shouted back at him, long past caring what he was going to do to her.

Cameron chuckled and moved a couple of paces to be in front of her. 'Well, yes, Marie, I will get away with it, because I'm dead.'

He turned to walk back to the middle, but stopped when she shouted back at him, 'Murderer!'

He moved right in front of her face. 'Call me a murderer? You murdered my baby, you bitch! And you call me a murderer?'

Marie was shocked at the viciousness in his face as he said it. Dean felt sure, in that moment, he'd blow her away. Sensing the danger, Dean tried to change the subject, 'So, how did you get Ryan embroiled in your scheme?'

The group waited, desperate for Cameron to take the bait of the question and move away from Marie.

Dean held his breath.

Finally, Cameron turned towards Dean. 'He didn't know he was helping me. You killed him for nothing, making you a murderer too.'

Cameron took pleasure in leaving that sentence hanging in the air as he composed himself again. 'You lot did me a massive favour by cutting him off. Even my little sister; she was the only one who knew why he'd chased after me that day.' He looked at her and smiled. 'But Ryan was the one with dignity in all of this. He could have told everyone what I'd done, to clear himself and besmirch my name. But he didn't.'

Cameron turned away from them momentarily and pointed to the hole that Ryan had recently gone through. 'Down there lies the only person in this goddam building with honour. And the irony is, he's going to get the blame for a dozen deaths.'

Dean was devastated. He'd killed someone needlessly, worse still – a friend. As he contemplated what he'd done, he temporarily lost interest in their predicament.

'I still don't see why Ryan's going to get the blame for all this?' Beth said, but immediately regretted it as Cameron walked over to her shouting, 'You really are a dumb bitch, aren't you! His little revenge game, breaking into homes, the paperwork, even following you all down here – it all points to him!'

'And because you're officially dead, they won't even be looking for you,' Marie said, despondently.

'It's perfect. It couldn't have worked out better. He teed you all up, and I smashed you away.'

'What would you have done if we hadn't cut him off, or if he wasn't stalking us?' Dean asked.

'Good point,' he said, 'but sometimes you need a little help and other times a plan B.'

The others looked bemused, but Cameron was enjoying his moment. 'I was just planning to come back to England and kill him. Simple as that. But I watched him for a bit and realised what he was doing to you lot and how I could use it to my advantage.'

He grinned widely. 'Let's finish it.'

* * *

'What's that?' Johnny declared as they approached Graham's body.

329

'Jesus!' Billy shouted as he started running towards it. As he got close, he slowed down – giving him time to survey the immediate area, then he bent down to examine the body.

'It's not Dean,' he declared with relief.

'Who is it?' Johnny asked.

'I think it's Graham. I saw the photos in his parents' house.'

'You mean grandparents?' Johnny tried to show-off. 'Well, at least you won't have to tell him they're dead.'

Billy shot Johnny a look that suggested now wasn't a good time for humour. 'Come on, there's more footprints this way,' Billy declared and moved cautiously through the mud and brambles.

They reached the barn within a couple of minutes and stopped about 20 metres away from the open door, in the clearing.

'What do you think?' Johnny managed as he struggled for breath.

'Let's go for it,' Billy declared, and they wandered through the open door into the barn.

Neither man saw the raven-haired lady standing behind a large oak tree, just a few metres away, watching as they entered the barn.

* * *

'So, it was you in the van, forcing Graham off the road?' Dean said; he wanted to keep Cameron talking for as long as possible. He wasn't sure how it would help, but he figured the longer it went on for, the greater the chance Cameron might make a slip. Dean surveyed the scene; he and Beth were the only ones with free movement of their arms and legs. Jack was now out of the game with his shoulder injury. Dean considered another dive forward but had absolutely no confidence that Beth would respond quickly enough.

'Of course, it was me,' he laughed.

'But, if you'd have killed us then, you wouldn't have been able to complete this plan?' Marie managed.

He laughed again. 'If I'd meant to kill you, you'd be dead.' He paused, looked around briefly and continued, 'I was following Pippa, I wanted to make sure you'd picked her up and then I had the urge to give you a fright. I have to admit, I was a bit worried when you were approaching that bridge, but even that stupid, uncoordinated husband of Marie's managed to control the car.' He looked at her as he said it, but she didn't give him the satisfaction of responding.

'And me, in the car park, did you mean to kill me?' Dean said solemnly.

Cameron turned to Dean and smiled. 'No. I don't think so. I wanted to stop you coming on the holiday, I thought you might pose a problem for me as you're undoubtedly the most competent member of the gang. I just got a bit crazy when I saw you. Perhaps I subconsciously knew you would make a move on Pippa. Believe it or not, I didn't really have the intention of killing you all. I just wanted to get revenge on Ryan.' He paused and turned towards Pippa. 'And, of course, for me and Pippa to be able to go away together.'

He took a pace backwards. 'It's time,' Cameron declared as he checked his watch. He walked back over to Dean and without warning, pistol-whipped him across the head.

Dean's screams rang out beyond the barn. Cameron's serious face returned. 'I wasn't going to kill you, Dean, but you've sealed your own fate by pushing yourself onto Pippa. Nobody, but nobody, takes her from me. I'm gonna make you pay for trying to take Pippa away from me.' Cameron had gone from calm and composed to psychotic in seconds. 'I was going to make Ryan suffer the most, but as you've killed him, you can have that pleasure. I'm going to make you watch as I kill your remaining friends one by one—' he smirked '—and then I'm going to kill you.'

He took a pace back, surveyed the scene briefly, and then shuffled towards Beth, ensuring he kept everyone in sight. He pointed the gun at her. 'You really are a dumb bitch. I'm doing you first, for the sake of human-ity.' He clicked the gun and started to squeeze his finger on the trigger.

The sound of the gun echoed around the barn – followed by screams. It was a direct, single hit to the head. Beth's face was covered in brains and blood.

For a split second, Dean thought she was dead, but then she breathed out; she wasn't dead. Dean saw a figure coming towards them and some words being said that he couldn't immediately comprehend. Finally, he looked down to see Cameron's body lying, with what remained of his head, on Beth's feet. Whether it was the shock, relief, or just the fact that the contents of someone else's head were splattered over her face – Beth screamed an hysterical scream, and then virtually stopped breathing.

Dean produced the first slap across Beth's face, and when that didn't work, he landed a second one, harder.

This stopped the loud screaming, instead she turned to Marie, planted her face in Marie's chest and sobbed.

Dean looked up at his uncle. He tried to think of something clever to say, but with his head throbbing and a trickle of blood running down his face, all he could manage was a weak, 'Thanks.'

'Hope you lot remembered travel insurance,' Billy said as he sat down to inspect his nephew's wounds. He carefully put his hands on Dean's bleeding head and reached into his pocket for a hanky.

Jack, who was still suffering from his shoulder injury, struggled up and sat on the hay bale. 'Did you know it was Cam?' he bellowed towards Billy.

He looked up and proudly nodded his head.

'How?' Dean asked.

'His dad said he was so disgusted in Cam that he couldn't even look at him when he identified the body.'

Dean thought for a minute. 'But surely there must be more than that,' he muttered.

'There is, but let's talk about it later. I have a feeling we're not quite at the end of this journey yet.'

Billy gradually went around each of the hostages, released their restraints and checked their injuries.

He surveyed the situation and announced the priority was to get Otis and Jack down the ladder.

Dean noticed Pippa; she was standing over her dead brother's body. Clearly sad, but not obviously emotional. He walked up to her and put his arm on her shoulder. She shrugged it off and moved slightly away, with this move he felt like he'd been hit in the gut again.

* * *

The raven-haired lady nonchalantly walked into the barn holding two glass bottles. Each was full of liquid and had a rolled-up rag tucked in the top. She popped one down, pulled out a lighter from her leather jacket and lit the one she still held. She drew back her arm and threw it into the hay under the mezzanine. She picked up the second bottle, walked a few steps back to the door, lit it and threw it at another pile of hay. Then she casually walked out of the barn.

* * *

'What's that?' Otis shouted as Billy and Marie attended to his legs.

Billy shot up, ran over to the edge of the mezzanine and looked over. 'FIRE!' he shouted and ran back towards the group.

The first bottle hit a large stack of eight bales, which stood directly below the part of the mezzanine where the group were gathered. The bottle landed in the middle of the stack and caught immediately. The fire burned through the dispersed fuel in seconds and quickly set about the hay. The second bottle, closer to the ladder, struck a smaller pile of hay but took just as quickly as the first.

Initially, the group couldn't register the threat, but quickly the realisation hit them as the smoke started to seep through the mezzanine floor. Beth and Pippa screamed as general panic set in among the seven. Otis remained flat on the floor but closed his eyes and took a deep breath.

Of the four separate haystacks that stood under the mezzanine, two had been hit by the bottles, and a third had now caught after the large pile tipped over. It had taken only seconds, but there was now a roaring fire covering most of the area under the mezzanine.

Billy took control. 'Quiet!' It didn't work first time. 'Shut the fuck up, everyone,' he followed up, and this momentarily stopped the panic.

'Listen to me and we'll get out of this,' he said confidently.

'Dean, take Jack to the ladder and help him down.' Dean didn't argue initially and started towards the ladder, collecting Jack. He helped him along a few paces but turned back towards his uncle as if to protest at being given permission to leave.

Billy wasn't in the mood for arguing. 'Just fucking do it, now!' and with that, Dean continued to support Jack towards the ladder.

Billy turned towards the others, assessing the situation. 'Girls, follow Dean.' No one moved for a second. 'Now!' he shouted and pulled Beth up from her slumber.

Beth and Pippa moved at pace towards the ladder, but Marie waited. 'What about Otis?' she questioned.

'I'll sort him,' Billy declared confidently, 'now go.'

Despite the flames having taken hold quickly and engulfed most of the underside of the mezzanine, miraculously, the flimsy wooden ladder remained temporarily untouched. Dean had worked his way onto the ladder first and guided Jack onto it above him, they gradually went down almost on top of each other. Jack winced every time he moved down a rung. About halfway down, Dean glanced at the position where Ryan had fallen, but could only see the flames engulfing the space.

'I'm not leaving without him,' Marie declared, and Billy gave up arguing.

'Women,' he muttered under his breath as he charged over to Otis.

'Come on then, grab his arm.' Billy grabbed Otis under his arm. 'This is gonna hurt, pal,' he said, but didn't give any time for the warning to register before he pulled him up.

Otis screamed with the searing pain, as Marie joined them and supported Otis under his other arm. 'Leave me, please leave me,' he protested, but they ignored him, not even acknowledging his request. They slowly dragged him a few paces, as they did, the mezzanine partially gave way from the exact position Otis had been lying. It caused the three of them to fall forward, but their section of the floor remained intact, for now.

It took Dean a couple of minutes to manoeuvre Jack down the ladder, by which time the whole mezzanine side of the barn was alight. Parts of the ladder were being licked by flames, but it stood firm.

The rest of the barn had only a dusting of hay, scattered about the floor and had only caught sporadically. 'I can see a path through to the door,' Dean declared as he helped Beth and Pippa off the ladder, 'follow me.' He didn't have time to think about Billy and Marie at this stage, he just wanted to get Pippa out.

They weaved their way through the parts of the floor which weren't burning, smoke causing each of them to cough in bursts. As they neared the large barn door, they were forced to weave closer to the mezzanine structure as an ill-placed hay bale had caught in front of them. As they squeezed past, Beth let out a yelp as a red-hot bale tumbled towards her. Pippa had spotted it seconds before Beth and managed to drag her out of the way in time. They reached the large barn door without further trouble, all four of them charging for the exit as if attempting to win a 100-metre race. They collapsed outside the barn, all coughing and spluttering as they recovered.

Billy struggled up from the floor and looked back at the hole in the floor as flames poured through. He caught his breath for a second and started to tug at Otis's arm. 'Come on!' he shouted at Marie as she remained on the floor. She looked at him, a certain resignation in her face that suggested she thought they had little chance of making it.

'Come on!' Billy shouted again, and this time she jumped up, grabbing Otis's other arm in the process. Both ignored his loud, pained screams.

They proceeded with greater pace, dragging Otis as they ploughed on. Within a few seconds, they reached the top of the ladder. Both paused as they looked below them – the entire ground level seemed like it was covered in flames.

Marie, struggling to breathe with the smoke, looked at Billy. 'GO!' he shouted and manhandled her onto the ladder. This time, she didn't argue, their predicament was beginning to look hopeless. She stepped onto the ladder, but screamed, the flames were beginning to jump through the rungs.

She looked up at Billy. 'Just go!' he shouted, and with that she moved a few rungs down. As she got one-third of the way down the ladder, a supporting beam gave way, causing the ladder to split in two. The bottom half of the ladder fell forward into the flames and for a few seconds, Marie thought she might hold on to the top half; she didn't. The top of the ladder crashed down to the floor, taking Marie with it. As she headed to the floor, her body caught fire. The momentum caused by the fall forced her body to roll through the inflamed hay and smash through the barn wall. Billy couldn't see her burning body from where he stood, but the screams died after a few seconds.

Dean had got Jack, Pippa and Beth away from the barn to a safe distance, but they were still close enough to hear the screams from within. Dean didn't hesitate, he charged back towards the barn, ignoring the screams of 'No' behind him. As he arrived at the barn, he was shocked at how badly the inside was engulfed. There was a loud crash as part of the roof collapsed and sent a wave of heat towards Dean. He jumped for cover and realised his chance of rescuing anyone inside was over.

Billy shouted in devastation as he watched Marie's body disappear below. He looked at Otis, coughing and spluttering as he continued to hold him upright. He quickly rotated his body around to survey the situation. The south side of the barn, from where they'd originally come in, was completely impassable. The floorboards had long since gone. This made up Billy's mind for him, and he set off towards the north side. No idea of whether he'd find a way out. He struggled to support Otis as the smoke filled his lungs, and he dropped him as they reached the scene of their confrontation with Cameron. He tried again to pick Otis up but collapsed as the smoke took hold.

'Leave me,' he heard faintly, 'leave me,' he kept hearing as he struggled for each breath. And all of a sudden, the smoke was so thick, he couldn't see Otis. He was crawling around now, trying to find him.

'Leave me, leave me,' he heard faintly. Then his arms gave way and Billy planted his face on the scorching hot boards.

The heat made Billy jolt up, bringing him around, but now he couldn't hear Otis. Billy tried to shout for him but couldn't speak – the smoke had taken his voice. Then he heard something louder, was it Otis? What was it?

'Billy, this way,' he could hear, 'Billy this way, follow my voice.'

He crawled slowly, pulling his body behind him, attempting to follow the sound. 'Billy, keep going this way.' He moved another couple of metres, then he could see something other than dark smoke – daylight!

'Billy, you're nearly there, come on,' then he realised it was Johnny's voice.

Johnny was perched on a ladder, propped up against the north side of the burning barn. There was a small hole in the wall, about 30 inches square, no hope of Johnny getting his large frame through it, but just enough space for Billy. Johnny was spluttering himself as the smoke bellowed through the gap. He kept dodging his head out of the way to draw breath before returning to scream for Billy.

Another two metres and Billy made it to the opening. Johnny reached in as far as he could to support Billy as he tried to lift his body to the hole. He wobbled precariously as he pulled Billy through the gap and guided him onto the ladder. Slowly he supported him as he struggled down each rung, pausing every few seconds to cough some more. They eventually made it to the bottom, with Billy collapsing in a heap at the base of the ladder. Johnny dragged him a few metres away from the barn as the fire finished it off.

* * *

The raven-haired lady ran the mile or so to where the 4x4 was parked and jumped in the passenger side.

She looked at the man sitting at the wheel and shook her head. The man, who was wearing sunglasses, tutted and spoke to someone on the phone. 'Mission failed, apprentice down,' then he looked back at the raven-haired lady and she nodded. The man spoke again, 'Agent Lilith confirms the clean-up was successful.'

The man put the car in gear, and they sped off.

* * *

On the south side of the barn, Dean sat on the ground with his arms wrapped around his knees, sobbing. He watched as the fire caused the barn to collapse. Jack, Beth and Pippa were huddled together, slightly away from Dean, silent as they watched the destruction; their friends had perished.

Johnny rubbed Billy's back in the hope it would help, but Billy still couldn't speak as he coughed continuously. Eventually, Billy managed to utter, 'Water,' and Johnny produced a bottle from his pocket, unscrewing the lid and pushing it to Billy's mouth. He took a few sips, spitting most of it back out and into Johnny's face.

Gradually the coughing subsided, and he managed to take in a few more sips of water.

'What the fuck just happened?' a voice came from behind Billy. He looked around but couldn't see through the tears as his eyes tried to recover from the smoke. It wasn't a voice he recognised, he looked at Johnny, who was sitting directly in front of him.

'I got him out,' Johnny said.

'Alive?' Billy managed among the spluttering.

'No, I'm a fucking ghost – you're dead as well,' Ryan said sarcastically. At that moment, Billy wouldn't have been surprised if he was dead.

'What are we going to do?' Pippa had quietly come over to Dean. The question didn't register with him. 'We've got to do something. We can't stay here forever.'

Still no response from him. 'Dean, DEAN!' she shouted in his ear, and he finally responded.

'Sorry,' he said quietly, 'what did you say?'

She put a hand on his shoulder. 'What are we going to do now?' she repeated. He shrugged his shoulder, forcing her hand off it, not deliberately, but she kept it retracted all the same.

'Surely we should make a plan?'

He didn't respond, and Pippa shuffled back to Jack and Beth. She shook her head but didn't say anything. Jack started to whisper something but stopped as he saw Dean stand up suddenly. Beth and Pippa turned to see what had taken Jack's attention.

Dean walked slowly towards the barn. He could see a figure coming from behind it. As he moved closer, he picked up the pace and was virtually sprinting by the time he embraced his blackened uncle.

The others jogged towards the pair as they embraced.

'Otis, Marie?' Pippa said as she reached Billy.

He looked at them and shook his head. He managed a weak, 'Sorry.'

Beth and Pippa embraced in tears. Pippa hadn't spotted Ryan as he came up behind her, putting his hand warmly on her back. Beth looked up first and jumped back from Pippa, releasing their embrace. Pippa wiped tears from her eyes as she turned around to see who it was, struggling to make out the person now stood in front of her. She screamed, this time with delight, and wrapped her arms around him.

CHAPTER 29

The storms had cleared, and the sunshine returned as Dean sat silently with his uncle on the damp ground. A blanket had been placed around them both as they stared at the burnt-out wreck of the barn. The area was now overrun with people and vehicles as the police and firefighters busied around the site.

Suddenly there was a commotion in the distance with raised voices and lots of gesticulating, a fireman shouted towards a paramedic, 'Elle est vivante!'

The female paramedic shouted back, 'Elle est vivante?' and started running towards the fireman.

Dean stood up and took a few paces towards the incident as several more paramedics ran towards the scene.

Billy joined his nephew. 'What's going on?'

'Not sure,' Dean said inquisitively. He tried to get closer, but one of the many police officers prevented him, and the police cordon was expanded.

Jack joined them. 'Vivante means alive,' he said as they all stretched to try and see what was going on. Jack started to converse with one of the policemen, and although Dean couldn't work out what they were saying, he got the impression it was good news.

'They say they've found a badly injured woman, alive,' Jack translated.

Dean looked shocked and turned to his Uncle. 'Marie?'

Billy shook his head. 'I don't see how. I saw her fall into the burning hay.'

Jack, spoke to the policeman again and then turned to Dean and Billy. 'They don't know who, but it's definitely a woman, and she's just about alive.'

'It must be Marie – thank God,' Dean said as they tried to move closer to confirm but were stopped again.

The three of them watched intently as the paramedics fussed around in the distance and eventually bundled the survivor into an ambulance. After a few minutes, a plain-clothed officer walked over to them and explained, in good English, that they had identified the lady as Marie Joseph from her passport. She was in a bad way, with significant burn injuries, but had a chance of making it.

Dean and Jack hugged with relief at the news, and Billy thanked the officer for the information, having gleaned the location of the hospital they were taking her to. Jack was persuaded to follow a medic into another ambulance so that his injured shoulder could be assessed properly.

As he waved off Jack, Dean began to feel tired again and returned to his blanket on the ground. Billy joined him, but neither said anything.

Dean's attention was drawn to two people huddled together a few dozen metres away; Pippa and Ryan sat next to each other, holding hands. Dean knew he'd lost her for good but decided that after everything Pippa and Ryan had been through, they deserved their happiness together. He knew he wouldn't be able to stand in their way, and even if he tried, it would be fruitless. Somehow, he'd have to live with it. Then unexpectedly, Dean thought about his son. For the first time in his life, he had a great urge to see him.

His daze was broken by Beth, who was being escorted by a paramedic. 'They're just taking me for a check-up,' she said as they passed, 'are you coming?'

Dean shook his head. 'No, feeling good as new.'

'Ok, see you later,' she said as she headed off. He watched as Beth disappeared into another ambulance and then looked in the distance as Pippa and Ryan were ushered away.

'Are you OK?' Billy said as he saw his nephew stare at the rekindled romance.

Dean shrugged his shoulders. 'Not really, but I'll live.'

Billy shuffled closer. 'That lad is incredibly resourceful. I'd suggest he could have a career as a private detective, but he's far too honourable.'

'I can't believe how close I came to being a murderer. I might have killed him, just because Cam had told Beth and Otis a pack of lies about Ryan being involved.'

'Yes, but you didn't. The pressure of the situation was immense, I think you deserve to go easy on yourself.'

'There's still a lot I don't understand,' Dean said to his uncle.

Billy just chuckled and shook his head.

'I don't understand how Cam faked his death,' Dean said, having realised Billy wasn't about to offer his view.

'It wasn't planned, that's for sure,' Billy finally offered, before continuing, 'but he took his opportunity when the avalanche hit.'

Billy coughed and took another swig of water before carrying on, 'He knew he'd never be able to go back to his old life when the news of Pippa's abuse hit, so he had to die.'

Dean nodded; this much made sense so far.

'He may well have been out on that mountain attempting to kill himself when it struck. I think he chanced upon someone that had been crushed, someone of similar age and build – there were two bodies never found, and one of those was similar to Cam. Anyway, I think he mashed the face up some more, changed the outer clothes and swapped IDs.'

Dean looked in amazement at his uncle. 'This sounds a bit too "MI5" for me. I mean, I've known Cam for quite a few years and he's not that resourceful. He never even came camping with me and Ryan.'

Billy nodded. 'Yep, that occurred to me too. It's also hard to believe Cam started the fire in the barn when he was already dead.'

Dean hadn't connected the timings in his head until then, he'd just mashed it all up as one event, but there was no way that Cam could have started the fire. He had that sinking feeling again, the one that suggested this perhaps wasn't all over.

Billy continued, 'There's someone I'd very much like to catch up with. Someone that I never did find in the UK, but they may well hold the key to this.'

'Who's that?'

'A girl that Ryan was seeing recently; she was mentioned by a few people. Someone called Lilith. I'd definitely like to have a chat with her.'

ABOUT THE AUTHOR

The author was inspired to write the story while on holiday in France with a group of close friends. The remote holiday cottage was plunged into darkness during a terrific lightning storm, a mystery figure could be seen in the grounds, and the author's imagination started to whirl...

Adam S. Dale was born and raised in Leicester, England before attending and graduating from the University of East Anglia while working as a lifeguard.

He has lived in Hertfordshire for over twenty years, where he juggles his time between his writing, a finance career and raising his son and daughter.